❦ 1 ❦

Jenny

I remember how it started, the beginning of the end. Of course I didn't know it then.

We were in southern Idaho and it was July. Daddy was working for the summer at a little campground that sat in a broad, grassy prairie between two mountain ranges. It was a nice place, hot and dry so you always had to carry a bottle of water with you. A curvy, slow-moving river ran just east of the campground, and lots of geese and ducks lived there. Sometimes we saw wild elk in the fields. Once at the river, I even saw a mother moose with her baby, standing on spindly legs in the water. If I'd had a camera, I would have taken a picture of them. I didn't have a camera, but I still remember how the mother glared at me as she stepped between Daddy and me and her baby. She was protecting him, I guess. That's what mothers are supposed to do.

Near the entrance to the campground sat a tiny, dusty restaurant called Zella Fay's Café. That's where we ate most of our meals. Zella Fay was an enormously fat old woman with a patch over her left eye and a bad temper. I never had the nerve to ask why she had an eye patch. She kind of scared me. But she made the best beef stew I'd ever had, and she always gave me an extra biscuit. Sometimes she let me take leftover bread from the restaurant to feed the ducks.

To the east, we could see the Teton Mountains from our campsite, with snow on the tops even in the summer. A boy who was staying at the campground in June told me that *Tetons* meant "titties" in French. Then he pinched my chest hard and laughed. I wanted to punch him. I let my hands curl into fists so tight my fingernails bit into my palms. But I didn't hit him, of course. He was a guest, and we had to be nice to the guests because they were paying to be there. They were paying for us to be there, too, Daddy said. Sometimes I hated that.

Anyway, that night in early July, I was lying on my bed—it was a shelf, really, in an alcove that jutted out of the trailer when we set up camp. I was staring at the roof, bored and kind of thirsty, wishing I could turn on the light to read. I was supposed to be asleep, but it was still light outside, even though it was almost nine o'clock. And it was still God-awful hot. I lay on top of the sheets below the screened window just over my bed, waiting for the breeze I knew would come eventually. We had air-conditioning in the trailer, but Daddy didn't like to run it at night. Once the sun set, it always cooled off so much I had to pull my quilt over me. Daddy said the fresh air was good for us both.

Outside, I heard Daddy talking softly and then laughing. I peeked out the window and saw him dancing in the grass with Emma, his arms wrapped around her waist. She tilted her head back to laugh and then saw me watching them from the window. Before I could drop the mini-blind, she smiled and winked at me.

I liked Emma. Actually, I liked her a lot. She took care of the horses at the campground, and she let me help feed them and sometimes brush them. Most days, she led the paying guests on trail rides into the surrounding foothills, telling them the history of the area, pointing out photo opportunities, and making sure they didn't get hurt . . . or worse, hurt the horses.

Emma knew every horse in the stable by name. She knew each one's likes and dislikes, its weaknesses and its stubborn streaks. She said the most important job she had was pairing a horse with a rider who would appreciate it. That and making sure that everyone got back to the campground in one piece.

For three years, Emma had been working at the campground. She was a year-round employee, taking care of the horses even after the campground closed for the season and the snow set in for months on end.

Daddy and I were only there for the summer. When the season ended and the campground closed, we would move on to the next place where Daddy could find work. Some people called us workampers, because we moved around so much and lived in a trailer. Daddy said we were modern-day gypsies or maybe even pioneers. He said stuff like that.

I was reading about the pioneers that summer. The week before, Emma had taken me to Victor, a little town that sat right up next to the mountains. We went to the Emporium for huckleberry shakes and then to the library to get some books about the people who'd come across the Teton Mountains in covered wagons to settle the area. Compared to those wagons, our trailer seemed pretty fancy. We had an electrical hookup and running water. We had GPS and even a satellite TV, which Daddy let me watch sometimes, but only after I had finished my lessons. Mostly, we used the TV to watch the Weather Channel. When you live in a trailer, you really do have to watch the weather.

Of course, compared to the houses I saw in the towns around the campground, our trailer seemed kind of shabby. There were some fancy houses in that valley, all brand-new and beautiful, with huge windows facing the mountains and sprinklers making "che-che-che" sounds as they sprayed water across the huge lawns. Zella Fay at the restaurant complained all the time about how much water people wasted on those lawns. They were mostly vacation homes, Daddy said. People built them just to come for a few months in the winter, when the ski hill was open. During the summer, they sat mostly empty, their windows glinting sunlight back at the mountains.

Still, our trailer was way better than the motels we used to live in, Daddy and me. Some of those places had been downright scary, with skittering roaches and mice. Once Daddy even killed a big gray rat that was hiding under our bed. And every few months, or even every few weeks, we'd move to another motel room and scrub it clean with Lysol and start all over again. At least with the trailer, we took all our stuff with us. And my bed in the alcove shelf was always my bed, with my own sheets and pillow and Bugsy Bear, the stuffed panda my mother bought for me before I was even born.

I raised the mini-blind again and peeked out the window. Daddy was kissing Emma's neck now and his hand was on her butt. Then I knew that she was probably going to be my new stepmom. For a minute, I let myself hope that she would stay. But almost as soon as the wish formed, it disappeared. I knew Emma wouldn't stay too long, no matter how much I wished. They didn't ever stay, not any of them.

Two weeks later, Emma moved her things from her room at the bunkhouse into the trailer. She didn't have a lot to move—just a duffel bag and a backpack. Daddy made space in a drawer beneath their bed for her things.

That night, I squeezed my eyes shut tight and tried hard to sleep, willing myself to see cartoon sheep or anything else I might count. There was no door to my little shelf/alcove and only a flimsy accordion door across the hallway into Daddy's bedroom. Like I said, a lot of women had come to live with us. And I really hated hearing them at night.

That night, Emma's voice rang out as clear as day.

"So Jenny hasn't ever been in a real school? Do you think that's a good idea?"

Daddy's voice was soft and low. He knew how everything worked in the trailer, knew I might still be awake. "She's doing a homeschool program on the computer. We move around too much to enroll her anywhere. She's better off this way."

"But . . ." Emma's voice trailed away. I heard Daddy kiss her.

"But nothing," he said finally. "We use an accredited program.

She has her laptop. We have the Internet. She's as smart as a whip. And she's fine."

"And you are more than fine." Emma's voice was breathy and soft.

I squeezed my eyes closed more tightly.

"Let me show you how fine I am." Daddy laughed.

❦ 2 ❧

Emma

Iknow it was stupid, moving in with Brannon so fast. But I was lonely before he came to the campground, and he was funny and sweet and so good with his daughter. And my God, he looked so *good*. When he and Jenny first arrived at camp, I watched him around the place for a few days before I talked to him, his dark hair just curling damp at the base of his neck, his arms and chest muscled and taut under his white T-shirts. He was something to watch, all right, so lean and tanned and glistening with sweat. Even Zella Fay at the diner said so, as we stared at him out the window over lunch one day.

"Yeah, he's a looker, all right." Zella Fay poured more coffee into my cup and almost smiled, watching Brannon outside, hauling wood to the fire pit for the big bonfire that night. "And the little girl seems like a good kid," she added, turning from the window. "She's real polite. Sometimes she even helps me with the dishes. I give her a dollar."

I'd seen the daughter around, too.

"How old do you think she is?" I asked.

"Ten," Zella Fay said. "Eleven in August."

"I wonder where her mother is." I was fishing now.

"Dead," Zella Fay said. "She died when Jenny was three."

I raised my eyebrows. Normally, Zella Fay didn't engage in gossip, but she was full of information today.

"Jenny hangs out here sometimes when it's too hot outside," she said. "Does her schoolwork at a booth or just follows me around. She seems kind of lonely."

"I'll bet," I agreed. "It must be hard on a kid, moving around the way they do."

Zella Fay nodded and swiped the counter with a towel.

"Seems like he's a good dad," she said, glancing out the window toward Brannon. He was stacking logs in the fire pit now, building a balanced pyramid. "I've never heard him raise his voice to her. He pretty much dotes on her."

"That's nice." I smiled to myself, watching Brannon build the pyramid. "It must be nice to have a dad who dotes on you."

When I left the diner that day, I stopped by the fire pit and introduced myself.

"Hey, I'm Emma. I work with the horses." I smiled at him.

He wiped his forehead with a blue bandana and grinned back at me—a crooked, beautiful, wide grin.

"I'm Brannon," he said, holding out his hand. "Brannon Bohner. Nice to meet you."

"Looks like hot work," I said, taking his hand and nodding at the pyramid.

"At least it's not muggy," he said. "Last summer I worked at a campground in Alabama. Imagine heat like this with ninety-percent humidity. It felt like I was working in a sauna."

"Zella Fay just made a fresh batch of iced tea," I said.

"That sounds good." He wiped his forehead again. "Will you join me?"

So I went back into the diner, where Zella Fay was still watching us, and sat down in a booth instead of at the counter.

"Can we get two iced teas, Zella Fay?"

She raised an eyebrow at me now, then poured two big glasses of tea and set them on the table before us.

"How 'bout some pie?" She halfway smiled at Brannon. "I got fresh peach pie today."

"That sounds good." Brannon smiled at her, his eyes crinkling at the corners. "Has Jenny been in this afternoon?"

"Not since lunch." Zella Fay waddled into the kitchen, returning with a huge slice of pie, topped with a scoop of vanilla ice cream. "She's down at the river with the kids from seventeen, the pop-up. Their mama's with them. She's all right."

He nodded before digging into the pie. Zella Fay stood at the table, watching him chew.

"Best peach pie I ever had," he said, swallowing.

She waddled back to the kitchen, smiling.

"So . . ." He turned his attention to me, that crooked smile thawing the cold places in my past. "Are you from around here?"

I shook my head. "Arizona," I said.

"Beautiful country," he said. "How did you end up at the Flying J?"

"Oh, that's a long story," I said, laughing. "I'll bore you with it sometime. How about you? How did you find your way here?"

He took a long drink of iced tea and sighed, relaxing into the red-vinyl booth. "We've been moving around for a few years now, my daughter and me."

"I've seen her around the place," I said. "She's a beauty."

He nodded, grinning. "She takes after her mom, that's for sure."

"Actually, I think she looks a lot like you . . . at least from what I've seen."

I felt myself blushing and hoped he didn't think I was some kind of stalker. But he just grinned again.

"She's a good girl," he said. "She's smart, too. And she seems to like it here."

"Maybe sometime she'd like to come see the horses?"

"I bet she'd love that," he said. "Thanks."

He rose and wrapped the bandana around his head.

"I'd better get back to work."

"I'll see you around, Brannon."

I watched him walk back to the fire pit. He was something to look at, all right. Behind me, I heard a snort. Zella Fay was laughing behind the counter.

"You be careful what you wish for, honey. That man is dragging around a whole lot of baggage."

"You mean his daughter?"

"For starters," she said.

I shook my head and smiled. "He seems like a nice enough guy."

"Just be careful," she repeated. She waddled back to the kitchen, glancing back over her shoulder. "Just you be real careful."

A week later, Brannon asked me to join him for lunch with his daughter. We were at Zella Fay's, of course. It was the only place close by to eat. I watched him order for himself and then for Jenny, shaking his head when she said she wanted a milk shake to drink.

"That's a dessert," he said. "You can have milk or juice with lunch."

"Juice," she said. "But can I have a milk shake after?"

"Let's see how you do with your lunch."

Zella Fay brought us big bowls of chili, a small plate of jalapeños, and a pan of cornbread. Her one good eye locked onto me, as if to say again, "Just be careful." I smiled at her.

"So," Brannon said, putting his arm around Jenny's shoulders. "Did you know that Emma works with the horses in the barn?"

"That's cool," the girl said.

I breathed in deep and said, "I was wondering if maybe you'd like to visit with them after lunch."

I smiled at her. After a long minute, she smiled back. It was a cautious little smile. It almost broke my heart.

"I'd like that," she said softly. "Thank you."

Jenny took to the horses right away. More important, the horses took to her. She was very gentle and spoke quietly to them, offering carrots and apple slices carefully in her outstretched palm. Sometimes I let her give them sugar cubes as a special treat. Before long, she became my constant shadow whenever I was at the barn. She shoveled hay and manure without my asking. I taught her how to brush down the horses, being careful never to stand behind them, where she might get kicked. And I discovered early on that Brannon had been right. Jenny was as smart as a whip.

"How do you know how much to feed them?"

Jenny was petting Buck's nose while I brushed the huge horse down.

"It depends on how big each horse is and how much exercise it gets," I said. "Buck here is almost two thousand pounds and he does the trail almost every day, so he needs more food. Angel"—I nodded to the dappled horse in the stall across the way—"she's a little older and a little bit smaller, and she doesn't get ridden as much, so she needs a little less."

"So it's a percentage of their weight?" Jenny looked at me with her startlingly blue eyes, so at odds with the dark hair curling to her shoulders.

I stared at her for a minute. It seemed a complicated concept for a ten-year-old.

"Yeah," I said finally. "It's a percentage of their weight, plus their activity. In the summer, they get most everything they need from grazing, and I supplement with some hay. Come winter, they'll get more hay plus a little bit of grain."

"Do you stay here all winter, too?" Jenny's blue eyes widened.

"Yep, I'm a full-timer here."

"You're lucky."

The little girl leaned her forehead against Buck's nose and sighed.

"It's plenty cold here in the winter," I said, watching her closely. "And we get a lot of snow. It's darned isolated, once the snow starts."

"I bet it's pretty, though." Her voice sounded far away.

"It is beautiful," I agreed. "But it's not for everyone."

"Daddy says we're going to Kentucky this fall. He's going to work in a big warehouse until after Christmas."

"That sounds nice," I said. "I've never been to Kentucky."

"We drove through it before. It's okay." Jenny shrugged. "It's a lot like everyplace else."

"So," I said, "how many places have you lived?"

She thought a minute before answering.

"We lived in Indiana first, I think. Then we bought the trailer and started moving. We've lived in Florida, Pennsylvania, Texas, Alabama, Tennessee, Kansas, and here. I think that's all."

"That's a lot."

She nodded.

"Do you like moving around? It sounds like a great adventure, like being a pioneer."

"It's okay." She shrugged her shoulders again.

"Kind of lonely sometimes?" I put my hand on her shoulder.

"It's okay," she repeated.

"Well, I'm glad you came west this time. You really are a great helper with the horses."

She smiled at me then, a smile to melt your heart, so hopeful and open. I hadn't seen her look like that before.

"Maybe me and Daddy could stay for the winter," she said. "I could help you with the horses, and Daddy can do whatever else needs to be done."

"I don't know," I said, sorry to disappoint that hopeful little face. "Boyd doesn't keep a lot of workers over the winter."

"Oh." Her shoulders slumped.

"But maybe you can come back next summer."

"Maybe," she said softly. "But probably not. We never go the same place twice."

She patted Buck's nose again, then kissed it.

"I better go," she said. "I still have to do my lessons. Thanks for letting me come."

"Thank you for helping." I smiled, watching her sprint for the door.

"Jenny?"

She turned at the doorway to look at me.

"You really are a great helper."

She smiled and ran toward the trailer she shared with her dad.

3

Jenny

After Emma moved in, we didn't eat at the diner nearly so often. Emma liked to cook, she said, and she actually was pretty good at it. Maybe not as good as Cara, but a whole lot better than Ami or Trish. Poor Trish caught a pan on fire once, and all she was doing was trying to boil some green beans. She left not long after that. Daddy said probably she was just embarrassed about it. I think maybe she left because I laughed at her. But honest to God, she was funny, grabbing the pan with a towel wrapped around her hand, jumping from one foot to the other, and screaming at me to open the door.

She got kind of snappy with me about it when I laughed, until Daddy told her to shut the hell up. I knew then that she would leave soon. I was eight when Trish lived with us, old enough to know that no one stayed around except Daddy.

On a Tuesday morning in early August, Emma swept into the trailer holding a plastic grocery bag triumphantly above her head.

"Hey, you!" She smiled at me, her green eyes sparkling bright. "Guess what I've got."

"Books?" Emma brought me a regular supply of books from the library.

"Nope." She opened the bag and pulled out a package of

bacon, almost full. Grinning, she set it on the table and reached into the bag again. Half a dozen eggs, an unopened quart of milk, and a carton of orange juice were deposited next to the bacon.

"The Andersons left just now, and they gave me the stuff out of their fridge. So I'm thinking we'll have breakfast for dinner tonight. How does that sound?"

"Great!" I loved bacon and eggs. We didn't have bacon often. It cost too much and Daddy said it wasn't very healthy. Mostly we had cereal for breakfast.

"I thought the Andersons were staying till Friday," I said.

Celia Anderson was a year younger than me, and we'd had fun in the week she'd been at the campground. Her mother took us on the lift up the ski hill once. She even paid for me to go. You could see forever from up there. Celia was afraid on the lift, but I loved it. It was almost like being in heaven.

"They're heading out below," Emma said, using the local term for leaving the valley. She stuffed the groceries into our tiny fridge. "They wanted to get out ahead of the storm."

We'd been watching the weather on television all morning. A front was building to our west, and we were supposed to get a gully washer—that's what the weatherman called it.

"The Dixons are leaving, too," Emma said. She turned to me and I guess I looked nervous, because she sat down across the table from me, took my hands in hers, and said, "We're going to be fine, honey. Don't you worry."

"But if we're fine, why is everyone leaving?"

"Not everyone," she said. "Just the Andersons and the Dixons. They're from places where storms mean tornadoes, I guess. But we don't get tornadoes in Idaho. I told them, Boyd told them, even Zella Fay told them it would be okay. But they left anyway."

I sighed. I would miss Celia.

"How are your lessons going?" Emma turned my math book toward her and frowned at the page. "Are these fractions?"

"Yeah."

I'd been plowing through the book all week. When I finished it, Daddy said he would take me to see a movie at the Spud—that was the drive-in theater in Driggs. It had a huge concrete potato on the

back of a truck out front. On weekends they played double fea-
tures, the movie dialogue interrupted regularly by someone calling
out on the speakers, "So and so, your Gladys burger is ready."
Daddy made me a bet at the start of summer that I wouldn't ever
make it through both movies without falling asleep. We'd been
twice so far, and both times I was asleep long before the second
movie had even started.

"This stuff would make me cross-eyed," Emma said. "I couldn't
help you if I tried."

"It's not so bad," I said. "Once you get used to it, it goes pretty
fast."

She shook her head.

"You're going to college someday," she said firmly, nodding at
me. "I can tell already you're going to be a college girl. You must
get your smarts from your dad."

"He didn't go to college," I said.

"Oh, I know," she said. "You don't have to go to college to be
smart. But you sure as heck have to be smart to go to college."

"Did you go to college?"

Emma laughed and rose from the table. "Me? Oh no, honey.
I'm not smart enough for college. I barely made it through high
school."

"You're smart about horses."

She bent to kiss the top of my head. "Thank you, Jenny."

"For what?"

"For being such a nice person."

I felt my cheeks redden.

"I've got to get back to the stables," she said, opening the door
and glancing at the sky. "I need to move out anything the wind
could pick up, and make sure the horses are okay. I'll see you at
lunch."

She strode toward the stables and I returned to my math problems. Emma wasn't worried about the storm, so I decided I wouldn't
worry, either.

By mid-afternoon the sky was a dark steel gray, and wind skit-
tered the brush and dry grass through the campground in small
whirlwinds.

Daddy came home and turned on the television while I watched the huge clouds towering in the sky out the window. Once in Texas we had seen a tornado and we didn't have time to go anywhere safe. It missed our part of the campground, but I won't ever forget the mess it left in its wake. Three trailers had been lifted right off the ground and thrown into a field nearby. Another lay on its side. Daddy helped a man climb out of that one. The firemen and police had to help some other people. No one died that day, but I always worried about bad weather after that.

"Should we go to Zella Fay's? She has a basement."

"Hmmm," he said, staring at the television.

"Hey, you guys!" Emma struggled to close the metal door behind her. Outside, the wind howled a long, low lament. "What are you doing sitting inside watching television, when Mother Nature is putting on such a great show out there?"

Daddy raised his eyebrows at her, frowning slightly. "When you live in a trailer, babe, Mother Nature's shows aren't always so great."

"We'll be fine," she said, dropping beside him on the bench by the table. "We don't get tornadoes in Idaho."

"Straight-line winds can be just as bad," Daddy said.

"Come on." Emma rose and pulled him up by his hands. "You have to see this."

We followed her outside and walked to the edge of the campground. In the distance, huge thunderheads rolled toward us. We could see the dark of the rain sweeping across the valley. Lightning arced across the sky to the ground, flashing again and again. It was beautiful in a terrifying kind of way. I held on to Daddy's hand tightly.

When the rain finally reached us, we ran back into the trailer. Heavy drops began rapping against the roof, not so bad at first, then louder and harder.

"Oh my Lord, it's so loud!" Emma gazed at the roof, her hands covering her ears. "I guess I've never been inside one of these when it rained."

She took Daddy's hand and grinned. "Come on. Let's go to

Zella Fay's. We can have some pie and watch the storm without all this noise."

We covered our heads with our jackets and ran through the downpour to the diner, where a half-dozen other campers sat drinking coffee and watching the storm outside.

"Pie?" Zella Fay filled two mugs with coffee and poured a glass of milk for me.

"Sure," Daddy said. "Jenny, do you want some pie?"

I shook my head, staring out the window at the storm. Daddy put his arm around my shoulders and hugged me tight. "We're okay, Jenny. We're just fine here. We're safe."

Zella Fay brought apple pie slices for Daddy and Emma and a couple of chocolate chip cookies for me. After a while, the wind stopped howling so loud and the deluge settled into a steady, hard rain.

"Come on," Emma said, rising from the table and holding out her hand to me. "Let's go see the gully washer."

Daddy smiled at her and rose, too. I took Emma's hand and followed her out into the rain, across the muddy parking lot and past our trailer.

"Where are we going?" I shouted, my voice muffled by the heavy rain.

"You'll see!" She led us up a slight hill, pulling me along by the hand. At the top, she stopped and pointed down into the ravine below. A small but vicious river whooshed through the little valley, a river that hadn't been there before now.

I stared at the rushing water and then at Emma.

"That's what they mean by a gully washer," she said, grinning. "The ground is too dry to soak in all the water, so it washes down the valleys like that."

"Cool!" I watched the river in awe.

"Yep, it's pretty cool," Emma agreed. "But it's dangerous, too. Look how fast that water is moving. You could get swept away in water like that."

I held her hand tightly and backed away from the edge of the rise where we stood.

"You're okay," she said. "I've got you."

A flash of lightning tore the sky open and I jumped. A few seconds later, thunder rumbled loud across the valley.

"Come on," Daddy yelled, pulling Emma's hand. "We'd better go back in."

We slogged back across the campground toward the diner, shielding our faces from the driving rain.

"You all look like drowned rats." Zella Fay shook her head as we entered. "Take those jackets off and drink something warm."

She poured more coffee for Daddy and Emma and brought me a steaming cup of cocoa with marshmallows.

"You've got to watch out for this one," she said to Daddy, nodding toward Emma. "She's got no more sense than the Good Lord gave a mule. Last summer, she almost got herself hit by lightning, out dancing in the rain."

Zella Fay shook her head and glared at Emma.

"But it was fun!" Emma smiled at her, then at me. "Besides, I had to make sure Jenny got to see a gully washer."

Zella Fay returned to the kitchen, muttering under her breath about damned fools.

"Did you really dance in the rain?" I asked, poking the marshmallows down into my cocoa and watching them bob back up to the surface.

"Sure I did," she said. "I like dancing in the rain. Haven't you ever done that?"

I shook my head. I hated rainstorms, the way the rain pounded so loud on the roof of the trailer and the wind shook the walls like paper.

"Well, come on then!" She rose again, laughing.

"I don't think so." Daddy shook his head. "Too much lightning out there."

"Come on," she teased. "You're not going to let a little lightning keep you inside, are you?"

Daddy shook his head again, so she turned to me. "How about you then, Jenny? Don't you want to go dance in the rain?"

I wanted to go with her, but I sat frozen in my chair, feeling my cheeks redden. Emma wasn't afraid of anything, it seemed. And I . . . well, I was afraid of just about everything.

"Jenny is *not* going out there until it stops storming," Daddy said firmly.

Emma tilted her head so that her red curls fell across her face. She pouted for a moment, then laughed again and sat back down beside Daddy.

Later that evening, after the lightning and thunder had crossed over the mountains, we did go outside and dance in the lingering rain, Emma peeling off her jacket and whirling across the grass. Even Daddy came out and danced. So did some other people who'd waited out the storm in the diner. By the time we were done, we were soaked all the way through our clothes, all the way to the bone. My teeth chattered as I spun around, holding hands with Daddy and Emma.

I can't remember a better day in all my life.

4

Emma

When Brannon asked me to go with him to Kentucky, I almost said no. It really was too soon, I hadn't known him very long, and I didn't want to leave the camp. I loved my job there, I loved the horses. I even loved the winters in Idaho, when the wind blew so cold and bitter-crisp it took your breath away.

"Come on," he said, rubbing my bare belly as we lay on his bed in the trailer, moonlight streaming through the open window across our naked bodies. "Don't you want to see the rest of the country? You've never been east of Wyoming, babe. There's a whole world out there you haven't seen."

"I know," I murmured. "It's just . . . it's awfully soon. I've only known you a couple months. And I like my job. Hell, I love my job. It took more than a year for Boyd to really trust me with the horses. I can't just leave them."

"We can come back here next summer, if you want."

I shook my head and avoided his eyes.

"You know I'm crazy about you, right?" He took my chin in his hand and made me look at him.

"I know." I nodded.

"And I'm pretty sure the feeling is mutual." He stared straight into my eyes.

"Yeah, it is," I said. "But . . ."

"But nothing. It's you and me, babe, all the way. We'll see the whole damned country together. I mean, Kentucky in the winter isn't exactly Shangri-la, but it's not too bad . . . rolling hills and funny little towns, oh, and distilleries, too. Maker's Mark, Jim Beam, Wild Turkey . . . think about it, honey. We can see all of them. And when I'm done at Amazon for the season, we can go anywhere you want to—Florida, Maine, New York, California, even . . . anywhere you want to go."

I closed my eyes, picturing the places we could go, being on the road with Brannon. I smiled a little, even as I shook my head again.

"But what if it doesn't work out?" I asked. "What if *we* don't work out?"

Brannon laughed and kissed my shoulder.

"Why shouldn't we work out?" he asked softly.

"Well, we don't really know each other that well."

"So, let's get to know each other." His voice was warm, cajoling. "We'll learn all about each other traveling cross-country. It will be fun. And . . ." he continued straight on as I opened my mouth with another, "What if?"

"And, if it doesn't work out, if you decide you don't want to stay in Kentucky, you can always come back here."

He nuzzled my neck, touched between my legs gently, ran his tongue across my breasts. "But I think you'll want to stay."

I moaned softly.

"And I know what you want right now, don't I?" he whispered, tracing his tongue slowly down my belly.

"Yes," I whimpered. "Yes."

Crazy as it sounds, that's how it happened. That's how I decided to leave behind Idaho and my beautiful horses and Boyd and Zella Fay and everything I knew and loved, to go with Brannon and Jenny to Kentucky, or to wherever else he wanted to go.

The next day I told Boyd I'd be leaving at the end of the season.

"You can't be serious," he barked, removing his sunglasses to stare at me. "You hardly know the man. You aren't really going to leave your job and just follow him to wherever? You're too smart for that, Emma."

Zella Fay said pretty much the same thing when I told her.

"I told you, didn't I? Didn't I tell you? The man's got baggage," she said, her mouth set in a firm, straight line. "And I ain't just talking about Jenny, either. Brannon, he's carrying a whole lot of junk."

But I would not be swayed. Come the end of October, I would leave Idaho and the west, and travel to Kentucky with Brannon and Jenny.

I did almost change my mind at the last minute.

Brannon wanted me to sell my SUV and ride with him and Emma to Kentucky in his truck.

"That's part of the fun, getting to know each other," he said, his hand on my knee. "We'll see the whole country together. It'll be great."

"But I'll need a car once we get to Kentucky," I said. "I don't want to be stuck in the trailer while you're at work every day."

"I'll walk to work," he said. "The campground is right next to the warehouse. So I'll walk and you can drive the truck."

The idea of a campground sitting right up next to a huge warehouse sounded awful. But the idea of being without my Chevy Tahoe was even worse. I'd worked hard and saved for over a year to buy it. That car was my pride and joy. Hell, it was my independence.

"We'll get you another car in Kentucky," Brannon said. "Another SUV, if you want. Or maybe a sedan, something that gets better mileage."

I shook my head and bit my lip. "I like my car."

"But it's just stupid to drive two cars all the way across country."

It was our first real disagreement, and both of us dug in our heels for a while.

Finally, I said, "Look, I'm giving up a lot to come with you, Brannon. I'm leaving a good job and my friends. I'm not leaving my car, too."

He stared at me for a long minute, and I thought he was going to tell me I should just stay behind. But then he laughed and shook his head, so that his dark curls brushed his collar.

"What the hell," he said. "Fine, keep the damned car. But it's going to be a long, lonely drive to Kentucky all by yourself."

He was pretty unhappy when Jenny decided to do the first leg of the trip with me, instead of in the truck with him.

"Well, great," he said. "That's just great. Now I've got two stubborn women on my hands."

He laughed, but I could tell he wasn't happy. And for just a minute again, I thought I wouldn't go, after all.

But then he kissed me on my forehead, my nose, my mouth. His dark eyes laughed into mine.

"Just be careful on the road," he said softly. "I'm trusting you with the most precious part of my life, you know."

I nodded and smiled back at him. He kissed me again, and I felt my knees tremble.

Lord, I was in trouble deep.

PART 2

KENTUCKY

5

Jenny

"Will you miss the horses?" I sat in Emma's SUV, staring out the back window at the campground that was disappearing in a cloud of dust behind us. Ahead of us, Daddy drove the truck, pulling our trailer behind him. We were on our way to Kentucky for the winter.

"Sure," she said. "But I'm ready for a new adventure. Aren't you?"

I shrugged my shoulders and turned in the seat to look at her. She was so pretty, her red hair tied back in a ponytail. Freckles sprinkled across her nose and cheeks. No makeup. Emma never wore makeup. Not like Trish or Cara or Jackie.

"How did you learn to take care of horses?" I asked, mostly to make conversation.

"My dad had horses," she said. "I grew up helping take care of them."

"Where did you live?"

"In Arizona; that's south of here."

"How come you came to the campground?"

She sat quietly for a minute and then sighed deeply. "I didn't get along with my folks. So one day, I left. I came north and ended up in Idaho."

I stared at her. "How old were you?"

"Seventeen," she said. She turned to smile at me, but the smile didn't reach her eyes. Her eyes looked sad. "Too young to be on my own, but too stupid to know better."

"Why didn't you get along with your parents?"

She shrugged, frowning at the road ahead. "They were . . . different. And I was bored, I guess. I didn't want to stay in the same little town my whole life. So, I left."

"Did you tell them you were going?"

She shook her head. "No," she said softly. "I left in the middle of the night while everyone was sleeping. Then I went down to the main road and caught a ride."

"You mean you hitchhiked?" My eyes widened. We sometimes passed hitchhikers on the road, but we never picked them up. Daddy said they must be either stupid or crazy to be out there on the road, and either way, we didn't want them in the truck with us. Daddy worried about stuff like that.

Emma nodded, her mouth set in a straight, tight line. "I know it was stupid. Like I said, I was seventeen and I thought I was invincible. It never even occurred to me that anyone would try to hurt me."

"Did they?" I whispered. "Did someone try to hurt you?"

"Let's just say I came across some good people and some not-so-good people. But mostly, I think, people are good."

"And that's how you came to Idaho?" I pushed further. "You hitchhiked here?"

"No." She shook her head, frowning slightly again. "At first I hitchhiked to Utah, to Salt Lake City. I got a job waiting tables in a little restaurant there and stayed almost two years. Then, I met a man who was really nice. Or at least I thought he was nice. I came with him to Rexburg in Idaho, that's where he lived. He owned a hardware store and I worked there for a while. But then . . . well, he turned out to be not so nice, after all. So I caught a ride to Driggs and I met Boyd there, and he gave me a job at the campground. That was three years ago."

"Don't you miss your mom and dad?" I asked.

She shook her head again. "Not really," she said. "Like I said, we didn't get along."

I sat back to think about that. How would I feel if I left Daddy and never came back? How scared would he be? I couldn't imagine it.

"They weren't very good parents," Emma said softly, as if reading my thoughts. "Not like your dad."

"Did you have any brothers and sisters?"

"Yeah," she said, her voice even softer. "I had a couple brothers and three sisters."

"Do you miss them?"

She was quiet for a minute and then sighed heavily. "I miss my sisters, I guess, especially my youngest one, Clarissa. She was only eight when I left. I do miss her."

"Why don't you go back to see her?"

"I can't." Her voice was firm. "I can't go back ever."

"I'm sorry," I said, touching her arm the way I'd seen Daddy do so often.

"It's okay," she said, smiling at me. "I'm going forward instead."

We drove all morning south through steep mountains, and then pulled onto I-80 to head east. After we stopped for lunch somewhere in Wyoming, I climbed into the truck to ride the rest of the day with Daddy.

"So, did you have a good ride with Emma?" he asked, pulling back onto the highway.

"Yeah," I said. "I like her."

"Me too," he said, grinning at me. "I think she might be the one."

Daddy always said that when he got a new girlfriend.

"I hope so," I whispered.

And I did hope so. I hoped against hope that Emma would be the one who finally stayed.

6

Emma

Lord God, I was so tired after that first day of driving. We did thirteen hours straight, finally stopping for the night outside of Hastings, Nebraska. We stayed there in a nasty dump of a campground, but not before Brannon got into it with the manager over the cost of parking my car.

"Twenty bucks? Are you kidding me? What a fucking rip-off!" His face was red, and the muscles at the base of his neck bulged.

"Sorry, buddy. That's the rate." The manager, an older man with a paunchy belly and red eyes, sounded bored.

"But you've got all those empty spaces." Brannon pointed to the half-empty campground.

"Twenty bucks for the extra car." The manager's voice was flat. "I don't make the rules. I just follow them."

"It's okay, Brannon," I said, as calmly as I could. I was so tired I would have paid twice that, just to be out of the car. "I've got it."

I handed the man a twenty and he took it without comment.

"Lot twelve," he said, pointing toward the back of the campground. "And you can park your car there." He pointed to a small, completely empty parking lot behind the camp store.

Brannon glared at the man and then at me before turning the

key in the truck's ignition. Beside him, Jenny sat absolutely still, staring out the window away from all of us.

I parked my SUV and walked across the campground, to where Brannon was maneuvering the trailer into lot twelve.

"Unbelievable! Just un-fucking-believable!" he spat at me, stepping from the truck. "Twenty bucks . . . wasted. This is why I wanted you to leave your damned car in Idaho."

"It's okay," I repeated. I tried to stay calm, but I could feel my voice shaking. I'd never seen Brannon angry like that. His dark eyes were wide, his mouth set in a tight, hard line.

"So it's okay with you? You think it's okay to just blow money?" His voice rose. Behind him, Jenny climbed down from the truck and stood watching us.

"It's not that much, Brannon." I was getting angry myself, now. After all, it was my money that got spent.

"Daddy?" Jenny's voice was soft, pleading. "I've got some money saved from my allowance."

Brannon turned to her, his face softening immediately. He ran his hand through his hair and sighed.

"Honey, no. You keep your money. It's okay."

He turned back to me and sighed again. "I'm sorry," he said. "I guess I'm just really tired."

"Me too," I said, draping my arms around his neck. "It's been a hell of a long day."

It didn't take much to set up camp, and soon I was boiling water on the stove for spaghetti and stirring a jar of sauce in a pan.

"That smells good," Brannon said, wrapping his arms around me from behind. I pushed a sweaty strand of hair from my eyes.

"It's just spaghetti and meat sauce. Nothing fancy."

"Well, it's better than anything I would have made." He kissed my neck and squeezed me tight. "I'm glad you're here, babe. I'm glad you came."

We sat on lawn chairs outside while we ate dinner, and I stared at the landscape stretching out flat in all directions.

"That was good," Brannon said, leaning back in his chair. "Jenny, wasn't that good?"

Jenny nodded and smiled. "Thanks, Emma."

She yawned and rose, taking her father's empty plate and then mine and walking toward the trailer.

"Wash up and get ready for bed," Brannon called after her. "We've got another long day of driving tomorrow."

He belched and rubbed his stomach, then smiled at me, that beautiful, crooked smile.

"Will we make it to Kentucky tomorrow?" I was definitely ready to be off the road.

"Nope," he said. "Tomorrow we'll stop in Indiana for the night."

"Why stop there?" I asked. "Why not just go straight on to Kentucky and get it over with?"

"I've got a storage unit in Indianapolis," he said. "I've got to pick up our winter gear and put away the summer stuff. It adds a few hours to the trip, but we need to get our winter things, Jenny's coat and all that. So, we'll stay in Indy tomorrow night, and then it's just a short drive to Campbellsville. We can get there by noon on Monday."

"Indianapolis, is that where you're from?"

Brannon hadn't talked much about his past. And thankfully, he hadn't asked much about mine.

"Yeah." He yawned and stretched again. "I grew up there."

"Is your family there?"

He paused and took a long drink from his water bottle.

"I don't have any family," he said quietly. "My mom was killed in a car accident when I was seven. After that I lived in foster care."

"My Lord, Brannon, I'm so sorry." I put my hand over his and squeezed.

"It was a long time ago," he said.

"Don't you have any other family?"

"Nope, Mom was on her own when she had me. I never knew my grandparents or anything."

"So, is Indiana where you met Jenny's mom?"

He nodded and ran his hand over the back of his neck.

"Once I was eighteen, I was on the streets and on my own. My foster parents couldn't wait to get rid of me. They were just in it for the money."

He took another long drink of water.

"I met Hailey in Greenfield, that's just east of Indianapolis," he said. "I was working in a lumberyard and she worked in the office. We started seeing each other. Then she got pregnant, so we got married."

"How did she die?"

I held my breath, waiting to see if he would keep talking. Like I said, Brannon didn't talk about his past.

He stared into the gathering dark for a long time and sighed deeply.

"She had a hard time with the delivery," he said finally. "She never really was strong or healthy after Jenny was born. She wasn't really healthy even before she got pregnant. And I wasn't home much. I was working twelve-hour shifts, trying to make ends meet and keep a roof over our heads. And then, right after Jenny's third birthday, Hailey came down with the flu. I didn't worry about it at first. I mean, it was just the flu, right?"

He rose and began pacing around the campfire.

"I came home one night and she was burning up with a fever. I took her to the emergency room, even though we didn't have insurance, but it was too late. She died the next morning."

I stood and wrapped my arms around him, pulling him close as if I might shield him from his pain.

"I'm sorry," I whispered.

He kissed my forehead and wiped a tear from my cheek.

"It's okay," he said. "I mean, it was hell then, especially for Jenny. But it's been a long time. We're okay now."

"Is that when you started moving around?"

He shook his head and stepped away from me, staring into the fire.

"We stayed in Greenfield for a few months, but I lost my job at the yard. Jenny was three, and I didn't want to leave her with someone I didn't know. So I missed a lot of work. And then it took a while to find something else, so I lost the apartment. Then the economy went to hell, and I couldn't find anything steady. So a guy I knew told me they were hiring seasonal workers at Disney World down in Florida. I wasn't sure how we'd get there, but he said he had a trailer he'd sell me. I'd been saving for an apartment, so I used that as a down payment. He let me pay him the rest after the gig at Disney. He was a nice old guy. He died a couple years ago."

He sat back down in his lawn chair and rubbed his chin. "Me and Jenny, we've been moving ever since."

"Do you ever think about settling down?" I asked, sitting back in my own chair.

"Sure," he said, nodding. "I'd like to, if I could find good, steady work. But with the economy the way it is, I have to take jobs where I can get them."

"It would be good for Jenny to have a real home, maybe go to school and make some friends."

"Yeah," he agreed. Then he rose. "But . . . look, it is what it is. And at least this way she gets to see a bunch of difference places. And she's happy, I think, especially since you moved in."

He held his hand out to pull me from my lawn chair.

"We probably should hit the sack. We've got another long day tomorrow."

I rubbed my stiff lower back and nodded.

"I sure wish you were riding with me," he said, nuzzling my neck. "It'd be a lot more fun."

I smiled and kissed his cheek. "But it will be worth it, having my own car in Kentucky," I said. "Don't you think?"

Brannon cupped his hand on my ass and smiled.

"Sure, babe," he said. "It'll be great."

7

Jenny

The next day I rode with Daddy in the morning, listening to country music on the radio. After we stopped for lunch in Iowa, I climbed into Emma's SUV for the rest of the day's ride. She looked kind of tired, but she smiled as we pulled out of the McDonald's parking lot.

"So, this is pretty," she said, nodding out the window at the rolling green hills. "It's so green."

"I guess so." It just looked like anywhere else to me.

She glanced at me and then was quiet. After a few minutes, she tried again.

"Are you excited to be going back to Indiana?"

I shrugged my shoulders. "Not really."

"Do you remember when you lived there? You were pretty little then, I guess."

"I remember we lived in some nasty places." I shivered, remembering the apartments and rooms with roaches and mice. "That was before Daddy bought the trailer."

"Do you go back to Indiana a lot?"

"Just when we need to get stuff from the storage place. We don't stay there long. I don't think Daddy likes it there."

"Maybe he has sad memories from there," she said softly. "That's where your mom died, right?"

I stared at her for a minute.

"How do you know about my mom?"

"Your dad was telling me about her last night, about how she got the flu and died when you were just three. I'm really sorry, Jenny."

"It's not your fault," I said.

She laughed a little. "I know. I'm just sorry it happened, sorry for you. You must miss her a lot."

I shrugged again.

"Do you remember very much about her?" Emma asked.

I shook my head. "Not much. I remember she sang to me sometimes. And sometimes when Daddy was at work late, she slept in my bed with me."

"That's nice," she said. "I bet she was a good mom."

I nodded. I was surprised Daddy had told her anything about my mother. He didn't like to talk about her. Sometimes when I was young, I'd ask him what she was like or how they met, and he got kind of mad. He always felt bad after, but he really didn't like to talk about her. That much I knew.

"Maybe we can put flowers on her grave while we're in Indiana."

Emma smiled at me. "Would you like that?"

I stared again, my mouth hanging open. "I don't think Daddy would like that," I finally managed.

"Well, I'll ask him. We'll see." She reached across the seat and patted my knee.

I just nodded. I didn't want to tell her what I thought. I didn't want to think about Daddy getting mad.

By mid-afternoon, the steady rumbling of the car had lulled me to sleep. I awoke with a start when Emma turned into the huge parking lot of a Walmart.

"Where are we?" I asked, rubbing sleep from my eyes.

"We're in Indianapolis," she said, pulling the SUV into a parking place beside where Daddy had maneuvered the trailer. "On the east side of town, I think. Your dad must need to buy some things."

I shook my head. I knew we weren't there to shop.

"Hey, sleepyhead!" Daddy opened the car door and stooped to hug me, pulling me from the car. "Time to rise and shine."

"Hey," Emma said, smiling at him across the top of the SUV. "Do we need to do some shopping?"

"Nope," Daddy said, grinning back at her. "This is where we're staying tonight."

Emma gazed around her and then looked back at him. On the road behind us traffic sped by. A car braked abruptly, its tires squealing. Another car's horn blared. In the distance, a siren wailed.

"We're staying here? In a Walmart parking lot?"

"Sure," he said, nodding. "Most Walmarts will let you park overnight, as long as you don't make a mess or too much noise."

"But, where will we plug in?" She stood staring at him, her green eyes wide, her freckled face pale.

"Tonight, honey, we'll rough it. We can use the facilities inside. We'll buy some sandwich stuff and have a picnic. The weather's warm. It'll be fine."

Daddy was already unhitching the trailer from the truck.

"Come on, Jenny," he said over his shoulder. "Hop to it."

We worked in tandem, just like always, while Emma stood watching in silence, her mouth still open. I felt bad for her, because I knew she was confused and probably disappointed. I always felt that way when we stayed at a Walmart, too.

After we'd set up, Daddy held his hand out to Emma and they walked into the store. I trailed behind them.

"Welcome to Walmart," an old lady grumbled at us.

"Thank you, ma'am." Daddy smiled at her.

The woman's eyes widened and finally she smiled back. Daddy was always nice to people. He said it was an easy way to make life a little better for everyone.

We filled a shopping basket with bread, sliced turkey, cheese, and tomatoes.

"Can we get some chips?" I loved potato chips, but we didn't have them very often.

"Sure," Daddy said. "Plain or barbecue?"

"Barbecue!" They were my favorite.

He smiled at me and touched my hair. He was in a good mood,

which kind of surprised me. Usually he was grumpy when we were in Indiana.

We picked up some apple juice and a six-pack of beer. Emma trailed behind us, not saying anything. I worried she was mad because we were spending the night in a parking lot.

We stood in a long line, waiting to pay for our stuff. Ahead of us an older couple unloaded their cart onto the conveyor belt. The woman bumped into Emma, then turned to smile.

"Excuse me, dear," she said.

Emma stared at her in silence, edging closer to Daddy.

"No worries," Daddy said, smiling at the woman.

He looked down at Emma, his forehead wrinkled.

"Are you okay, babe?"

She nodded, still watching the woman in front of us.

After we paid for our things, we carried the bags across the parking lot to the trailer. Still, Emma said nothing. She gazed around her at all the people pushing carts. She looked like she might cry.

"Okay, what's wrong?" Daddy asked, unlocking the door.

Emma stepped into the trailer and put her bag on the table. She was quiet for a minute, then she whispered, "There are so many black people here."

Daddy's eyes widened and then he laughed. "No more than anywhere else," he said.

Emma sat down at the table. "A hell of a lot more than I ever saw before."

I pulled the bag of chips from a sack and opened them. "Didn't they have black people in Arizona?"

"Not the part I'm from."

Daddy stood for a minute with his hands on his hips. Finally, he said, "Please don't tell me you're a racist, babe. Because where we're going, there'll be all kinds of people."

She looked up at him, her eyes wide.

"I'm not a racist," she said firmly. "I'm just not used to being around people . . . like that."

It occurred to me then that we hadn't seen a black person all summer.

"There weren't any black people at the ranch," I said.

Daddy shook his head. "I guess Idaho isn't known for its ethnic diversity."

"Mexicans," Emma said. "There are lots of Mexicans there, especially in Rexburg."

"Well, you'll meet all kinds of people in Kentucky," he repeated. "Blacks, Hispanics, Africans, Asians . . . you name it. Seasonal workers are a diverse bunch of folks. That's not going to be a problem, is it?"

Emma shook her head and forced a small smile. "No," she said. "It will be an adventure."

"Good!" Daddy started opening packages and making sandwiches. "You'll see, babe. People are pretty much all the same. We all want the same things. We all want to be happy. We all want a better life for our kids. We're all just people."

I sat down beside Emma at the table and opened the juice, wondering why there were no black people in Idaho.

After we ate, Emma cleaned the kitchen while Daddy and I pulled all of our clothes out and made piles, some to take with us and some to go into storage. I sighed when I put my swimsuit in the storage pile, wondering if it would still fit me when I got it back.

I climbed into my bed that night with Bugsy Bear and listened to the traffic of the street.

"It's so noisy," I heard Emma say.

"It's just for tonight." Daddy's voice was low. "Tomorrow, we'll be in Kentucky."

"I hope it's quieter there."

Daddy laughed. "It'll be fine," he said. "You'll see."

The next morning when I got up, Daddy had already left to take our summer clothes to the storage unit. Emma cut a piece of coffee cake for me and poured juice.

"Your dad will be back in a while," she said. She sipped black coffee from a Styrofoam cup.

"I hope my winter stuff still fits."

"I'm sure some of it will. The rest, we'll just replace."

I nodded. "There's a Goodwill down the street from here."

She smiled at me. "So this is your regular Indiana camping place?"

I nodded again. "We always come here to get our stuff."

"Maybe someday you'll settle down somewhere for good."

I shrugged my shoulders. "Maybe."

"Wouldn't you like that?" she asked.

"I guess."

She smiled and rose, pacing the narrow aisle of the trailer.

"Do you want to go back to the store?" I asked, thinking it would be nice to be out of the trailer.

"No," she said, her voice firm. "I don't want to go back in there. Not without your dad."

"Are you scared of black people?"

She sat back down and sipped her coffee. "I'm just not used to them, I guess."

"They're okay," I said. "Last winter in Georgia, the family in the trailer next to ours was black. They were really nice."

"It'll be an adventure," she said again, but she sounded worried.

8

Emma

I was glad to leave the Walmart behind. Jenny asked if she could ride with me, but I told her she should ride with her dad. I needed some alone time, just to think.

I know it surprised Brannon, the way I acted at the Walmart when I saw all those black people. I'm sure he thought I was crazy. But honestly, I never saw a single black person before I was seventeen, except sometimes on the television when I was very little, before we got rid of it. And living in Utah and Idaho, I hadn't seen many since, except on TV and in the movies.

How could I explain to Brannon the way I was raised? He would never understand. I mean, I lived it and I still don't understand it.

The drive south was dull, until we left the interstate and took to the back roads. We wound up and down rolling hills ablaze in yellows and reds and oranges. I had a hard time focusing on the road, the trees were so colorful. I felt like I had left the black and white of Kansas and entered a Technicolored Oz, where anything might happen. Signs for distilleries and churches flashed by, more kinds of Baptist churches than I ever knew existed—Southern Baptists, Independent Baptists, Missionary Baptists, Evangelical Baptists,

Primitive Baptists. Who knew there were so many kinds of Baptists?

I knew already that Brannon wasn't religious, and I had sure as hell had enough religion in my childhood to last through all eternity. But the little white churches were pretty, scattered along the road amid the autumn colors.

Finally, we saw a sign for Campbellsville. I followed Brannon's trailer past the outskirts of a small city. Then we turned left and I gaped at a huge, sprawling warehouse. It looked almost as big as the city itself, with hundreds of cars in the fenced parking lot. Across the road behind another little church, we pulled into an equally huge gravel lot, stair-stepped up a hill. A sign proclaimed it the Heartland RV Park, but it looked nothing like the campgrounds I'd worked in out west. No green space, no trees, no lake or even a pond, just acres of gravel punctuated by RV hookups. A few dozen trailers were scattered across the lot, some of them much nicer than ours, others far shabbier.

Brannon parked in front of the rental office. I parked beside him and got out of the car, stretching. I felt like we'd been driving for weeks, instead of just three days.

"So, this is it," he said, holding his hand out to me. "Home, sweet home until January."

I stared at the barren lot and tried to smile. A small terrier yapped at the end of a chain. A dark-haired woman with a baby on her hip yelled at the dog to shut up. Down the hill, someone was grilling hamburgers for lunch. My stomach growled and I swallowed hard.

Brannon went inside to check in while I stood staring. I felt Jenny's hand touch mine.

"It's kind of ugly," she said.

"Yeah," I agreed. "But maybe it'll be prettier when it snows."

"Maybe," she said. Her voice sounded doubtful.

"Do you decorate the trailer for Christmas?" I asked.

"We put up lights," she said. "I mean, more lights than we usually do."

I nodded, remembering the plastic lanterns strung from the canopy in Idaho.

"I have to go to the bathroom," she said.

"We'll get set up soon."

"I can't wait. Will you go with me?"

We walked into the building, where Brannon was laughing with a young blond woman who wore a skin-tight sweater and too much eye makeup.

"Here they are," he said, waving at us. "This is Emma, and this is Jenny."

"She's just as pretty as you said," the woman said, smiling at Jenny. She didn't look at me.

"I have to pee," Jenny said softly.

"The restroom's next door, honey." The woman pointed to a low building outside. "Showers and laundry are in there, too."

"Thank you," I said, willing her to acknowledge me. But she was already bent over her desk, pointing out our spot on a map for Brannon.

Jenny and I walked to the shower building and I pushed open the door cautiously. It was clean and well lit and smelled of bleach. I sighed with relief.

When we walked back outside, Brannon was already in the truck. The blond woman leaned against the cab, pointing down the hill to our spot.

"Thanks," I heard Brannon say. "Thanks a lot."

"Anytime, sugar." She backed away from the truck and watched him pull the RV onto the gravel drive, smiling like she was pleased with herself.

Jenny and I climbed into the SUV and I gunned the engine a little, just to let the blonde know I was there.

"She looks trashy, doesn't she?" Jenny said in a small voice.

"She sure does."

"She looks kind of like Trish."

"Trish? Is that a friend of yours?"

"No," she said, staring out the window. "She was one of Daddy's . . . friends."

"Oh." I glanced at her, but she didn't look toward me. "Did she live with you guys?"

Jenny nodded. "Just for a while."

I felt like the wind had been knocked out of me. I hadn't thought about it much, but of course I probably wasn't the first woman Brannon had been with since Jenny's mother died. How many had there been? I started to ask and stopped myself. We were already pulling alongside the RV. And I didn't want to pump Jenny for information. She was, after all, only eleven.

Then Brannon was opening the car door and pulling me out to kiss me. He smiled that crooked smile and I felt my doubts subside. Of course he had a past. I had a past, too. They didn't determine our future.

After we set up camp, we climbed into the truck and drove into the city of Campbellsville. It was a pretty little town, and when we parked and walked onto Main Street it felt almost like we were stepping back in time. Brick storefronts lined the street, many festooned with wreathes in fall colors. Window boxes overflowed with mums and jack-o-lanterns, stone planters bloomed on the sidewalks, light poles were wrapped in cornstalks and ribbons, and a banner draped across the street proclaiming, MAINSTREET SATURDAYNIGHT!

"It's so pretty! Like being in a 1950s movie or something."

"Mayberry, U.S.A." Brannon smiled.

"What's Mayberry?" Jenny asked.

"That's a little town from an old TV show," Brannon explained.

"Look!" Jenny pointed to a storefront window painted with hamburgers, french fries, and milk shakes.

"Happy Days." Brannon read the sign aloud. "That's another old TV show."

"Can we eat there?" Jenny looked at her dad, her eyes wide.

"Sure," he said. "A late lunch . . . or maybe an early supper."

We settled into the vinyl seats of a booth with a red-checkered vinyl tablecloth. A pretty young woman with blond hair piled on top of her head approached, carrying menus.

"Welcome to Happy Days," she said, smiling. "I'm Resa and I'll be taking care of you today. Ya'll ain't from around here, are you?"

"Just got in," Brannon said, smiling back at her. "I'm working at Amazon for the season."

"Well, I hope you like it here." She smiled at Jenny and then at me. "Campbellsville is a good place to live."

I laughed when I opened the menu and read the selections, all themed from the old sitcom.

When the waitress returned, Jenny ordered the Love Me (Chicken) Tenders and Onion "Rings of Fire." Brannon asked for Chachi's Chili Cheeseburger. I got a veggie wrap.

"That's not very authentic," Brannon said, laughing. "You should at least try some fried pickle chips."

"Not if I plan to stay in these jeans," I said.

"Honey, if I could fit into those jeans, I'd eat until I burst wide open." The waitress looked down at her own curvaceous figure. "I wasn't that size when I was her age." She nodded at Jenny.

We all laughed.

"So, what is there to do in Campbellsville?" Brannon asked.

"Not much," she said.

"What about Main Street Saturday Night?" Jenny asked.

"That's over for the season. Ya'll missed the last one just last week."

She paused then, looking at Jenny's disappointed face. "Still," she said, "there are some fun things to do around here. Let's see, there's Green River Lake. That's real pretty. You can go boating or fishing, if it's not too cold. Or you can take a horseback ride."

"We did that all summer," Jenny said, her lower lip drooping just a bit.

"Well, there are a lot of Civil War sites close by, and there's the place Abe Lincoln was born. That's a fun trip."

Jenny sighed.

"Sounds great," Brannon said, his voice just a shade too loud. "We'll find lots of fun stuff to do." He put his arm around Jenny's shoulders. "I'll bet you and Emma will have lots of great adventures."

9

Jenny

I didn't like Campbellsville much at first. The town was okay, but I hated the campground. It was gray and dusty and there was nothing to do; it didn't even have a swing set. I guess they didn't get a lot of kids staying there.

Daddy worked the night shift, ten hours at a time, four nights a week—unless there was overtime. Then he worked five nights. When he came home we had breakfast together, and after breakfast he went to bed.

Emma usually took me to the library to do my schoolwork. I loved the library in Campbellsville. It was in an old church and still had stained-glass windows. I brought my laptop and did my work while Emma read books or looked at magazines. At lunchtime we walked to Main Street and ate, sometimes pizza at the Snappy Tomato, but more often at Happy Days. I loved their onion rings and Emma liked the salads. After lunch, we went back to the library until two o'clock. Then we'd go home, where Daddy would just be getting up.

On a sunny, warm afternoon in early November, we walked home from the library, each carrying a book.

"There are my two favorite girls!" Daddy sat at the table in his sweatpants and a T-shirt, drinking coffee. "How was your morning?"

"Okay." I plopped down beside him. "Just the usual."

"Did you finish your lesson?"

I nodded, reaching for a cookie. "Emma checked it for me."

Daddy raised his eyes to Emma. She smiled and nodded.

"It's just English today," she said. "I figure I can handle that."

Daddy laughed. "So, what's the plan for today?"

"Well, since the weather's so nice, I thought we could go to the lake," Emma said. "Maybe take a picnic?"

"Sounds good," he said. "Let me just grab a shower first."

Outside, we heard the rumbling of a motor. I opened the door to watch a big RV maneuver itself into the lot next to ours, a Coleman with bright stickers from around the country covering its door. An old VW Bug was hitched behind it. I watched as a woman climbed out of the RV.

"Daddy!" I hollered after him as he closed the bathroom door. "The Johnsons are here!"

I opened the door, hopped down the step, and ran toward the truck. "Hi, Mrs. Johnson! It's me, Jenny, from last winter."

The woman turned and grinned. "Well, hey there, Jenny. We didn't know you'd be here. How've you been?"

"I'm good," I said. "Where's Lashaundra?"

Before the woman could answer, I saw Lashaundra running around from behind the RV.

"Hey, Jenny!" She threw her arms around me and hugged me tight. "Are you staying here, too?"

I nodded, feeling a flood of relief. It was so good to have a friend, someone I'd met before.

"How's your daddy?" Mrs. Johnson asked.

"He's okay. He's taking a shower."

"How's Jackie? Is she inside?" Mrs. Johnson took a step toward our trailer, then stopped suddenly. I turned to see Emma standing in the doorway, watching us.

"Oh," Mrs. Johnson said. "Um, hello."

Emma opened the door and stepped down. "Hi," she said. Her voice sounded stiff.

"I'm Angel, Angel Johnson. And this is my daughter, Lashaundra. We camped beside Brannon and Jenny last winter, in Georgia." She extended her hand. After a slight pause, Emma shook it.

"I'm Emma," she said.

A man walked around the RV carrying a small boy.

"And this here is Michael," Mrs. Johnson said, waving toward the man. "And our boy, Malcolm."

"Nice to meet you." Mr. Johnson put the boy down and extended his hand. Again another pause before Emma finally took his hand.

"Well, hey, you guys!" Daddy appeared on the step, grinning. "I didn't expect to see you here."

"Good work, good pay," said Mr. Johnson, shaking Daddy's hand. "How're you doing? Where you been working?"

"We've been out west, working at a campground in Idaho. How about you?"

"Dollywood," Mr. Johnson said, shaking his head.

"We did that a few years back. When was that, Jenny?" Daddy turned to me.

"That was when I was seven," I said. "Cara was there."

There was a sudden silence. I saw Mrs. Johnson raise an eyebrow slightly at Mr. Johnson, who said kind of loudly, "Well, we won't be going back there anytime soon."

"Yeah," Daddy agreed. "Not much of a setup."

"Still, it paid pretty well."

"Let me give you a hand, Michael." Daddy and Mr. Johnson began unhooking the car from the RV.

"Well," Emma said, stepping back toward our trailer. "It's nice to meet you."

"Can Lashaundra come with us to the lake?" I asked.

"I . . . um, I don't know, Jenny. She probably has to stay and help her mom."

"Can I go, Mom?" Lashaundra grabbed her mom's hand. "Please?"

Mrs. Johnson stood quietly for a minute. Then she said softly, "I don't think so, honey. We just got here. We've got a lot to do."

"Please?" Lashaundra repeated.

"Maybe I could stay and help you set up," I said. "Is that okay, Daddy?"

Daddy turned from the hitch and wiped his forehead. "It's okay with me if it's okay with Mrs. Johnson."

She smiled at me. "Well, that would be fine, Jenny. More hands, fewer chores."

She turned to look at Emma. "I hope that's all right with you?"

Emma looked from Brannon to me to Mrs. Johnson and finally said, "If Brannon thinks it's okay then I'm good with it."

She turned and walked into our trailer, the door clanging shut behind her.

Mrs. Johnson put her hand on my shoulder and smiled. "It sure is good to see you and your daddy again."

"I'm glad you're here," I said. "I missed you guys."

With Daddy helping, it didn't take long for Mr. Johnson to hook up the RV. Then Lashaundra and I helped Mrs. Johnson set up inside. Soon, the place looked just like I remembered it from the year before.

Daddy and Emma climbed into her SUV with a picnic packed in a brown paper bag.

"You sure you don't want to come with us?" Emma asked.

"No, I'm gonna stay here with Lashaundra," I said.

"It's all good, babe." Daddy put his hand on her shoulder. "It's good for her to have a friend. And it's good to have a little time, just us."

He winked and waved at me and they drove up the dusty road, Emma watching me through the back window.

"Is she your new mom?" Lashaundra asked, waving at them.

"Yeah."

"She's prettier than Jackie."

"She's okay." I shrugged my shoulders. "I like her all right."

I could see Mrs. Johnson in the window of their RV, and I knew she could hear us. I wasn't sure if I should talk about Emma or not.

Daddy always said what happened in our family was our family's business and no one else's. But the Johnsons were friends. Last year, Daddy and Jackie had spent a lot of time with Mr. and Mrs. Johnson, playing cards and drinking beer. We even celebrated New Year's Eve together.

"Where's the playground?" Lashaundra asked, looking around.

"There isn't one," I said. "There isn't anything, really, at least not here. But downtown is nice. There's a great restaurant called Happy Days. You'll love it."

Mrs. Johnson called out the window. "You girls want to come with me to the store?"

We piled into the Bug. Malcolm stayed at the RV with Mr. Johnson, but he wasn't happy about it. He wriggled in Mr. Johnson's arms, trying to climb into the car with us.

"You stay here, baby. You stay with Daddy. Mama will be back after a little while." Mrs. Johnson kissed Malcolm through the window. He was hollering like crazy when we drove off.

Mrs. Johnson wheeled a cart through the Kroger, pointing to things for us to pick off the shelves. I found the creamed corn and Lashaundra got the whole-kernel corn. Then we ran in search of corn muffin mix and cheddar cheese. Mrs. Johnson made the best corn casserole ever.

When the cart was full, we stood in the checkout line behind a lady who seemed to have a coupon for everything in her cart.

"Can we get some gum, Mama?"

"No, baby. It's bad for your teeth."

"Even sugarless?" Lashaundra smiled at her mother, her dark eyes wide.

"All right." Mrs. Johnson sighed and put a package of gum in our cart.

"So," she said, not looking at me, "what happened to Jackie? I'm surprised she's not with you."

"She left," I said. "When we went to Idaho, she didn't come with us."

"Is that where you guys got Emma?" Lashaundra asked.

"Yeah."

"Well, that explains that," Mrs. Johnson said so softly I could barely hear her.

I watched her move items from the cart to the checkout counter and thought of the woman in Walmart, the one who'd bumped into Emma.

"She's not racist," I said. "She's just not used to being around black people. There aren't any black people in Idaho."

"Mmm-hmm." Her back was to me.

"Honest, Mrs. Johnson, Emma's really nice. She's just shy, I guess."

She turned to look at me then, cupped my chin in her hand, and smiled. "I'm sure she's nice, honey. Is she nice to you?"

I nodded. "She worked with the horses at the campground we were at, and she let me help. I know all about taking care of horses now."

"Well, that's good, Jenny. That's just fine."

I slept that night in the Johnsons' RV, sharing Lashaundra's bed like I had so often the winter before. Daddy kissed me good night, while Emma watched from the trailer doorway. They must have been tired from their picnic, because they turned out the lights even before Lashaundra and I went to bed.

"Did you like Idaho?" she whispered to me under the covers.

"Yeah," I whispered back. "It was really pretty and there were mountains and a river. And we saw lots of deer and ducks and stuff, even a moose one time."

She sighed. "I wish we could have gone there instead of stupid Tennessee. That campground was awful . . . worse than this one."

We giggled for a minute.

"The campground in Idaho was nice. Lots of grass, and they had bonfires at night, and we swam in the river."

"How come there aren't any blacks there?" she asked.

"I don't know," I said. "But I didn't see anybody but white people the whole time we were there."

"Maybe that's why we didn't go, too."

"Maybe."

"Do you miss Jackie?"

I nodded. "Sometimes. She was funny."

"I liked her. She told the best jokes." Lashaundra yawned. "Why did she leave?"

"I don't know. She just left, like they all do."

"Do you think Emma will leave?"

I nodded again. "They all do."

Long after Lashaundra fell asleep I lay awake, listening to Malcolm snore in the bunk below. Finally, Mr. and Mrs. Johnson turned off the television and the light.

"So, what do you think about Brannon and that woman?" Mrs. Johnson's voice carried softly across the RV.

"She's a looker, all right."

I heard a slap and a laugh. "That's not what I meant and you know it."

The bedsprings creaked.

"I don't know, Angel. Brannon says she's real good with Jenny."

"Jackie was good with Jenny." Mrs. Johnson's voice was sharp.

"And she left." Mr. Johnson sounded tired.

"Well, this new one sure has issues."

"Brannon says she grew up in some weird town in Arizona and never has been anywhere except there and Idaho."

"Hmmph." Mrs. Johnson sounded unconvinced.

"She can't be too bad, honey. She let Jenny spend the night."

"That wasn't her choice. That was Brannon."

"Well, we're stuck with her for a few months. So we might as well make the best of it."

There was a long silence. At last, Mrs. Johnson said quietly, "I'll be nice. You know me, I'm always nice. But if she says anything to hurt my baby . . ."

"Go to sleep, Angel. It'll be fine. You'll see."

"Michael?"

"Hmm?"

"I love you."

"I love you, too, honey."

I lay in bed awake for a long time, wondering what it would be like to have two parents who both stayed.

10

Emma

"Ya'll want the usual?" Resa called out as we walked into the diner.

"I think I'll have a chef's salad today," I said.

"You want dressing, or are you eating it naked?" She pulled her pad from her apron pocket.

"Italian," I said, sliding into our usual booth.

"How 'bout you, hon?" She smiled at Jenny. "The usual?"

Jenny nodded and smiled back. It was impossible not to smile when Resa was around.

She took our ticket to the kitchen and returned with our drinks.

"So, what are ya'll up to?"

"We've been at the library," I said, taking my iced tea. "Jenny's working on a big science paper."

"Good girl," she said, placing Jenny's milk on the table. "Study hard, get good grades, go to college, and get yourself a real job that pays real money."

"What do you think I pay you?" Harlan yelled from the kitchen. "Monopoly money?"

Resa laughed and rolled her eyes. "You don't pay jack shit, and you know it," she called back to him. "If you did, maybe Carol Sue wouldn't have quit."

"Carol Sue quit?"

"Yeah," Resa said, leaning against our table. "Last night she walked out in the middle of the dinner shift. Told the old man to take the job and shove it."

She sighed. "So now we're shorthanded for the evening shift. You know anyone looking for a job?"

"Actually," I said, "I might be interested."

Jenny stared at me. "But who will take me to the library?" she asked.

"I will," I said. "If it's the dinner shift, I can work while you're with your dad."

"You got any experience?" Resa asked.

"Yeah, I've waited tables before. Did a couple years at a truck stop in Utah. It would only be until we leave in January, but it'll give you some time to find someone permanent."

"Well, let me get you an application," she said. "Like I said, it don't pay much, but it's better than nothing. And of course, you'll get all the pleasure of working with me!"

I guess I thought Brannon would be happy when I told him about the job. But he wasn't, not at all. That night, before he left for his shift, he let me know just how unhappy he was. Thankfully, Jenny was at the Johnsons'.

"I can't believe you took a job without even talking to me about it first!"

"It's just the dinner shift, and it's only three nights a week. We can use the money."

"Damn it, Emma! I am the man in this family, and I can take care of the money."

"But I thought . . ."

"I don't care what you thought. I'm telling you I don't want you working at that goddamned diner!"

He slammed his fist on the table so hard the whole trailer shook. I stared at him in disbelief. I'd never seen him so mad.

I took a long breath and said as calmly as I could, "Look, I'm sorry I didn't tell you first. I didn't know you'd be so upset. I just thought the money would be helpful with Christmas coming up.

We can use it to get Jenny some nice things, maybe a new coat. Her old one is getting too small for her."

He stared at me for a long minute, his face red. Then he, too, took a long, deep breath and seemed to deflate.

"Oh, Emma," he said finally, "that's sweet, honey, that you want to buy stuff for Jenny. I'm sorry I lost it, babe. Really, I'm so sorry."

He drew me into a hug and held me until both of us were breathing normally again.

"Why would you get so mad about me working?" I asked, easing away. "I worked when we were in Idaho. I've always worked. I like working. I like pulling my own weight."

He took my hands and was quiet for a minute. Then he said, "Last year, I met a woman named Jackie. You probably already knew that, right?"

I nodded, still holding his hands. "She lived with you," I whispered.

"Yeah, she did. And I thought it was going to work out. We got along great; we had fun. She seemed to love Jenny. I thought maybe she was the one, that maybe we'd even get married."

"So what happened?"

"She took a job at a gas station in the town where we were. Said she wanted to make some extra money. And then, boom, she decides she's in love with the guy she works for. He owned the station. A real loser, if you ask me. But she left me, she left without even telling Jenny good-bye."

He sat down at the table and dropped his head into his hands. "I was pretty hurt, but Jenny . . . God, Jenny was just devastated to lose her. They'd gotten really close."

I sat down across from him and put my hands on his. "That's not going to happen to us," I said firmly. "I promise you, Brannon, I'm not going to leave you for anyone else."

He raised his head and I saw a tear slide down his cheek. My heart nearly broke.

"I love you, Brannon," I said, brushing away that tear. "I love you and I love Jenny, and I'm not going anywhere without you."

He rose and pulled me to my feet, then wrapped me in a tight embrace.

"I love you, too, babe." He kissed my forehead, my cheek, my nose. He drew me into a long, deep kiss.

"Ewww!"

Jenny stood in the doorway, Lashaundra beside her. Both girls looked pretty much horrified.

I stepped back, feeling my cheeks redden. We didn't kiss like that in front of Jenny.

"Can Lashaundra sleep here tonight?"

"I have to work tonight, honey," Brannon said. "So I guess it's up to Emma."

He looked down at me and smiled. "Is that okay with you?"

"Sure," I said, returning his smile. "That's fine with me."

After Brannon left for work, Jenny and Lashaundra ran to the Johnsons' to get her overnight things. A short time later, I heard a knock at the door.

"Come on in, silly!" I was washing dishes in the sink.

"Excuse me?"

"Oh!" I said, turning toward the door. "I'm sorry . . . I thought you were Jenny."

Mrs. Johnson stood in the doorway, hands on her hips, frowning at me.

"She's at our place," she said. "I wanted to talk to you before I let Lashaundra spend the night here."

"Okay." I wiped my hands on a dish towel. "Have a seat."

We sat at the table.

"Can I get you some tea?"

"No, thank you. I just . . . I want to be upfront about some things before my little girl stays here with you."

She cleared her throat and looked directly into my eyes.

"It's pretty obvious you're a racist," she said. "And that's your problem, it's not mine. But you'd better be damned certain that you are *not* going to do anything or say anything to hurt my child. You got that?"

I felt like someone had punched me in the stomach. Her words took my breath away. I stared at her, feeling her anger wash over me like a cold wave. Her dark eyes never even blinked as she stared back at me. At last, I found my voice.

"Look, I'm not . . . I mean, I don't think I'm a racist. I don't want to be, anyway."

She said nothing, simply watching me.

"Where I was raised, we were taught some pretty weird things. Awful things, actually. And . . ."

"I know what it's like to be raised to hate," she said softly.

I stared at her, my mouth hanging open.

"What, you think white folks are the only ones who can hate? My daddy hated white people. He grew up in the South under Jim Crow. He took a whole lot of crap from the police, got beat up, even went to jail once. And it made him hate anyone who wasn't like him. He disowned me when I married Michael."

She must have seen my confusion.

"Michael's mother is white," she explained. "My daddy couldn't handle that. So, I know about being raised that way. But that doesn't mean *I* have to be that way. And it doesn't excuse you, either."

"But I'm not . . ."

"I saw you the day we got here," she continued. "I saw your face when you looked at my daughter. And I could hear the word screaming in your head. *Nigger.* That's what you thought when you saw my Lashaundra. That's what you thought when you saw Malcolm. I know the look when I see it."

I felt my cheeks beginning to burn. "I . . . I'm sorry," I whispered. "I didn't mean to look like that. I didn't mean to even think it."

"But you did."

The words hung between us, heavy in the air. I rose and began pacing the aisle of the trailer. My head was aching from too many thoughts. Finally, I sat back down and took a deep breath, trying to exhale all the fear and vitriol and garbage from my head.

"I grew up in the FLDS," I said. I hadn't told anyone that in a long time. I hadn't even told Brannon yet.

She simply looked at me.

"Fundamentalist Mormon," I said. "The kind you see on that television show, *Big Love.*"

"You mean the one with that man and all his wives?"

Now it was her turn to stare at me with her mouth open.

I nodded.

"Where I was raised, we were completely cut off from the rest of the world. We were told that everyone outside our church was going to hell, and that people with dark skin were the children of the devil. I know it sounds crazy, but that's what I was taught when I was a little girl. And you and Lashaundra . . . well, you're the first black people I've ever actually talked to. There were no blacks where I came from. After I was four, we didn't even have a television. The prophet, I mean the guy in charge of the whole town, he made us get rid of our TV. He said it was full of evil influences. So the only thing I knew about blacks was what I was taught in school. And the school was run by the church, so I got a pretty biased education."

I rose and poured water into the teakettle. I needed something to do.

"Are you for real?" She sounded skeptical.

"Honest to God, that's the truth."

I put the kettle on the stove and lit the flame. Then I sat back down across from her, a black woman at my kitchen table. My mother would have died!

"I ran away when I was seventeen. I left and I never looked back. And I set out to learn everything I could about the outside world. But even after I left, I didn't meet any black people. There just aren't very many out there.

"When I lived in Utah, a friend of mine took me to see *The Pursuit of Happyness*. Did you see that movie? It starred Will Smith, and my God, it blew my mind! I mean, here he was, this good guy, this good father who was trying so hard to make a better life for his son. After I saw it, I went home and cried for at least an hour, because I realized I had spent so much of my life being afraid of black people and thinking they were evil, when they really are just like us. I am . . . I'm sorry, I mean that you are just like me."

The teakettle began whistling, so I got up and poured water into two cups.

"Herbal okay?"

She nodded, still staring at me like I was from Mars.

I put the cups on the table between us and sat back down.

"After that, I watched lots of reruns of *The Cosby Show*. It was on at eleven every night. And I always ended up crying, thinking how I'd been so stupid. I mean, my family was a nightmare. Really, just a nightmare. But oh, they put on a show like they were just the best family in the world. And here was this *black* family with a great mom and dad, and the kids were all happy and got along. I felt like I'd been lied to my whole life. I *was* lied to my whole life."

I stirred sugar into my tea and sipped it.

"So, yeah . . . I don't know how to be around black people. And I *hate* that I still have all that stuff in my head. But I'm trying, I'm really trying, Mrs. Johnson. I'm trying to learn it all over, or to un-learn it, or . . . whatever."

I looked at her and tried to smile. "Does that make sense?"

She nodded and smiled back. It was the first time she'd really smiled at me, and it was a beautiful smile.

"It's Angel," she said. "Mrs. Johnson is my mother-in-law."

We both sipped our tea quietly for a minute. Then I said, "I promise you, Angel, that I will never say or do anything on purpose to hurt your daughter. I'm really glad that Jenny has a friend. I hope you believe me."

She nodded again. "I believe you, Emma."

"Thank you."

We drank our tea in silence. When her cup was empty, Angel rose and said, "Well, you've signed on for some chaos tonight. I hope you know that."

I smiled at her, so grateful that I almost cried.

"Thank you," I said again. "I think we'll be fine."

❧ 11 ❧

Jenny

That Thanksgiving in Campbellsville was the best I can remember in all my life. Emma roasted a turkey breast in the oven and made real mashed potatoes, not the instant kind, and green beans cooked with bacon.

In the morning, before the turkey went into the oven, she baked two pecan pies, and I proudly carried one of them to the Johnsons', still warm from the oven.

"Come on in." Mr. Johnson held the door open for me, smiling broadly. "It's cold out there."

"Hi, Jenny!" Lashaundra grinned at me from her bunk bed, laying aside the book she was reading. "Can you eat dinner with us?"

"No," I said. "Emma's cooking and I'm helping. She wanted me to bring you a pie."

I set the pie on the table beside a huge bowl filled with chopped sweet potatoes and a bag of brown sugar.

"Well, isn't that sweet of her."

Mrs. Johnson turned from the oven and smiled at me.

"And I guess it's true that great minds think alike, because I've got one for you-all, too."

She handed me a pumpkin pie from the counter, whipped cream piled in the center.

"Thanks, Mrs. Johnson!"

I carried the pie back to our trailer and put it on the table.

"Look what Mrs. Johnson sent."

"Hell yeah!" Daddy said. "Now my Thanksgiving is complete. Pumpkin *and* pecan pie for dessert. Is there anything better?"

I looked at Emma, who was staring at the pie, her cheeks reddening.

Oh no, I thought. *Please, Emma, don't send the pie back just because it was made by a black woman. Please don't hurt Mrs. Johnson's feelings.*

Then I saw a tear roll down her cheek, and she smiled.

"It really is nice," she said softly.

Daddy wrapped his arms around her from behind.

"They're good people," he said.

"Yes," she agreed. "They're the best."

We sat down to a full table that day. It smelled heavenly. I picked up my fork and reached for a roll.

"Shouldn't we say . . . something before we eat?" Emma asked.

"You mean like a prayer?" Daddy's forehead wrinkled. We'd never said a prayer together. Daddy said prayers were for ignorant, superstitious people.

"No, just . . . I don't know, just something." Emma shook her head and smiled. "Never mind, I guess I'm being silly."

"No," Daddy said. "It's okay. We can say . . . something."

Then we sat a moment in silence, and I wondered what to say.

Eventually, Daddy said, "How about we each just say what we're thankful for this year? Will that work?"

"That would be nice." Emma smiled and took his hand.

"Well, I know what I'm thankful for," Daddy said. "I'm thankful for the two of you, my best girls." He winked at me. "And I'm thankful for a job and a place to live."

"I'm thankful that Lashaundra is back," I said. "And for you guys. I'm thankful for both of you," I added.

Daddy and I both looked at Emma then, waiting. She sat quietly for a long time, then took a deep breath, reached for my hand, and squeezed it tightly.

"I am so grateful that I finally have a family," she said, her voice soft, her eyes filling with tears.

Daddy leaned over and hugged her, then opened an arm for me. We all hugged and Emma cried some more and I thought to myself, *Please, God, if you're really there, let that be true. Please let us really be a family.*

So one of us did say a prayer that day, after all.

And then we ate, and we ate some more. And then, we ate some more.

After we'd eaten as much as we could possibly eat, Emma rose and began clearing the dishes from the table. I watched as she stacked and began washing them in the sink, Daddy standing next to her with a towel, drying as she washed. I just sat watching them and letting myself feel happy and a little bit hopeful for the first time in a long time. Daddy was happy. Emma was happy. Maybe this time it would last. *Please, God . . .* I began again.

A knock at the door startled all of us. I ran to open it and found Lashaundra standing on the step, her coat wrapped tightly around her. A bitterly cold wind whipped at her braids.

"Come in, Lashaundra," Emma called. "And close the door! Good Lord almighty, it's cold out there!"

"This from the woman who lived year-round in Idaho," Daddy said, flicking her bottom with a dish towel.

"That's a different kind of cold," she said, smiling at him. "It's cold, yeah. But the cold doesn't seep into your bones like it does here."

"That's the humidity," Daddy said. "Dry cold is better than wet cold, just like dry heat is better than wet."

"Your pie was really good," Lashaundra said, rubbing her belly and beaming at Emma. "Daddy said it's the best pecan pie he ever ate."

"Well, your mom's pie was amazing!" Emma smiled back at her. "I think Brannon ate half of it in one sitting."

"Do you want to spend the night?" Lashaundra turned to me. "Mama's gonna make spiced cider."

I licked my lips, remembering Mrs. Johnson's cider.

"Can I, Daddy?"

"Sure," he said, leaning back in his seat.

"She said you-all should come, too," Lashaundra said.

"Not to spend the night," she added quickly. "Just for cider."

"That sounds like a plan," Daddy said.

And so we all spent the evening together, eating the last of the pie and sipping Mrs. Johnson's spiced cider.

By the time we climbed into Lashaundra's bunk, my tummy was aching from so much food.

"Guess what," she whispered.

"What?"

"Daddy says we might be staying here for good."

"Really?" I stared at her. "How come?"

"There's talk at the warehouse about some of the temp workers staying on. If Daddy gets asked to stay, we'll sell the RV and move into a real apartment."

"Wow." I thought about it for a minute. "Do you think my dad will get asked, too?"

"I don't know." Lashaundra sighed. "I hope so. Wouldn't it be great if we both stayed? Then we could go to school together and everything."

I nodded. It would be great to stay in one place and to have a real friend.

"Mama said we should pray real hard about it."

I nodded again. Would that work? If I prayed, would that help Daddy get a real job, so we could live in a real house and I could go to a real school?

I thought about what Daddy always said about people who prayed. Then I thought about Emma wanting to say something at lunch. She didn't seem ignorant or superstitious. Neither did Mrs. Johnson, and she prayed all the time.

I shut my eyes tight and held Lashaundra's hand.

"Dear Lord," she said softly, "please let Daddy get a permanent job. And let Mr. Bohner get one, too, so Jenny and I can be friends forever. Amen."

"Amen," I said.

Long after Lashaundra was asleep, I lay awake listening to the sounds in the RV and wondering about praying. Finally, just before I fell asleep, I whispered, "Dear God, if you're there, can you please help my dad get a real job? If you do, I'll be really good for the rest of my life. I promise."

I waited a minute more, but couldn't think of anything else to say. So I just said, "Amen."

❧ 12 ❧

Emma

"Order's up!" Harlan called from the kitchen.

I picked up the plates and carried them to a table, managing to set the right order before the right customer.

My first couple shifts at the diner had been pretty bad. I messed up so many orders, I thought Harlan was going to fire me on the spot. But then I started getting the hang of it. And Resa was fun to work with.

"Ya'll got room for some dessert?" Resa asked the table behind me.

"I'll have the apple pie with ice cream," the man said loudly.

"How 'bout you, Shirley?" Resa smiled at the woman sitting in the booth.

"It all looks good," she said softly.

"Well, your fat ass sure as hell don't need no dessert." The man's voice boomed through the restaurant. Other people stared at their plates. I felt my cheeks redden.

"How 'bout some more coffee, then?" Resa asked.

The woman nodded in silence, her head low.

I followed Resa into the kitchen. "Who's that?" I asked, nodding at the table she'd just left.

"That's Damon Rigby and his wife, Shirley. Poor thing, she just ain't got no backbone at all." Resa shook her head. "If I was married to Damon, one of us would be dead by now, and it sure as hell wouldn't be me!"

"Ya'll keep your gossip to yourselves," Harlan growled from behind the counter, slamming down a slice of pie and a cup of coffee. "Ain't none of our business."

He handed me another plate. "Table seven," he said.

I carried the plate to the table and smiled at the young man in the booth. His greasy hair hung low over his forehead and he slouched like he was half-asleep.

"Anything else?"

He shook his head. "Thanks, Emma. I'm good."

As I worked the dinner rush, I kept glancing at the table where Damon Rigby was shoveling pie and ice cream into his mouth, while his poor wife sipped decaf and never raised her eyes. It made me angry, angrier than I'd felt in a long time.

When they finally left, I bused the table, collecting a very small tip for Resa, not even ten percent. What a jerk!

That night as we cleaned tables and mopped the floor, I asked Resa, "So what's the deal with that Rigby guy?"

"He's bad news," she said, grimacing. "A real bully, always has been. Even when we were kids in school he was mean. I don't know why Shirley stays with him. Don't know why she married him in the first place, except maybe because he had money. He owns that car lot out on Greensburg. Inherited it from his daddy."

I sighed, thinking of the women I'd known as a child. "Maybe she doesn't think she has a choice," I said.

"Honey, this is the United States of America!" Resa leaned against the mop and frowned at me. "Of course she's got a choice. She just ain't got no backbone."

"I knew a lot of women like that back home," I said. "They didn't feel like they had any choice. It's the way they were raised. If no one ever treats you like a real person, you kind of start thinking maybe you're not. Like maybe nothing good happens to you because you don't deserve it."

She stared at me. "Well, hon," she said after a pause, "you are the living proof that you always get a choice. You could've stayed where you were and been like that. But you didn't. You got a spine.

I don't see you staying with a man who treated you the way Damon treats Shirley."

I bent over to wipe a table. I didn't want Resa to see my cheeks, which were hot and red.

"Sometimes, it takes a little help, is all," I said.

"Now you listen to me, Emma." She walked over and put her hand on my shoulder. "I know it ain't pretty to watch, but Shirley's marriage is her own problem. Don't you go getting any ideas about trying to save her. Damon Rigby is bad news. You don't want to cross him."

"Resa's right about that," Harlan yelled from the kitchen. "You stay the hell out of his way."

I nodded. "I'm not going to do anything stupid," I said.

"That's my girl." Resa beamed at me. "I knew you were a smart one the minute I laid eyes on you. Well," she laughed then and flicked me with her washrag, "when I could tear my eyes off that man of yours. Lord God almighty, he is a fine-looking man."

I smiled at her and then laughed. "He is nice to look at, isn't he? I feel pretty lucky."

"And your little girl's a beauty, too."

"Oh," I stammered. "Jenny's not my daughter. I'm kind of her stepmom, I guess. But not really."

"Ya'll ain't married?" Resa looked me up and down.

I shook my head. "We only met in June."

"Well, I'll be damned," she said. "I thought you were an old married couple. And the way that little girl looks at you, you could be her mama."

I smiled and shook my head again.

"Don't wait too long," she said, walking toward the kitchen. "A man like that, you gotta snare him up while you can. Make him put a ring on your finger."

I laughed again and followed her to the kitchen.

"I'm good," I said. "I'm happy just the way things are."

"That's because you're still young and pretty," Resa said. "Wait another ten or fifteen years and you'll wish you'd married him before you got old. Hell, when I was your age I'd already been married and divorced. I knew if I didn't get married again soon, I'd be an old maid all my life. Probably turn into one of those crazy old ladies they find dead in a house with twenty cats or something."

"If you don't finish up here and get yourself home, Earl might just be gone," Harlan said. He sounded mean, but he was grinning at her. "You could still get in on that crazy-cat-lady thing."

She laughed and swatted at him. "The day Earl McCoy tries to leave me is the day you'll find him dead with his balls cut off and mounted on the wall. Ya'll ready?"

Harlan turned out the lights and locked the back door, then walked with Resa and me to our cars. He was a cantankerous old man, but he walked us to our cars every night.

"Good night, Emma," he said, nodding at me. "You did a good job today."

I smiled as I drove home, surprised at how much that small compliment had raised my spirits.

Jenny was spending the night with Lashaundra and Brannon had left for work by the time I got home. So I got a can of beer from the fridge and sat down to watch *Criminal Minds* on the television. Brannon always laughed at my addiction to the show.

"That's going to give you nightmares," he said again and again. "I don't know how you can watch that stuff."

"I don't like the gory parts. I just like watching how the team solves the crime. It makes me feel better, somehow, to know there are people like that in the world, people who can solve murders and things."

He just laughed. "It's TV, babe. It doesn't work like that in the real world."

I wondered if he was right. But I still watched the show every week, hoping that there really were people like ones in the behavioral analysis unit, people who could track down and catch the bad guys. I wished they were in Campbellsville, Kentucky, right about now. I wished I could call them and ask them to check in on Shirley Rigby.

❦ 13 ❦

Jenny

After Thanksgiving, Daddy started working a lot of overtime. At first it was five ten-hour days a week, then five twelve-hour days. Emma and I didn't see him very much. He dragged home in the morning, kissed Emma and me, and went right to sleep. And because he was going into work earlier, there was no one at home on the nights Emma worked at the diner. Some nights I spent at Lashaundra's. But sometimes I just went to the diner with Emma. I ate dinner and sat in a booth, watching whatever was on the television or reading until closing time.

"Hey, Jenny, do you want a brownie?" Resa asked as she walked by my table.

"No thanks."

"Well, how 'bout some cocoa with marshmallows?"

"Okay," I said, smiling at her over my book. "Thank you."

"What are you reading?" she asked as she set the cocoa on the table.

The Sisterhood of the Traveling Pants." I held the cover up for her to see.

"Traveling pants? How do pants travel? Is that like Harry Potter?"

"No." I laughed. "It's about these four girls who are best friends.

And they travel different places during the summer, and they send the pants back and forth. And the pants fit all of them, even though they're not all the same size."

Resa shook her head. "Why would anyone write a book about a pair of pants?"

"It's more about the friendship," I explained.

"Oh," she said, nodding. "That makes more sense. You've got to have friends. They're the most important thing in the world."

Emma stopped by on her way to the kitchen. "Friends are important," she agreed.

"Daddy always says family is the most important thing." And by family, he meant me and him.

"Honey, let me tell you something." Resa plopped down in the booth across from me and rested her elbows on the table.

"Boyfriends come and go. Hell, sometimes husbands come and go. But your girlfriends are your girlfriends forever, no matter what. Don't you forget that when it comes time for you to start dating. Don't ever let a boy get between you and your girlfriends. You hear me?"

I nodded solemnly, even though I didn't have any girlfriends except for Lashaundra, and I was *never* going to date a boy.

"Order's up!"

Emma and Resa hurried back to the kitchen and I returned to my book. The pants were in Greece right now with Lena. And so was I.

Later that night, I yawned and watched while Resa mopped and Emma wiped down tables.

"You know," Emma said, "husbands don't always come and go."

Resa laughed. "I know, honey. But sometimes they do. I mean, look at my ex. He took off with a younger, thinner, blonder girl while I was pregnant with my first. He never even looked back."

"That was mean," I said.

"Well," she said, smiling at me, "he was just my practice husband. You know, the first pancake?"

Emma laughed, but I just looked at her.

"The first pancake?"

"Okay, listen," Resa said. "You know how when you make pancakes, the first one always gets thrown away? Either the griddle's too hot and the pancake burns, or it's not hot enough and the batter spreads out too thin. Either way, the pancake ends up in the trash. That's how my first husband was. I practiced on him. Hell, we've all got a first pancake."

Emma laughed, and I looked at her, suddenly afraid.

"Is Daddy your first pancake?" I asked, before I could stop myself.

"Oh, Jenny." She leaned down to hug me. "Don't worry. Your dad isn't my first pancake."

"You mean you were married to someone else?" I stared at her. Resa stopped mopping and turned to look at Emma, too.

Emma's cheeks colored and she stood for a minute not saying anything. Then she sat down beside me and wrapped her arm around my shoulders.

"I got married when I was very young," she said. "I wasn't even sixteen. And . . . it didn't work out. So I left."

"But I thought you ran away from home when you were seventeen." My head was spinning.

"I did," she said. "But not from my parents' home. I ran away from my husband. He was not a nice man."

"Ah," Resa said softly.

"Yeah." Emma nodded. "That's why I got so upset about the way Damon Rigby was with his wife. Because his wife . . . well, that was me when I was fifteen."

"Does Daddy know?" I whispered.

Emma sighed and squeezed my shoulders.

"Not yet," she said. "I wanted to tell him. I know I should have told him. But . . . it never seemed like the right time."

"Well, you're gonna have to tell him now." Resa's voice was firm.

"She's right." Harlan's voice made us all jump. He stood behind the booth, a towel in his hands. "The man's got a right to know. And, if he's a real man, it won't matter a lick."

As we drove home, I watched Emma carefully. She looked the

same as always, but different, too. She got married when she was only four years older than me, to a man who wasn't nice to her. I'd always thought that Emma was strong, but she seemed afraid now.

"Are you scared to tell Daddy?" I finally asked.

She nodded, and then smiled at me.

"A little bit, I guess. I should have told him a long time ago."

"Why didn't you?"

She sat still a moment and then sighed heavily.

"I was embarrassed, I guess. It seems so stupid now. It's just, where I was raised getting married that young was normal. And people don't understand it. Some people I told early on treated me like I was a freak after they knew. I didn't want to do that with your dad."

She sighed again. "I guess I just want us to be normal, like a normal family."

"Do you think he'll be mad?" I asked.

"I don't know," she said. "But I have to tell him. I should have told him before I told you."

"You don't have to tell him that I know."

"No," she said, shaking her head. "I don't want to lie to Brannon. That's no way to maintain a relationship. I'll just . . . tell him, I guess."

We came home to a dark trailer. Daddy was at work.

Emma changed into her pajamas and made a cup of tea. I watched her from my bed.

When she turned out the light, I said, "I don't care about it, you being married before. And I don't think Daddy will care, either."

She walked to my alcove, leaned over, and kissed my cheek.

"Thanks, Jenny. That means a lot."

"Emma?"

"Yeah?"

"I love you."

I squeezed my eyes shut and waited to see what she would say. I heard her take a quick breath and when she spoke, I could tell she was crying.

"I love you, too, Jenny. And I love your dad."

She walked to the bedroom, but she didn't close the door. I sat up in bed and looked down the hall, to where she sat on the bed, her head in her hands. Then I saw her kneel on the floor beside the bed, fold her hands, and bow her head. She was praying.

So I prayed, too.

Dear God, if you're there, please let Emma stay. Please don't let her go away.

❧ 14 ❧

Emma

The day after I told Jenny about my past, I woke up feeling anxious and tired. I'd had bad dreams all night, dreams of Colorado City, my parents, my husband, my little sister. I tried so hard not to think about the past, to let it stay in the past. But the conversation at the diner had stirred it all up again.

I rose and made coffee, sitting at the table in the trailer, listening to the soft sounds of Jenny sleeping. She was so beautiful, her dark hair tangled around her shoulders, so quiet and innocent. She was the same age Clarissa had been when I left. God, Clarissa would be almost eighteen now. I hadn't seen her in more than six years.

The door opening startled me, and Brannon came in, the cold wind following him through the door.

"Hey, babe." He bent over and kissed me, then dropped into the seat across from me.

"Hey," I said, rising. "Let me get you something to eat."

He leaned back in his seat and yawned, stretching.

"I've got leftover meatloaf and potatoes, or I can make you some eggs."

"Leftovers are good," he said. He rubbed the back of his hand across his eyes and yawned again.

"How was work?"

"Same as always," he said. "It's getting busier every day, more people on the floor. Some guy almost ran me over with a cart."

"I hate that you're working so many hours." I put a plate into the microwave and stood behind him, rubbing his shoulders.

"It's good money," he said. He took one of my hands and kissed it. "But I sure do miss you."

I kissed the top of his head and whispered in his ear, "Well, Jenny was up kind of late last night, so she's sleeping pretty soundly. We could . . ."

He kissed my hand again and shook his head. "I can't, babe. I'm sorry. I'm just beat."

"It's okay. Maybe tonight Jenny can stay at the Johnsons' and we can have some time to ourselves when you've had some sleep."

It was Saturday. Brannon wouldn't go back to work until Monday night.

"That sounds good."

He tilted his head back and I leaned in to kiss him. Even exhausted and dusty, he was beautiful to look at.

After he'd eaten, he headed for bed, and I heard him start snoring almost the minute his head hit the pillow.

After Jenny got up and we'd had breakfast, we climbed into the SUV to drive to the local Walmart. We were going to buy decorations for Christmas, and I wanted to get Brannon's Christmas gift.

"These are cute." I held up a strand of star-shaped lights. Jenny nodded, and I put them into the cart.

"Look!" She pointed toward the Christmas trees, all brightly lit and shining with ornaments and tinsel. "I wish we could have one."

"I know," I said. "But none of those will fit inside the trailer."

We walked among the trees, each one prettier than the one before. At the very back, we saw it—a small tree, just two feet tall, with lights of blue, purple, green, and gold. Tiny glass ornaments hung from the branches, sparkling in the lights.

"That one would fit," Jenny said, touching an ornament with one finger.

"It's perfect. Let's get it."

"Really?" She looked at me, her blue eyes wide.

"Sure, why not?" I found a boxed tree and we gathered lights and ornaments. Jenny was as excited as I'd ever seen her.

"We've never had a real tree before. Can we get a star for the top?"

We put a small silver star into the cart. I couldn't help smiling, watching her prance up the store aisle. It was one of the only times I'd seen her really act like a kid.

"Now," I said, "we need to get something for your dad."

"You mean like a tie or something?"

I shook my head, laughing. "What would Brannon do with a tie?"

"I don't know," she said. "I never got him anything before. Not from the store, anyway. I used to make him stuff for his birthday."

"Homemade gifts are the best."

She shook her head. "I want to buy him something this year. I've been saving my allowance. I've got twelve dollars."

We wandered through the store, looking at and rejecting several shirts, world's-best-dad coffee mugs, colognes, and baseball caps. None of them seemed right.

"Maybe we could get him some fishing gear. He likes to fish." She looked up at me. "What do you think?"

"I think that would be a great idea if I knew anything about fishing gear. But I don't know what he has already and what he wants."

"How about some lures? He always likes to get lures."

We walked through the sporting goods aisle and stopped before a vast array of fishing lures. Jenny picked them up one by one, examining each as if it were a piece of jewelry.

"They cost more than I thought," she said, laying aside a colorful feathered lure.

"Well, I can help out some," I said. "Just choose one you think he'll like and we'll get it."

"Really?" She launched herself into my arms. "Thanks, Emma!"

After several minutes, she settled on a beautiful green lure with a red feather tail. We added it to the cart.

"What are you getting him?"

"I'm not sure," I said. "I mean, there are things I know he'd like, but we don't have a lot of space. So . . ." I shrugged. "Any ideas?"

"You could get him a lure, too."

I shook my head. "No, that's a special gift just from you. I'll think of something else."

We wandered through the vast store, but nothing popped out at me.

"Can we look at the books?" Jenny was already making a beeline for the book aisle. I followed her, laughing. She didn't know it, but she was choosing her own gift just then. I watched her pick up one title and then another.

"Look!" She held up a book. "They have the second Traveling Pants book. I keep looking for it at the library, but it's always out."

"Hmm," I said, trying not to smile.

"Oh my God! They have the whole set in a box!" She held the box up and ran a finger along the book spines. "All four of them."

She looked at the price, sighed, and returned the box to the shelf.

I stood watching her, wishing I could give her the books right then and there. Instead, I would stop by after work one night that week to buy them.

I looked at the bargain books, idly wondering what Brannon might be getting for me. And then I saw a hardcover collection of Edgar Allan Poe's works. Brannon told me one time that the only thing he had liked in high school was English, and that Poe had been his favorite.

I put the book in the cart and smiled at Jenny, still browsing. This was going to be the best Christmas I'd ever had.

That night, Jenny slept over at the Johnsons' so I made a special dinner for Brannon—steaks seared then broiled to medium rare, baked potatoes with real butter and sour cream, a chopped salad, and some rolls.

"That smells good," he said, nuzzling my neck.

"Well, I wanted you to have a special treat. You've been working too much."

"It's only another month," he said. "After Christmas I'll be lucky to get any hours at all."

I prepared our plates and set them on the table. Then I uncorked a bottle of red wine.

We raised our glasses, and Brannon winked and said, "To Emma, my beautiful, beautiful girl. Thanks, babe. This is great."

I took a sip of wine and a deep breath, preparing myself to finally tell him about my past. But before I could say anything, he spoke again.

"I've been thinking about where we should go next. Michael says they're hiring at Disney. Would you like to spend the rest of the winter in Florida?"

"Sure," I said. "I could use some Florida sunshine after this Kentucky cold. But—" I paused, not sure if I should go on. "Angel said they may be staying here even after the season, that there's talk of a few permanent jobs."

"There's always talk," he said. "Never any jobs, though."

"Okay. Are the Johnsons going to Florida, too?"

"Maybe." He cut a bite of steak and raised his fork. "This is perfect, Emma. Just the way I like my steak."

"I'm glad."

I took another deep breath and plunged in.

"So, I've been thinking it's time to tell you about my past."

"We've all got pasts, babe. The only thing that matters is now."

I took a sip of wine and another breath.

"I know, but . . . well, I want to tell you."

He chewed his steak, watching me with one eyebrow raised. "Okay," he said finally. "Shoot."

"You know I was raised in Arizona."

"Yeah."

"And I told you the town I came from is very small and kind of . . . actually, very weird."

He nodded.

"Well, the thing is, I was raised in the FLDS, the fundamentalist Mormon church."

"Is that like fundamentalist Baptist?" he asked.

"No, it's like . . . nothing else. The town where I was raised is called Colorado City, and pretty much everyone who lives there is part of the church. The church owns all the land and runs the school and almost everything else."

He set his fork down and leaned forward, frowning slightly. "Like a cult?"

"Yeah," I said, nodding. "Exactly like a cult. The FLDS broke away from the Mormon church after the Mormons banned polygamy."

"You mean, like one guy with a bunch of wives?"

I nodded again.

"My dad has four wives. My mom is his third."

"God, Emma. That's just . . . why would any woman marry a man who's already got two wives?"

"Like you said, it's a cult." I struggled to keep my voice steady and wished to God I hadn't started talking at all. How weird would Brannon think I was when he knew the whole truth?

"We were completely cut off from the outside world and taught from infancy that people outside the church were evil and wanted to hurt us," I explained. "And the only way for a woman to get to heaven was through her husband. I know, it sounds crazy. But like I said, we were isolated. The leader of the church, we called him the prophet, his word was law, and he decided who got married to who and when. So when the prophet told my mom to marry my father, she did. It was all she knew, and she was only eighteen. I mean, we didn't have news from outside, we didn't even have televisions. We were completely isolated."

He watched me, his eyes wide.

"So, how did you get out without getting married?" he asked.

"I didn't."

He stared at me, his mouth open.

"You were married?"

I nodded.

"When I was fifteen, I was married to a man named Micah. He already had four wives. He was sixty-three when I married him. And he was as mean as a snake."

I watched Brannon absorb this, willing myself to go on.

"And that's not all."

He said nothing, just stared at me.

"When I was sixteen, I got pregnant."

"Oh my God! You have a kid?"

Brannon rose now, staring down at me.

"No, that is, I mean . . . I did. I had a baby. His name was Andrew. He only lived a few weeks and then he died of respiratory failure. Micah wouldn't let me take him to the hospital. Instead, he prayed over him and told me that would make him better. But it didn't. My baby died."

Brannon sat down again and reached for my hands.

"Oh my God, Emma," he said. "That's awful. I mean, it's unbelievable. You had a baby at sixteen and then lost him? I'm . . . I don't even know what to say."

I squeezed his hands, feeling the tears start.

"After Andrew died, I decided I was going to die, too. I didn't want to live. But I was too afraid. I was afraid if I killed myself, I'd go to hell for all eternity, and then I'd never see my baby again. But something in me broke when he died, and I knew I had to get out of Colorado City, out of the church, and away from Micah. I just couldn't stay.

"Micah started talking about having another baby almost as soon as Andrew was dead, like that would just make it all fine. He said the next time I'd be a better mother and have a healthy child, that it was my lack of faith that killed my baby. And I *hated* him! My God, *he's* the reason Andrew died. He wouldn't let me take my baby to the doctor. And I thought if I had to have sex with him even one more time, I'd probably kill him and then I'd kill myself.

"So one morning when Micah was in Canada on church business, before everyone else in the house got up, I snuck out. I stole one of Micah's cars and drove to the interstate. It was only an hour away, but it felt like forever. I was so scared someone would see me and stop me. Even the police force there is part of the church. If I got stopped, I'd be taken back and I probably wouldn't ever have another chance to leave."

My shoulders shook and I let the tears fall. I didn't even bother wiping them away. It had been years since I'd told anyone about Micah. Just saying his name out loud was scary. I took a deep breath to steady myself. Brannon stared at me.

"Anyway," I continued, "when I got to the highway, I left the car on the shoulder and started walking north. I'd walked a couple hours when a woman in a van stopped and asked if I needed a ride.

At first I said no. I thought she might be from the church, or that she might try to hurt me. Like I said, we were taught that outsiders were evil. But she asked again, and then she asked if I was all right. Should she call the police for me? I didn't want her to call the police! We were still too close to Colorado City. So I got in her car and she drove me up to Salt Lake City.

"A cousin of mine who left the church a long time ago lives in the city there, so I looked up her name in the phone book and called her. She helped me find a job and a place to live. I was always afraid Micah would come find me, but I guess I was too much of a bother. Thank God of it! Anyway, I left Colorado City, and I never went back. I haven't seen my mother or my sisters or anyone from there in more than six years."

I waited for what felt like a very long time, waited to hear what Brannon would say. Part of me just knew he would kick me out right then and there. I waited to see "the look" cross his face—that mix of pity and fear and horror I'd seen the few times I'd told anyone about my past. I waited and I cried and I prayed.

And then he stood and pulled me to my feet. He wrapped his arms around me and kissed my forehead and my cheeks. And I saw tears streaming down his face, too.

"Oh, Emma," he whispered. "Oh, babe, I can't stand that you had to go through all that. I can't stand that you lost your baby. I wish I could give him back to you. I wish I could kill the bastard you married, or your father, or the damned prophet! I wish I could kill them all!"

I leaned into his chest and cried, more relieved than I'd ever felt in my life. He knew, Brannon knew, and he still loved me.

"I'm so sorry," I said.

"Don't!" His voice was loud. It shook with anger, and I stepped back.

"I'm sorry," he said more gently. "I just can't stand for you to apologize for things that weren't your fault. You were just a kid, Emma."

He took my chin and raised it, so that I had to look him straight in the eyes.

"You were a child, and someone should have protected you. Your father should have protected you. Your mother should have protected you. None of it is your fault, and you have *nothing* to apologize for."

"I'm sorry I didn't tell you before."

"Oh, babe," he crooned, hugging me tightly. "It's okay. It's all going to be okay. We're together now, and I will never, *never* let anyone hurt you again."

"I love you," I said into his chest. "God, Brannon, I love you so much. And I love Jenny, too. I just feel so lucky to have you guys."

"Shhhh," he said, pulling me toward the bedroom.

We left our steaks mostly uneaten on the table and made love as the last of the late afternoon sun streamed through the small window. And after, I lay with my head on his chest knowing that finally, I was safe. I was home.

❦ 15 ❦

Jenny

On Christmas morning, Emma and I went with Mrs. Johnson, Lashaundra, and Malcolm to Happy Days for breakfast. Daddy and Mr. Johnson both had to work the night before, so they were still sleeping.

"You can't even stay away from us on Christmas?" Resa grinned at us as we walked in.

"I'm just glad you're open," Emma said, hugging her. "We had to get the kids out before they woke up Brannon and Michael. Merry Christmas!"

"Merry Christmas to you, hon!" Resa hugged her back, then hugged me and Lashaundra. Then she hugged Mrs. Johnson and Malcolm.

"I'm surprised so many people are out on Christmas morning," Mrs. Johnson said. The restaurant was about half full.

"Well, a lot of folks are like you," Resa said, showing us to a table. "Their men work nights, and they got to get the kids out of the house in the morning. We do pretty good business on Christmas."

"Order's up!" Harlan's voice called from the kitchen, and Resa disappeared to the back.

"Hey, Emma, can I get some coffee?" A man sitting in the next booth grinned at her.

"She ain't working today, dumb ass!" Resa swatted the man as she passed, carrying a tray.

Emma smiled and sat down beside me.

"How long have you been working here?" Mrs. Johnson asked.

"Just a month," Emma said.

"Well, it seems like everyone knows you."

I looked around the restaurant, and Mrs. Johnson was right. Everyone there did know Emma, and they knew me, too, because I came in with her so often. I grinned at Jerry Burns and his wife, Coral, sitting in the booth across from us and they smiled back.

"Merry Christmas, Jenny," Coral called.

"Merry Christmas, Mrs. Burns!"

It felt good to be someplace where everyone knew me. It felt like home.

"Goddamn it, woman! Look what you done!" A man's voice rang through the restaurant. I looked toward the front and saw Damon Rigby rise from his seat, wiping coffee from his lap. Standing before him, Merilee held a coffeepot. Merilee was the oldest waitress at Happy Days. I guessed she must be in her eighties, but Emma said, no, she was only fifty-nine.

Merilee immediately began wiping off the table. "I'm sorry, Damon," she said. "Let me get you a fresh cup."

Mr. Rigby simply glared at her, then glared at his wife.

"Get your coat, Shirley," he yelled. "This place has gone to the dogs!"

He stared hard at Merilee, then turned and stared directly at Mrs. Johnson and Lashaundra.

Mrs. Johnson said nothing. She simply returned his stare, her eyes never dropping. After a long minute, Emma rose and stood between them.

"Let me get you some more coffee," she said, walking toward Mr. Rigby.

But he only pushed her aside and stomped out the front door, his wife still struggling to get her coat on.

"Goddamn it, Shirley!" His voice boomed from outside. "I said let's go!"

Mrs. Rigby started digging through her purse to pay the bill, but

Merilee touched her hand, shook her head, and smiled. "Go on, Shirley. It's on the house."

Emma came back and sat down in the booth. Resa stood with her hands on her hips, glaring at the front door, then went on with her order. Eventually, people went back to their breakfasts, talking in low voices about what a jerk Mr. Rigby was.

"You all right?" Emma asked softly.

"I'm fine," Mrs. Johnson said, nodding at her. "Not the first time, won't be the last time. Now"—she smiled at her children—"what do you-all want for breakfast? You want pancakes, Malcolm?"

After a huge breakfast, we walked around downtown for a little while. Colored lights twinkled from the trees and lampposts under a light dusting of snow. Finally, we headed back to the trailer park. Lashaundra hugged me and made me promise to come over later so we could compare notes on what we got for Christmas. Then Emma unlocked the trailer door and tiptoed inside.

Daddy was already up, drinking coffee. He'd turned on the Christmas lights, and the room sparkled in shades of blues and greens.

"Merry Christmas, babe!" He rose and wrapped his arms around Emma, then pulled me into the hug. "Merry Christmas to my two best girls!"

"I didn't think you'd be up yet," Emma said. "If I'd known, we'd have waited for you."

"Couldn't sleep." He smiled at her and kissed her cheek. "It's Christmas, and I feel like I'm a kid."

"Can we open presents?" I asked, fully expecting him to say no, we should wait until later.

Instead, he laughed and nodded. "Sure, honey. Let's open some presents."

I ran to my bed and pulled out the two packages I had wrapped in bright red pepper.

We sat in the tiny living room, where our little Christmas tree held center stage. Looking around the room that morning, I was happier than I ever remembered being. I had a friend. People in town knew me. Emma and Daddy were happy. It felt like we were a real family.

"Here, open this first!" I handed Daddy a box.

"Hmmm," he said, shaking the box and holding it to his ear. "What is it?"

"Open it and see!"

"No clues?" He grinned at me and I shook my head.

"Well, okay then." He tore off the paper and opened the box Emma had found to disguise the shape of the lure.

"Hey!" He grinned again. "That's great, Jenny. How did you know that's just what I wanted?"

He opened his arms and I ran into them and we hugged.

"Now you open yours," I said, handing Emma another box.

"You got something for me?" She took the box and kissed my cheek. "Honey, you didn't need to do that."

I just smiled at her, watching her unwrap the present.

She opened the box and took a sharp breath. Then she held up the glass ornament of a horse, and tears spilled down her cheeks.

"Oh, Jenny," she breathed. "It's beautiful! Thank you!"

"Daddy helped me choose it," I said.

"It's perfect!" Emma rose and carefully hung the tiny horse on the Christmas tree. Then she stepped back and admired it, not even bothering to wipe away the tears dripping from her chin.

"Now you!" Daddy handed me a box wrapped in gold and blue, with a big gold bow. "Open this first. It's from Emma and me."

I tore away the wrappings and opened the box. A beautiful blue sweater with a matching hat and gloves lay inside.

"They're really pretty. Thank you."

"Now this one." Daddy handed me an even bigger box wrapped in green with a red bow.

"What is it?" I asked, taking the box.

"No clues!" Daddy said. Emma laughed.

"I love it!" It was a purple parka coat with white fur around the hood. "Thank you!"

I ran to hug Daddy, then hugged Emma, too. It was the best Christmas I'd ever had.

"Wait," Emma said, winking at Daddy. "I think there's one more."

She pulled a smaller box from behind her, this one wrapped in red, and handed it to me. "I hope you like it."

I held the box for a minute, feeling its shape, wondering and then hoping. Finally, I tore away the paper and shrieked.

"The Traveling Pants books! All four of them! Oh, wow! That's . . . you're the best, Emma!"

I hugged her tight, felt her tears plop down on my head. Then I hugged Daddy, too. It really was the best Christmas ever.

I tore away the plastic wrap, pulled the books from the box, and immediately opened book two.

"Hey, you!" Daddy's voice interrupted me. "It's not time to start reading yet. There's another present here. This one is for Emma."

But she was holding a present out to him, too. He looked surprised, then took the package and smiled.

"You didn't need to get me anything," he said.

"I know." She kissed him. "But I wanted to."

He tore away the gift wrap and a grin spread across his face.

"How did you know I liked Edgar Allan Poe?"

"You told me once it was the only thing you liked in high school."

He rose and hugged her. "Thank you, Emma. I love it. I love that you remembered that."

He opened the book and read something written on the first page, smiling.

"No reading yet!" I called out. "If I can't start reading, you can't, either."

"Okay!" Daddy laid the book aside and handed Emma a small box, wrapped in silver with a pink bow.

"For me?" She took the box and held it for a minute, just staring at it. Her cheeks were pink and her eyes sparkled. Then she carefully pulled the wrapping paper off to reveal a small jewelry box.

For just a second, she paused, staring at him. And I let myself think, in that second, that he'd bought her a ring, that maybe they would get married, that Emma would be my mom forever. I swallowed hard.

She opened the box and pulled out a heart-shaped locket made of silver. My heart sank, my eyes stung, a huge lump rose in my throat.

"Oh, Brannon," Emma said, her voice shaking. "It's beautiful."

"It's inscribed," he said, turning the locket over.

"Brannon and Emma, Jenny and Andrew." Her voice was so soft I could hardly hear her.

I opened my mouth to ask who Andrew was, but they were kissing now and I had to look away. When I looked back, Daddy was smiling at me over Emma's shoulder. Then he raised one finger to his lips as if to shush me and winked. I tried to smile back, but I felt like throwing up.

Because I knew then what I didn't want to know. Emma wasn't different from Jackie or Trish or Cara or Ami or any of the others. At least she wasn't different to Daddy. He'd given her the same gift he'd given each of them in turn.

Emma wouldn't stay. None of them ever stayed.

❧ 16 ❧

Emma

We celebrated the new year with the Johnsons and a few other families from the campground. We all rented rooms at the Holiday Inn Express, ate dinner together, and then the kids played in the pool. The staff even kept the pool open until midnight for us.

I sat in a lounge chair, watching Brannon laugh in the hot tub with a young woman who worked at Amazon. She was pretty, with long jet-black hair and flashing dark eyes. I watched as she touched his shoulder, laughing at something he'd said.

"You okay?"

Angel plopped down into a chair beside me, dripping from the pool.

"Yeah," I said.

She followed my eyes and took my hand. "I think he's crazy about you."

I smiled at her. "I hope so."

"Why don't you put on your suit and go in?"

I shook my head. "I'm crampy and bloated and I feel like I'm going to start my period any minute. Plus, my boobs hurt."

I wrapped my arms across my chest, still watching Brannon and the woman.

"Could you be pregnant?"

I shook my head again. "No, I'm just PMS-ing. We always use a condom."

"Well," she said, eyeing the woman in the hot tub, "I wouldn't worry about her. She's not his type."

I raised my eyebrows.

"Seriously, she's got kind of a hard edge," Angel said. "From what I've seen, she's not Brannon's type."

"Where I'm from, we'd say she looks like she's been rode hard and put up wet." I said it without thinking, and immediately felt bad. I didn't know anything about the woman, after all.

Angel laughed. "I think that's a pretty good description."

She stood and yelled at the pool, "Lashaundra, you stay close to your brother!"

I smiled, watching her. She was a good mom.

"Can I ask you something?" I said as she sat back down.

"Shoot," she said.

"What was Jackie like?"

She paused for a long minute, then said, "She was nice, friendly. She joked around a lot, teased Brannon something awful. We liked her. She was good with Jenny."

"Do you think Brannon loved her?" I glanced back toward the hot tub, where the dark-haired woman was standing, squeezing water from her hair. She wore a tiny string bikini, and her breasts were just level with Brannon's eyes.

Another long pause.

"I'm sorry," I said. "I don't mean to put you in an awkward spot."

"It's okay." She turned to look at me and smiled again. "I don't know if he loved her or not. They seemed happy, but . . . well, she's not here, is she?"

"She left him for another guy."

Her eyes widened; her mouth opened and then closed.

"I . . . really?"

I nodded. "Brannon said she got a job at a gas station and fell for the man who owned it."

Angel shook her head. "I can't believe that," she said softly. "She was crazy about Brannon, and about Jenny. I don't remember her working anywhere."

We sat in silence for a while, then Angel said, "But we weren't really close or anything. I mean, I didn't know everything about her, obviously."

She touched my hand, then took it and squeezed it hard.

"I think Brannon is crazy about you. And I think Jenny is, too. What's past is past. Let it rest."

I nodded and squeezed her hand back. "I know. I'm just . . . I'm PMS-ing, like I said. It makes me think crazy things."

"Like worrying about that rode-hard woman?" She grinned and winked. "I understand, I get that way sometimes, too. But deep down, I know Michael would never cheat on me."

We both turned to watch as her husband swam toward Lashaundra and Malcolm, surfacing just in front of them and splashing them both.

"Yeah," I said. "Michael is a keeper."

Long after midnight, Brannon and I climbed into bed. In the bed next to us, Lashaundra and Jenny were already asleep. I knew Malcolm was staying the night with a friend. We tried to trade off with the kids, those of us who lived in the trailer park, giving each other time alone. There's not much privacy when you live in a trailer, after all.

"Did you have fun tonight?" I asked, resting my head on his chest.

"I'd have had a lot more fun if we'd just stayed here in the room."

He wrapped his arms around me and kissed my forehead.

"We could still have some fun," he whispered. "They're out for the night." He nodded at the bed where the girls slept.

"I have cramps," I said. "I'm sorry."

"It's all good, babe."

He kissed me and turned out the light. Within minutes, he was snoring with his back to me.

I lay awake, staring at the dark, listening to Brannon snore, and wondering at how far away I was from everyone and everything I'd ever known.

It was the start of a new year, and it felt like the start of a whole new life, somehow.

After a while, I rose cautiously and went to the bathroom—still no sign of my period. I stared at myself in the mirror and wondered about my mother and Clarissa. Were they okay? Was Clarissa already married off to some old man? For a brief instant I thought about calling them, but the thought went by as quickly as it came. As much as I missed them, as much as I wanted to know they were okay, I couldn't bring myself to call. I still couldn't risk Micah knowing where I was. Even all these years later, he scared the hell out of me.

I tiptoed back into the room and knelt by the bed. Officially, I had left the church. I *had* left the church. But sometimes it felt like the church hadn't ever really left me. Part of me still wanted to talk to God, to believe there was a God, to believe I mattered to God. I would never admit it to anyone, but I still prayed a lot. And I thought about my mother and my sisters every single day.

Dear God, please take care of Mama and Clarissa and Elizabeth and all of them. And please bless Brannon and Jenny and Angel and Michael and Lashaundra and Malcolm and Resa. And please, God, if you have an extra minute, please let everything be okay with me and Brannon. Thank you, Lord. Amen.

I climbed back into bed and winced at the weight of the blankets against my breasts. Maybe I would pick up a pregnancy test at the pharmacy this week. Just to be sure.

Two days later, I left Jenny with the Johnsons and drove to the nearby drugstore, glancing around to make sure no one saw me as I stood before the array of test kits.

"Excuse me?" I said as the pharmacist walked by. "Do you know which of these is the most reliable?"

"They're all pretty much the same," the woman said, smiling at me. "Basically, you pee on the stick and watch to see what color the stick turns. It's pretty simple."

I picked up a box and handed it to her. She smiled again and rang up the purchase.

"Are you excited?" she asked, handing me my bag.

"Um, yeah," I murmured. In reality, I was more scared than anything.

"Well, good luck," the pharmacist said. "And you have a blessed day."

I stared at her stupidly for just an instant, then stammered, "Thanks, you too."

This was a Southern thing, for sure. Even in Colorado City, people didn't tell complete strangers to have a blessed day. Still, it made me smile a little.

I drove back to the trailer and locked the door behind me. Brannon was asleep and Jenny was still next door with Lashaundra.

As quietly as I could, I closed the bathroom door. I felt like I should pray, but I wasn't sure what I would even pray for. So I just said, "Please, God." That's all.

I sat in the tiny bathroom staring at the test stick while the color slowly changed from white to blue. I checked the stick against the picture on the box and then checked again—definitely blue.

My mind seemed to spin in a thousand directions at once. I was pregnant . . . again. I was pregnant with Brannon's baby, a baby I desperately wanted. But what would Brannon say? We'd never even talked about having kids.

I wrapped my arms around my stomach and rocked back and forth, watching snow fall outside the small window. And I let myself hope that it would be okay. Brannon was great with Jenny, after all. Hell, he was probably the world's best dad. Surely he would love this baby, too.

I patted my belly and smiled at the thought of the tiny life growing inside.

"Don't worry, little baby," I whispered. "Mama is here and I will always protect you and I will always love you, no matter what."

A banging at the trailer door startled me to my feet. Shoving the test kit back into the box, I buried it deep in my purse. Then I put my purse in the drawer under the sink and went to let Jenny and Lashaundra inside, out of the cold.

❧ 17 ❧

Jenny

I was sitting in the trailer doing schoolwork when I heard a banging on the door. Emma opened it, and Lashaundra ran inside, grinning.

"Daddy got a job!" She grabbed my hands and pulled me to my feet, hugging me tightly. "We get to stay here, in one place. And Mama says we'll get an apartment and I'll go to school and everything!"

"Really?" I pulled back to stare at her. "You're gonna stay here?"

She nodded, her eyes sparkling with tears. "And I'll have my own room and maybe we're even gonna get a dog!"

"That's wonderful!" Emma smiled at her.

"Yeah," I said. I was trying really hard to be happy for my friend.

"Maybe your dad will get one, too," she said, nodding as if that would make it so. "Daddy said they're hiring a few people."

"Do you think so?" I turned to Emma. She smiled and shrugged her shoulders.

"Maybe," she said. "I hope so."

*   *   *

When Daddy got home the next morning, Emma and I were both waiting to hear if he, too, had been offered a permanent job.

"Hey, here are my favorite girls." He kissed my forehead and then Emma's. "You're up early."

"Lashaundra's dad got a permanent job," I said, watching him closely.

"I know," he said, smiling. "He's pretty happy about it."

I looked at him, waiting. He took off his jacket and sat at the table. "Do we have any orange juice?" he asked, looking at Emma.

She nodded and took a bottle from the fridge. She didn't say anything, but I could see her eyes were watery just like mine. Daddy hadn't been offered a permanent job. Soon, maybe next week even, we'd move on.

"Hey," Daddy said, smiling at me. "Why are you so gloomy?"

"I'm not," I said, trying to smile back.

"Were you hoping we'd stay, too?"

"No, Daddy. It's okay. Florida will be fun."

"That's my girl." He leaned back in his seat and took a long drink of juice.

"Do you want some eggs?" Emma's voice was soft.

"That would be great, babe. Maybe scrambled with some cheese and onions?"

She nodded and opened the fridge again.

"Babe?" Daddy was watching her back. "You okay?"

"Sure," she said, turning toward him. "I'm fine."

After Daddy had his eggs and was asleep, I walked to Lashaundra's and knocked on the door. She answered immediately, but she didn't look me in the eye.

"Daddy didn't get a job," I said, shrugging off my coat.

"But . . ." Lashaundra began.

Mrs. Johnson hugged me lightly. "It's okay, Jenny," she said. "There will be other jobs."

"But, Mama," Lashaundra began again.

I looked up just in time to see Mrs. Johnson shake her head firmly.

"Why don't you girls go check on the laundry," she said. "It should be about time to move it to the dryer."

I put my parka back on and Lashaundra put on her coat.

"Can I go?" Malcolm asked.

"No, baby," Mrs. Johnson said. "You're going to stay here and help Mama snap green beans."

We ran to the laundry building, our breath puffing in the cold air.

"I'm sorry," I said, as we closed the door behind us. "I wish we could stay, too."

"You could," she said. "Your dad got offered a job, too. But he turned it down."

I stared at her, my mouth hanging open like an idiot's.

"It's true!" she continued, her voice rising. "Daddy said Mr. Parker offered your dad a job, and he turned it down."

I shook my head. "That can't be right. Daddy said he didn't get a job."

She took my hands. "I'm not lying," she insisted. "That's what Daddy said. Your dad told Mr. Parker he already had a job lined up in Florida. And he told my dad he didn't want to stay in Kentucky. Mama told me not to tell you."

She stopped abruptly and dropped her eyes. "She said not to tell you. But you're my best friend. I had to tell you." Her voice was low now, almost a whisper.

"Don't tell Mama I told you, okay?"

"Okay."

We sat down in front of the washing machine, which was still chugging away.

"Why do you think he doesn't want to stay here?"

I shrugged. I couldn't imagine a reason why.

"Maybe he doesn't like the job," I said. "Or maybe he doesn't like this park."

"But if he had a permanent job, you wouldn't have to live in this park. You could get an apartment like us, maybe even right next door. And we could go to school together and everything."

I shook my head, felt tears stinging my eyes. It sounded like a dream. Why wouldn't Daddy want to stay where we could live in an apartment like a real family?

Finally, the washing machine chugged to a stop. We moved clothes into the dryer, put in a dollar's worth of quarters, and ran back to Lashaundra's.

"Remember," she said before we walked inside. "Don't tell Mama what I told you."

I nodded miserably. I wanted to ask Mrs. Johnson if it was true, but I didn't want to get Lashaundra in trouble.

"Do you girls want to go into town?" Mrs. Johnson asked. "I have to go to the post office and pick up some things at the store."

"Okay," Lashaundra said.

I shook my head. "I have to go home," I lied, not meeting her eyes. "I have to help Emma with . . . something. I'll see you later."

Before Lashaundra could say anything, I was out the door, down the steps, and running for home. I wanted to wake Daddy up and ask him if it was true, if Mr. Parker had offered him a permanent job. And why he'd said no. But of course I couldn't, not without telling on Lashaundra.

"Hey!" Emma looked up in surprise when the door slammed closed behind me. "I thought you were hanging out with Lashaundra."

"She has to run errands with her mom, and I have that paper I'm supposed to do."

I avoided her eyes as I pulled off my coat.

"That paper isn't due for two weeks," she said. I could feel her eyes on me.

"Did you two have an argument?" Her voice was gentle.

I shook my head, squeezing back tears.

"Jenny, what's wrong?"

I felt her hands on my shoulders and turned to lean into her arms.

"Daddy got offered a job, a real job," I said, letting the tears finally come. "And he didn't take it."

"What?" She drew back to look me in the face. "I think you've heard something wrong, honey. Your dad didn't get the job."

"He did," I said, struggling to keep my voice low. "Lashaundra's dad told her he did. Mr. Parker offered him a job and we could have stayed here and I could have lived by Lashaundra and gone to school and not lived in a trailer anymore!"

"Oh, Jenny." Her voice was calming, soothing. "I'm sure Lashaundra got it wrong. Your dad told us he didn't get the job. And it's okay, honey. We'll go to Florida and it will be warm and sunny there and you'll make new friends."

I let her shush me for a while, then pulled away from her, gathered my laptop and books, and climbed into my alcove to work on school stuff, anything to keep from thinking about why Daddy had turned down a job, a real job, a permanent job in a place where we could stay, a place where I knew people and they knew me, a place where I had a real friend.

❧ 18 ❧

Emma

I prowled around the trailer in silence all day, waiting for Brannon to wake up. Jenny stayed in her bed, working on the computer, not talking and not looking at me even once. I felt claustrophobic, like the walls were closing in on me. Surely Jenny was mistaken. Or Lashaundra was mistaken. Or Michael was mistaken. Surely Brannon hadn't turned down a full-time, permanent position.

I took my cell phone outside and called Resa at the diner.

"Hey, can you find someone to cover my shift tonight?" It was a Thursday. Brannon would be off work for the next three days.

"Sure, honey," she said. "You okay?"

"I'm fine," I lied. "Just tired and feeling a little bit puny."

"I'll call Merilee," she said. "She's been wanting more hours. You just relax and take a nap and enjoy some time with that hunk of a man of yours."

"Thanks, Resa."

I went back inside, shivering from the bitter cold, and resumed pacing the narrow aisle of the trailer. What had felt like a cozy little home in the summer had become a kind of prison with the onset of winter.

Sometime late in the afternoon, Brannon emerged from our bedroom, rubbing sleep from his eyes.

"Hey, you," he said, nuzzling my neck. "I thought you'd be at work by now."

"Merilee needed more hours," I said. "So I let her take my shift."

"Hey, pumpkin." He smiled at Jenny, who was still stretched out on her bed, pecking away at the laptop. "What are you up to?"

"School stuff," she said, not raising her eyes from the computer. Brannon lifted his gaze to me and shrugged slightly.

"Everything okay?" he said, softly enough so that Jenny couldn't hear.

"It's all good," I said, smiling at him. God, he was so beautiful. "I'm thinking I'll make stew for dinner. How does that sound?"

"That sounds good." He kissed me and disappeared into the bathroom.

Jenny was silent all evening, not even smiling at her dad's jokes when we sat down for dinner.

"What's up with you?" he finally asked.

"When are we going to Florida?" Her voice was flat, her eyes fixed firmly on her plate.

"Probably the week after next," he said. "I've got to finish out next week, and then we'll head south."

I rose and began picking up plates and piling them in the sink.

"You'll like Florida." Brannon's voice was easy and cajoling. "It'll be sunny and warm. And maybe we'll get some comp passes to Disney World. You'd like that, wouldn't you?"

Finally, Jenny looked up from the table and met his eyes, un-flinching.

"I'd rather stay here with Lashaundra."

"I'm sorry, honey. It just didn't work out this time."

She rose from the table and grabbed her parka from the hook by the door.

"Can I go to Lashaundra's?" she asked, looking to me for per-mission.

"Sure," I said. "As long as it's okay with Angel."

She left without another word. Brannon stared at the door and then turned to me.

"Seriously," he said, confused. "What's wrong with her? Do you think she's getting ready to start her period or something? Isn't she still too young for that?"

I smiled and shook my head. I sat down beside him at the table and took his hand.

"Lashaundra told her today that you'd been offered a permanent job at the warehouse, and that you turned it down. I told her Lashaundra must be wrong or something. But I don't think she believed me."

"Oh." He leaned back, his face impassive, and stretched his arms. "I wondered if that was it."

I sat in silence for a minute, then turned to him.

"So, is it true? Did you get offered a permanent position?"

"Yeah." He nodded, rubbing his neck.

"And you turned it down?"

"Yeah, I did. Hey, babe, could you get me a beer?"

I didn't move, and after an instant he turned to look at me.

"Why didn't you tell me?" I felt my stomach clench.

He sighed. "Oh, babe, it's just a job, a crap job. There'll be other jobs. Besides, it's on the day shift, and that pays a dollar an hour less. That's forty dollars a week less than I'm making now."

"But . . ." I stammered, stopped, took a deep breath. "But why didn't you at least talk to me about it? I mean, we're a couple, right? I thought we made decisions together. That's what couples do, right?"

He smiled and put his arm around my shoulders.

"Sure we're a couple. We're solid," he said, his voice tired and flat. "But it's my job and my decision. Besides, you and Jenny will love Florida."

I rose abruptly, pulling away from his arm.

"It's your job, yes. But where we live and whether we stay or go, those are things we should decide together, Brannon. And Jenny . . ."

"Jenny is *my* daughter." His voice was low and firm. "*I* decide what's best for her. I've taken care of her for the past eleven years, and she's doing just fine."

"But, Brannon . . ." I sat down opposite him and leaned across the table toward him, reaching for his hands. "Jenny really wants to stay here. She wants to be near Lashaundra. She wants a real house. She wants friends. She wants to go to school."

"Jenny is a kid," he said, not taking my hands. "She doesn't know what's best for her. I'm her dad. I make those decisions."

"But what about me?" I asked, shaking my head. "I've got my job at the diner. I've made friends here. I *like* it here."

"Then stay," he said, rising from the table, his voice and his face expressionless. "Stay if you want to, but Jenny and I are going to Florida."

I felt like I'd been slapped, like I'd had the wind knocked out of me. I stared up at him, letting the tears drip down my cheeks.

"I thought you loved me," I whispered.

He turned his back to me and walked toward the bedroom while I stared.

"I love you, Emma," he said, just before he closed the door behind him. He didn't turn to look at me. "But I'm the man in this family, and I make the decisions for my daughter. If you can't live with that . . . well, then maybe we aren't a couple like I thought."

I sat for a long time at the table, my shoulders shaking, my eyes streaming. A million possibilities ran through my head. I could go back to Idaho. I still had my car. I could go back and ask Boyd to hire me again. But he probably wouldn't, not now that I was pregnant. I couldn't work with the horses while I was pregnant.

I could stay in Campbellsville and keep working at the diner. But that didn't pay enough to live on, especially not with a baby. Not even if Harlan took me on full-time.

And could I really leave Brannon? Could I leave Jenny? They were the only family I had now, the only family I'd had for a long time. I loved them.

I cried until my head ached. And after what felt like a long time, I rose, walked to the bedroom, and pulled open the accordion door.

Brannon was lying on the bed, paging through an old issue of *Time*. He looked up at me, set the magazine on the nightstand, and said nothing.

"I'm pregnant," I said quietly. I didn't say anything else, just that.

The knowledge settled between us like a silent explosion in the room, in our lives, in the universe.

He stared at me for a long minute, his face unreadable.

"You're what?"

"I'm pregnant, Brannon. I'm going to have a baby."

For another long minute, I waited, wondering if he would kick me out right then and there.

"Are you sure?" He rose, walked to me, and took my hands.

I nodded.

"Oh, babe!"

He wrapped his arms around me tightly and lifted me off my feet. "Emma, baby . . . that's great! How far along are you? Why didn't you tell me? Do you feel okay? Here . . ." He lowered me back to my feet and pulled me to sit beside him on the bed. "Sit down. Are you okay? Are you sick? . . . God, a baby! Emma, that's so great!"

I started crying again. I leaned into his chest and sobbed great, heaving, gulping sobs.

"Oh, babe, it's okay. You're okay. We're okay," he crooned.

"I wasn't sure what you'd think," I mumbled into his chest. "I thought maybe you'd be mad, that maybe you wouldn't want another kid, that . . . I don't know."

"Are you kidding?" He tilted my chin up and kissed my nose, his face lit up like the Christmas tree we'd just packed away. "A baby that's half you and half me, Emma, that's . . . that's perfect. Oh my God, Jenny will go bananas!"

I smiled at him and thought what a mess I probably looked, with a red, runny nose and red, weepy eyes. I was grateful, so grateful that he wanted the baby, that he still wanted me. But the way he could go from happy to angry and then angry to happy again in zero flat . . . that confused me. That always confused me.

"So, are you feeling okay?" he asked again, his eyes crinkling in a worried kind of smile.

"I'm fine," I said, my arms wrapped across my belly. "Just tired and kind of scared . . . or not scared, more nervous, I guess."

"Did you see a doctor yet?"

I shook my head and bit my lip. Then I took a deep breath and plunged in.

"Brannon, we don't have insurance."

He said nothing, so I went on.

"If you took the job with Amazon here, we would have insurance. And we could move out of this trailer and into an apartment big enough for us and Jenny and the baby."

Still he said nothing. And, afraid to spoil the moment, I stayed quiet.

After a minute, he rose and walked out of the bedroom. I sat on the bed silently, waiting, willing him to come back. And in a minute he was back, carrying a big glass of milk.

"Okay," he said, smiling as he held the glass toward me. "Okay then, we'll stay."

Tears filled my eyes yet again and I bowed my head, not wanting him to see me cry all over again.

"Hey," he said, his voice low, "it's all good, babe. We'll stay here in Campbellsville. We'll put Jenny in school. We'll get insurance and we'll get a crib and diapers and a car seat and . . . and whatever else we need."

He kneeled before the bed and took my hands in his, squeezing them tightly.

"We'll get married, Emma. We'll be a real family, and we'll be happy. Is that what you want?"

I could only nod and cry. The lump in my throat was too big to get any words out.

He wrapped his arms around me and I cried into them. When I finally looked into his face, I was surprised to see tears running down his cheeks. My heart clenched and my breath caught in my chest. This was real. This was actually happening. I was finally going to have the family I'd always wanted with a man I loved beyond belief.

"I'll go in tomorrow and tell Parker I want the job," he said. "I hope it's still available."

I nodded again.

"And then we'll go to the courthouse and we'll get married."

I stared at him, trying to take it all in.

"That's okay, right?" he asked. "I mean, there's no reason to wait, is there?"

Again I nodded. I felt so full of love and happiness and sheer gratitude, I almost couldn't breathe.

I reached for his hand and pulled him toward me as I rose, kissing his face, still wet with tears. We both stood, crying against each other. Then I fell back onto the bed and opened my arms.

"Come here," I whispered.

He smiled and lay down beside me, kissing my forehead and then my cheeks.

"I love you, Brannon."

"I love you, too."

I nestled against him, running my hand across his chest, then allowing it to drift toward the zipper on his jeans. He rolled slightly away from me.

"What's wrong?"

"You're pregnant, babe."

"I know," I said, smiling. "That doesn't mean I'm untouchable."

He raised himself onto an elbow and caressed my cheek gently.

"I think we should wait until you talk to a doctor," he said. "We don't want to do anything to hurt the baby."

"But . . ." I began.

"Shhhh," he whispered, holding my body against his. "It's going to be okay. It's going to be great, babe. I'll take care of you. I'll take care of you and our baby."

I sighed, relaxing into him.

"God," he said, and even his voice seemed to be smiling. "I can't wait to tell Jenny."

~19~

Jenny

I didn't go home the next morning. I was so mad at Daddy that I didn't want to see him. And I didn't want to hear Emma tell me that I must be wrong about the job.

Lashaundra knew the truth and I knew the truth. We'd both cried before we went to sleep the night before. But we couldn't even talk about it, because I didn't want to get her in trouble for telling me. So we just pretended everything was okay. Every once in a while, I could see Mrs. Johnson watching us, her forehead wrinkled. I knew she was worried. And I wished for the millionth time that she was my mother, that I had a mother.

Finally, not too long after we ate lunch, I had to go home. Mr. Johnson worked the same schedule as my dad, four nights on and three off. He had the day off so he got up early, and they were all going into town. I almost asked if I could go with them, but I knew I had to go home.

I opened the door to the trailer, and Emma was standing there in front of me, a big grin on her face.

"We're staying!" she said. Then she scooped me into a hug so tight I almost couldn't breathe.

"What?" I pulled away and looked up at her. Her cheeks were pink and her eyes sparkled.

"Your dad is going to talk to Mr. Parker today, to take the job. We're going to stay here in Campbellsville with the Johnsons. And you can go to school!"

I stared at her in disbelief, willing myself to believe her but not really accepting what she said.

"But Daddy . . ."

"We talked last night." Emma pulled my coat off and hung it on a hook. "And it's all settled. Your dad is taking the job and we'll stay here and look for an apartment, or maybe even a house to rent. Wouldn't that be great, a house with a yard and everything?"

I couldn't say anything at first. I felt numb. And then I started shaking, first my hands and then my whole self.

"Seriously?" It was all I could croak out.

She nodded, smiling like her face might just split in two.

I leaned into her arms and hugged her. Could it really be true? Were we finally going to stay in one place, not live in the trailer anymore? Was I finally going to have a friend I didn't have to leave? Was I really going to school?

"Hey, pumpkin!"

I looked around Emma to see Daddy standing in the doorway to the bedroom. He was smiling, too.

"Are we really staying?"

"We really are." Daddy knelt down and opened his arms and I ran into them. He rested his chin on top of my head and held me for a long minute while I tried hard not to cry.

"Are you sure?" I had to ask, even though it felt mean. I had to be sure.

"Well," he said, standing up and pulling on his jacket, "as long as the offer's still good. I'm heading over to talk to Parker now."

"But what if it's not?" I stammered, suddenly sure the job offer was gone.

"It will be," he said, smiling again. "Trust me, Jenny. He wants me. I just have to say yes."

He kissed Emma and left, the metal door slamming behind him.

I stood a minute, just taking it all in. We were staying in Kentucky. We would live in an apartment instead of the trailer, or maybe even a house. I would see Lashaundra every day, not just for the next week but for forever.

Then I turned to look at Emma. She was sitting at the table, her hands curled around a coffee cup, watching me.

"So . . ." she said, just before I ran and threw myself at her.

She hugged me and held me while I cried and laughed and shook all over.

"You're magic!" I finally said. "How did you make him do that?"

She laughed. "Oh, Jenny, I'm not magic at all. Your dad just loves you. He wants you to be happy. He just had to realize that staying was what's best for you."

I shook my head, tears stinging my eyes. Because I knew what she didn't. Daddy had gotten job offers before. He didn't think I knew, but I did. He just never took them. I wasn't sure why, but he never wanted to stay in one place.

≈ 20 ≈

Emma

Two days later, on a cold but sunny January morning, we stood in the courthouse waiting to see the justice of the peace. I wore my only dress, a pale blue one with a slightly scooped neckline. The locket Brannon gave me for Christmas hung around my neck. Brannon wore jeans, a white shirt, and a dark jacket. Jenny danced around us, her dark hair tied in a red ribbon that matched her dress.

"Brannon Bohner?" An older, heavy woman appeared in the doorway, frowning and holding a clipboard in her hands.

"That's me." Brannon shook her hand and we all followed her into a small room.

"Do you have your license?" the woman asked.

Brannon gave it to her and clasped my hand.

"Justice Benson will be right in." The woman took the license to another desk and sat down. We all stood, waiting for a long minute until a short, round man waddled into the room. He smiled at me over his wire-rimmed glasses.

"So, you're here to get married?"

"Yes, sir." I nodded and squeezed Brannon's hand.

"The license?" He looked at the woman sitting at the desk. She nodded and held it out to him.

"Well then," he said, scanning the paper quickly, "everything looks in order. Let's get started."

It was over in less than ten minutes. I was no longer Emma Kingston, illegal fifth wife of Micah. I was now Emma Bohner, the legal and only wife of Brannon and official stepmother of Jenny. We stepped out of the courtroom into a brilliant, sunny, bitterly cold day. I held Brannon's hand tightly, still in disbelief that we were really married.

"Let's get some lunch," he said, smiling at me.

"Pizza!" Jenny cried.

"No," Brannon said, taking her hand. "Not pizza. Pizza is not a good wedding lunch."

"Nothing fancy," I said, laughing. "I'm happy with pizza, if you-all want that."

"Let's go to the diner," he said, winking at Jenny as we walked.

He held the door open for me and I stepped inside and stopped short, staring around me.

The restaurant was full of people, all of them applauding and smiling. Candles flickered on every table. A banner hung across the back wall, proclaiming, CONGRATULATIONS, BRANNON AND EMMA!

Resa stepped forward to hug me. "Congratulations, honey! We're so happy for ya'll."

I turned to see Brannon grinning widely. Jenny was watching us both, smiling hugely.

"Come on in," Resa said, pulling me by the hand. "Your table is ready."

She led us to a booth, where a huge bouquet of red roses dominated the table.

"Now you just relax," she said. "Your lunch will be ready soon."

"Did you do this?" I asked, staring at Brannon as he sat down across from me.

He laughed and shook his head. "This is all Resa and Jenny."

"It's your wedding reception!" Jenny slid into the booth beside me. "And look, there are presents and everything!"

She pointed to a table by the counter, while held a stack of beautifully wrapped packages.

Tears filled my eyes as I hugged her.

"Thank you, Jenny," I whispered. "You're the best."

Resa returned with plates and set them grandly on the table before us. I stared at the steaks, baked potatoes, French-cut green beans, and warm rolls. This was not the usual fare at Happy Days.

"Harlan made it special," Resa said.

I looked back toward the kitchen and saw Harlan standing in the doorway, watching us.

"Thank you!" I called. He winked and disappeared into the kitchen.

"And this is from me and Merilee." Resa placed a bottle of red wine on the table, and Merilee appeared with two wineglasses.

"Not for Emma," Brannon said, pushing a glass back toward her.

"It's okay, Brannon," I said, my cheeks reddening. "One glass won't hurt."

He frowned and shook his head. "Emma will have some milk."

Resa's eyebrows arched and she took my wineglass away, returning with two large glasses of milk, one for me and one for Jenny.

As we ate, people came by the table to say congratulations and give us good wishes.

"I can't believe all these people know you," Brannon said in a low voice. "We've only been here a few weeks."

"I think everyone in Campbellsville knows everyone," I said. "Especially here at the diner."

"Attention! Attention! . . . Okay, ya'll, listen up!" Resa hollered, waving a red-checked napkin over her head. "It's time for the first dance. Brannon, Emma, come on out here."

I blushed as we walked to the small space cleared in the center of the restaurant. People clapped and shouted encouragement. Then Resa put money in the jukebox, and music filled the room.

We swayed to the strains of "Love Me Tender," my head resting on Brannon's shoulder, his arms firm around my waist. I thought I might burst from sheer joy.

After the dance, we opened presents—a cast-iron skillet from Merilee, embroidered dish towels from Resa, pretty frames and a set of pans and a quilt and so many other beautiful things. I hugged more people than even I could remember, and then we sat back down in the booth at Resa's direction. Then, with much applause and whistling, Harlan rolled in a cart with a three-tiered wedding cake frosted in white, a tiny plastic couple on top.

"Oh my God," I breathed, staring from him to Resa to Merilee to Brannon to Jenny. "It's beautiful!"

"Mama made it!" I looked up to see Lashaundra grinning at us. "And I put the people on top."

I rose to hug her and then went to hug Angel. She and Michael sat with Malcolm, all of them smiling.

"Thank you," I said. "It's perfect."

"Be happy," she said, with a small catch in her voice. "Just be happy."

"You didn't bake that cake in your trailer," I said.

"Harlan let me use the kitchen." She smiled. "In fact, Ms. Jensen from the bakery just offered me a job, decorating cakes."

I hugged her again, my eyes filling.

"That's great," I said. "That's so great."

After we'd eaten cake and made another sweep of the restaurant hugging people, it was time to go.

"Thank you," I said again and again, hugging Merilee and Resa. "This was just perfect."

"Jenny, you'd better put that coat on," Brannon said. "It's cold out."

"I'm going home with Lashaundra," she said. She smiled shyly at us, then looked at the floor.

"Oh." Brannon smiled and kissed her on the forehead. "Well, then, I guess we'll see you tomorrow."

He turned and shook Michael's hand. "Thanks, man," he said.

"No problem." Michael grinned. "We thought you-all might like a little time to yourselves."

I put on my coat, picked up my purse, and turned to see Harlan standing directly in front of me. He held out a white envelope.

"I'm not much for presents," he said. "But I thought ya'll could use this to help you get settled."

Before I could even say thank you, he turned and strode back to the kitchen.

In the car with Brannon, I opened the envelope and gasped.

"What is it?" Brannon asked.

His eyes widened as I pulled four one-hundred-dollar bills from the envelope.

"Wow!" He took the bills and laid them out on the seat between us. "That will be a good start on our rent."

I could only nod, my eyes filled with tears yet again. So many people in Campbellsville were so good to us. It felt like we'd lived there forever.

When we got home, Brannon took a beer from the fridge and sat down, patting the seat beside him.

"So, Mrs. Bohner," he said, "did you like your wedding reception?"

"My gracious," I said. "It was perfect. I can't believe Jenny and Resa did all that. And Merilee and Harlan and Angel . . . we have so many good friends here."

He put his arm around me and kissed my cheek.

"Everyone loves you," he said. "But nobody loves you as much as I do."

I rose and held out my hand to him.

"How about we get undressed and you show me just how much you love me?"

He smiled but didn't rise.

"Not until you see the doctor," he said. "I want to make sure everything is okay with the baby."

He picked up the remote and flipped on the television and took a long drink of beer.

I stood a minute, feeling deflated and a little bit foolish. Then I put on the teakettle and made some chamomile tea and we watched the evening news.

So much for a romantic wedding night.

Still, I was happy. I had a good job with good friends, a wonderful stepdaughter, a husband I loved, and a baby on the way. Pretty much, life that day was perfect.

21

Jenny

"I love this one!"

The little green rental house had a porch with a swing and a small yard.

"It's nice," Emma agreed.

"Let's wait till we see inside," Daddy said.

Mr. Marshall unlocked the front door and we went inside. The pale yellow living room, filled with sunlight, opened into a small dining room. Behind it, the kitchen was tiled in turquoise and white.

"Do the appliances come with it?" Daddy asked.

"Yep." Mr. Marshall opened the refrigerator and then the oven. "Everything here stays."

"That's better than the last place," Emma said.

We walked through three bedrooms and a bathroom with a red claw-foot tub. Then Mr. Marshall unlocked the back door and we stepped onto a screened porch overlooking a fenced backyard. Behind the fence a garage opened onto a wide alley.

"Not much storage space," Daddy said.

I stared at him. It was so much more space than we had in the trailer.

"Well, there's the basement," Mr. Marshall said. "The washer and dryer are down there. And then there's storage in the attic."

We went back inside and peeked into the dark basement. It smelled damp. Then Mr. Marshall walked into the hallway, opened a trap door in the ceiling, and pulled on a cord that hung down. A ladder unfolded through the door and extended into the hallway. Daddy climbed up and looked into the attic. When he came back down, I climbed the ladder and looked into the room. Light from a small window showed a dusty, warm space with sloping walls. I could just stand in the center of the room.

I could read up here, I thought. I'd put some pillows on the floor under the window and maybe a lamp. It would be my own private hideaway.

When we'd seen the entire house, Mr. Marshall walked back to his car to let Daddy and Emma talk on the porch.

"What do you think?" Daddy asked.

"I love it," Emma said. "It's definitely got more room than anything else we've seen. And I love the yard. We could put in a garden, grow our own vegetables. Then Jenny and I can do some canning. That'll save money in the long run."

"How about you, kiddo?" Daddy looked over to where I was sitting on the swing.

"I love it," I echoed Emma. "I really love it."

"Okay then," Daddy said, his arm around Emma. "It looks like we've got a winner."

We moved in two days later. There really wasn't a lot to move, just our clothes and linens and kitchen stuff. We didn't even have any furniture yet. So for the first week we slept in the trailer, which Daddy had parked in the alley behind the house.

Over the next few days, Emma and I went to all of the thrift shops in town. We bought a table with four chairs for the dining room, an old couch and a chair for the living room, and a futon to put on the floor in my room until we could buy a bed for me. We made shelves out of cinderblocks and boards and a desk from two sawhorses and an old door. Emma hand-sewed curtains for all the windows. Then Daddy and Emma went to Sam's Club and bought a box spring and mattress for their room, with a dresser and a bed-side table. Soon the house began to feel like a real home.

"We need to get Jenny enrolled at school," Emma said one night at dinner. "Angel enrolled Lashaundra last week, and she says it's a good school."

"I don't know," Brannon said. "Starting in the middle of the school year might be kind of tough. Maybe we should wait until fall."

"She'll be fine," Emma said. "She'll make friends."

"What do you think, Jenny?" Daddy turned to me.

"Can I be in the same class as Lashaundra?"

"I don't know," Daddy said. "I guess we can ask."

I thought a long minute. I'd always wanted to go to school. But now that it was real, I was a little bit scared.

"If I can be in Lashaundra's class, then I want to go, I guess."

The next Monday morning, Emma and I walked into Camp-bellsville Middle School. Kids ran past us, shouting to one another and laughing. My stomach felt like a giant twisted knot. I really wanted to hold Emma's hand, but I didn't want to look like a baby, so I just clutched my notebook to my chest and tried hard not to look too scared.

We walked to the front desk, where a woman was talking to a boy who looked much older than me.

"Jasper, I have told you before you cannot wear your pants like that."

I looked down and saw his jeans sagging almost off his hips.

"They're my pants," the boy said. "I can wear them any way I want to."

"Maybe at home, but not at school," the woman said firmly.

She rose from her chair and walked around the desk, a stapler in her hand.

"What are you doing?" the boy shouted.

She said nothing, just began stapling the waist of his pants to his shirt.

"You're gonna ruin my shirt!" The boy tried to step away from her, but she simply held his arm in one hand and continued stapling with the other.

"My dad is gonna be pissed!" the boy shouted. "You just wait and see. He'll get you fired for this."

The woman walked back around the desk and sat down.

"Your father can come talk to me any time," she said calmly. "Now go on to class, or you'll be late."

The boy stalked off, still shouting. "My dad's gonna get you fired, you old bag. You just wait and see."

The woman looked up at us and smiled.

"Good morning," she said. "Can I help you?"

"We've come to enroll my daughter," Emma said. "We just moved here."

"That's fine," the woman said. "My name is Mrs. Murphy. Do you have her birth certificate and proof of residence?"

Emma handed her a stack of papers. Mrs. Murphy scanned them, then smiled at me.

"Well, Jenny, welcome to Campbellsville Middle School. What grade are you in?"

I stared at her in silence. I didn't even know what grade I was in.

"She's been homeschooled," Emma said, her hand on my shoulder. "We've traveled around a lot. Here are her transcripts."

She handed Mrs. Murphy another stack of papers. Mrs. Murphy scanned the pages and her eyes widened.

"You're eleven?" she asked.

I nodded.

"Well, you're working well above your grade level. These are very impressive scores."

"She's a smart girl," Emma said, smiling at me.

"So, we have two options," Mrs. Murphy said. "According to her age, she should be in the sixth grade. But with these test scores, she could easily go into the seventh grade."

"I want to be in the same class as Lashaundra," I said.

"Lashaundra Johnson?"

I nodded.

"She enrolled last week. She's in the sixth grade."

"Then I want to be in the sixth grade."

Mrs. Murphy looked at Emma. Emma smiled and shrugged her shoulders.

"Lashaundra is her best friend," she said. "It would be nice if they could be in the same class."

Mrs. Murphy nodded. "I can certainly put her on the same team, so they'll have some classes together. But I can't guarantee they'll be in all the same classes."

Emma filled out some papers while Mrs. Murphy wrote out a schedule. Then she rose and shook Emma's hand.

"Thank you, Mrs. Bohner," she said. "I'm sure Jenny will have a good experience here."

Emma hesitated, then kissed my forehead.

"Okay, Jenny. You go with Mrs. Murphy and she'll show you what to do. I'll be here to pick you up at three."

I watched her walk away, my stomach churning.

"Come on, Jenny." Mrs. Murphy put her arm around my shoulders. "Let's get you a locker and then I'll walk you to your first class."

Everyone in the room looked up when Mrs. Murphy pushed the door open. I followed her into a classroom filled with kids. I'd never been around so many kids before. I felt like I might throw up. And then I saw Lashaundra. She grinned and waved at me.

"This is Jenny Bohner," Mrs. Murphy said to the man standing at the chalkboard. "She just moved to Campbellsville."

"Welcome, Jenny. I'm Mr. Thomas."

He extended his hand and I shook it.

"Why don't you take a seat," he said. "We're just doing some review on the U.S. Constitution."

I walked to the back of the room and sat down at a desk beside Lashaundra.

I opened my notebook, pulled out a pen, and stared around me. Finally, I was in a real school.

The morning passed in a blur. I got lost twice moving from classroom to classroom amid a sea of faces I didn't know. Thankfully, I had two classes with Lashaundra, and when I got to the lunchroom, I found her waiting for me. We stood in a long line to get our food. The noise in the room was unbelievable. Finally, we filled our trays and found seats together at a crowded table.

"How do you like it so far?" Lashaundra opened her little carton of chocolate milk and took a long drink.

"It's okay." I stared at the food on my plate—a slice of turkey, mashed potatoes with brown gravy, and some canned fruit. It looked disgusting.

"It's a lot better than the last school I was at," she said, spreading potatoes over her turkey slice.

"Where was that?" I took a tentative bite of potatoes.

"Alabama," she said. "That place was terrible. Everything was old and dirty. The kids were mean. I hated it."

"How many schools have you been to?"

She paused a moment, chewing, then said, "This is the fourth. How about you?"

"This is my first."

She stared at me. "Really? You never went to school before?"

I shook my head. "I just did my lessons at home."

She nodded. "I did that, too, sometimes. But when we stayed anywhere for more than a couple months, Mama always sent me to school. This one is pretty nice."

"It's so loud," I said.

"Yeah, but you'll get used to it."

"I'm really glad you're here." I couldn't even imagine what I would do if she wasn't there.

"Me too," she said. "It's nice to know someone."

Another blur of classes passed and I walked outside to see Emma waiting for me, her arms wrapped around her stomach. It was bitterly cold out. But I didn't care. I had made it through my first day of school.

"How was it?" she asked.

"It was okay. Pretty loud."

"Yeah." She nodded. "Did you see Lashaundra?"

"She's in four of my classes, and we have lunch together."

"Good," she said. "Was everybody nice to you?"

I shrugged. Mostly I had been ignored.

"One girl in my English class shared her book with me."

"That's nice. Didn't you get your own book?"

"They had to order it."

We got in the car and drove toward home.

"So do you think you'll like it?" she asked.

"Yeah," I said. "I think I will."

22

Emma

"Mrs. Bohner?" A nurse called my name and we followed her to an exam room.

"The doctor will be right with you," she said.

"Thank you." Brannon grinned at her and she beamed back at him.

After a few minutes, Dr. McLaren walked in and smiled at us.

"Well, it's official. You're pregnant. Congratulations!"

"Thanks, Doc!" Brannon shook his hand. "When is she due?"

"Mid-September, I'd say. How are you feeling?"

"Fine," I said.

"No morning sickness?"

"No, I feel pretty good."

"Is this your first pregnancy?"

"Um, no. I had a baby, a boy. He died."

"I'm so sorry." Dr. McLaren put his hand on my shoulder. "Was he stillborn?"

"No, he lived five weeks. But he never was very strong and then he got a respiratory infection and . . . and he died."

Dr. McLaren wrote something on my chart.

"Well, we'll monitor you very carefully and do everything we can to make sure you have a healthy baby."

"Thank you."

"In the meantime, I want you to start taking prenatal vitamins, get plenty of rest, avoid stress, and eat a good, healthy diet."

"Can I still have coffee?"

"Yes," he said. "But not more than one cup a day unless it's decaf. Decaf is okay."

"What about work, Doc?" Brannon asked. "She works at the diner and is on her feet all day. I think she should quit and stay home, right?"

"That's really up to Emma," the doctor said. "If it starts to be too much, she should at least cut back her hours. But there's no reason for her to quit if she doesn't want to. The more active she stays, the healthier she and the baby will be."

I smiled at Brannon. He'd been talking about me quitting my job ever since he found out I was pregnant. But I didn't want to quit. I loved my job. I loved the people I worked with, I enjoyed the customers, and I certainly didn't want to be stuck at home all the time.

"We'll want you scheduled for monthly visits," Dr. McLaren said. "Vickie will set that up for you. Do you have any other questions?"

"Well," I mumbled, feeling my cheeks redden. "Actually, I was wondering . . . I mean . . . is it still okay for us to . . ."

"Sex is fine," he said, laughing. "As long as you feel like it, it's fine. Some women have sex right up into the ninth month."

"Okay, good." I glanced up at Brannon. He wasn't smiling like I thought he'd be. In fact, he looked angry.

"Okay." Dr. McLaren shook my hand and then Brannon's. "We'll see you next month."

Brannon didn't say anything as I made my next appointment with the receptionist or as we walked out to the truck.

"Are you upset about something?" I finally asked.

He turned to me and his eyes were hard.

"I can't believe you asked the doctor about . . . about sex," he spat. "Good God, Emma. You're pregnant. You're a mother now, not a slut."

I stared at him, feeling myself getting flushed.

"But I thought . . ."

"I know what you thought," he spat. "You thought you'd just humiliate me in front of the doctor by acting like a whore."

He revved the engine as I reached for the door handle. Before he could say anything else, I was out of the truck and walking away from him.

"Emma!" he yelled after me. "What the hell are you doing? Get back in the truck right now!"

I kept walking, my eyes blurring with tears. Behind me I heard the truck door slam and Brannon's footsteps closing in on me. He grabbed my arm and turned me to face him.

"What the hell is wrong with you?"

"What's wrong with me?" I yelled. "What the hell is wrong with you? I am not a slut, Brannon. I am a wife who loves her husband and wants a real marriage with sex and the whole deal. And I will *not* be talked to like that. Not by you, not by anyone!"

His face reddened, his hands gripped my arms.

"Get back in the truck," he hissed. "We don't need to talk about this in public."

I glanced around and saw Mrs. O'Hearn standing in the doorway of the flower shop, watching us.

"Let go of me," I said softly. "You're hurting my arms."

He released his grip, took a deep breath, and stepped back. "Okay, look," he said, "I didn't mean to yell. I'm sorry. I just couldn't believe you would talk to the doctor like that. It's not . . . proper to talk about sex with your OB. It's . . . God, it's almost obscene."

I stared at him for a long minute and then sighed. "Brannon, I think Dr. McLaren knows we have sex. I mean, I am pregnant."

He smiled a little then and ran his hand over his eyes. "I know that. It just doesn't sound very ladylike, in your condition."

"My condition is pregnancy, honey. Not leprosy."

He reached for me again, this time more gently, and pulled me into a hug.

"Okay," he said. "I'm sorry. I guess I'm just old-fashioned about some things. Will you get back in the truck now?"

I kissed him and smiled. "Yes, I will get in the truck, but only if you promise to take me to lunch. I'm starving."

"That's what I like to hear," he said. "What do you want to eat?"

"Pizza," I said firmly. "I believe I would kill for a mushroom-and-jalapeño pizza."

That afternoon, we told Jenny about the baby.

"No way!" she yelled, hopping from one foot to the other. "For real? You're really having a baby?"

"Yep, we are," Brannon said. "In September you'll be a big sister."

"Is it a boy or a girl?" she asked.

"We don't know yet," I said. "The doctor said he'll do an ultrasound at four months, but even then we might not be able to tell. So . . . it will be a surprise."

"I hope it's a girl!" she said. "I really want a little sister."

"Well, we can't promise you that," Brannon said, laughing. "But whether it's a boy or a girl, you will be a big sister."

"What are you going to name it?"

Brannon looked at me and I looked at him. We hadn't even talked about names yet.

"I don't know," I said. "To be honest, I haven't thought about it."

"Well, I think we should name her Mia," Jenny said. "Mia or Sasha, those are my favorites."

Brannon laughed, shaking his head.

"Hold your horses there, ma'am. We don't even know if it's a girl. And I'm sure as hell not naming my son Mia or Sasha."

"Well, obviously not if it's a boy," she said, rolling her eyes. "If it's a boy, we should call him Isaac."

I laughed, watching the two of them. They were both so excited they were almost giddy. I rested my hands on my flat belly. *This is your family, baby,* I thought. *And we already love you so much.*

"Hey, you," Brannon said. "Are you okay?"

I nodded even as tears dripped down my face.

"I'm just really happy."

"Me too, babe," he said.

"And me!" Jenny yelled. "I'm happy, too! Can I call Lashaundra and tell her about the baby?"

"Sure," Brannon said. "I think that's okay, isn't it?"

He turned to me.

"It's fine," I said.

And it was. A lot of women don't tell people they're pregnant until after the first trimester. But I knew this baby would be healthy. Our baby would be strong and happy and loved more than any child in the world.

❧ 23 ❧

Jenny

"What about Seth?" Lashaundra had been listing baby names for the last half hour while we ate lunch.

"I like it," I said. "Are you going to eat your pickle?"

She shook her head, forked the pickle, and dropped it onto my plate.

"Or maybe Wesley. No, not Wesley. How about Cameron?"

I laughed. "I don't think my dad would go for Cameron. He likes names like Bill and Paul, you know, old-fashioned, boring names."

"What about Emma? What kind of names does she like?"

"I'm not sure," I said. "Emma hasn't said any names she likes."

"My mom has already started knitting a blanket for the baby. It's green and white. Then if the baby is a boy she'll trim it in blue, and if it's a girl she'll trim it in pink."

"Your mom knows how to do a lot of stuff, doesn't she? I mean, she bakes and she decorates cakes and she knits. You're really lucky."

Lashaundra grinned and dipped her last french fry in a small puddle of ketchup.

"She's okay," she said. "She's teaching me to knit. Maybe she'll teach you, too."

We stood up to take our trays to the counter, when a big boy walked right into Lashaundra. Her tray crashed to the floor. Everyone stopped talking to stare.

"Hey, watch where you're going!" Lashaundra said.

"Why don't you watch where you're going? And while you're at it, why don't you just go back to Africa where you belong, jungle monkey?"

Several people around us laughed and the boy grinned at them.

I recognized him now, the same boy I'd seen on my first day of school, the one with the saggy pants. Now he was dancing around like a monkey in front of Lashaundra. I stared in disbelief as she drew back her fist and slammed it into his stomach.

Immediately, two teachers came running. One put her arms around Lashaundra, the other grabbed at the boy's arm to keep him from hitting her back.

"Both of you, to the office right now!" one of the teachers yelled.

"It wasn't Lashaundra's fault!" I said. "He was being really mean to her."

The teacher holding Lashaundra turned to me and said, "You come along, too. We'll let the principal figure this out."

I followed them down the long hallway to the principal's office, my stomach clenching, my palms sweating. I had only been at school a couple weeks and I was already in trouble. Daddy would be so disappointed in me.

The principal looked up as we entered his office.

"These two were fighting in the lunchroom," the teacher holding the boy's arm said.

"Jasper Rigby," the principal said, looking over his glasses at the boy. "This is the fourth time this year you've been in my office for fighting."

"She hit me!" the boy yelled. "I didn't hit her."

"Only because I stopped you," the teacher said.

The principal looked at Lashaundra. "And what is your name, young lady?"

"Lashaundra Johnson, sir," she said.

"Did you hit Mr. Rigby?"

"Yes I did, sir. But he deserved it."

"Okay, why don't you-all sit down and tell me what happened."

The two teachers who had brought us to the office left, and Lashaundra and I sat down. I reached over to hold her hand. Jasper stood staring at the principal, sneering.

"Mr. Rigby, I asked you to sit down." The principal stared right back at him until Jasper finally sat down with a thud.

"Now, Miss Johnson, tell me what happened."

"She hit me!" Jasper yelled again.

"I asked Miss Johnson to talk. You'll get your turn to talk next." Jasper sighed loudly.

"He ran right into me and made me drop my tray," Lashaundra said. "Then he called me a jungle monkey and told me I should go back to Africa."

"Is that true?" The principal turned to Jasper.

"She's the one who ran into me," he said. "And she's the one who hit me."

"Did you call her a jungle monkey?"

Jasper didn't reply. He just kept sneering.

The principal sighed now and shook his head. Then he looked at me.

"And why are you here?" he asked.

"The teacher told me to come with her," I said. "And he did call Lashaundra a jungle monkey." I nodded at the boy as he glared at me. "And he was scratching his belly and acting like a monkey and everything."

"Mr. Rigby," the principal said, turning toward the boy, "you will apologize to Miss Johnson immediately."

Jasper sat in silence, staring hard at the principal, and then at Lashaundra and me.

"I asked you to apologize," the principal repeated, his voice low.

Still Jasper said nothing.

Finally, the principal took a deep breath and turned back to Lashaundra.

"Miss Johnson, I appreciate that Mr. Rigby insulted you. He

was very wrong to do that. But hitting is never an appropriate response. I will be calling your parents to tell them what you've done, and I think you will need to stay after school today in detention."

"Yes, sir." Lashaundra's voice was soft.

"You two go back to your classes," he said.

We rose and Jasper got up, too.

"Not you, Mr. Rigby. We're not finished here."

When I told Daddy and Emma what had happened, Emma's eyes grew wide.

"Is Lashaundra okay?" she asked.

"Yeah," I said. "But I'll bet she's in trouble at home."

Daddy shook his head. "Well, he sure had it coming, didn't he? Frankly, I'm glad Lashaundra punched him. He deserved it."

He laughed and shook his head again. "Imagine, little Lashaundra punching out a bully. Good for her!"

"Did you say the boy's last name is Rigby?" Emma asked.

I nodded. "Jasper Rigby."

"I'll bet he's Damon Rigby's son. He's a bully just like his father."

"Who's Damon Rigby?" Daddy asked.

"He's a jerk who comes into the diner sometimes. He's always yelling at his wife, just humiliating her every chance he gets. And he's a bigot, too. You should see the way he looks at Angel when he sees her."

"Jasper is the boy we saw that first day of school," I said. "The one with the saggy pants."

"Well, I'm kind of sorry Lashaundra crossed him. You stay out of his way, okay? It sounds like he's a bully just like his father, and the farther away you are from him the better." Emma put her hand on mine.

"Okay." She didn't really have to tell me that. I already knew I wanted nothing to do with Jasper Rigby.

24

Emma

"Emma, that's wonderful, honey! When are you due?" Resa hugged me tightly.

"The middle of September," I said.

"Is Brannon just over the moon?"

I laughed. "He's pretty excited. So is Jenny."

"I bet they are." She pulled back to look me up and down. "Are you feeling okay?"

I nodded. "I'm fine. No morning sickness or anything yet."

"Let's hope the Good Lord keeps it that way," she said. "I puked my guts out when I was pregnant, every single time. I even ended up in the emergency room with Justine. I was so sick they had to give me one of them IV drips. I wouldn't wish that on my worst enemy."

"So far, I'm good," I repeated.

"Well, if you've got any questions, honey, you just ask. I been through it four times, so I guess that makes me a pro. Who's your doctor?"

"Dr. McLaren."

"He's good." She nodded. "Real nice."

Harlan emerged from the kitchen.

"You gonna keep working for a while?"

"Sure," I said. "I feel good; I like my job. There's no reason to quit."

"All right," he said. "But if you get tired, you take a break. No arguments." He raised his hand as I opened my mouth. "You get tired, you sit down. You got that?"

"Yes, sir!" I saluted him like a soldier would a drill sergeant.

He shook his head and walked back into the kitchen.

"Have ya'll thought about names yet?" Resa asked as she filled a saltshaker on a table.

"Not really. We just found out a couple weeks ago."

"Naming is the fun part. I had all kinds of names I liked when I was pregnant. I liked Caroline and Lorelei and Madelyn for girls. But Earl didn't like any of them. He's kind of particular about the naming."

I smiled. Resa's husband was a quiet, easygoing man with a soft voice and a gentle grin. I couldn't imagine him being particular about much of anything.

"When you're ready," she continued, "the mission store has lots of maternity clothes, real good prices. I got most everything there. St. Vincent's, you know it? It's on Central. Oh, and Fabulous Finds has good stuff, too. I'll take you sometime if we ever get a day off together."

"Thanks, Resa."

"Like I said, I've done it four times. You got questions, you just ask."

"Um . . . actually," I stammered, feeling myself start to blush. "When you were pregnant, did you and Earl . . . did you, I mean . . ."

"Did we what?" She looked confused.

"Did you still have sex?" It came out almost in a whisper.

"Oh, yeah," she said, laughing. "We had sex right up till the day Sam was born. In fact, I think that's what finally started my labor. I was past due with him."

"So, Earl still wanted to?"

"Honey, Earl always wants to. I think I could weigh eight hundred pounds and be on a respirator, and he'd still want to jump my bones."

She paused and then asked, "Don't Brannon want to?"

"Not since he found out I was pregnant," I said, my cheeks burning. "It's like he's afraid he'll hurt the baby."

"Some men are like that, I guess. Not my Earl, of course. Lord knows there's been times I wish he would lay off, but he's always ready to go. But some men don't like sex when their wives are pregnant."

She reached for another saltshaker and laughed again.

"What you need, darlin', is a BOB."

I stared at her, not understanding.

"A battery-operated boyfriend," she said, grinning at my red cheeks. "It don't talk back, it just hums."

My eyes widened and I knew I looked like an idiot.

"Brannon would kill me if I came home with a . . . a vibrator."

"Not if he don't know," she said, moving to another table. "Sometimes a girl's got to take care of her own self, if you know what I mean."

I shook my head. In a million years I could not imagine myself walking into one of those kinds of stores and buying a vibrator.

"If you ladies have some time on your hands, how about opening shop?" Harlan's voice made me jump. I looked back just in time to see him disappear into the kitchen.

"Oh my God," I said. "Do you think he heard us?"

Resa laughed as she unlocked the restaurant's front door.

"Don't worry, Emma. It'll take more than a vibrator to embarrass old Harlan. Trust me, honey, he's heard it all before."

When school was over, Jenny and Lashaundra came to the diner. Angel was working at the bakery now, so they often came in to have a snack and do their homework.

"Ya'll want some pie?" Resa asked.

"No, thank you," Lashaundra said, smiling up at her.

"Yes, please!" Jenny said.

"How about some cocoa, then?"

"Yes, thank you."

"Those girls are so polite," Resa said as she passed me. "You and Angel are good mamas."

"I can't take much credit," I said. "Brannon's the one who raised Jenny."

"Well, he's done a fine job. My kids think they're doing you a favor to say please or thank you."

I laughed. Resa's four children were all well mannered, if a little bit rowdy. When they came into the diner, it was like a hurricane of noise and motion.

I picked up plates from a table and pocketed the tip, then headed for the kitchen when I heard the chimes on the door. Glancing back, I saw three boys enter. One of them looked familiar.

"What do you have to do to get service around here?" one of the boys, the biggest one, shouted as they all sat down at a booth.

"Hold your horses!" Resa called back. "I'll be right with you."

I put the plates into the dishwasher, picked up an order, and walked back to the front of the diner. The three boys were sitting in a booth toward the front.

"Hey, Emma," Jenny hissed at me as I passed the table where she sat with Lashaundra. "That's Jasper Rigby, the one who called Lashaundra a jungle monkey."

I eyed the boys at the table, wishing I could ask them to leave.

"Just be quiet and stay out of his way," I said softly.

Jenny nodded and dropped her eyes to the social studies book in front of her. Lashaundra turned in the booth to look at the boys.

"Hey, it's the jungle monkey!"

The biggest boy rose from his seat and began walking toward the table where the girls were sitting. I stepped in front of him.

"Why don't you sit down and I'll take your order," I said, forcing my voice to remain flat.

"I'm not sitting in any restaurant that serves niggers." The boy stared past me at Lashaundra and Jenny.

"Jasper Rigby, that's enough out of you!" Resa stood behind me, her hands on her hips. "You sit back down and behave yourself or I will call your mother."

Jasper rolled his eyes at her and stood still for a long minute. Then he turned abruptly and walked back to the table where his friends sat.

"Let's go," he said. "Nothing but niggers and nigger lovers in here."

The two boys in the booth rose and they all left, slamming the door behind them.

"Are you okay?" I asked, walking back toward the girls.

Jenny nodded. Lashaundra sat in silence, her fists gripped into two tight balls.

"Don't you worry, honey." Resa put her hand on Lashaundra's shoulder. "He'll get what's coming to him. Bullies always do."

Jenny's eyes were wide as she watched Lashaundra's face. Lashaundra said nothing for a minute, then looked up at Resa and said, "I've heard worse."

"He's a pig, just like his daddy," Resa said. "He's not even worth your time."

Both girls nodded.

"My dad said he was glad you hit Jasper," Jenny said. "He said Jasper had it coming."

Lashaundra smiled then. "My daddy said he was proud of me, too. But boy, Mama was mad."

"Just try to steer clear of him and his friends," I said. The sheer hatred on Jasper's face as he stared at the girls had shaken me.

"Don't worry, Emma." Lashaundra gazed up at me, her dark brown eyes wide and clear. "I won't let him bother Jenny."

Just before we closed that evening, the front door slammed open so hard the windows rattled.

"Resa Lane McCoy!" Damon Rigby yelled as he stalked into the restaurant. "I want to talk to you."

"Hey, Damon. Do you want some coffee?" Resa's voice was calm.

"Did you kick my boy out of here today?" Damon stopped directly in front of Resa, his red, angry face just inches from hers. He reeked of alcohol and tobacco.

"No, Damon. I did not kick Jasper out. I just asked him to sit down and behave himself."

Damon stared at her, breathing heavily. Then he looked pointedly at the booth where Jenny and Lashaundra sat, watching him with wide eyes.

"Well, he ain't coming back in here no more, and neither is anyone else in this town that's got any sense. Not while you keep en-
couraging *that*."

He pointed at Lashaundra and Jenny.

"You talking about the cocoa, Damon?" Resa asked with a smile
set firmly on her face. "Because lots of folks hereabouts like Harlan's cocoa just fine."

"I'm talking about race mixing, and you know it, you stupid
bitch!"

"That's enough, Damon." Harlan stood at the back of the
restaurant, slowly removing his white apron. "We don't need no
trouble in here."

"I ain't the one with trouble," Damon shouted. "You are!"

"Go on home now," Harlan said, his voice soft but steely.
"You've had too much to drink. Go home before I call the sheriff
to come get you."

Damon's nostrils flared as he ran a hand through his thinning
hair. After a long, tense standoff, he turned and stalked out the
door, slamming it hard behind him.

Resa locked the door behind him.

"I better call Shirley and warn her," she said. "He's in a bad way."

"Should we call the police?" I asked.

Harlan sighed and began clearing dishes from a table.

"Won't do no good," he said. "He'll go home and sleep it off.
Just steer clear of him."

I nodded.

"Thanks, Harlan."

He gave me half a smile and returned to the kitchen.

"Come on, girls," I said. "Help me clear this place up and we
can go home."

I dropped Lashaundra off at the apartment Michael and Angel
had rented. Michael waved from the doorway as we drove away.

"Why is Mr. Rigby so mean?" Jenny asked.

"I don't know, honey. Some people are just born that way, I
guess."

"Should we tell Daddy about it?"

I thought for a minute before answering.

"I guess we should," I said. "He'll probably find out from Mr. Johnson tomorrow anyway."

Brannon turned off the television as we walked into the house.

"There are my favorite girls," he said. "How was school today?"

"Okay," Jenny said.

"Just okay?"

"School was okay," Jenny said. "But after school wasn't."

"What happened?" Brannon looked from Jenny to me as Jenny began telling him about the scenes with Jasper and then Damon Rigby. Brannon's face grew darker by the minute. He rose and began pacing the living room.

When Jenny finished talking, Brannon stood quietly, his fists clenching and unclenching.

"Don't worry, Jenny," he said softly. "I'll take care of it."

"What are you going to do?" she asked.

"I'm going to let Damon Rigby and his thug of a son know that they can't talk to you or about you like that."

"Harlan and Resa said we should just stay out of Damon's way," I said, touching his arm.

He pulled his arm away and spun to face me.

"No one talks to my little girl like that," he yelled, his face red.

He stormed out of the house and a minute later we heard the truck's motor roar to life.

"Where's he going?" Jenny asked, her voice trembling.

"Probably just to cool off," I said, hoping she would believe me.

"What if Mr. Rigby shoots him?"

"I'm sure that's not going to happen."

But my stomach was churning, just like hers probably was.

"Come on," I said, holding my hand out to her. "Let's get ready for bed. Your dad is probably just driving around for a while to cool off."

Long after Jenny had gone to bed I sat in the living room, waiting for Brannon to come home. Finally, just after two in the morning, I heard his truck in the driveway.

He came in quietly, locking the door behind him.

"Hey," he whispered. "Why are you still up? You should be in bed. You're sleeping for two now, remember?"

"I was worried," I said. "Where have you been?"

"I drove around," he said. "I needed to clear my head."

"I was afraid you were going to Damon Rigby's," I said. "I was so afraid he might hurt you or . . . or something."

"I'm fine." He wrapped his arms around me and held me against his chest. "Don't worry about me, babe. I'm just fine."

❧ 25 ❧

Jenny

We were conjugating verbs in Spanish the next morning when the principal's voice came over the speaker system.

"Attention, students. I have some very sad news to tell you. One of our students lost his father last night. Damon Rigby, Jasper's dad, was killed in a car accident. I hope you will all keep Jasper and his family in your prayers. The school counselor is available for anyone who wants to talk with her about it."

I stared at Lashaundra and she stared back at me. Neither of us liked Mr. Rigby, but it was still sad to know he was dead. At least I thought so. Then, as I watched in disbelief, a small smile spread across Lashaundra's face. She composed herself quickly and we listened as Señora Mitchell droned on for a while about what a tragedy it was and how we should all be extra nice to Jasper when we saw him.

When the bell rang at the end of class, I walked with Lashaundra to our lockers.

"I know he was mean, but it's kind of sad that he died," I said.

"He deserved it," she said softly but firmly. "I'm glad he's dead."

She took my hand and squeezed it. "I mean, I'm a little sorry in a way, I guess. He was a person and all. But at least now we don't have to be scared of him anymore."

I thought about Mr. Rigby's wife. I wondered if she would be sad he was dead, since he was so mean to her.

"Are you going to pray for Jasper?" I asked. I knew Lashaundra prayed a lot.

She shrugged her shoulders. "I guess so," she said. "I know I'm supposed to."

We rummaged through our lockers for folders and homework.

"I'll see you at lunch," she said.

The cafeteria was just as noisy as always. Nobody seemed particularly sad about Jasper's dad.

"Hi, Jenny." Sarah Lindner stood by the table where I sat. "Can I sit with you and Lashaundra?"

"Sure."

She put down her tray and sat.

"Pretty weird about Mr. Rigby, huh?" She took a bite of her chicken salad sandwich.

"Yeah," I said. "Pretty weird."

"Hey, guys." Lashaundra sat down opposite Sarah.

"Hi," I said.

"He was pretty mean," Sarah continued. "But it's still weird that he's dead."

"Mr. Rigby," I said to Lashaundra.

"He *was* mean," Lashaundra said, nodding. "He was a bully and a racist. And Jasper is just like him."

"Jasper can be nice sometimes, though," Sarah said. "One time he gave me lunch money when I forgot mine. And he helped Megan with her math all last year."

We ate in silence for a minute. Then Sarah said, "I think Jasper was afraid of his dad, just like everyone else was. My mom says Mr. Rigby was mean his whole life, even when he was a kid. And sometimes when we were in grade school, Jasper used to come to school with bruises on his legs. One time he even had a black eye."

"You think his dad hit him?" I asked.

"Yeah," she said, nodding. "He hit Jasper a lot. He hit Mrs. Rigby, too. Everyone knew it."

"Why didn't anyone stop him?" I asked.

She shrugged. "It's his family," she said. "My mom always said it was none of our business."

That sounded familiar to me. Daddy used to say that what happened in our family was nobody else's business.

"Do you think Jasper is sad that his dad is dead?" I asked.

Sarah nodded. "Yeah," she said. "Mr. Rigby was plenty mean, but Jasper was always trying to make him proud, you know? I guess he thought if he was just like his dad, maybe his dad would like him more or something."

"That's pretty sad." Lashaundra's voice was softer, less hard than it had been before.

"Yeah," I agreed. My dad got angry sometimes. I'd seen him get really mad. One time he even slapped Jackie when he thought I was asleep. He slapped her so hard she fell down. But he would never hit me. And no matter how mad or upset he was, I always knew Daddy loved me.

After school, Emma was waiting for me in the car. It was her day off.

"Mr. Rigby died," I said as soon as I got in.

"What?" She turned to stare at me. "How? What happened?"

"He got in a car crash last night and died. Some kids are saying he was drunk driving."

"He had definitely been drinking," she said. "We probably shouldn't have let him leave the restaurant. We should have called the police or something."

We drove a ways in silence, then she sighed.

"His poor wife," she said. "I wonder what she'll do now."

"Maybe she'll be happy he's dead," I said. "At least he can't hit her and Jasper anymore."

She shook her head.

"It's more complicated than that," she said. "Even if he wasn't good to her, he was her husband. She stayed with him all those years. She must have loved him at least a little."

"Sarah said Jasper loved him. She said the reason he was a bully was because he was trying to be like his dad, so his dad would be proud of him."

"I wonder what they'll do now," Emma said.

"A girl in my math class said Mrs. Rigby has a sister who lives in Bardstown, and maybe they'll move in with her now."

Emma shook her head and sighed again.

"I hope they'll be okay."

"Me too."

When we got home, Emma walked into the kitchen and began rummaging through the pantry.

"What are you doing?" I asked. It was too early to start cooking dinner.

"I'm looking for a cake mix or something I can make to take to the Rigbys."

"You don't even hardly know them."

"I know," she said. "But when somebody dies, that's what you do. You take the family food. It's a tradition."

I watched as she pulled out a bag of flour, some sugar, and bananas.

"Banana bread," she said, smiling at me. "That will be okay."

I helped her make two loaves of bread. When they were in the oven, she said, "Go ahead and get your homework started."

Then she called Resa to get Mrs. Rigby's address.

Just before dinner, we got into the car and drove to another part of town where the houses were fancier than ours and the yards bigger. We pulled into a driveway behind several other cars, got out, and walked up to the porch. Before we could ring the bell, the door opened and Mrs. Rigby reached out to hug Emma.

"We are so sorry for your loss," Emma said, handing her the loaves of banana bread.

"Thank you, Emma. You're such a sweetheart. Come on in."

We followed her into the living room, where more than a dozen people stood around talking softly. Resa saw us and came over to hug Emma.

"It's real good of you to come," she said. "I know you don't really know Shirley, and you didn't much like Damon. But she needs all the help she can get right now."

I looked around the crowded room, but I didn't see Jasper.

"Are you looking for Jasper, hon?" Mrs. Rigby touched my shoulder. "He's out back. I'm sure he'd love to see you."

I swallowed hard. I didn't want to see Jasper, actually. But Mrs. Rigby smiled at me like she was grateful and pointed down the hallway toward the back door.

"Go on," she said. "Don't be shy. I'm sure he'll be glad to see a friend."

Emma nodded at me and Resa smiled. So I took a deep breath and walked down the hallway to the door. When I opened it, I saw him sitting on a tire swing that hung from a huge oak tree. His shoulders slumped and his head was lowered, so his hair hung down over his eyes. He didn't look up as I approached.

"Hey," I said softly.

He raised his head to glare at me.

"What do you want?"

"I just . . . I don't know, I guess I just wanted to say I'm sorry about your dad."

He said nothing. He only lowered his head again.

"My mom died," I said. "It was a long time ago, when I was little."

He raised his head and looked at me.

"You have a mom," he said.

"Emma is my stepmom. My real mom died when I was three. I know it's hard. And I'm sorry."

I started to walk back to the house.

"Hey," he called.

I turned and was surprised to see his face soften.

"What did you do? After she died, I mean."

I thought for a minute.

"I cried a lot. And then I got really mad. I was so mad at her for going away."

He nodded.

"It gets easier after a while."

He wiped a hand across his eyes, climbed out of the swing, and sat down on the grass.

"Everyone hated my dad," he said.

I sat down and waited.

"Everyone thought he was such a jerk. But he wasn't always that way, you know?"

I nodded.

"Like sometimes when I was little, he took me fishing on his boat. And he came to all my baseball games. And . . . sometimes he was really nice."

He looked up at me and stared for a minute, like he was seeing me for the first time.

"What was your mom like?" he asked.

"I don't know, really. I was little when she died. I remember she had blond hair. And she used to sing to me. That's all, I guess."

"That sucks."

I nodded again.

"At least you'll always remember your dad," I said. "That's something."

"I guess." He sighed heavily.

"I better go." I rose, wiping grass from my jeans.

"Hey," he said. "What's your name, anyway?"

"I'm Jenny," I said. "Jenny Bohner."

"I'm Jasper," he said.

"I know."

"You're the one with the nigger friend."

"She's not a nigger!" My voice rose. "Her name is Lashaundra, and she's the nicest person I know."

I turned and walked quickly back into the house. This time he didn't stop me.

"Can we go now?" I asked.

Emma looked down at me and smiled.

"Sure," she said. "Let's go make dinner."

26

Emma

"Are we doing okay?" Brannon sat at the table, writing checks for our bills. His forehead furrowed deep.

"It's tight," he said, not looking up at me. "It's always tight."

He sighed.

"I could ask Harlan for more hours."

"No," he said, smiling at me, his brow relaxing a bit. "You work too many hours as it is. We just need to cut back on our spending a little."

"What's that one?" I asked, pointing at the bill he held in his hand.

"It's for the storage unit."

"How much is it?"

"Not much." He put down his pen and stretched, yawning.

"How much is not much?"

He sighed again.

"It's sixty bucks a month," he said finally.

My eyes widened. "That's a lot of money."

He shrugged.

"Seriously, Brannon, that's almost an entire week's worth of groceries every month, every single month."

He raised an eyebrow at me but said nothing.

"Okay," I said. "Now that we have a house, why don't we go get the stuff from the unit? We've got the space for it."

He shook his head. "It's a four-hour drive each way, babe. I don't want to waste an entire day on it."

"I'll go with you."

He didn't say anything.

"Seriously, honey, we can go this weekend. It'll be fun . . . a mini–road trip."

He shook his head again.

"Brannon." I heard my voice rise, even as I tried to stay calm. "Honey, that's sixty dollars a month out of the budget. That's worth a day of driving, isn't it?"

"We'll manage."

I sat down across from him at the table.

"Look," I said, keeping my voice flat. "Jenny has grown an inch just since October. Her winter clothes are getting too small, and you know the things she wore last summer aren't going to fit her come spring. She needs some new clothes, honey. And pretty soon I'm going to be needing some fat-lady clothes."

He laughed and took my hands. "You are *not* going to be a fat lady. You're going to be a pregnant lady."

"Well, this pregnant lady is going to need some maternity clothes. And I'm thinking I'm going to need them sooner than I'd like. I'm already gaining weight. And sixty dollars a month, honey, that will go a long way toward our bills."

He looked at me in silence and then sighed heavily.

"Okay, fine," he said. "I'll go on Saturday. Maybe I'll get the truck washed before I go. Don't want to put all of that stuff in it as dirty as it is."

"Jenny and I will come with you. We'll make a day of it. Maybe we can have lunch in Louisville . . . or dinner on the way home."

"Jenny has that thing at the library on Saturday," he said. "I'll go, and you can stay here and hold down the fort."

"Okay, that's a deal."

* * *

Brannon left early on Saturday morning, right after breakfast. Not long after he left, Jenny called to me from the living room.

"Emma, there's a dog on our front porch."

I looked out the window and saw a beagle scratching at the door, whimpering pitifully.

"I think he belongs next door," I said. "I've seen him in the yard."

I opened the door and the beagle ran into the house, sniffing me and then Jenny and then the furniture, his tail wagging frantically.

"Hey, buddy," I crooned, reaching out my hand for him to sniff. "What are you doing here?"

The dog licked my hand and then my face as I knelt to scratch his ears.

"Should we take him home?" Jenny sat down on the floor and began stroking the dog's head as he licked her face.

"That's probably a good idea."

I scooped up the dog in my arms, and we walked to the house next door and knocked on the door.

A face appeared in the window—a very old, wrinkled face with very blue eyes.

The door opened and a tiny woman stood before us, smiling, those blue eyes boring straight into me.

"Beauregard!" she cried, reaching for the beagle. "How did you get out of the yard again?"

The beagle wriggled into her arms and she looked up to smile at me.

"He's a bad one for digging, he is," she said. "Seems like I'm always chasing him all over the neighborhood."

"He was scratching on our door," Jenny said. "We live there."

She pointed to our house.

"He was great friends with the little boy who lived there before you. Thank you for bringing him home."

"I'm Emma," I said. "And this is Jenny."

"It's a pleasure to meet the both of you." The woman shook my hand and then Jenny's.

"I'm Lilah," she said. "Lilah Figg. Won't you come in?"

She held the door open.

Jenny looked up at me and I smiled and nodded.

"We'd love to," I said.

We followed Mrs. Figg into the house, and Jenny suddenly stopped short just in front of me so that I walked right into her. She let out a startled yelp.

"Don't mind the animals." Mrs. Figg smiled, waving her hand toward the mantle.

Several cats perched on climbing towers. Beauregard barked at another beagle, wagging his tail.

"That's Daisy." Mrs. Figg pointed to the second beagle. "And those are Felix and Tabby and McGuffy and Little Bit. Ain't she just the most beautiful cat you ever saw?"

One of the cats, I don't know which one, sauntered over to rub itself against Jenny's leg. But Jenny was staring toward the fireplace, where several more cats and two more dogs were posed, seemingly frozen.

"And those are my loves, the ones who've passed on," Mrs. Figg said, smiling fondly at the stuffed animals. "I can't bear to let them go. So . . . a friend embalms them for me. And here they are."

She walked to the hearth and put her hand on the head of a large stuffed hound. "This here is Amos," she said. "And that's Tipper." She pointed toward another dog, this one of undetermined breed, maybe a Labrador–golden retriever mix?

"And the kitties there are Jemimah, Clovis, Maeve, Picasso, Moses, and Piper."

"They're dead," Jenny said breathlessly.

"Yes, dear. I know that." Mrs. Figg moved one of the cats slightly, so that it faced more squarely into the room. "But they're still my babies."

"It's beautiful work," I said, staring closely at the hound. "I had an uncle who did taxidermy when I was a kid, but he mostly did wild animals . . . after people shot them. These are beautiful."

"Yes, Horace does good work. And he don't charge me a thing for it, either. I just make him a pie or some scones or muffins. He wants me to marry him, you see. He's been after me to marry him for almost twenty years now, ever since my husband died."

She shook her head.

"He's persistent, Horace is. I'll say that for him. Now, can I make you a cup of tea, dear? I've got some nice scones, fresh out of the oven."

We walked into the kitchen and Jenny yelped again.

"That there's Petunia," Mrs. Figg said, smiling at the stuffed pig that sat by the back door, its snout pointed toward us. "She was such a good little pig. Vietnamese potbelly, she was. Sweet as sugar and smart as a whip. Smarter than most dogs, I'd bet. And oh my, she just loved to swing."

"What?" Jenny stared at her with wide eyes.

"She loved to swing," the old lady repeated. "We put a baby swing in the backyard, and Petunia loved to be in it and swing. Oh, she wasn't afraid at all, Miss Petunia. She loved that swing."

We sat down at the table and Mrs. Figg put a kettle on the stove.

"Do you have any children?" I asked, already certain of the answer.

"Oh no," she said. "The Good Lord didn't see fit to bless us with babies. I don't know why. But we always had the animals. Jacob, that's my late husband, well, he was as crazy about them as I am. He's the one who put up the swing, you know."

She set a plate of cranberry scones on the table. They smelled heavenly.

"I've been meaning to come by and introduce myself," she said. "And welcome you to the neighborhood. But I was feeling poorly for a while. Got the diabetes, you know."

She held her leg up as some kind of proof. So I nodded.

"Sometimes it makes me poorly. But I'm better today, especially now that ya'll are here." She smiled at me and at Jenny, and slathered butter onto a scone.

We drank tea and ate scones while the beagles begged for bites and Mrs. Figg chattered away, telling us about the family who lived across the street—they weren't friendly at all, she said. And they played their music too loud.

"How long have you lived here?" I asked when she paused to sip her tea.

"Oh, I been here ever since I married Jacob," she said. "That was in 1951. We bought the house right after the wedding. He'd been saving, you know. Smart man, my Jacob was. We thought we'd fill it up with children, of course. But that didn't happen. . . . Still, it's a good house."

She beamed at the kitchen, with its antiquated appliances and faded, peeling wallpaper.

"It's a good house," she repeated.

After we'd eaten our scones, I stood.

"We should probably be going," I said. "Jenny has a craft party at the library today."

"Oh, a craft party, that's nice." Mrs. Figg nodded enthusiastically. "And the library is nice, too. I just love those big stained-glass windows."

We walked back into the living room, where Jenny eyed the animals on the hearth with suspicion.

"Before you go, let me show you one more thing!"

Mrs. Figg walked into the dining room, motioning for us to follow.

"This here is my pride and joy," she said, touching an old, dark, upright piano.

"Do you play?" I asked.

"Oh no, dear." She smiled at me. "I don't have to. This piano plays itself."

She opened a wooden cabinet beside the piano and pulled out a roll of paper. Then she opened the front of the piano and put the roll inside. She flipped a switch, and the piano began playing on its own. Jenny stared at it, her eyes wide, as Mrs. Figg sang along to the tune, a song about sitting in the shade of an old apple tree.

When the song had finished, she beamed at us.

"That's so cool!" Jenny said.

"It is, isn't it?" I agreed.

Smiling, Mrs. Figg carefully removed the roll from the piano and placed it gently back into the case.

"Thank you so much," I said, shaking her hand again. "The scones were wonderful."

"Here," she said, shuffling back into the kitchen. "Let me get you some to take home with you. Lord knows I can't eat them all."

She returned with several scones wrapped in a cloth napkin.

"You come back any time, you hear? You won't bother me at all. I love company."

She shook my hand yet again and put a gnarled palm on Jenny's hair.

"You're a beauty," she sighed. "Like a young Elizabeth Taylor, you are."

She watched from the porch as we walked back to our house.

"What a lovely lady," I said.

"She's kind of weird," Jenny said. "I mean, all those dead animals would give me the creeps."

I laughed. "Those are her babies, I guess. I think she's probably just really lonely."

"And a little bit crazy."

Jenny ran to her room to gather her things for the library and I looked out the window at the house next door, where Mrs. Figg still stood on the porch smiling.

~~ 27 ~~

Jenny

"That's really pretty," Lashaundra said, watching me dab paint onto a candle.

We were making Valentine's Day presents for our moms. I was kind of proud of mine. The lines were clean and straight. I hoped Emma would like it.

"Yours is good, too," I said.

Lashaundra's candle was sort of a mess.

She shook her head. "No, mine's not near as pretty as yours."

I smiled at her. "I think your mom will love it."

She smiled back. It felt so good to have a friend.

"All right, ladies. It's time to start putting things away."

Mrs. Hensley walked from table to table, inspecting our work.

"Why, that's beautiful, Jenny," she said. "Just beautiful."

She turned to look at Lashaundra's. "Yours is nice, too, Lashaundra."

We closed the paint cups and started washing the paintbrushes.

"Just leave your candles on the shelf here to dry. Next week we'll make something for your fathers," Mrs. Hensley said. "And then we'll make wrapping paper for your gifts, just in time for Valentine's Day!"

Mrs. Johnson was waiting outside the library for us.

"Did you have fun?" she asked.

"Yes, ma'am," I said.

"What did you make?"

"It's a surprise," Lashaundra said.

"I want a surprise!" Malcolm yelled.

"It's not a surprise for you," Lashaundra said. "It's for Mama."

He stuck his tongue out at her.

"Well, I can't wait to see it." Mrs. Johnson smiled at us. "Jenny, are you having supper with us tonight?"

"No, thank you. I can't," I said. "I'm helping Emma make vegetable soup."

Mrs. Johnson dropped me off in front of our house, and I ran inside to find Emma stretched out on the couch, fast asleep and snoring. She woke up when she heard me and smiled, sitting up and rubbing her eyes.

"Are you okay?" I asked. I'd never seen Emma asleep during the day before.

"I'm just tired," she said. "Being pregnant makes you tired, I guess."

We chopped carrots and onions and potatoes for the soup.

"Should we add some sage?" I asked.

Emma looked up at me like she was surprised.

"I'm sorry," I stammered.

"It's okay," she said, smiling and reaching for the spice drawer. "I never put sage in my soup before. Where did you learn to cook?"

I shook my head, my cheeks reddening.

"Jenny, honey, it's okay if someone else taught you to make soup. Was it Jackie?"

I shook my head. "Jackie didn't like to cook."

"Oh." Her voice was soft.

"Before Jackie lived with us, and before Trish, there was Cara."

I didn't look up at her. I didn't want to see her face. I didn't want to tell her about Cara or Jackie or Trish or Ami. I wished I'd never volunteered to help with the soup.

"And Cara taught you to make soup?"

I nodded.

"Well," she said, "I'll be glad to use her recipe if you liked it."

I looked up at her then and she smiled at me.

"It's okay," she repeated, her voice gentle. "I know your dad had friends before me. That's his past. It doesn't matter now."

She put an arm around my shoulder and kissed my cheek.

"He didn't marry any of them," she said. "He married me."

I smiled at her in relief.

"Cara put thyme in the soup, too."

"Well, then, get me some thyme."

We'd just put the soup on the stove when we heard Daddy at the front door.

"How's my favorite girl?" he asked, kissing me on the head.

"I'm good," I said.

"And how's my other favorite girl?" He kissed Emma on the mouth.

"I'm okay," she said, yawning. "Tired, but okay. Did you get all your stuff?"

"It's in the truck."

"Do you need help bringing it in?" Emma wiped her hands on a dish towel.

"Jenny can help me."

"I can help, too," Emma said, laughing.

"No heavy lifting for you, pregnant lady."

Daddy kissed her again and nodded at me. "Come on, Jenny."

I put on my parka and followed him out to the driveway, and we began carrying boxes and bags inside. Pretty soon the living room looked like a small warehouse.

"Where are we going to put all this stuff?" I asked.

"Some of it in the basement and the rest in the attic."

Daddy walked back outside and returned carrying a big wooden rocking chair. Pale pink-and-yellow cushions covered the seat and back. He put the chair in the corner, right next to the fireplace. It looked like it belonged there, like it had been there forever.

"Hey, that's beautiful." Emma touched the wood with one finger. "But it needs a good dusting."

She disappeared into the kitchen and returned with furniture polish and a rag. Before long, the oak wood of the rocker gleamed.

"That was Hailey's," Daddy said softly, looking at the rocker with a small smile. "When she was pregnant with Jenny, she used to rock in it all the time, just singing to her belly. And then when Jenny was born, she rocked Jenny in it."

"That was my mom's?"

I sat down in the chair, running my hand over the smooth wooden arm.

"It's beautiful," Emma repeated. "And you kept it all these years."

"I couldn't get rid of it." Daddy put his arm around her shoulder. "Most of the stuff I had before we started moving around, I sold. But this . . . this I had to keep."

Emma kissed his cheek and stroked his face. He smiled at her with tears in his eyes.

"And now you can rock our baby in it," he said.

She nodded and I could see tears sparkling in her eyes, too.

"Is this everything?" she asked after a minute, surveying the stacks of boxes strewn around the room.

"Yep, everything we own in the world is right here. It's not too much," Daddy said, shaking his head. "But it's enough."

I got out of the chair, walked up to a box on top of a stack of boxes, and began tearing away at the masking tape holding it closed.

"Not now, Jenny," Daddy said, his hand on my shoulder. "The unpacking can wait till tomorrow. I'm going to have to go through all of these boxes and figure out what goes where. And Lord knows there will be a lot of things to pitch. But right now, I think I'm going to take a shower. I'm beat."

"I'll bet you are," Emma said, kissing his cheek. "Soup's on, so whenever you're ready, we'll eat."

"Thanks, babe."

Daddy smiled at her and disappeared into the bathroom. Pretty soon we heard the water running in the shower.

"Come on," Emma said. "Help me set the table."

We ate vegetable soup with sourdough bread Emma bought at the bakery.

"This is really good, babe," Daddy said, ladling a second helping of soup into his bowl.

"Jenny helped me with the spices," she said, winking at me. "It'll be even better this summer, when we have vegetables fresh from our garden."

He grinned at her. "I guess then we'll be Old MacDonald and his wife."

"And their daughter," I said.

"The whole MacDonald clan then." He nodded, laughing.

He rose suddenly and walked into the living room, returning with a photograph in his hand.

"I thought you might get a kick out of this."

He handed the picture to Emma. She looked at it for a minute, and then snorted.

"Oh my God!"

She held the picture out to me. It was Daddy, but he was much younger in the picture. His long hair was dyed blondish with black ends, and it was slicked back in the front. In the back it was short and spiky.

"That's funnier than a pig on a swing." Emma winked at me and I started laughing, too.

Daddy stared at us, confused.

"What did you say?"

"I said, 'That's funnier than a pig on a swing.' "

Emma threw her head back and laughed out loud, and that made me laugh even harder.

"Okay," Daddy said, "what are you two on?"

That just made both of us laugh even harder. I laughed so hard I thought I might pee my pants.

"Hey!" Daddy rose, his face dark, his voice almost angry.

I stopped laughing.

"Just exactly what is so funny?"

Emma winked at me again and stood, taking Daddy's hand in hers.

"So this morning, we met our neighbor," she said quietly. "The old lady next door. She's kind of wonderful and pretty much . . . well, I guess you'd say she's a little bit eccentric."

"She has a whole bunch of pets," I chimed in. "Dogs and cats and a pig even! Some of them are alive and a lot of them are dead and . . . stuffed."

"Stuffed?" Daddy looked more confused than ever.

"Taxidermy," Emma said, reaching for his hand. "Every pet she's ever owned is there. She has them stuffed and puts them all over the house."

Daddy sat back down in his chair, staring from Emma to me.

"She sounds crazy," he said finally.

"I know!" I yelled triumphantly.

"I think she's just really lonely," Emma said, sitting back down in her chair. "She never had any kids, so the animals are her babies. And . . . and when they die she has them stuffed and keeps them. Like I said, she's a little bit eccentric."

"She has a pig in the kitchen," I said. "A stuffed pig; it's dead. But when it was alive, her husband made a swing for it, a baby swing.

"Seriously," I said, because Daddy was staring at me now as if I was crazy, too. "He put up a swing. And the pig, her name was Petunia, she loved the swing. Honest, Daddy, that's what Mrs. Figg said. The pig loved being in the swing."

He shook his head, but he was smiling now.

"So," he said, looking from me to Emma, "so I'm as funny as that pig in a swing?"

"No," Emma said, "you're not that funny. But God, Brannon, look at your hair!"

She took the picture back from me and smiled at it.

"You were beautiful," she said softly. "Not as beautiful as you are now, but damn, honey, you were hot!"

28

Emma

Brannon was already sorting through boxes when I got up the next morning.

"You want some help with that? I've got time before my shift."

I was already dressed for work.

"No thanks," he said, not looking up from the folder that lay open in his lap. "I've got it covered."

"Angel says it's okay if Jenny comes to their house while I'm at work. I can drop her on my way, if you want."

"That would be great."

Still, he didn't look up.

"Brannon?"

"Yeah?" Finally, he raised his eyes.

"I love you."

"I love you, too." He smiled, set aside the folder, and rose to hug me.

"Sorry," he said. "I guess I'm just kind of distracted with all this." He nodded toward the boxes.

"It's okay."

"I'll have all of it put away by the time you get home tonight."

"Have you found any more pictures you want to share?" I smiled at him.

"After the whole pig-on-a-swing bit? I think I'll just keep my pictures to myself, thanks."

"Are you sure you can get all these boxes up into the attic?" I asked. "It might help to have an extra set of hands."

"I'll be fine." He kissed me. "You just go on to work and I'll get this stuff sorted out and put away."

I dropped Jenny off at the Johnsons' and went to work, still feeling a little bit groggy. I hadn't slept well the night before.

"Did you hear?" Resa asked as soon as I walked into the diner.

"Hear what?" I asked.

She followed me to the back room where I hung my coat on a hook.

"The sheriff's saying Damon's accident might not have been an accident at all."

"What?" My eyes widened. "Why does he think that?"

"Good Lord, Resa," Harlan's voice bellowed from the kitchen. "Don't you go starting no rumors now. Wiley said it's possible, but he still thinks it's more likely Damon had an accident. God knows he was drunk enough in here that night. And after he left here, he went to the tavern and drank some more."

"Well, but what about those tire marks?" Resa put her hands firmly on her hips.

"Could be a coincidence," Harlan said.

"What tire marks?" I asked.

"There were two sets of tire marks on the road. One of them was Damon's. But they don't know whose the others were."

"Could have been someone swerving to avoid Damon," Harlan said. "Or those other marks could have been there a long time before. No one knows for sure."

He waved a spatula at Resa over the stove. "What this town don't need is you spreading rumors and talking crazy. Poor Shirley's got enough on her hands without worrying over whether it was an accident or not. Just leave it alone, Resa."

She shook her head at me, her lips pursed together, and said in a low voice, "I know what I heard. Wiley ain't convinced it was an accident."

"But who would drive Damon off the road?" I asked, swallowing hard, forcing myself to breathe.

"Who knows?" Resa said. She tied an apron around her waist and patted her bleached-blond hair. "A lot of folks around here didn't like Damon, that's for sure. He was a mean old cuss. Just a couple weeks ago he fired three men from the car lot. Said they weren't making their sales quotas. More likely he was just in a foul mood."

She shook her head darkly. "A lot of people had it in for Damon."

"Will you please stop with the gossip and open the shop?" Harlan yelled from the kitchen. "I ain't paying you to run a gossip mill."

"You ain't paying me diddly squat," Resa shot back, winking at me.

The day seemed to drag on and on. Business was slow for a Sunday, and I had plenty of time to wonder about who might have run Damon Rigby off the road. Brannon had been gone a long time that night. And he was certainly furious at Damon. But still, I couldn't imagine Brannon ever hurting anyone. Sure, he got mad sometimes, but this was Brannon. I'd known some violent men in my life, and Brannon was nothing like any of them.

"Emma!" Harlan's voice broke through the noise in my head. "Order's up."

I took the plates from the counter and carried them to the booth by the front door.

"I asked for ketchup," a boy in the booth said.

"And I wanted onion rings, not fries," said another.

"I'm sorry. I'll take care of that right away."

"You okay?" Harlan asked when I returned to the kitchen for the onion rings.

I nodded. "I'm just tired," I said.

And it was true, I was tired. I was tired and anxious and worried. My stomach churned and my head ached.

"Don't you let Resa get you all upset," Harlan said. "She's got a big mouth and too much time on her hands. Everyone knows Damon was drunk as a skunk that night. He didn't need any help driving his car into that ravine."

"It's just so awful to even think about. That someone might do something like that."

"The world is full of awful, Emma. But there's more good than bad. That's what I think, anyway."

We had just locked the front door when someone knocked on it loudly.

"Who is that?" Harlan yelled from the kitchen.

"It's the sheriff," Resa yelled back.

She unlocked the door and a man in a uniform walked in.

"Hey, Wiley," Resa said. "You need some coffee to go?"

"Not tonight, Resa," the sheriff said. "I just wanted to ask Emma here a couple questions about last week, the night Damon was killed."

"Sure thing," Resa said. "You got any new leads?"

"Resa McCoy, you sound like you think you're on *Law and Order*. Let the man ask his questions and be done with it." Harlan stood in the middle of the restaurant, a dish towel over his shoulder.

"It won't take but a minute," Wiley said.

He looked at me and raised his eyebrows.

"You okay to answer some questions, Emma?"

I nodded. I had served Wiley and his wife several times at the diner.

"Were you here last Wednesday night?"

I nodded again.

"Can you tell me anything about that night?" He opened a notebook and stood with his pen poised.

"Well," I stammered. "Damon's son was in earlier, and he was making kind of a commotion."

"He was teasing some girls who were here, right?"

I nodded. "My stepdaughter, Jenny, and her friend Lashaundra. I guess he and Lashaundra had a run-in at school, and he was being pretty rude to her."

"And then what happened?"

"Resa told him to behave himself or she was going to call his mother."

Wiley grinned at Resa and winked. "I've heard that threat before."

Resa smiled back. "Honey, everyone who's ever been in here has heard that threat."

The sheriff nodded and turned back to me. "And then . . . ?"

"Then Jasper and his friends left."

"What happened later?"

I looked from Harlan to Resa. I knew they had already answered the same questions. I wondered if either of them had mentioned Damon's not-so-veiled threat.

"Damon came in just before closing," I said. "He was pretty mad and he yelled at Resa, said she'd kicked Jasper out of the restaurant. Resa told him what had happened, and then he made a comment about race mixing, because of Jenny and Lashaundra. And Harlan told him to leave."

The sheriff nodded and made some more notes.

"Did you smell alcohol on Damon when he was here?" He looked up at me.

"Yes," I said. "He smelled like bourbon and cigarettes."

"Well, bourbon was Damon's poison of choice, that's for sure." He smiled at me. "Thank you, Emma. I'm just covering all the bases."

"What about them tire marks?" Resa said.

"Probably a coincidence," Wiley said. "No evidence at the scene of anything but an accident."

"There," Harlan said, flicking Resa with the towel. "I told you it was an accident. Now maybe you can stop with all the gossip and concentrate on your job."

"So that's it?" Resa asked. She sounded a bit disappointed. "It was just an accident?"

"That's what it looks like," Wiley said. "Sorry to disappoint you, Resa." He laughed.

"I am not at all disappointed, Wiley Ruben!" Resa sounded indignant now. "Lord knows I didn't *want* it to be murder. No one would want that."

"You're right," Harlan said flatly. "No one at all would want that."

I picked up Jenny from the Johnsons' on my way home, grateful that I had put a chicken in the Crock-Pot before I'd left for work. I was bone-tired and the thought of cooking was almost too much to bear.

"Hey, Emma." Angel smiled at me in the doorway. "You look half-dead."

"That's about how I feel." I sank gratefully onto the couch in the living room.

"The girls are upstairs," she said. "Do you want a cup of tea or a soda?"

"No, thanks, Angel. I'm okay."

"Well, I wanted to tell you something before the girls come down." She sat down beside me on the couch.

"The sheriff was here earlier, asking about the night Damon Rigby died."

I stared at her.

"It's okay," she said. "He just wanted to know about what happened with the girls at the restaurant. And then he asked if Lashaundra had told us about what happened."

"He came to the diner tonight, too," I said.

"I guess he has to look at everything," she said. "But then he asked Michael where he was that night."

My stomach lurched. "Why?" I asked, my voice choking in my throat.

"Because we're black," she said flatly. "It's always the black man, you know. No matter what happens, they always come for the black man."

"But he didn't have any reason to think that Michael would . . . hurt Damon Rigby."

"No, except that Michael's black."

I could tell she was working hard to keep her voice steady and calm.

"Anyway, thank God, Michael was working that night. He'd pulled an extra shift at the warehouse, and about a hundred people can vouch for the fact that he was at work all night."

I nodded and reached for her hand.

"I'm so sorry, Angel," I said.

"You've got nothing to apologize for," she said. "It's the way of the world, I guess. But the girls were here when the sheriff came. So Jenny might have some questions. I just wanted to give you a heads-up."

"Thanks, Angel. And thanks for keeping Jenny today. Brannon was up to his eyeballs in stuff when I left, and I think he really was glad Jenny wasn't home all day."

Angel smiled. "Jenny said he'd gone to get all of their stuff out of storage. That's good. That means he finally feels at home."

I nodded and smiled back at her.

"Yep," I said. "We are finally at home."

Jenny started talking as soon as we got into the car.

"The sheriff came to ask Mr. Johnson a bunch of questions," she said.

"I know," I said. "He came to the diner, too. He has to cover all the bases, I guess."

"But I thought Mr. Rigby was driving drunk and had an accident."

"That's exactly what happened," I said. "But the sheriff has to fill out all the paperwork, and that means talking to everyone who might have any information."

"But Mr. Johnson didn't have any information."

"I know, honey. It's just procedure."

"Because Mr. Johnson is black?"

I sighed and shook my head. "There's a lot of prejudice in the world, Jenny. I know that. But I think the sheriff was just asking questions because of the way Mr. Rigby was to you and Lashaundra that night in the diner. That's all."

I pulled into the driveway and parked.

"It's okay," I said. "The sheriff said Mr. Rigby's crash was an accident. It's over and done with now."

Please, God, let that be true.

I unlocked the front door and stopped to stare. The room was cleared of boxes and bags. The rocker sat by the hearth, where a fire burned brightly. And above the mantel hung a huge painting of white and yellow daisies against a brilliant blue sky.

"Welcome home," Brannon said, emerging from the kitchen with a cup of tea in his hand. "It looks good, doesn't it?"

"I can't believe you got everything put away," I said, sinking into the rocker and taking the tea from him. "Where did you put it all?"

"Most of it's up in the attic," he said.

"Where did that come from?" Jenny pointed at the painting of daisies.

"I've had that a long time," he said. "But there wasn't any place for it in the trailer. Do you like it?"

"It's pretty," she said.

"Your mother painted it."

Jenny stood with her mouth open, staring at the picture.

"My mother painted?" she finally asked. "How come I didn't know that?"

"I guess it never came up."

"Well, it's beautiful." I rose and touched the frame lightly. "She was very talented."

"Yeah," he said. "She did some nice stuff. That one was my favorite."

"Are there any more?" Jenny asked.

"In your bedroom."

Jenny ran down the hall and shrieked.

"Oh my God! It's so pretty!"

Brannon and I followed her into the room, where another big painting dominated the wall above Jenny's futon. A single tree covered in white blossoms stood in a field of tiny yellow flowers. It really was beautiful.

"There was a field behind the apartment building where we lived," Brannon said, his arm around Jenny's shoulder. "Your mom liked to carry her canvas and paints out there and do her thing. That's spring. She did one for each season."

"Where are the others?" Jenny turned to look at him, her eyes sparkling.

"I'm sorry, honey," he said. "I sold the others. After your mom died, we really needed the money. I hated to do it, but I had to."

"Oh," Jenny said, her voice soft.

"But I saved this one for you."

"And it's beautiful," I said. "Maybe we can buy a bedspread and curtains to match the colors. Would you like that?"

Jenny nodded. "I wish we still had the others," she whispered. Her eyes were bright with tears.

"I know, honey. But how wonderful that you have this one, and the one in the living room. You must be really proud to know that your mom painted those," I said.

She nodded again.

"Thank you, Daddy," she said in a small voice, wrapping her arms around him. "I love them both."

"You're welcome, honey. I love you."

"That chicken smells good," I said. "Who's ready to eat?"

29

Jenny

I stared at the painting above my bed for a long time that night. My mom was an artist, a painter, and I never even knew it.

I thought about the candle I'd painted for Emma. Maybe I had inherited some of my mother's talent. What would that be like?

There was so much I didn't know about my mother. Daddy didn't like to talk about her. It made him sad, so I didn't ask him too many questions. But now I knew she was an artist. And I couldn't stop wondering what else there was to know about her. Maybe now that Daddy had Emma in his life and was happy, he would tell me more about my mom.

People always said I looked like Daddy, and I guess I did. My hair was dark like his and our noses looked pretty much the same. But his eyes were dark, dark brown, and mine were blue. He used to tell me I got my eyes from my mom.

I stood up for probably the twentieth time since going to bed just to touch the painting, feeling the texture of the brushstrokes. My mother made those strokes. It felt funny to touch something she had touched . . . funny, but nice in a weird kind of way.

My mother had painted in the field behind the apartment where she lived with my dad. I lay back down again and closed my eyes, trying hard to remember that apartment, where we had all lived together when I was so little. But the only thing I could remember was her voice, singing to me.

"You are my sunshine, my only sunshine . . ."

She was brushing my hair and singing. I think it was a sunny day. I think I remember feeling the sun on my face, but I could just be making that up. I know she was brushing my hair, though, and singing. I think she sang to me a lot. I hoped so, anyway.

I opened my eyes and looked around my room. I had a real bedroom for the first time I could remember, my very own room. And now I had a painting from my mother. But instead of feeling happy, I felt restless and kind of nervous, like I couldn't settle down.

Why hadn't Daddy ever told me that my mother was a painter? Why hadn't he ever told me anything about her?

As soon as the thought formed in my head, I felt guilty. Daddy was the one who had raised me and loved me. He cooked for me sometimes, not very well, but at least he tried. He made sure I did my schoolwork. He tucked me into bed every night and kissed me good night. He was Daddy. And if he couldn't bring himself to talk about my mother, maybe it was just because he loved her and missed her so much.

At least he'd kept the paintings.

I rose yet again and padded softly into the living room, where the picture of the daisies hung above the mantle. I turned on a lamp and stood, just staring at those daisies. My mother painted those daisies.

"Jenny?"

Emma's voice was low. I turned to see her rubbing the back of her hand across her eyes. She looked really tired.

"Are you okay?"

"I'm okay," I said. "I just wanted to see the picture again."

She smiled and sat down on the couch.

"Your mom was a pretty amazing artist," she said. "I mean, that is just beautiful. And the one in your room, God, that's gorgeous."

I sat down beside her and she put her arm around me.

"I'm sorry she died," she said quietly. "I'm sorry you didn't get the chance to know her."

"I didn't even know she painted," I said. "I don't know much about her at all."

"Well, maybe we can ask your dad to tell us about her."

"Really?" I stared at her. I guess I was surprised that she would want to know about my mother.

"Yes, really," she said. "She was your mom, and your dad loved her. And he's been so sad for so long. And now, well, now maybe he'll be ready to talk about her."

I leaned into her and she squeezed me tight.

"Thanks, Emma."

"Oh, Jenny," she said, and I heard a catch in her voice. "You don't have to thank me. I'm the one who should be thanking you. I mean, I haven't known you for very long, and you could have been really mad at your dad and at me when I moved in. But instead, you've been . . . well, you've been wonderful. I feel so lucky to be your stepmom. You are the best stepdaughter ever."

"I love you," I whispered.

"I love you, too," she whispered back. "I love you so much, and I love your dad, and we're all going to love this baby." She patted her stomach and kissed my head.

"We are probably the luckiest family in the world."

30

Emma

The next day, while Jenny was at school, I drove to the Walmart and bought some fabric to make curtains and a cover for her comforter. We didn't really have the money for it, but I wanted her room to be pretty. I really wanted her to feel at home in the house.

Standing in line waiting to pay for my things, I felt a tap on my shoulder. I turned to see Shirley Rigby in line behind me.

"Hello, Emma," she said, smiling. "I just wanted to say thank you again for coming by the house last week and bringing the banana bread. It was delicious. I think Jasper ate an entire loaf all on his own."

"You're welcome," I said. "How are you doing, Shirley?"

"I'm all right. Tired, mostly. And relieved that the funeral is over."

"Resa said it was a lovely service. I'm sorry we didn't come."

"That's okay." She paused and cleared her throat.

"I heard what Damon said to your daughter and her friend, and I want you to know that I'm so sorry."

"It's all right, Shirley. He'd had too much to drink and he was angry."

"He was always angry," she said softly. "I like to believe that wherever he is now, he's not angry anymore."

I nodded.

"I also wanted to tell you that your little girl was a real help to Jasper at the house that day."

"Jenny?" I asked, surprised.

"She told Jasper she had lost her mom when she was little. I think it helped him to know he's not the only person in the world to lose a parent."

"I'm glad she was helpful," I said.

"I know Jasper hasn't been very nice to Jenny, or to her friend."

I nodded. I wasn't sure what to say.

"Anyway, it was sweet of her to talk with him that day. You and your husband have done a wonderful job of raising her."

"Oh, I can't take any credit," I said, smiling. "Brannon raised her alone for most of her life."

"Well, he must be a very good father to have raised such a thoughtful young lady."

"He's a good dad," I agreed.

"Ma'am?" The cashier was waiting for me.

"Oh, sorry," I said. I pulled cash from my wallet and paid for my things.

"It was nice seeing you, Shirley," I said, taking my receipt.

"You too," she said.

I started to walk away.

"Emma?"

I turned back to her. She smiled at me.

"I know you're new in Campbellsville. So if there's anything you need, anything I can do to help get you settled in, you let me know. Okay?"

"Thanks, Shirley."

"Maybe we could get a cup of coffee sometime?"

She looked so anxious, like she almost expected me to say no.

"I'd like that." I wrote my phone number on a slip of paper and handed it to her.

"I'll talk to you soon," she said, smiling as she took the paper.

"I look forward to it."

I walked to my car, wondering how such a lovely woman could have ended up with a man like Damon Rigby.

I spent the morning stitching curtains, wishing I still had my old sewing machine. After lunch, I started on the coverlet. The fabric was yellow and white. It matched the daisies in the painting perfectly. I was just getting ready to hang the curtains when I heard a soft knock at the door. I opened it to find Mrs. Figg standing on the porch.

"Hello, dear," she said. "I'm sorry to bother you, but I wonder if you could help me with something?"

"Sure," I said. "What do you need?"

"Well, I've been trying to bathe the kitties today. They surely do need bathing. And I've got most of them done. But Little Bit, well, bathing her is a two-person job. She's tiny, but she's got a fierce will, you know."

"You're giving the cats baths?"

"Yes, dear. Every couple of months they get their baths. They roam around in the basement, you see. And there's an old coal bin down there, from way back in the day. And oh, don't they just love that old thing. They get that coal dust all over themselves. So, they have to take their baths."

I laughed, picturing tiny Mrs. Figg wrangling all those cats into the sink.

"Let me just get my jacket," I said, then followed her to her house.

From a corner in the living room a large orange cat stared balefully at us, his wet fur clinging to his skin. Another cat streaked by as we walked in, leaving a trail of water droplets behind.

"That's fine, McGuffy," Mrs. Figg crooned. "You run off some of that energy and you'll feel better in no time."

She hung our coats on a coat tree by the door and looked around, hands on her hips.

"Now where do you suppose Little Bit is?" she asked. "She's hiding somewhere here. Can't be in the basement, because I closed the door."

"Little Bit?" I called. "Here, kitty, kitty, kitty."

"Don't do no good to call her," Mrs. Figg said. "She's deaf as a doorknob. She's white, you see, with blue eyes. Those are always deaf."

"Then how do you find her?"

"We'll start in here." Mrs. Figg got down on her knees and looked under the sofa. I watched for a second, trying not to laugh, then got on my knees and began looking under tables. Little Bit was not in the living room, so we headed into the kitchen. She wasn't there, either.

Finally, I spotted her in the dining room, under the buffet.

"Here she is," I called, reaching for the small white cat.

"Oh no, dear," Mrs. Figg said. "You can't just pull her out. She'll scratch you to pieces. She knows it's bath time. She doesn't want to come out."

The old lady lay down on the floor in front of the buffet.

"Now here's what we'll do," she said. "You take that broom and shoo her toward me, and I'll catch her with this."

She held out a bath towel.

I nodded, not convinced the plan would work. Then I took the broom and stuck it under the hutch. The cat hissed.

"All right, Little Bit," Mrs. Figg said softly. "Just come to Mama. Come on, sweet girl."

Finally, the cat had enough of my prodding and made a run for it. With surprising speed Mrs. Figg lunged at her, covering her with the towel, then scooping the cat and towel into her arms. Inside the towel, the cat was clawing frantically and meowing.

"She's the loudest cat I ever had," Mrs. Figg said, smiling fondly at the moving bundle in her arms. "I reckon that's because she can't hear herself. Now then, come along. I've got the bath ready."

I followed her up the stairs and into a bathroom.

"Close the door," she said. "We don't want her getting out."

The tub was partly filled with water.

"Now," she said, "I'll put her in, and then the real fun begins. You stand there." She pointed and I moved to stand just behind her. "There's the shampoo. You hand it to me when I say so, okay?"

I nodded.

"Here," she said, shoving the wriggling bundle into my arms. "Hold her for a second so I can get ready."

I stared as the old lady pulled on long rubber gloves.

"This way she can't scratch me," she said, winking.

"Okay, here we go."

She dropped the cat into the water and it immediately began clawing at Mrs. Figg, trying to get out.

"There you go, darling," she said, scooping water into a cup and pouring it over the cat. The cat was screaming now. I'd never heard anything like it.

"Shampoo, please."

I handed her the shampoo and watched as she poured it onto the cat's white fur.

The cat yowled and hissed and jerked and twisted every which way, but Mrs. Figg never let go.

"Almost done now," she said, pouring more water onto the angry cat.

"Now, dear, if you could just pick her up with that towel, we'll be done."

I stared at her in disbelief. There was no way I was going to try touching that cat. It was screaming like a mental patient.

"Don't be afraid," Mrs. Figg said. "I'll let go and she'll hop out and you just drop the towel on top of her and hold her down until I can get these gloves off."

Before I could say a word, she released the cat. It snarled at her and leaped from the tub, skidding when it hit the tile floor.

"Go ahead, dear, get her with the towel."

Mrs. Figg was unplugging the drain, completely oblivious to the snarling mess of wet fur frantically clawing at the door.

I took a deep breath and dropped the bath towel over the poor thing, then struggled to hold it down until finally Mrs. Figg knelt down beside me and picked up the cat, towel and all.

"There, Miss Little Bit of a Cat," she crooned. "All clean. Doesn't that feel better?"

She rubbed the towel all over the cat, while it screamed at her and tried its level best to sink its teeth into her hand.

"All right, then." Mrs. Figg released the wet cat, which now looked like nothing more than a wet, white gremlin.

She opened the bathroom door and the cat shot out, ran down the hall, and disappeared into a bedroom.

"That wasn't so bad, was it? With two people it's easy. But I can't manage on my own. The other kitties behave much more politely in the bathtub."

She ran the towel over the wet floor and dropped it into a hamper. "I could use a cup of tea," she said. "Would you like some?"

"That sounds great." I turned to follow her and felt my foot slip out from under me. I landed with a heavy thud on the wet tile. Pain shot up my leg like lightning.

"Oh dear," Mrs. Figg said. "Are you all right?"

I grimaced, trying to squeeze back tears.

"Here, take my hand." Mrs. Figg held out a gnarled hand to me and I took it and tried to pull myself up, but as soon as I put my left foot on the ground, I collapsed back onto the floor.

"I think I sprained it," I said.

"It looks swollen, all right." Mrs. Figg sat down on the floor beside me and touched my ankle gently. "Do you think you can . . ."

Her words trailed off and I looked up to see her staring, wide-eyed, to where I sat. A small dark stain seeped down the leg of my pants.

"Oh no!" I cried. "Oh God, no!"

"You sit still, dear." Mrs. Figg rose and padded down the hallway. "I'll call for an ambulance."

"Please, God, please don't let this be happening," I begged, clutching my arms tight around my stomach. "Please let my baby be okay."

"Are you sure you're okay?" Brannon's face was white and his hands shook as he brushed the hair from my forehead.

"I'm all right." I smiled up at him. "I've got a sprained ankle, but the doctor said the baby is fine. I had some spotting, but I'm not going to miscarry or anything like that. They just want me to stay overnight, to be on the safe side."

"What happened?" he asked. "How the hell did you fall?"

I shifted in the hospital bed. "I was helping Mrs. Figg give her cat a bath, and the bathroom floor got wet and I slipped."

Brannon stared at me for a long minute, his face slowly changing from white to red.

"You were giving her cat a bath? What were you thinking?" he finally asked. "You don't need to be doing stupid shit like that while you're pregnant. God, Emma! You almost lost the baby."

"I'm fine," I said softly. "I was just clumsy, I guess. But I'm okay and the baby is okay. Everything is fine, honey."

He paced around the small room, running his hand through his dark hair.

"Everything is not fine," he said, his voice low and flat. "What the hell is wrong with that woman? If she can't take care of her own damned animals she shouldn't have them. Asking you to put yourself in danger so she can give her damned cat a bath. And you . . ."

He turned to face me. "You of all people should know better. You know how easy it is to lose a kid. What kind of mother puts her baby at risk like that?"

My cheeks burned as if he'd slapped me.

"It was an accident," I said, struggling to keep my voice steady. "It's nobody's fault, Brannon. Sometimes things like this happen."

"It wouldn't have happened if you had the sense God gave a goose." His voice rose.

"Mrs. Bohner?" A nurse stood in the doorway, eyeing Brannon distastefully. "Is everything okay in here?"

Brannon stared at her for a long minute, then ran his hand through his hair and smiled at her.

"Sorry," he said. "I guess I lost it for a minute. I'm just worried about my wife."

"Well, I think the best thing for her right now is to get some rest," the nurse said firmly.

Brannon nodded and smiled again. "You're right," he agreed. "She definitely needs her rest."

He leaned down to kiss my forehead, then smiled at me. But his eyes were still hard and cold.

"I'll come back after dinner and bring Jenny," he said. "You get some sleep."

"I love you," I called after him, but he just kept walking away.

"He's just upset about the baby," I said to the nurse.

"Mm-hmm," she said.

"Really," I went on. "Brannon is a wonderful father and a good husband. He just got scared."

The nurse smiled at me and patted my hand. "I'm sure he is," she said. "Now, you should get some rest."

"Which cat were you washing?" Jenny perched on the side of my bed, holding my hand tightly.

"Little Bit, the white one with the blue eyes."

"She's the prettiest," Jenny said.

"She wasn't very pretty today," I said, laughing. "She looked more like a gremlin than a cat. And the noises coming out of that little body were just . . . freakish."

Jenny laughed.

"I ran into Shirley Rigby this morning, too," I said. "She wanted to tell me how glad she was that you talked to Jasper at the calling last week."

"You went to the calling for that bastard?" Brannon stood at the foot of the bed, staring at me hard. He'd hardly spoken since they arrived, and I could feel his anger from where he stood.

"I didn't go for him," I said. "I went for Shirley. It's what you do when someone dies."

"Why didn't you tell me about it?"

"I guess I didn't want you to get angry," I said, "like you are now."

He took a deep breath and sat down in the chair by the bed.

"Okay, I'm not mad," he finally said. "I'm just . . . surprised. You don't even know the woman, Emma. And her son has been a real prick to Jenny."

"I know." I nodded. "But it's not Shirley's fault that her husband was a bully. And even if Jasper has been a jerk, he's still a kid who just lost his father."

"He was okay that day," Jenny said. "I mean, he called Lashaundra a nigger, but other than that he was okay."

Brannon shook his head. "I don't want you to get friendly with either one of them. The dad was a bully and the son is just like him. And the wife . . . well, she just stood by and watched while they behaved like animals."

"It's not her fault," I repeated. "She seems like a nice person."

He shook his head again.

"Nice people don't raise kids who are racist bullies. Besides, you need to be thinking about yourself right now. Your job is to take care of yourself and the baby, not run around trying to take care of everyone else in this damned town."

I turned to touch Jenny's cheek. "Thank you so much for the daisies, honey. They are just beautiful."

I didn't want to argue with Brannon, especially not in front of Jenny.

31

Jenny

"It's snowing!"

Big white flakes were falling fast. The backyard was covered in a blanket of white.

"Yes it is."

Emma hobbled into my room carrying a mug of coffee. She was still wearing her pajamas.

"Are you feeling better today?" I asked.

She'd only been home from the hospital for two days.

"I'm good," she said, grinning at me. "You have a snow day today. School is closed, so we have a whole day to do whatever we want."

"Does Daddy have to work?"

"He's already gone," she said. "I let you sleep in, since we have a day off."

"It's so pretty." I pushed aside my new yellow curtains to take in the view. "I don't think I've ever seen this much snow."

"This is nothing compared to Idaho. They get feet of snow at a time out there. When the roads get too bad, people just get around on their snowmobiles."

"So, what are we going to do today?"

She tilted her head and smiled.

"We can do whatever we want," she said, "as long as we do it here. I don't want to drive anywhere. We don't have a snowmobile." She laughed.

"Can we make pancakes for breakfast?"

"Sure we can. You brush your teeth and I'll get started on breakfast."

After we ate, I watched television for a while. Emma sat in my mother's rocking chair looking at magazines about babies.

"Can I ask Lashaundra to come over?"

I was getting bored with cartoons.

"You can ask her," Emma said. "But I'm betting Angel won't want to drive in this weather any more than I do."

Lashaundra picked up on the first ring.

"Hey," I said. "Do you want to come to my house?"

"Let me ask," she said.

A moment later she was back on the line.

"Mama doesn't want to drive," she said. "Can you come here?"

"No," I said. "Emma doesn't want to drive, either."

"I guess I'll see you at school tomorrow."

I fidgeted for a while, half watching the television but mostly wondering what to do with myself.

Then, I had an idea.

"Hey, Emma?"

"Hmmm?" She didn't look up from the magazine in her lap.

"Can I go up in the attic?"

She raised her eyes and arched one eyebrow.

"Why do you want to go up there?"

"I think it would be a good place to read."

She laughed.

"Your room is a good place to read," she said. "Or right there on the couch is a good place to read."

"I know," I said. "But I like the light up there. I could take some blankets and pillows. It would be like having a clubhouse, only inside the house."

She smiled. "Honey, if you want to build a fort in the attic and read, that's fine with me. But do me a favor and sweep the floor before you start taking up blankets and pillows. It's pretty dusty up there."

I ran to the kitchen to get the broom and dustpan, then walked into the hall and stared at the door in the ceiling. I wasn't tall enough to reach the handle.

"Will you open the door for me?" I called to Emma.

"Hang on," she said.

After a minute, she limped into the hallway and pulled open the door. Then she yanked the cord that brought down the ladder.

"Be careful," she said as I climbed the ladder, broom in hand.

"I will."

She handed me the dustpan and hobbled back to the living room. I stood in the funny little room. It looked smaller now that all of Daddy's boxes were stacked there. Still, there was a nice spot just under the window where I could make a reading nest.

I swept the floor under the window, carried the dustpan carefully down to the kitchen, and dumped it in the trash. Then I grabbed two blankets from the closet in the hallway and carried them up the ladder. Finally, I took the pillow from my bed and picked up the copy of *Little Women* I was reading, and I carried them up the ladder, too.

I piled the blankets and pillow under the window and curled up to read. I was just to the part where Mr. Laurence had given Beth the piano. But the room was so warm and the blankets so cozy, that I felt my eyelids drooping closed.

I shook my head and rose. This was my first snow day ever. I didn't want to waste it sleeping. I yawned and stretched and looked out the window at the snow that was still falling fast. It wasn't even lunchtime, and I was bored.

I sat down on one of Daddy's boxes, wondering what I should do next. I ran my hand along the packing tape holding the box closed, and then I started picking at it. Before long, I had torn all the tape off. I hesitated for a minute. Daddy had told me not to go digging around in the boxes. He had them organized, he said, and didn't want me to mess with them. But now the untaped box seemed to call out to me.

I pulled the top open and stood, just looking, at first. The box was full of folders and envelopes, neatly stacked. And then I saw the spine of a photo album, blue and gray, wedged between the stacks of folders and the side of the box. Surely Daddy wouldn't mind if I just looked at the pictures in the album.

I pulled the album from the box and sat back down in my nest of blankets and pillows. I took a deep breath, opened the album, and stared open-mouthed at a picture of my mother. I don't even know how I knew it was her. I had never seen a picture of her before. But I was certain the woman in the photo was my mother.

She sat in the wooden rocking chair that was in the living room downstairs now, her hands folded over her hugely pregnant belly, smiling at the camera. I touched the picture with one finger. My mother . . . she was beautiful. Straight blond hair fell just past her shoulders. Her eyes were a brilliant deep blue. Her smile revealed even, white teeth. Other than her belly, she was tiny. She didn't look much bigger than me.

I turned pages of the album, staring at images of my mother standing in a small kitchen holding a spatula, sitting on a porch swing with an open book in her lap, posed before an easel with a blank canvas. There were pictures of her with Daddy, his arm draped around her shoulders, her head resting against his chest.

And then there were a bunch of pictures of her holding a tiny, dark-haired baby, smiling proudly. That baby must have been me. More pictures showed her cradling me in the rocking chair, spooning baby food into my mouth, holding my hands as I took steps across the floor, brushing my hair, kissing me good night—all the things a mother does.

I felt my throat tighten, and then I was crying. My mother had loved me. My mother was beautiful. My mother was dead.

Why hadn't I ever seen this photo album before? Why had Daddy never shown me the pictures? All my life I had wondered what my mother was like, what she looked like, what she did, who she was. But Daddy had never wanted to talk about her.

I remembered asking him once if he had any pictures of her. He'd shaken his head and looked really sad.

"No," he'd said. "I wish I did, but we didn't have a camera. That was before cell phones. I always meant to get a camera, but we never had the money. And then she died."

And I had believed him.

"Jenny?"

Emma stood at the bottom of the ladder.

"Are you okay up there?"

"Yes," I called back.

"Well, it's time for lunch. Do you want some tomato soup?"

"Sure."

"I've got some chocolate chip cookies, too," she said.

I closed the photo album and rose, still holding it. I knew I should put it back in the box, but I couldn't. I couldn't just leave it there, now that I knew about it.

I closed the box and smoothed down the packing tape I had pulled up. Then I carried the album down the ladder and into my room. I put it in a dresser drawer under some sweaters.

"Hey," Emma said when I walked into the kitchen. "Are you okay? You look like you've been crying."

"I'm okay. My nose is kind of runny. I think it's because of the dust."

We sat at the table to eat soup and crackers, and then cookies still warm from the oven.

"So, what do you want to do this afternoon?" she asked.

I shrugged. "Maybe read some more."

"Why don't you put on your coat and mittens and play outside for a while?"

"It's too cold."

"The fresh air would be good for you."

I sat for a minute thinking about it.

"Can I go see Mrs. Figg?" I asked. "Maybe she'll let me play music on the piano."

She smiled at me.

"I think that's a lovely idea," she said. "I'm sure Mrs. Figg would enjoy some company."

I put on my parka and mittens.

"Why don't you take her some cookies?"

Emma put some cookies on a paper plate and covered them with plastic wrap. I took the plate and walked next door, then pounded on Mrs. Figg's door. I could hear the dogs baying inside, but Mrs. Figg didn't answer. I pounded again, then turned and trudged back home through the snow.

"Back so soon?" Emma looked up from the couch where she was laying with her foot propped up on pillows.

"She's not home." I took off my jacket and hung it in the closet.

"Are you sure?" she asked, sitting up. "I can't imagine her going out in this weather."

"I knocked twice," I said. "The dogs were barking like crazy, but she didn't answer the door."

"Do me a favor," she said. "Go look out the back window and see if her car is in the driveway."

I ran to the kitchen and looked out the window. Mrs. Figg's old car sat behind her house, just like it always did.

"It's there," I yelled.

"I hope she's okay." Emma stood behind me, leaning against the doorframe.

"Maybe she's visiting that man who wants to marry her."

"Maybe." She didn't sound convinced.

"I'll go back later," I said.

"Thanks, honey."

She limped back to the living room and dropped onto the couch heavily.

"I don't know about you," she said. "But I think I'm ready for a nap."

"I'm going to read some more," I said.

"Okay," she said, flopping onto her back. "Will you wake me in an hour? I don't want to sleep the whole afternoon away."

Within minutes, I heard her breathing settle into a soft, regular snore.

I pulled the photo album from the drawer I'd hidden it in, and lay on the futon in my bedroom, staring at pictures of my mother. My beautiful, dead mother whose blue eyes I had inherited.

32

Emma

I woke with a start from a dream, a bad dream about Micah and Andrew. A dream about losing my baby.

Judging by the angle of the sun in the window, it was late afternoon. How long had I been asleep?

"Jenny?" I called.

She emerged from her bedroom.

"What time is it?"

"Four," she said.

"God, I can't believe I slept so long. I thought you were going to wake me up."

"I'm sorry," she said. "I was . . . reading."

"Oh, well." I sat up and rubbed sleep from my eyes. "So much for getting anything done today."

"Can I have another cookie?"

"Sure." I rose from the couch and hobbled into the kitchen, where the plate I'd made for Mrs. Figg still sat on the table.

"Why don't you take those over to Mrs. Figg's first?"

Jenny pulled on her jacket and boots, took the plate, and slogged through the snow while I watched from our front porch. She banged on the door and waited. I could hear the beagles baying from inside the house, but no one answered.

"She's not here," Jenny called.

"Look in the window," I called back, worried now. Where was Mrs. Figg?

Jenny looked through the front window and then turned and yelled, "She's on the floor at the bottom of the stairs!"

"Try the door!" I yelled, then stepped inside to pull on my own coat.

I limped across the yard, praying that I wouldn't slip and fall again, while Jenny jiggled the handle to Mrs. Figg's door. It swung open as I reached her front porch.

"Wait," I said to Jenny. "Stay here."

I stepped past her as one of the beagles bolted out the door.

"Catch the dog!" I yelled to Jenny. I walked into the house and the other beagle jumped up on me, whining piteously. Mrs. Figg lay on the floor, not moving.

"Mrs. Figg?" I knelt beside her and touched her shoulder, but she didn't respond.

"Is she okay?" Jenny stood behind me, staring.

"Call nine-one-one," I said. Mrs. Figg's face was cold and ashen-looking. I felt for a pulse while Jenny dialed the phone.

"We're at our next-door neighbor's house," she said. "I think she fell down the stairs. She's not moving. . . . I don't know, I came over after lunch but she didn't answer the door then."

She stood staring down at Mrs. Figg's lifeless body, her eyes wide.

"Here," I said, "let me talk to them."

I took the phone, gave the dispatcher the address, and slapped Mrs. Figg's cheek lightly. But I could see she was already gone.

The beagle beside me was licking Mrs. Figg's face, whimpering.

"Why don't you put this one on a leash and take him out to find the other one," I said. I didn't want Jenny just standing there staring at a dead body.

"Is she okay?" Jenny made no move to leave.

"No, honey," I said, my voice soft. "I think she's gone."

Jenny sank to the floor beside me, wrapped her arm around the beagle, and touched Mrs. Figg's face with one finger. A tear slid down her cheek.

"She must have fallen down the stairs," I said, putting my arm around Jenny.

"Do you think if I had checked earlier we could have saved her?" Her voice shook.

"I don't know, honey. Probably not. We don't know how long she's been laying here."

The beagle that had bolted out the front door was now scratching to get back inside. I rose and opened the door and the dog ran to Mrs. Figg and lay down beside her. Both dogs whimpered softly.

"Poor Daisy," Jenny said, stroking one of the dogs. "You miss her, don't you?"

The ambulance arrived within minutes. The paramedics asked some questions, then gently covered Mrs. Figg's body with a sheet.

"Looks like an accident," one of them said. "The sheriff's on his way."

Sheriff Wylie arrived minutes later.

"Oh, Lilah," he said, his voice gentle. "Poor old girl. I told her years ago she shouldn't be living here all by herself."

He turned to me. "You found her like this?"

I nodded. "Jenny brought a plate of cookies for her." I pointed to the plate she had dropped on the front porch. "She came right after lunch, and Mrs. Figg didn't answer the door. Then she came again, and when she still didn't answer I got worried."

"How did you get in the house?" He had his notebook open now and was writing in it.

"The front door was unlocked," I said.

He cocked his head and raised an eyebrow.

"That's not like Lilah."

I shrugged.

"Did you see anyone around here today? Anyone on her porch?"

"No," I said. "But I wasn't watching or anything."

"Do you think someone killed her?" Jenny's voice came in a whisper.

"No, honey." Wylie smiled at her. "I'm just covering all the bases. It looks like she fell down the stairs. I'll have the medical examiner look at her, of course. But it looks like an accident."

"What's going to happen to her pets?" Jenny's arm was still around the beagle.

"I'll call animal control," he said. "They'll find homes for them, don't worry." He smiled at Jenny again.

"You-all can go home now. We'll take it from here."

Jenny rose and took my hand. We paused at the front door and she looked back into the house.

"Good-bye, Mrs. Figg," she whispered.

We walked back to our house and left our coats and boots by the door.

"Do you want some cocoa?" I asked.

She shook her head and sat down by the front window, staring across the yard to Mrs. Figg's house.

"It's sad, honey. I know it makes you sad, but she lived a long life."

"I hate that she died all by herself," she said.

I wrapped my arms around her and hugged her.

"Daisy and Beauregard were with her," I said. "I'm sure they never left her side."

"Poor Daisy," she repeated.

We sat for a while just watching the house next door. We watched as they wheeled Mrs. Figg's body out to the ambulance, put her inside, and drove her away. Then a big white van pulled up in front of the house, and two men got out and began unloading pet carriers.

"That must be animal control," I said.

"I hope they find good homes." Jenny was crying again.

"Hey, what's going on?" Brannon walked in from the kitchen. We hadn't even heard him come in through the back door.

"Mrs. Figg died," Jenny said. "Now they're taking all her animals away."

Brannon looked out the front window and shook his head. "What happened to her?"

"They think she fell down the stairs," I said. "I sent Jenny over with some cookies and she didn't answer the door. So we got worried and went inside."

"You went in her house?"

"Yes," I said. "She was lying on the floor by the stairs. We called nine-one-one, but she was already dead."

"You took Jenny into a house with a dead person?" Brannon's voice rose. "You let my daughter see that?"

"I was worried about Mrs. Figg," I said. "We could hear the dogs barking and her car was in the driveway, but she didn't answer the door."

"So instead of doing what a normal, sane person would do, you took an eleven-year-old into the house to see a dead body?"

I stared at his angry face and felt a rush of anger myself.

"A woman died, Brannon. I did what I had to do."

He returned my stare for a long, tense minute, then wrapped his arms around Jenny.

"I'm sorry you had to see that," he said softly.

"They're taking the dogs away," she said, staring over his shoulder out the window.

A man walked from Mrs. Figg's house with the beagles on leashes.

"Please, Daddy," Jenny said. "Can we take Daisy?"

"What?" Brannon stepped back to look at her. "No, honey, we can't take any of the old lady's animals. Hell, she probably tripped on one of them and that's how she fell down the stairs."

I stared at him, and a small shiver ran up my spine. First Damon Rigby and now Mrs. Figg . . . Death seemed to be following us somehow.

I wrapped my arms across my belly and shook my head. *Accidents happen,* I thought. *You're pregnant and hormonal and letting your imagination run wild.*

Brannon rose and wrapped his arms around me.

"How are you feeling?"

"I'm okay," I said. "I took a long nap this afternoon."

He smiled and kissed my forehead.

"How about we order pizza for dinner?" he said. "That way you don't have to cook."

"That sounds good."

He dialed his cell phone and walked into the kitchen. I sat in the rocking chair and closed my eyes, trying to erase the image of Mrs. Figg's lifeless body on the floor. Jenny cried softly, watching out the window until long after the animal control truck had driven away.

33

Jenny

"What did she look like?"

Lashaundra's eyes were wide.

"She looked like she was asleep, I guess, except she was on the floor."

"I never saw anyone dead before."

I shrugged.

"Well, she's in heaven now."

Lashaundra sounded pretty sure of herself.

"What do you think heaven is like?" I asked. I hadn't thought much about it before. Daddy always said dead is dead, and only fools believe anything else.

"Heaven is like everything you ever wanted all the time," she said, smiling. "Mama says it's better than anyplace in the whole world."

"Do you think Mrs. Figg's husband is there, too?"

"Probably," she said. "If he believed in God and stuff."

We sat on her bed, our English homework spread out, untouched, beside us.

"What if he didn't believe in God?"

"I guess then he'd be in hell," she said. "But I'm sure he believed in God. Almost everyone believes in God, right?"

"I guess so."

I didn't tell her what Daddy said about people who believed in God.

"And he must have been a good person," she continued. "I mean, he let her have all those animals."

"He even put up a swing for the pig," I added.

"I'm sure he's in heaven, and she's there with him."

She sounded so sure of it all.

"Do you think Damon Rigby is in heaven?"

She raised her eyes and stared at me for a long minute.

"I don't know," she said finally. "He was pretty mean."

"Yeah," I agreed. "But even so . . ."

"Mama said he was mean to his wife and his kids, and that's why Jasper is the way he is. Mama says we should try to forgive Jasper, even if he is a jerk."

"Maybe Mr. Rigby's dad was a jerk, too," I said. "Maybe that's why he was so mean."

"Maybe, but he was an adult. He didn't have to be like that."

I stared at the notebook in my lap, but all I could see was the picture of my mother holding me in the rocking chair. Had she believed in God? Was she in heaven? Would I see her one day when I died? And if I did, would she even recognize me? I had changed a lot since she died.

"Mama is taking us to the animal shelter this weekend to get a cat," Lashaundra said. "Maybe we'll get one of Mrs. Figg's."

I sighed heavily. "I wish Daddy would let me take Daisy. She's such a sweet dog."

"Maybe Emma could ask him," she said.

I shook my head. "No, she'd better not. He already said no, and if she asks him again, he'll probably just get mad."

"He gets mad a lot, doesn't he?" Lashaundra's voice was cautious.

I shrugged.

"My daddy said he gets in a lot of arguments at work. He almost punched a guy last week, because the guy got in his way and made him drop a package."

"He doesn't usually get mad," I said.

I was lying, I guess, but I felt like I should stick up for Daddy. He was my dad, after all.

"I heard Mama and Daddy talking one night, when we were still in the trailer. She said she heard him yelling at Jackie one time. She said she almost called the police, but then he stopped yelling. And she said Jackie was fine the next day."

"He yells sometimes, I guess. But not at me. He hardly ever gets mad at me."

"Well, Daddy said the guy who got in your dad's way at work is a jerk, anyway. So maybe that's why he got mad."

I smiled at her. Lashaundra was my best friend.

"Does your dad ever get mad?" I asked.

"Sometimes, I guess. But he doesn't yell. When he gets mad, he gets really quiet."

"Was he mad when the sheriff came to your apartment after Mr. Rigby died?"

She shook her head. "I don't think so. He didn't act mad, anyway. But Mama was pretty upset. She called the sheriff a cracker."

I raised my eyebrows.

"Why did she call him that?"

"That's what she calls people who are racists. She says they're redneck crackers."

"He was nice when he came to Mrs. Figg's house after she died," I said, remembering Sheriff Wylie's kind smile.

"Well, you're white." Lashaundra's voice was flat. "He's probably nice to most white people. But when something bad happens, crackers always blame black people. That's what Mama says."

"She doesn't think that Emma's a cracker, does she?"

"No." Lashaundra smiled. "I think she did when we first got here, but she likes Emma pretty well now."

I smiled back at her. Who wouldn't like Emma, after all?

∽ 34 ∽

Emma

I was sitting in the rocking chair a couple weeks after Mrs. Figg died, making lists of baby names I liked, when the phone rang.

"Hello?"

"Emma? Hi, this is Shirley Rigby."

"Hi, Shirley."

"I was wondering if you could meet me for coffee this afternoon?" Her voice was soft and sounded anxious. "Maybe one o'clock at the diner?"

"That sounds great," I said. "I have to pick Jenny up from school at three, so that gives us a couple hours."

"Perfect, thank you!" she said. "I'll see you then."

She was waiting at a booth when I walked in.

"I ordered coffee for us," she said, smiling at me hopefully.

"It's decaf." Resa set a cup in front of me. "No caffeine for you."

She set another cup in front of Shirley.

"Emma's expecting," she said.

"How wonderful!" Shirley reached across the table and put her hand on mine. "I'll bet your husband is just over the moon."

"We're pretty happy," I said.

"There's nothing better than bringing a child into the world. I remember when Della was born, that's my first-born. I couldn't believe how much love I could feel for something so tiny."

I nodded, thinking about Andrew.

"Is Jenny excited, too?" Shirley nodded at me, anticipating my reply.

"She is," I said. "We're all excited."

"Well, of course you are. Why wouldn't you be?"

She sipped her coffee, her cheeks reddening slightly.

"How many children do you have?" I asked.

"Seven," she said. "Well, six that lived. I lost one."

"I'm so sorry." Now I put my hand over hers. "I know how hard that is. I lost a baby, too. There's nothing worse in the world."

"What happened to your baby?" she asked, not meeting my eyes.

I sat a moment, wondering if I should tell her the truth. Then I took a deep breath. I'd told the truth to Resa and to Brannon. And neither of them had abandoned me.

"My first husband was abusive," I said, straining to keep my voice calm. "My baby, Andrew was his name, he got a respiratory infection when he was still just tiny, and my husband wouldn't let me take him to the hospital. And . . . he died."

She stared at me now, her eyes wide.

"So you know . . . I mean . . . you know what it's like?"

"I do," I said. "I got married very young, and Micah, my first husband, he was mean as a snake. I was pretty much scared to death of him."

"What happened to him?" she asked.

I shrugged. "As far as I know, he's still in Arizona being mean to some other woman. After Andrew died, I left. I left while Micah was out of town and I never went back."

"I left Damon once," she said. "When I was pregnant with Della, he hit me so hard he knocked me down. I left while he was at work the next day. I went up to stay with the nuns at the convent in Loretto. I was raised a Catholic. I even went to Catholic school until high school. Of course, when I married Damon I joined his church. He was a Baptist, you know. They don't like the Catholics much. He said I wasn't going to raise his children to be Pope followers, so that was that. I had to become a Baptist before he'd marry me. I did miss the nuns, though. They were always kind to me.

"Anyway, my sister Theresa worked in the kitchen at the convent in Loretto. So I drove up and stayed a few days. The sisters were so kind to me. I could have stayed there forever. But Damon figured out where I was. It wasn't hard for him to guess. And he came and got me. He promised me he'd never hit me again. He promised we'd be happy."

She took another sip of coffee.

"I almost left another time. When I was pregnant with my third, he came home drunk one night and beat me up bad, real bad. I lost the baby."

"Oh God, Shirley, I'm so sorry."

"I wanted to leave," she said. "I even started packing up my suitcases. But Della started to cry, and I had to sit down and rock her a bit. And I realized then, I already had two babies, and I didn't know where I could go that he wouldn't find me. Besides, I didn't think I could support myself, let alone the kids. I never had a job, you know. I didn't even finish high school. And Damon made good money."

She sighed. "I stayed because I couldn't figure out how to leave."

"Where are your children now?" I asked.

"Well, Jasper is still at home. You met him. He's in the seventh grade. And he misses his daddy something awful. I don't know what to do about that. Of all my kids, Jasper was Damon's favorite. And even though he was hard on Jasper sometimes, Jasper really did love his daddy."

She paused and blew her nose into a napkin. Then she took a deep breath and plowed ahead.

"My Lucy is a senior up at the high school. She's already applied to college at the University of Kentucky. I'm sure she'll get in. Lucy is my smart one.

"And then Della, well, she lives up in Cincinnati. She doesn't come home very often. She didn't even come for her daddy's funeral. She's mad at him still, I guess. He was plenty hard on her. She inherited Damon's stubborn streak, so she caught it a lot. And she's pretty mad at me for staying with him."

"What does she do?" I asked.

"She works in a day-care center. Della loves the little ones. She's married and got three of her own. They're six, four, and two. She's a good mama, Della is."

"She must have learned that from you," I said, smiling at her. She just looked so beaten down and anxious.

"Lord knows I wasn't a good mama," she said. "If I'd had some sense in me, I'd have taken the kids and run a long time ago."

She took another deep breath.

"Lucas, he's my fourth, he's in Louisville. He's a plumber and he's got two kids. And Maryanne and Julie live in Florida. They share an apartment in Jacksonville. They don't come home much, either. But I did get to go down to see them once, a couple years back. They live a block from the beach, so they're happy."

She sighed. "I did the best I could to protect them, but I guess I didn't do a very good job."

"It's not your fault," I said. "You were a victim, too."

"But I was their mama. My job was to protect them."

"Maybe things will get better, now that Damon's gone?"

She nodded. "I hope so. I miss my girls something awful."

She sipped her coffee and swiped her hand across her eyes.

"I'm sorry," she said. "I don't mean to complain. A lot of folks got it worse than me."

"So," I said, smiling at her. "What are you going to do now?"

She smiled back. "I'm not sure. I've got enough money to stay in the house till I die, if I want to. Damon was a good provider, I'll say that for him. And I don't want to move Jasper away from his friends, especially now. I was thinking I might try to get a job, just to have something to do, someplace to go, you know?"

I nodded.

"What kind of job?" I asked.

"Lord God almighty, there's the problem." She smiled but her cheeks reddened again. "I got no skills at all. I can't type or use the computer. I don't know who'd hire me."

"Shirley Rigby!" Resa's voice made us both jump.

"Don't you let me hear you go on about having no skills," she said, slamming her hand down on the table. "You got lots of skills. You can sew. You can cook. You do the prettiest flower arrangements anyone ever saw. What you do with those flowers at the church every Sunday, that's surely a gift from God himself. I bet Rosie O'Hearn would hire you at the flower shop, if you asked her."

"Do you really think so?" Shirley looked startled.

"Honey, Rosie is always talking about what a gift you got with the flowers. You call her up, and I guarantee you she'll give you a job."

Shirley smiled. "I wish I had your gumption, Resa. I always envied you that."

"Well, it's never too late to grow a spine," Resa said firmly. "With Damon gone, you can do what you want to now. Why, you could even go back to your church, the one you grew up in."

"Oh, I couldn't do that." Shirley's voice wavered. "Damon would have a fit!"

"But Damon ain't here, is he?" Resa asked. She poured more decaf into my cup. "Damon don't get a vote no more."

Shirley sat quietly for a long minute.

"Do you really think I could just go back?" Her voice was barely more than a whisper.

"I know you can." Resa smiled and put a hand on Shirley's shoulder. "You can do whatever you want now, honey. Ain't nothing holding you back anymore."

"Order's up!" Harlan's voice called from the kitchen.

"Hold your horses!" Resa hollered back. She winked at me and smiled.

"It would be something to go to Mass again." Shirley's eyes were fixed firmly on Resa's back. "I haven't been in more than twenty-five years. I expect a lot has changed since then."

"Well, there's only one way to find out," I said.

She smiled at me.

"I'm glad I called you," she said. "Thank you for coming."

"I'm glad, too," I said. "It's nice to have a friend."

35

Jenny

As soon as I got home from school every day, I ran to my bedroom to check the drawer and make sure the photo album was still there. Most days I sat in class half wondering if I'd just dreamed it up, conjured it out of thin air. Maybe it wasn't real at all.

But there it lay, safely tucked beneath my sweaters. I wondered if I should tell Daddy about it. In fact, I had almost decided during algebra that day that I should give it to him. It was his, after all. And I shouldn't have been snooping through his things. I knew that, too.

But then I thought about all the times I had asked him about my mother, all the times he could have told me about her, all the times he'd lied about not having any pictures. By the end of that class, I had changed my mind. If he discovered the album was missing from the box, then he could just ask me about it. In the meantime, I could hardly wait to get home and look at the pictures again.

"Do you have any homework?"

Emma stood in the doorway, her hand on her lower back. She looked tired. She always looked tired anymore.

"Um, not very much," I said, shoving the photo album back into the drawer. "Just some algebra problems."

"Well, I can't help you with those," she said, laughing. "God knows, I'm math-impaired. If you need help, your dad can help you after dinner."

"What are we having?" I asked.

"Beef Stroganoff with noodles and creamed peas," she said.

"Do you need any help?"

"No, sweetheart, I'm good. You get started on your homework."

I heard her banging pans around in the kitchen. I didn't want to look at the photo album there in my room. What if she walked in again?

"Emma?" I called. "I forgot I have some English homework, too. I have to read a couple chapters in my book."

"Okay," she called back. "What are you reading?"

"Bridge to Terabithia," I yelled back.

It's true, that's what we were reading in class. But I had finished the entire book the week before.

"I never heard of that." Emma appeared in the kitchen doorway. "Is it good?"

"Yeah, it's good," I said. "I really like it."

"That's good." She smiled.

"I think I'm going to read up in the attic again. Is that okay?"

She tilted her head and raised her eyebrows.

"Are you sure? Last time you were up there it set off your allergies."

"I'm sure. It's a good place to read. Quiet and . . . well, it's really quiet."

"All right then."

She pulled the cord to bring the ladder down and disappeared back into the kitchen.

As soon as she was gone, I pulled the photo album from the drawer, grabbed the blanket and pillow from my futon, and climbed into the attic.

For a while I just paged through the album again, staring at the pictures of my mother. She looked so young. I had never asked Daddy how old she was when she had me. Or how old she was when she died. She looked like she was just a kid herself, holding me in the rocking chair. Hailey. Her name was Hailey. . . . Hailey what?

I stared hard at a picture of her sitting at a picnic table in what looked like a park. I sat in a car seat on the table in front of her. She was holding my toes. She was my mother. And I didn't know her middle name. I didn't even know what her last name was before she got married to my dad.

I stared hard at the box where I'd found the photo album. I knew I wasn't supposed to go through the boxes in the attic. Daddy had been pretty clear about that. In fact, he'd told me several times to stay out of them.

But maybe there were more pictures in that box, maybe even something with my mother's name—her last name, her full name. She had to be more than just Hailey. And she was my mother. I had a right to know her name, didn't I?

I pulled the box open and stared down into it. Then I picked up the folder that lay on top of the stack and opened it. Income tax returns from last year . . . boring. I set the folder aside and opened the next and then the next one. More tax stuff, something from an insurance company, the title to the trailer. I sighed. Maybe there was nothing interesting in there, after all.

Then I found a big brown envelope addressed to Daddy. I opened it, and pulled out a stack of papers. At the top of the first page I read, *St. Elizabeth/Coleman Pregnancy & Adoption Services.* What was this?

I sat down in my blanket nest and squinted to read the small type on the first page.

> *Dear Mr. Bohner,*
> *Thank you for your inquiry regarding your birth sister, Jennifer Adele Bohner. Our records indicate that she was adopted in 1992. According to state law at that time, the adoption records were sealed, so we cannot give you any more information about her. What we can do is put a letter from you into her file here, where it will remain in the event that she wants to find out more about her birth family.*

*I am sorry we cannot be of more help to you. I
understand that you were separated in the foster care
system, and that you want to locate your sister. But she
was only four years old when she was adopted, and she
may have no memory of her early years. Be assured that
she was placed into a stable home, with qualified, loving
parents.*

*If you wish to include a letter in her file, please
forward it to me at this address.*

Sincerely,

Kendra Parkinson

I stared at the letter for a long time. Jennifer Adele Bohner . . . that was my name. And that was Daddy's sister's name? Daddy had a sister? Why hadn't he ever told me about her? And foster care. I knew he'd been in foster care after his mom was killed. I heard him tell Emma about it once, although he'd never talked about it to me. But he'd never even mentioned a sister . . . a sister with the same name as me. My head ached from all the questions I couldn't answer.

I looked through the rest of the papers in the envelope, but all of them were from before the letter I'd already read—Daddy's first letter to St. Elizabeth's, which got returned because it had the wrong address. His next letter and a reply saying there was a fee to do a search for Jennifer Adele Bohner. Then another letter with a photocopy of a check stub from a bank in Alabama. That's where we lived with Trish. Did Trish know that Daddy had a sister? Was I the only one who didn't know? Did Emma know?

I shoved the papers back into the envelope and stood up, feeling sick and kind of dizzy. What else was in the box? What else did I not know about my mother, and my father, and the aunt I'd never even heard of? I reached into the box for another folder, but Emma called from downstairs.

"Hey, Jenny? Can you come down here and help me with something?"

I sighed and returned the envelope with the adoption papers to the box, then patted the tape down. Of course, it wouldn't stick.

I'd pulled it apart too often. I would have to get some tape and redo it, once I was done looking through the stuff inside.

Emma stood in the kitchen. Her face was so pale I could see all of her freckles more clearly than ever. She smiled weakly.

"Would you please open the fridge and get me the ground beef, butter, an onion, the mushrooms, and the sour cream. Wait!" she yelled as I reached for the refrigerator door. "Wait till I'm in the other room, please."

She ran out of the kitchen, holding her nose. I stared after her, wondering why she couldn't open the fridge on her own. Then I pulled out the things she needed and set them on the counter. When I had closed the fridge door, I called to her.

"Okay, they're out."

She walked cautiously back into the kitchen, still holding her nose. Finally, she took a sniff, gagged, and ran to the bathroom. I could hear her throwing up in the toilet.

"Are you okay?" I called.

After a couple minutes, I heard the toilet flush and Emma walked unsteadily back into the kitchen.

"I guess the morning sickness has finally kicked in," she said. She smiled a little and sat down at the table. "Could you pour me a glass of water, please?"

I poured the water and set it before her.

"But it's not even morning," I said.

"I know." She took a tiny sip of her water and grimaced. "I guess my body doesn't know that. I was fine until I opened the refrigerator. The smell set me off. God! I don't know what that smell is. I never smelled it before. But it's awful."

"I didn't smell anything," I said. I rose and started to open the refrigerator to smell again.

"Don't!" Emma's voice froze me.

"Please don't," she repeated more softly. "I think it's because I'm pregnant. I read that pregnant women are hypersensitive to smells and taste. I guess the fridge is going to be a problem for me."

She rose, her hand on the table to steady herself, then abruptly sat back down.

"Okay," I said, hands on my hips. "You tell me what to do, and I'll cook the Stroganoff."

She smiled. "Thank you, honey. That would be a big help."

That's how I had the first of many cooking lessons. Over the next couple months, Emma dictated from the kitchen table or sometimes from the living room, while I constructed our meals.

"I honestly don't know what I would have done without her," she told Daddy that night. "I guess we'd have been eating out."

"You did a great job, Jenny." Daddy smiled at me.

I tried to smile back, but it felt fake, even to me. I kept thinking about the photo album, the letters from the adoption agency, the aunt with my name.

Thankfully, Daddy didn't seem to notice if I seemed different. He was worrying over Emma, coaxing her to eat some peas, drink some milk, take one more bite of Stroganoff. After we'd eaten, he rose and pulled Emma to her feet.

"Off to bed, you," he said firmly.

"I'm okay," she said, but her voice was tired.

"No, you're not," he insisted. "You go to bed. Jenny and I will clean up the kitchen."

She protested a couple more times before finally trudging off to bed.

"Okay, kiddo," Daddy said. "Let's get the dishes done, and then you can start on your algebra."

Daddy washed the dishes while I dried and stacked them.

"You okay?" he asked.

"Yeah," I said, nodding. "I guess I'm kind of tired, too."

"How's school?"

"Okay."

It was quiet after that, the first time I ever remember that I couldn't think of anything to talk about with Daddy.

Actually, I had plenty I wanted to talk about, lots and lots of things I wanted to ask him. But I couldn't do it. One time I even opened my mouth, but no words came out.

Finally, I dried the skillet, put it in the cupboard, and yawned.

"I think I'm going to do my algebra in my room," I said.

"Do you need any help?" He smiled at me, the familiar smile I'd known all my life.

"No," I said. "I'm good."

I kissed his cheek and returned to my room, closing the door behind me. I could have used his help on a couple of the problems, but I couldn't bring myself to ask. It felt almost like I was afraid, like if I asked him about an algebra problem then I'd blurt out questions about my mother, my aunt, the photos. And then he'd know that I'd been in the boxes. And maybe he'd move them out of the house, and I'd never get the chance to look through them all.

Maybe he'd get really mad at me. Or worse, maybe he'd get really mad at Emma for letting me go into the attic.

So I stayed in my room and did the best I could on my homework. When I'd finished, I opened the drawer and pulled out the photo I had removed earlier from the album, the one of my mother holding me in the rocking chair. I put it under my pillow, turned out the light, and squeezed my eyes shut. But it was a long time before I finally fell asleep.

36

Emma

"You look like hell." Resa tilted her head to look at me. "Are you okay?"

"The morning sickness has finally kicked in," I said. "I'm okay, just really tired."

"Kind of late, isn't it? You're almost three months now, aren't you?"

I nodded. "I guess I'm a late bloomer."

"Well, what the hell are you doing here?" she asked, shaking her head at me. "Why aren't you at home on the couch with your feet up watching soaps?"

"We need the money," I said, staring down at my belly, which was just beginning to pooch out. "I'm going to need some maternity clothes pretty soon. Plus, I think I'll feel better if I keep busy. It seems like just when I lay down to rest, that's when it gets worse."

"You need some vitamin B6," she said. "And some real ginger ale. Not the stuff you get at the store, though. That stuff doesn't have any ginger in it at all. You need ginger ale made with real ginger. My mother-in-law made it by the gallon for me when I was pregnant."

"I didn't know you could make ginger ale," I said.

"I'll make you some," she said firmly. "Nothing settles your stomach like ginger. In the meantime, drink lots of peppermint tea. Peppermint's good for your stomach, too."

I nodded and began filling the saltshakers on the tables.

"I bet you're having a girl," Resa continued. "Morning sickness is always worse with girls. Lord, when I was pregnant with Becky I ended up in the hospital with an IV, I got so dehydrated. But with Sam, I was hardly sick at all."

"Really?" I stood and put my hand on my stomach. Was I really carrying a little girl?

"Everyone knows girls cause more morning sickness than boys. Ask your doctor, he'll tell you." She nodded firmly. "Ya'll better start thinking on girls' names."

"Jenny would love a little sister," I said, smiling.

"You think she'll be jealous?"

"No," I said. "She's really excited about the baby."

"Well, kids are always excited about the baby before it comes. Once it's here, taking up all the attention, sometimes they're not so thrilled after all. And Jenny, she's had her daddy's full attention her whole life. She might have a hard time at first."

I shook my head again. "I don't think so. I think she's old enough to become like a second mother to this little one. She'll be twelve by the time the baby is born."

Harlan emerged from the kitchen carrying a mug of steaming tea.

"Peppermint," he grumbled, shoving the mug at me.

"Thanks, Harlan." I took the tea and sniffed. It smelled surprisingly good.

"You-all have been so good to me," I said.

"You just remember the rule," Harlan said as he walked back to the kitchen. "You get tired, you sit down."

Resa grinned at me. "He likes to think of himself as a lone wolf, but he's just a big old softie."

A slight tapping at the door made us both turn. It was still ten minutes before opening time.

Shirley Rigby smiled at us and waved, so Resa unlocked the door.

"Hey, Shirley. You okay?"

"I'm fine, Resa. I'm just fine. In fact, I start my new job today!"

"Yay!" I said. "Where are you working?"

"At the flower shop." She beamed first at me, then at Resa. "I never would have thought to ask Rosie for a job. Thank you!"

She threw her arms around Resa and squeezed, then turned and hugged me.

"I feel like a whole new person!"

"Good for you, Shirley." Resa patted her shoulder. "I knew you could do it."

"And that's not all," Shirley said, grinning widely. "Della is coming to visit next week. She's even bringing her kids!"

She looked like she might just cry from sheer happiness.

"Well, you'd best get on to work, ma'am!" Resa shooed her out of the store. "You can't be late on your very first day."

She locked the door again and turned to grin at me.

"Well, I'll be damned. Good for Shirley!"

"I hope she likes the job," I said.

"She will. Now that Damon's gone, it's like she's got a whole life again."

She picked up her broom and walked toward the kitchen.

"If someone really did run Damon off the road, they did Shirley a favor. Hell, they did this whole town a favor."

"No gossip!" Harlan's voice boomed from the back.

Resa laughed and turned to wink at me. I tried to smile back. But it chilled me even to think that someone could have run Damon Rigby off the road.

I sighed and took a sip of tea. Wiley had said it was an accident. Just like Mrs. Figg's death was an accident. He surely must be right. He was the sheriff, after all. He knew about things like that.

"Nine o'clock!" Harlan called. "Let's open up."

I unlocked the front door and carried my tea to the back, ready to start a new day.

Just before three I hung my apron on its hook, pulled on my coat, and walked to my car. The cold air felt good on my face, waking me up just a bit. I didn't remember being so tired when I was pregnant with Andrew as I was now.

"That's because you're carrying a girl," Resa kept saying all day.

I wondered if she could be right. A girl, a daughter . . . a child of my own.

"Girl or boy is fine," I said out loud to myself. "As long as it's healthy."

I drove to the middle school and parked, waiting for Jenny to emerge from the building. After a few minutes, she came running down the walkway toward me, hand in hand with Lashaundra.

"Hey!" she said as she climbed into the car. "Can Lashaundra come to our house?"

"It's okay with me," I said. "But she'll need to call her mom."

"She already did," Jenny said. "We used the phone in the office."

I laughed, unsure whether to be put out that they hadn't asked me first or pleased that Jenny felt comfortable enough with me to ask her friend over.

The girls giggled and whispered in the backseat, while I concentrated on the roads, still slippery from snow and ice. When we reached the house, Jenny jumped out of the car almost as soon as it stopped.

"I'm going to show Lashaundra the attic," she said. "Will you pull down the ladder?"

I followed them into the house and shrugged off my coat.

"I don't know if your dad would want you guys playing up there," I said. "Why don't you just play in your room?"

"Please, Emma! I just want to show it to her. We'll be careful, and we won't touch any of Daddy's stuff."

I sighed, picturing my bed, the covers pulled down, beckoning my aching body.

"Oh, all right."

I pulled the cord to release the ladder and watched them climb up and disappear into the attic.

"I'm going to take a little nap," I called. "If I'm not up by four, will you please get me up?"

"Okay." Jenny's head appeared in the opening. "Are you sick?"

"I'm fine," I said. "I'm just really tired."

She smiled at me and disappeared. I trudged down the hall and dropped onto the bed, not even taking the time to pull off my shoes. Before I could pull the blankets up over me, I was fast asleep.

I woke with a start to Brannon's voice, loud and angry.

"What the hell are you two doing up there?"

I sat up, feeling dizzy, and looked at the clock. Five forty-five. Damn! Jenny had forgotten to wake me up.

"We were just playing." I heard Jenny's voice now, soft and pleading. "We weren't touching any of your stuff."

"Get on down here right now. Where's Emma?"

"I'm here." I stumbled into the hallway, rubbing sleep from my eyes.

"Did you tell them they could play up there?" He stared hard at me, his mouth an unyielding line.

I nodded.

"Jenny likes to read up there," I said. "It's okay. I had her sweep up the dust first."

Behind him, I saw Jenny climb down the ladder, followed by Lashaundra, who was staring at Brannon with wide eyes.

Brannon stared at me for a long time, not saying anything. Then he turned abruptly and barked at Lashaundra, "You'd better call your mother and have her come pick you up now."

He stalked past me into the bedroom, slamming the door behind him.

"It's okay," I whispered to the girls. "Lashaundra, why don't you call your mom? Jenny, bring your things down from the attic. I'll talk to your dad."

"I'm sorry." Jenny's voice was barely audible. Her blue eyes were wide in her pale face.

"It's all right," I repeated.

I took a deep breath, turned, and walked to the bedroom. Brannon was sitting on our bed with his back to me, breathing hard. He didn't turn to look at me, so I closed the door behind me and walked to the bed to sit beside him.

"Hey," I said softly. "I'm sorry you're upset."

His nostrils flared slightly, but he said nothing.

"Jenny likes taking a blanket and pillow up there to read. She says it's like having her own fort right inside the house."

He finally turned to look at me.

"I told Jenny and I told you that I didn't want either of you going through my boxes." His voice was hard and clipped.

"She's not going through your boxes," I said. "She's just been reading her books up there."

I reached to touch his shoulder and he jerked away.

"I told you," he repeated. "Why can't you ever just do what I ask you to? Why can't you just take care of Jenny like you're supposed to? What the hell have you been doing, while she's taking her friends up there and getting into my stuff?"

I rose and put my hands on my hips.

"I was asleep," I said firmly. "I was exhausted after work, and I needed a nap. Jenny is eleven years old. She's old enough to entertain herself for an hour or two without me hovering over her."

"She's a child!" His voice exploded into the room. "She's a child, and you're supposed to take care of her!"

I stared at him and took a step back away from him.

"I do take care of her," I said, my voice pleading now. "I was right here if she needed me. But, honey, I have to take care of this baby, too." I put my hands across my belly protectively, as if to shield our child from his anger.

He took a deep, ragged breath and ran his hand through his hair. And as I watched, I could see the anger drain from him. His shoulders dropped, the muscles in his neck loosened, his breathing slowed. When he looked up at me again, he looked like my dear Brannon.

"I'm sorry," he said, his voice gentle now. "You need to take care of yourself and the baby. I know that. But I'm not comfortable with Jenny and her friends being alone, unsupervised. And I really do not want her messing with my stuff."

"Okay," I said, feeling my own anxiety ease. "I won't let her go into the attic anymore."

He opened his arms and I walked into them, relieved like I always was when his anger passed.

He kissed my forehead and stroked my cheek. Then he said softly, "Tomorrow I want you to quit that damned job."

"But . . ." I began, but he simply held me closer and repeated, "Tomorrow, you are going to quit that job, Emma. It makes you too tired. You need to take better care of yourself and the baby. We can manage on my salary. I can pick up some extra hours and we'll be fine. But you are done working."

I leaned my head against his chest and squeezed my eyes closed against the tears.

"Okay," I whispered after a long minute. "I'll call Harlan tomorrow and tell him."

He leaned in to kiss me, his arms tight and warm around my back.

"That's my girl," he whispered.

❧ 37 ❧

Jenny

I sat down to dinner that night as nervous as a cat at the dog pound. I didn't want to see Daddy's anger at Emma, didn't want to hear the cutting remarks I knew would come about her cooking or her bad housekeeping skills or her stupid ideas. I'd heard them all before. I knew they were the start of a bad time that would end up with Emma leaving. I chewed my lip and prayed silently, waiting for Daddy to come to the table.

But when he sat down, Daddy seemed okay, just like . . . normal. He smiled and touched my shoulder.

"Sorry I lost my temper."

"It's okay," I said. "I'm sorry I was playing in the attic."

Emma walked into the kitchen then and smiled at me. I could see her eyes were a little bit red, but otherwise she seemed fine.

"How about leftover spaghetti and meatballs?" she said.

"Sounds good." Daddy smiled at her and patted her butt as she walked past him.

I stared at them for an instant in disbelief, then rose and walked quickly to the fridge.

"I'll get it," I said.

Emma smiled again and walked from the room.

"I wonder what it is that she smells in there?" Daddy asked, peering into the refrigerator.

"I don't know," I said, pulling out the spaghetti, butter, and parmesan cheese. "But it makes her puke every time she smells it."

I put the spaghetti and sauce in the microwave and fanned the air in the kitchen.

"Okay," I called. "You can come back."

Emma walked back in and kissed my forehead.

"Thanks, honey."

Daddy beamed at the two of us.

I set the table while Emma pulled dinner from the microwave. When we sat down, Daddy reached for our hands and said, "I know it's not Thanksgiving or anything, but let's take a minute to just say what we're grateful for."

I stared at him openmouthed and he laughed.

"Okay, I'll start," he said, squeezing my hand. "I am so grateful for you two and for the baby coming."

"I'm grateful for my life," Emma said softly. "For you guys and for this baby and for good friends."

She turned to smile at me.

I opened my mouth, but nothing came out. A giant lump filled my throat. I couldn't put into words what I was grateful for just then—that Daddy wasn't being angry and mean, that Emma was still here, that we were still a family.

"It's okay," Emma said, squeezing my hand. "Let's eat."

I watched Daddy laughing with Emma as she tried to explain the smell in the fridge. He held her hand across the table, stroking her wrist with his finger. He buttered a second slice of bread for her, and urged her to eat it.

The phone rang, and Emma rose to answer it.

"Hi, Angel." She turned her back to the table slightly.

"Oh no, it's fine. Everything is fine," she said. I saw Daddy watching her back as she talked.

"No, no. He's not mad at Lashaundra or Jenny or me or anybody. He was just surprised when he came home and I was out like a light and the girls were in the attic. . . . Yes, I know. It's okay. He just worried about them being up there. It's dusty and there's a bunch of old junk up there. . . . Okay, thanks, Angel. Tell Lashaundra it's okay. 'Bye."

She turned and smiled at Daddy.

"You made quite an impression on Lashaundra," she said.

"I'll apologize to Michael tomorrow," he said.

She kissed his forehead.

"Thank you," she whispered.

That night I lay awake on my futon for a long time, wondering and worrying and praying.

Maybe Emma really was magic. She'd been with us for over eight months. That was longer than anyone I could remember. And even though Daddy had gotten mad today, she was still here and they seemed okay. Maybe she was the one who would stay and be my mom forever. Maybe when the baby came, we could finally just be like a normal family.

The next morning, Emma was up and dressed by the time I woke up, just like always. But she was wearing old jeans and a flannel shirt and tennis shoes.

"Aren't you going to work?" I asked.

She shook her head.

"I'm not going to work for a while," she said. "Your dad and I think it's a good time for me to stay home and just take care of things here."

"But I thought you really liked your job."

"I do. I mean, I did. But it's not good for me to be on my feet so much and be so tired all the time. Maybe once the baby is born, I'll go back to work."

"So what are you going to do all day?" I asked, watching her carefully.

"Well, today I think I'll sew some new curtains for the baby's room. And maybe I'll learn how to bake bread. Wouldn't that be good, homemade bread?"

"Sure, I guess."

"But for right now, you need to get ready for school or you'll be late."

By the time I had gotten myself dressed and walked into the kitchen, she was standing at the stove, stirring a big pot of oatmeal.

"I was going to make eggs," she said. "But I didn't want to open the fridge."

"Oatmeal's okay."

We ate in silence and I wondered if she really had wanted to quit her job, or if she was doing it just to please Daddy.

"Is your dad still mad?" Lashaundra asked at lunch.

"No," I said, shaking my head. "He got over it pretty fast."

"I never saw him look like that before. I mean, I've seen my dad get mad, but never like that. He was kind of . . . scary." Her eyes were round.

"He doesn't get mad very often," I said. "But when he does, it's pretty bad."

"Is he mad at Emma?"

"No. By the time we had dinner, he was just like normal."

"Good," she said, smiling at me. "I'm glad he's not mad anymore."

Behind me I heard something drop to the floor. I turned to see Jasper Rigby, staring at me. When he saw me looking back, he gave a small, awkward wave and looked away. I turned back to Lashaundra, who was staring at his back.

"What was that about?" she asked.

"I don't know," I said. "Maybe he thought I would pick up his fork for him."

"As if," she said, laughing. "Like you would do anything for him."

I laughed, too.

"I liked your reading nest," she said. "I'm sorry we got in trouble. Does that mean you can't go up there anymore?"

I shrugged. "I guess so."

It seemed a small price to pay for peace in the house and Emma staying with us. If that was what it took to keep Daddy happy, then that was exactly what I would do.

Just like Emma quitting her job, I thought. *We're both just trying to keep Daddy happy.*

The thought made my stomach ache. What if someday Emma

got tired of doing things to make Daddy happy? What if she wanted to go back to work after the baby was born?

Please, God, I began my silent and constant mantra. *Please let Emma stay. Please.*

"Are you okay?" Lashaundra was looking at me, her head tilted.

"I'm okay," I said. "Just thinking."

"Do you want to come to my house after school? Mama's making corn casserole. She said you could come for dinner, if you want."

"No." I shook my head. "I better go home."

She tilted her head to look at me again.

"I want to make sure Daddy's really not mad," I said.

"But you said he was okay at dinner."

"I know." I paused, trying to think of the right words. "But I just need to make sure he's not mad at Emma. You know . . ."

She nodded. "Like with Jackie?"

"Yeah," I said. "And all of them."

I was waiting in front of the school for Emma. Lashaundra had already gone with Mrs. Johnson. They'd offered me a ride, but I told them Emma was coming to pick me up. Now she was late.

"Hey."

I turned to see Jasper Rigby standing beside me.

"Hey," I said.

"Are you waiting for your mom?"

I nodded.

We stood in silence. I wondered why he was standing there with me. He hadn't said a word to me or to Lashaundra since his father died. Frankly, it had been a welcome silence.

"My mom got a job," he said finally. "At the flower shop with Mrs. O'Hearn. She said your mom and Resa helped her get it."

"Oh."

"And she likes it, I guess."

I stood still, wondering what he wanted me to say.

"Anyway, thanks, I guess." He didn't meet my eyes. "I mean, thanks to your mom and Resa."

"Okay," I said.

I stared up the street, willing Emma to arrive in her Chevy Tahoe and get me away from Jasper. Just standing next to him felt weird, like maybe I was being disloyal to Lashaundra.

"Um, so . . ." He paused, staring hard at the ground. "So . . . I heard you talking to your friend at lunch."

"Lashaundra?" I asked, waiting, just waiting for him to call her a jungle monkey or a nigger or something else hateful. My fists were clenched, and so were my teeth.

"Yeah, Lashaundra," he said. "And I thought . . . I mean, what she said about your dad."

He raised his eyes to mine and then dropped them again.

"Does your dad hit you?"

He blurted it out quickly, never looking up from the ground.

"What?" I stared at him.

"It just sounded, I mean from what Lashaundra was saying, it sounded like maybe he . . . did. Hit you, I mean."

"No!" I yelled it at him, my face flushed. "My dad doesn't hit me!"

"Okay," he said quickly, stepping away from me. "Geez, I just thought . . . never mind."

He turned and stalked away and I stared at his back. He seemed to get taller as he walked.

I sat down on the step and leaned my face into my hands, feeling tired and antsy and afraid. After what seemed like a very long time, Emma pulled up in front of the school and honked. I ran to the car and climbed in.

"Sorry I'm late," she said. "I fell asleep in the rocker."

"It's okay," I said.

"I'm making smoked sausage and scalloped potatoes for dinner tonight. Does that sound good?"

I nodded, still thinking about Jasper Rigby and what he'd said, what he'd asked me. Why would he ask me that?

"Hey, Jenny?" Emma's voice was low. I turned and looked into her wide green eyes.

"Yeah?"

"Can we not tell your dad I was late picking you up? I mean, I don't want him to worry and . . ."

"Sure," I said. I knew exactly what she meant. "There's no point telling him. It's okay."

I smiled at her, and she smiled back. She looked relieved.

I thought about Jasper Rigby's question again. I'd answered it honestly. My father had never hit me, not even once.

"I love you, Emma."

She turned and looked at me in surprise.

"Thank you, Jenny. I love you, too."

She squeezed my hand and her shoulders seemed to relax.

"Can we make some biscuits to go with the sausage and potatoes?" I asked.

Daddy loved biscuits.

"Sure," she said. "That's a good idea."

She smiled again.

"I love you, too, Jenny," she said again. "I love you, too."

∽ 38 ∽

Emma

I stared at the soggy mess of dough on the kitchen counter. It certainly didn't look like the picture in the recipe book. The bread dough in the picture was round and firm. Mine was a wet, shaggy mess. I'd grown up watching my mother bake bread, but I'd never tried it myself. So far, it was turning out to be a disaster.

I sighed and shifted weight from one foot to the other. My feet hurt, my back ached, and I felt the beginnings of a headache in my temples.

I looked at the clock. Only noon. How could time pass so quickly at the diner and so slowly here at home?

A soft rapping on the front door startled me. When I opened it, Resa stood there, holding a plastic pitcher.

"Brrr," she said, shaking her head. "It's plenty cold out there."

"Come in, Resa. What are you doing here?"

"I came to check on your progress with the bread," she said, smiling.

"How did you know I was making bread?"

I stared at her, wondering if she was psychic or something.

"Jenny told me yesterday when she stopped in at the restaurant. I brought you some real homemade ginger ale. It's good for what ails you."

"Thank you!" I smiled at her as I took the pitcher. Then I looked back at the dough on the counter and sighed.

"Well, so far all I've made is a big mess."

"Bread's tricky at first," she said, patting my hand. "It takes a little while to get the hang of it. But after that, it's the easiest thing in the world."

She walked into my kitchen and stared at the lumpy mass on the counter.

"Yeah," she said, nodding. "That ain't good."

She picked up the entire mass of dough and dropped it into the trash can. It landed with a heavy thud.

"Okay then, let's start over."

"Oh, Resa," I began. "That's okay. You don't have to . . ."

"Nonsense," she said firmly. "I been baking bread my whole life. I taught my girls how to do it. I can surely teach you."

And so I started pulling out the flour and yeast and salt. Then I washed down the countertop and scrubbed my biggest bowl clean.

"First thing is, you got to proof your yeast."

She poured warm water into a measuring cup and stirred in the yeast and some sugar.

"The book said to do that, but I wasn't sure what it meant."

"You've got to let it set a few minutes and see if it bubbles up. If it doesn't, that means your yeast is old."

I stared at the liquid and watched as tiny brown bubbles began forming on the surface of the water.

"Good," she said. "The first mistake lots of folks make is using old yeast. Your bread won't rise at all without good yeast."

I reached for the flour and sifter, and she put her hand on my arm.

"Oh no, honey. You don't sift flour for bread. Let me show you."

I watched her measure a cup, chopping and scraping the excess from the top. Then she watched as I measured another cup and stirred in some salt.

"Now, put in some water and stir it hard."

I poured and stirred, watching a soggy mass form, while she sprinkled a heavy coating of flour on the counter.

She poured in the yeast mixture, then added more flour. I stirred as best I could, but it was hard work.

"Okay," she said. "Here we go."

She took the bowl from me and dumped the dough onto the flour she had sprinkled on the counter.

"Now here's the important part," she said. "You got to knead the dough till it feels right. See how I do this?"

I watched for a minute as she folded and pounded the dough, turning it and adding more flour. Then she stood aside and watched me knead until my arms were tired. After what felt like an hour, she touched my arm.

"Now, we test it."

She poked two fingers into the ball of dough, and the indentations bounced back immediately.

"That's how you know you're done kneading," she said. "See how it feels? See how it comes right back after you poke it?"

The ball of dough on the counter looked just like the picture in the cookbook, and nothing like the mess I had made before.

I buttered a bowl and dropped the dough into it. Then I covered it with a towel and put it on top of the fridge to rise.

"Thank you, Resa," I said, watching as she washed first her hands and then the mixing bowl and wooden spoon.

"It's no trouble at all. I love to bake. I can teach you all kinds of things, if you want."

"I'd like that."

"I hate that you left the diner. It's lonely there without you."

I nodded. "I know, but with the baby coming, Brannon thought . . . that is, we thought it would be better for me to stay home."

"Well, I reckon you're lucky to have a husband who loves you so much he wants to take care of you."

She smiled at me as I took her place at the sink to wash my hands.

"Yes, I'm pretty lucky."

We sat down at the table and I poured two glasses of ginger ale. Then I rose and walked to the cupboard.

"I have some oatmeal cookies," I said. "They're not homemade, but they're pretty good."

I put some cookies on a plate and set it on the table in front of her.

"Next time, I'll teach you to make your own oatmeal cookies," she said, staring doubtfully at the plate. "Cookies are the easiest thing in the world."

After we'd had our ginger ale and cookies, she pulled her coat on and gathered her purse and gloves.

"Check that dough in an hour," she said. "When it's about doubled in size, you're going to punch it down and knead it again. Then put it in the pan and let it rise again for a while. When it's up over the top of the pan, put it in the oven at three hundred and fifty degrees."

"Thank you, Resa," I said, holding the door open for her. "Honestly, thank you so much."

"Well, you're welcome, honey." She took my hand and squeezed it. "You call me if you need anything, you hear? And come see me at the diner sometime soon."

I watched her pick her way down the snowy sidewalk to her car, then turn and wave back at me. She was so kind. I felt so lucky to have friends like Resa and Angel.

When Brannon came home from work that night, the whole house smelled wonderfully of fresh bread. Jenny had already eaten a huge slice with butter and honey.

"Did you make this?" he asked, his eyes wide as he stared at the loaf on the counter.

"Yes," I said. "But I had some help."

"Good girl!" He turned and smiled at Jenny.

"Not me, Daddy," she said. "Resa helped."

"She came by to bring me some homemade ginger ale," I said. "And I had made a huge mess of the first batch of dough."

I opened the trash can and pointed to the glob of dough.

"What is that?" Brannon stared at it cautiously.

"That's my first attempt."

He wrinkled his nose.

"Anyway, Resa saw it and said she'd help me make a new batch. And that's what happened."

"Well, thank God for Resa." He grinned and wrapped his arms around me.

I relaxed into his embrace.

"So how was your day? Did you enjoy just being at home?"

"It was nice," I said.

I didn't mention how lonely I'd been, how the day had dragged by before Resa came to the rescue.

"I told you," he said, smiling. "It's better for you to be at home, taking care of yourself and Jenny and me, like the good mother you are."

I hoped Brannon was right, but I wasn't sure I was cut out to be a homemaker. I'd worked too hard for too long to stand on my own two feet.

Then I looked over his shoulder and saw Jenny grinning at us, and I let my shoulders relax again. She needed me. Brannon needed me. The baby needed me. And that was enough.

39

Jenny

I didn't go back up into the attic for a long time. I wanted to. I wanted to go through more boxes and see what else I could find out about my mother and about Daddy's sister. But I didn't. I couldn't risk getting Emma in trouble again. Not now, when things were going so well. Daddy seemed happier than I'd ever seen him. Emma was learning to bake, and she seemed a lot less tired than before. She was also starting to show now, her belly rounding out beneath her T-shirts and sweaters.

But I still had the photo album, tucked safely away in my sweater drawer. And every day I pulled it out at least once, just to look at the pictures of my mother.

On a sunny, almost warm afternoon in mid-April, I was sitting in the kitchen after school, drinking orange juice and working on algebra problems, when the phone rang. Emma answered it.

"Hello, Shirley. How are you?"

I sat quietly, just listening.

"Oh my," Emma said. "Is he all right?"

I set my pencil down on the table, listening.

"Sure, I can do that," Emma said. "No, really, it's no problem at all. . . . Okay, I can be there in half an hour. . . . I'll see you soon."

She hung up and turned to look at me.

"Jasper Rigby had an accident on his bike last night," she said. "He's home from school with a broken leg."

"Oh." I hadn't even noticed his absence.

"Anyway, his mother doesn't want to leave him alone because he can't get around. So I'm going to run to the store and pick up a few things to take over there. Do you want to come with me?"

I stared at her for a minute.

"Why did she ask you?"

"Well, she tried a couple other people but no one else is available."

"Daddy won't like it," I said. I remembered what he'd said about Mrs. Rigby and Jasper.

Emma frowned slightly.

"It's just a neighborly thing to do," she said. "And if I go now, I can be back before your dad gets home."

My eyes widened.

"What if he finds out?" I whispered.

"Don't worry. It will be fine. I'll only be gone an hour."

I nodded, but my heart was pounding hard.

"So, do you want to come with me?"

"Can I stay here?" I asked, looking down at my algebra book. "I've got a lot of homework."

She hesitated just a minute, then nodded and kissed my head.

"Okay," she said. "Finish your homework. And if you need anything just call me."

"Okay."

Emma pulled on a jacket, picked up her purse, and paused again at the door.

"You sure you'll be all right?"

"I'll be fine," I said. "I'm just going to do these stupid problems."

She smiled again and left, locking the back door behind her.

I watched through the window as she pulled her car out of the driveway, and then sat back down and surveyed the kitchen. I'd never been alone in the house before. Daddy wouldn't be home until later. Emma would be gone for an hour, she said.

I should do my algebra.

I bent over the book and stared at the problems, but all I could see was the box in the attic, a box full of things that might tell me more about my mother.

After a few minutes, I gave up trying to work on my algebra. I rose and walked into the hallway, staring up at the door to the attic. Then I returned to the kitchen and dragged a chair into the hall. Standing on it, I could reach the cord that released the ladder.

I went back to the kitchen and got a knife from one drawer and packing tape from another. Then I climbed the ladder, listening carefully for the sounds of Emma returning, or worse, Daddy. But the house was quiet.

The box I'd already been through was taped securely shut. I was so glad I'd done that before Daddy caught Lashaundra and me up there. But several more boxes were stacked around the room.

I took a deep breath, listened again, and walked to a box in the back. It was big and had a lot of tape holding it closed.

I slit the tape, set the knife down on the windowsill, and pulled the box open.

Daddy's summer clothes were folded neatly inside. I sighed and started to fold the lid shut. Then I saw the corner of another box peeking out from under the clothes.

I started pulling clothes out of the box, stacking them on the floor, praying they wouldn't pick up too much dust. Then I reached in and pulled out the other box, which had even more tape on it.

I sat down on the floor and held the box for a long minute. Daddy would be furious at me, and at Emma, if he caught me going through his things. I knew I should put the box back and go downstairs to do my homework. But I thought about the letters from the adoption agency and the pictures of my mother, and I slit through the layers of tape and pulled the smaller box open.

A glint of silver caught my eye. I reached in and pulled out a locket like the one Daddy had given Emma for Christmas. Turning it over, I read, *Brannon and Jackie*. I felt tears sting my eyes, remembering how excited Jackie had been when Daddy gave her the locket. She wore it all the time after that, even in the shower. She must have given it back when she left Daddy for that other man.

Another glint of silver, another locket, this one's chain tangled with yet another's. *Brannon and Trish. Brannon and Ami.* Then another—*Brannon and Laura.* I didn't even remember a Laura. A couple more lockets lay in the box, but I was pulling out a big envelope now.

I opened the envelope and found several smaller envelopes inside, each holding a letter. The one on top was addressed to Mrs. Hailey Bohner on Pippin Road in Cincinnati—my mother! The return address listed Mrs. Imogene Wright on North Layman Street in Indianapolis, Indiana. I pulled the letter from the envelope and stared at the date: February 2, 2006. My hands shook so hard I had to lay the letter down on the floor and bend over to read it.

> *Dear Hailey,*
>
> *I was so glad to get your letter, I about cried when it came. I know you said never to write back to you, but honey I am scared for you and I need to know if you are OK.*
>
> *I know things were bad between us before, but I am your mother and I always will be. Nothing will ever change that.*
>
> *Hailey if you are scared then please come home. Bring the baby and just come home. Use this money and get on a bus and come back home. If you don't want to live with me you can live with Mary Anne and Bill. They have plenty of room and they would love to have you and Jenny stay with them.*
>
> *Please at least write back to me and let me know you are OK.*
>
> *I love you,*
> *Mom*

I read the letter twice. Then I read it again. My hands shook, my stomach knotted so that I thought I might throw up. A letter to my mother from her mother. My mother had a mother, a mother named Imogene Wright. I had a grandmother.

Why was my mother afraid? And why didn't she want her own mother to write to her?

I put the letter back into the envelope and pulled out another, this one addressed from Mrs. Hailey Bohner to Mrs. Imogene Wright. It was dated February 7, 2006.

> *Dear Mom,*
> *I am fine. I am sorry I worried you. Brannon and*
> *I had an argument, that's all. We are OK now.*
> *Sometimes he just gets so mad and his eyes get this*
> *look, and I think maybe he'll hurt me. But he would*
> *never do that. I know that now.*
> *Thank you for the money. I hope it is OK if I keep*
> *it. We are kind of tight right now. Jenny is growing up*
> *so fast, and she always needs new clothes.*
> *Please don't write to me again. Brannon would be*
> *mad at me if you did.*

The letter ended there. There was no signature, even; it just ended. I stared at the paper. My mother wrote that letter. But why was it here in the box? Why hadn't she ever mailed it? Or even signed it?

I looked back into the box and saw another box, even smaller, like the ones Daddy got from the bank with his checks in them. Setting the letters aside, I pulled the check box out and opened it. Inside, right on top, Jackie's face smiled at me from a small plastic rectangle. It was her driver's license. Beneath it were more licenses—Trish's and Ami's and Cara's. There were two more, women I didn't know, or at least didn't remember. Why did Daddy have Jackie's driver's license? Surely she would have taken that with her when she left.

I held the licenses in my hand, staring at them, willing my mind to come up with an explanation.

"Jenny!"

I shoved the licenses into my pocket as I spun to see Emma's head in the doorway to the attic.

"What in heaven's name are you doing up here?"

I closed the check box quickly and shoved it back into the box with the lockets and letters.

"I just . . . I wanted . . ." I stammered, but no words would come. I had no idea what I could even begin to say.

"Put that stuff back right now!" She emerged through the door and frowned at me. "Quick," she said. "I don't want your dad to know you were up here again."

I stuffed things back into the box and taped it. Then I put the box into the larger box and began putting Daddy's clothes back inside. Finally, I taped the big box shut and turned to face Emma. Her face was pale, her eyes wide.

"How could you do this?" she asked. "You know how mad your dad would be if he found out!"

I picked up the knife and tape, still saying nothing.

"Get yourself downstairs, right now!"

She followed me down the ladder, then pushed it back up into the trap door.

"I'm sorry," I whispered.

She looked at me for a long minute, and I waited for her to start yelling. Instead, she took the knife and tape from me and sighed.

"Go change your clothes and take a shower," she said. "You're a mess."

She was right. I was covered in dust. Before I undressed, I took the driver's licenses from my pocket and shoved them into my underwear drawer. Then I showered and washed my hair.

When I padded back to my room, my dirty clothes were gone and I heard the washing machine start in the basement.

I dressed and toweled my hair, then sat down on the futon. My hands were still shaking; my stomach was in knots. I had so many things I wanted to know, and no one to ask. No one except Daddy, of course. But I couldn't do that. That much I knew.

"Hey."

Emma stood in the doorway. She'd changed her clothes, too.

"I'm sorry," I said again. "I just . . . I just wanted to see what was up there."

"I know," she said. "I know you're curious. I get that, I really do. But you promised your dad, and I promised your dad. And you have to promise me now that you will not go up there again."

I sat not looking at her for a long time. I wanted to promise her, to make her happy. But what about the letters and the lockets and the driver's licenses? What if there was more stuff up there about my mother?

"Jenny?"

At last, I raised my eyes to meet hers.

"I promise," I whispered.

"Okay, then." She nodded and held her hand out to me. "Come on and help me get dinner started."

"Did you get the stuff for Mrs. Rigby?" I asked, following her into the kitchen.

"Yes," she said. "And I saw Jasper, poor thing. He's in a cast up to his hip, and he'll be out of school for a while."

I never thought of Jasper as poor anything, but I did feel bad about his leg.

"I'll tell you what." Emma turned to me and tilted her head. "Both of us did something today we probably shouldn't have done. And neither of us wants your dad to know. So for this one time, we'll keep our secrets, okay?"

I nodded and smiled at her.

"But just this one time," she said firmly. "No more sneaking, no more lies. Okay?"

I nodded again.

She smiled at me and pulled me into a hug.

"I know you're curious," she repeated. "But your dad just wants what's best for you . . . what's best for both of us. He loves us, that's all."

I nodded. I hoped against hope that she was right.

❧ 40 ❧

Emma

I sat in the waiting room at the doctor's office, trying to concentrate on the parenting magazine in my lap. But my mind kept returning to the day before. To Jenny, digging through Brannon's boxes in the attic. What was so fascinating up there that she would risk Brannon's anger? I felt vaguely guilty, not telling Brannon about it. But how could I, when I was keeping something from him, too?

Shirley had become a real friend in the last couple months. We'd had coffee several times and once I'd gone to her house for lunch. With Damon gone, Shirley was coming into her own, becoming the person she had always wanted to be. And she'd been so helpful to me, teaching me to arrange flowers and helping me find the best bargains on maternity clothes and baby things. She'd even given me a big box of baby clothes that had been her kids'. Most of them looked brand-new.

I hoped Jasper's injury wouldn't interfere with her job. She loved working at the flower shop almost as much as I had loved working at the diner. God, I missed Resa! I even missed Harlan bellowing, "Order's up!"

"Mrs. Bohner?" A nurse with a clipboard stood smiling at me. "The doctor will see you now."

I followed her to the exam room, undressed, put on the hospital gown, and sat on the table, waiting and wishing that Brannon were there with me. He'd been taking on extra hours since I left my job at the diner, and I didn't want him to miss work. He knew I had a doctor's appointment, of course. It had been on the calendar for a month. But I hadn't told him it was a special appointment. I wanted to surprise him.

"How are you feeling, Emma?" Dr. McLaren smiled and extended his hand.

"I'm good," I said, shaking his hand.

"Is the morning sickness subsiding?"

"Yeah, it's a lot better."

"Good," he said, writing on the chart. "Are you ready for your ultrasound?"

I nodded and smiled.

"Okay, then," he said. "Let's have a look at that baby."

I lay back on the table and a nurse pulled aside my gown and smeared a cold goo on my belly. Then the doctor placed the sensor on my stomach and a sound filled the room, a whoosh, whoosh, whoosh—the sound of my baby's heart.

"There's your baby." Dr. McLaren pointed toward a monitor and I stared in wonder.

"Here's the head, and those are the hands and feet."

"Oh my God," I breathed. I'd never seen anything so beautiful.

"And . . . do you want to know the baby's sex?"

"Yes!"

"Well, it looks like you're having a girl. Congratulations."

A girl . . . a baby girl who was half me and half Brannon, a little sister for Jenny.

Tears stung my eyes. I couldn't speak because of the huge lump in my throat. My daughter was beautiful and tiny and perfect.

"Is she okay?" I finally croaked.

"Everything looks good," he said, smiling at me. "She looks right on track in terms of size. I think you'll have a healthy little girl."

After he'd turned off the machine and left the room, I cleaned the goo off my belly and sat, just letting tears drip down my cheeks for a minute. Then I got dressed, scheduled my next appointment, and drove toward home. Outside, the sky seemed bluer than I'd ever seen it. The returning robins sounded sweeter. The breeze felt warmer and fresher. I felt happier than I'd ever been. I stopped at Walmart and bought a pair of tiny pink booties with white ribbons. Then, on impulse, I picked up a new nightgown, long and sheer and pink, with a dangerously low-scooped neckline.

I couldn't wait to tell Brannon.

When I got home I called Angel.

"Can you pick Jenny up after school?"

"Sure," she said. "Are you feeling okay?"

"Yeah," I said. "I'm fine. In fact, I'm great. I just . . . I would really appreciate it if she could have dinner at your house tonight. I need some time just with Brannon."

"That's fine," she said. "What time should I bring her home?"

"I'll come get her," I said. "Is nine okay?"

"That's fine," Angel repeated. "You have a nice evening with Brannon."

"Thanks, Angel. I will."

When Brannon walked through the front door that night, he stopped and looked around in surprise. I'd set up a small table in the center of the living room, with a tablecloth and candles and two place settings. A bottle of white zinfandel stood by one plate, already uncorked, alongside a single wineglass. Soft music played from the radio. I smiled at him from across the room.

"Welcome home, handsome."

He grinned and shook his head.

"Where's Jenny?"

"She's having dinner with the Johnsons tonight."

"What's all this?"

"I just felt like having a nice dinner with my husband," I said. "Is that okay?"

"Sure!" He walked toward me and stopped, looking me up and down.

"What are you wearing?"

"I got it at the store today. Do you like it?"

"Uh, yeah, I guess so. Aren't you cold?"

He kissed me briefly. When I leaned into him, he pulled away slightly.

"I'm fine," I said, smiling up at him.

"Dinner is almost ready. Why don't you take a shower and shave?"

He smiled at me uncertainly and headed for the shower.

I stood a minute, steeling my nerves. Tonight, I wanted to celebrate with my husband. I wanted to feel close to him, to be close to him. And by God, that's what I was going to do.

In the kitchen, I pulled the roasted chicken from the oven and moved it to a platter. Then I arranged the potatoes and carrots around it and garnished it with a sprig of parsley. I put the rolls in a basket and carried them to the living room. There wasn't room on the little table for everything, so I set up a TV tray next to the table and put the rolls and the platter of chicken on it. Finally, I took the pats of butter I'd been chilling in the fridge and arranged them on a small plate.

I stood back to admire the effect. It was pretty. Romantic. Definitely not a typical Tuesday night dinner.

I went back into the kitchen and pulled the cheesecake from the freezer. I wished I'd had time to make one myself, but store-bought would be okay. I had a few strawberries and some chocolate syrup to drizzle on top.

I checked my reflection in the mirror and thought briefly about putting on some lipstick. But I couldn't remember the last time I'd worn lipstick, and I wasn't sure where the one stick I had might be. So I dragged the brush through my hair and patted my cheeks. Then I sucked in my belly and looked again. If I stood just so, you could hardly even tell I was pregnant.

"What are you doing?" Brannon was watching me from the hallway, smiling.

"I'm trying to look like something other than a fat, pregnant lady."

"You're not fat," he said, shaking his head and laughing. "But you are pregnant. You are pregnant and beautiful and wonderful."

I walked into his arms and he held me as we swayed slightly to the music, a song I didn't know.

"That looks really good," he said, eyeing the food. "I'm starving."

"Well, let's eat then."

I carved the chicken and put some on each plate, along with potatoes and carrots. Then I handed him a roll and the butter.

"What's the special occasion?" he asked as he dug into the chicken.

"Just a good day," I said, smiling.

"Did you see the doctor?"

"I did."

"And everything is good?"

"Everything is perfect."

He raised his eyebrows at me and forked a potato.

"Okay," he said, grinning at me. "I give. What's up?"

I smiled and reached under the table to pull out the tiny booties. I set them on the table beside his plate.

"We're having a girl!"

He stared at the booties, and for just an instant I saw what looked like disappointment cross his face.

"Brannon?"

He looked up at me and smiled.

"A girl? That's great, babe! That's just . . . great."

"You don't sound very sure of yourself." I felt a lump growing in my throat.

"No, seriously, Emma. That's great."

"Did you want a boy?"

He sat a moment and took my hand. "It might have been nice to have another guy in the house," he said. "But a daughter is great. Really."

I sighed just a little. I'd hoped he would be as excited as I was.

"So . . ." he said softly. "You had an ultrasound today?"

I nodded.

"Why didn't you tell me?"

"I wanted to surprise you."

He looked at me in silence.

"I didn't think you'd want to miss work," I added.

Still he said nothing, just took another bite of chicken and began chewing.

"Brannon? Are you mad?"

"Not mad," he said quietly. "Disappointed, I guess."

"I'm sorry. I guess I should have had you come with me."

"It's okay."

Clearly, it wasn't okay. He was unhappy. But there didn't seem to be anything I could do about it.

"Anyway, we're having a girl. I brought home a picture of the ultrasound."

I handed him the picture and he stared at it. Then he smiled at it.

"She's a beauty, isn't she?"

"I think so," I said, relieved. "And I think Jenny is going to be so excited to have a little sister."

He nodded and took another bite.

"The chicken is good," he said.

We ate without talking for a while. I felt hot and uncomfortable. The music that had been so beautiful before was simply annoying now.

"So," I said finally, unable to bear the silence. "How was your day?"

"Okay," he said. "Just a day."

He finished his chicken, buttered another roll, and ate, never even looking up at me.

"Brannon, I'm sorry. I didn't mean to upset you."

"It's all good, babe."

He rose and picked up his plate.

"Are you finished?" he asked, reaching for my plate.

He carried the dishes into the kitchen and I followed him.

"We've got dessert," I said, pointing to the cheesecake thawing on the counter. "I've got strawberries and chocolate to go on top."

He turned and tilted his head, smiling.

"That's Jenny's favorite," he said. "I should go get her and she can have some with us."

"Oh." I couldn't think of any reason to object, or at least any reason he might listen to. "Okay."

He scooped his car keys from the counter and walked to the back door, then turned.

"You should probably change clothes before we get back."

I nodded and he was gone. After he left, I lay on our bed and cried until my stomach ached, not sure what had gone wrong, what I had done to upset him. And then, lying on my back, I felt a tiny flutter, almost like a small moth was flying around in my stomach. I put my hand on my belly and lay very still. Another flutter. The baby was moving. Our tiny daughter was moving inside of me.

"Don't worry, baby," I crooned. "Mama's here. Mama will take care of you always."

Then I rose, hung my beautiful new nightgown in the closet, and pulled on a pair of sweats.

By the time Brannon returned with Jenny, I'd cut the cheesecake into slices and topped each with a strawberry and a drizzle of chocolate.

Jenny burst through the door and flew at me, throwing her arms around my expanding waist.

"I can't believe we're gonna have a girl! I knew it! I knew it was a girl! Aren't you happy, Emma?"

And I was. Standing in my kitchen with Jenny's arms around me and my baby safe in my womb, I was happy for the first time since Brannon had come home that night.

I looked over her head to see him standing in the doorway, watching us. He winked and smiled at me, then mouthed, "I love you."

I smiled back at him, kissed Jenny's forehead, and we sat down at the kitchen table to eat dessert.

∞ 41 ∞

Jenny

"You should tell Emma."
Lashaundra's eyes were wide and worried.

"I don't know," I said. "I can't. I mean, she's pregnant and everything. I don't want to worry her."

We sat on Lashaundra's bed, the driver's licenses from the check box spread out like a fan on the blanket between us. Emma had some errands to run, she'd said. I think she was out buying baby clothes, baby girl clothes. So I had come home with Lashaundra after school again. Down the hall, I could hear cartoons blaring from the television in the living room. Malcolm loved *Curious George,* and he loved to watch it with the sound up loud.

I took a drink of my soda. Lashaundra just kept staring at me.

"Seriously, Jenny, you *have* to tell Emma. I mean, what if your dad . . ."

Her words trailed off, but her eyes never left my face.

"My dad loves Emma," I said. "He would *never* hurt her. Honest, Lashaundra, my dad would never hurt *anyone.*"

"Then why does he have Jackie's driver's license in a box?" she asked. "Why does he have all of these?" She nodded toward the plastic squares on her bed. "Where did he get them?"

I shook my head. I didn't have any answers for her.

"I don't know," I said finally. "But I'm sure there's a reason why he has them."

"Like what?"

"Like . . . I don't know," I said. "Maybe they were expired or something. Maybe he was just keeping them in case . . ."

I shrugged. In case of *what?* Even I knew that wasn't an answer. I stood up and shook my head again hard.

Lashaundra stood and took my hands in hers, holding them tightly.

"Look, Jenny. You have to tell Emma, you know you do," she said again. "Or we can tell my mom and dad."

"No! You can't tell your parents. Promise, Lashaundra! Promise me you won't tell anyone."

She said nothing for a minute, just looking at me. Then she sat back down on the bed and picked up her laptop.

"What are you doing?" I asked.

"Googling Jackie," she said. "Maybe we can find out where she is or . . . or something."

She held Jackie's driver's license in one hand and typed with the other.

Jackie Marlin, Birmingham, Alabama.

We waited while a list loaded, but none of the items was about the Jackie I knew.

I drew a deep breath. I wasn't sure if I was relieved or disappointed.

Lashaundra just picked up another driver's license and began typing again.

Cara Montgomery, Knoxville, Tennessee.

"Look!" Lashaundra pointed to an entry on the screen that read, *Missing adults in Tennessee.*

She clicked on the link and began scrolling through the profiles there.

"That's her!"

I recognized her as soon as I saw her.

I stared at the picture of Cara, smiling brightly into the camera, wearing a blue sundress and long, dangly silver earrings. I remembered those earrings.

"Missing since 2010," Lashaundra read.

"That's when she lived with us," I said softly.

My stomach lurched, just looking at her picture. Cara had been so nice to me, and she was a really good cook. She made the best fettuccine Alfredo I'd ever had. And she always made garlic bread to go with it.

Lashaundra stared at me hard for a minute. Then she began typing again.

Briana Simpson, Erie, Pennsylvania.

Several items came up this time. At the top was a newspaper article from the *Erie Times-News.* She clicked on the link and we both stared at the screen.

LOCAL WOMAN'S REMAINS IDENTIFIED

ERIE, PA—Police in Erie confirmed yesterday that the unidentified remains of a woman found near Dallas, Texas, on February 7 are those of a missing local woman, Briana Simpson.

The remains found in Cedar Hill State Park, about 10 miles southwest of Dallas, were sent to the University of North Texas Center for Human Identification for DNA analysis.

An investigation into Simpson's death is ongoing.

The Erie woman had been missing since December 2007. Her mother, Linda Simpson, became a regular on local news programs in the years after her daughter's disappearance. She made several pleas in the media for information on Briana's whereabouts.

Nia Michaels, a spokesperson for the Simpson family, told reporters today, "We are just heartsick about Briana's death. We've always held out hope that someday she would come home to us."

Friends held a candlelight vigil outside the Simpson home last night, many holding signs with Briana's picture and the words, "We will not forget you!"

"It's just so terrible," said Candace Reynolds, a high school friend of Briana's. "She was a wonderful person. I can't believe she's really gone."

I stared at the photo onscreen of a smiling, young blond woman. I hadn't seen Briana since I was five years old, but I remembered her now. She'd had a guitar and a beautiful voice, and she sang me to sleep at night in the trailer when Daddy was at work.

"Jenny?"

Lashaundra was staring at me now, her eyes round.

"Are you okay?"

I wasn't okay. I was shaking like a leaf in a thunderstorm and feeling like I might throw up.

I lay back on the bed and closed my eyes tight, remembering Jackie and Cara and Briana and Ami and Trish.

"What about Trish?" I said, sitting up and shaking my head. "Look for her."

Trish Alexander, Topeka, Kansas, Lashaundra typed.

Nothing came up on the screen. I sighed with relief.

"I guess no one is looking for her," Lashaundra whispered.

"I have to go!"

I stood and started grabbing the driver's licenses from the bed, shoving them into my backpack.

"Hey, wait!" Lashaundra said. "Don't you want to look up the others?"

"No. I just want to go home."

"Jenny, wait. You *have* to tell Emma now. You know that, right?"

"I'll see you tomorrow." I pulled my jacket on and ran from the room.

"It everything okay?" Mrs. Johnson called from the kitchen as I ran through the living room.

"I have to go home," I yelled.

I slammed the door behind me and ran through the parking lot of the apartment complex.

Don't think! Don't think! Don't think!

I repeated it to myself with every step pounding onto the sidewalk.

By the time I got home, I was out of breath and sweating, but I felt really cold.

Emma wasn't home and the front door was locked, so I went around to the back of the house and pulled the spare key from under the doormat. I unlocked the door, stepped inside, and then locked the door again behind me.

I stood in the kitchen for a long time, just trying to feel my feet underneath me. Then I sank into a chair, staring blankly at the yellow painted walls, the ceramic canisters on the counter, the little chalkboard stuck on the refrigerator. Emma kept a running grocery list on it. Just then, it read: *bread, tomatoes, toothpaste, onion powder, laundry soap, basil.*

There. That was my world. That was normal. That was real.

Emma's grocery list on the fridge in our kitchen, where we all lived together, that's what was real. Me and Daddy and Emma were a real family, just like I'd always wanted. We were a real family and we lived in a real house and I went to a real school, just like I'd always dreamed about. Daddy loved Emma and he loved me. And Emma loved me. Emma was having a baby, a baby girl. I would be a big sister soon. *That's* what was real.

I breathed in and out deeply, again and again, just staring at the grocery list.

"This is real," I said out loud. "This is our house, our kitchen. Emma and Daddy and me . . . that's what's real."

I closed my eyes and rested my head in my hands on the table. It would be okay. Everything was fine.

Then Briana's face floated before my closed eyes. And Cara's. And Jackie's. And Ami's. And Trish's.

They had been real, too. Each of them had been part of my family, at least for a while. And now . . . where were they?

Briana was dead.

That was real.

I opened my eyes and stared hard at the refrigerator, but not even Emma's grocery list could erase the article Lashaundra had found online.

Briana was dead. Cara was missing. And Jackie and Trish and Ami and . . . what was the other woman's name? What had happened to them?

I reached into my backpack and pulled out the driver's licenses, looking at one after another.

Laura—that was her name, the one I couldn't remember. Laura Parker.

I stared at the photo on the driver's license, but no memories came to me. The date on the license was 2005. I was just two then, and my mother was still alive.

My mother . . . a wave of nausea swept over me, and I barely made it into the bathroom before I threw up in the toilet.

My mother died when I was three.

That's what Daddy had told me, anyway. She died of the flu. We lived in Greenfield, Indiana, in an apartment with a field out back where she painted beautiful pictures of a tree.

Except . . . except the letter from her mother, from Imogene Wright in Indianapolis, Indiana, had been addressed to Mrs. Hailey Bohner on Pippin Road in Cincinnati.

Daddy had never said anything about us living in Cincinnati.

I stood and walked unsteadily back into the kitchen. I stared hard at the driver's licenses on the table, each of them a mute scream inside my head. I grabbed a knife and tape, dragged a chair into the hallway and stood on it, pulled the cord that released the attic door, and climbed the ladder.

I opened the big box first and dug through Daddy's clothes to pull out the smaller box with the lockets and letters. I resealed the box and turned to the one I'd opened first, the one I'd found the photo album in. I cut the tape and pulled out the folder with the letters from the adoption agency. I looked through some other folders, but didn't see anything interesting. So I resealed that box, too.

I opened box after box, but they were filled with clothes and other things, nothing I was interested in. I sealed each one after I'd opened it. When I had looked through all the boxes, I took the things I'd pulled out—the box with the lockets and the adoption file—and I climbed back down the ladder. I put the knife and tape away, closed the door to the attic, and dragged the chair back into the kitchen. Then I sat down to wait for Emma.

I had no idea what I would say to her, but I knew I had to show her what I'd found. Maybe she would have some explanation for it all. Maybe Daddy had told her all about the adoption stuff and the driver's licenses. Maybe . . . but probably not.

When I heard Emma's key in the door, I stood and then sat back down immediately. My legs were shaking so hard they wouldn't even hold me up.

"Hey!" she said. "What are you doing here? I thought you were at Lashaundra's."

"I came home," I said.

"Well, you've got to see what I bought!"

She opened a bag and began pulling baby clothes out, little ruffled dresses and a bonnet and some sleepers.

"Aren't they adorable? I know I probably spent too much, but I . . ."

She stopped and stared at me.

"Are you all right? You look like you've seen a ghost."

I took a deep breath and swallowed hard.

"I've been in the attic," I said. "And I found some things you should see."

"Jenny! You promised me you wouldn't go up there again. Your dad will be furious!"

"Emma, wait. Just look at this."

I opened the small box and pulled out the lockets, all tangled together.

"What are those?"

She sat down at the table and took them from me. I watched as her eyes widened and her face grew pale as she read the inscriptions. When she finally looked up at me, I saw tears in her eyes.

"He got the same locket for all of these women? The same one he got me?"

I nodded.

"There's more."

I pointed to the driver's licenses laid out on the table.

Emma's hand was shaking when she picked them up. Her face paled even more.

I handed her the envelope with the letters then. She didn't say anything, just took them and began reading.

"Oh my God," she whispered. "Oh my God."

Tears dripped onto the letter my mother had started to my grandmother.

"Lashaundra and I Googled those women," I said, fighting back my own tears. "Cara is listed as a missing person. And . . . and Briana is dead. They found her body in Texas. That's where we were when she lived with us."

Emma stared at me, her mouth open. She began crying harder, dropping her head into her hands. Her shoulders shook and a low moan rose.

I rose and walked around the table, and draped my arms around her.

"What should we do?" I asked.

She raised her head and looked at me.

"We have to get out of here," she said, her voice shaking. "We have to get out of here now, before your dad gets home."

She rose and steadied herself against the table.

"It's four fifteen," she said, looking at the clock. "Brannon won't be home for a couple hours. We'll pack some clothes and go . . . somewhere. Oh God, Jenny. Oh my God, where will we go?"

"We could go to the Johnsons'," I said.

"No." She shook her head. "He'd find us there. We have to go someplace he can't find us, until . . . until we figure out what to do."

She wrapped her arms around me and hugged me tight.

"You go pack a suitcase," she said. "Bring some clothes and your laptop, and whatever else you need."

I stood staring at her stupidly.

"Hurry!" she yelled. "Do it now!"

I ran to my room and pulled my suitcase from the closet. I shoved clothes into it, then my toothbrush and toothpaste. I pulled the photo album from the drawer and put it in the suitcase. Finally, I stuffed Bugsy Bear in it and closed it.

I dragged the suitcase into the kitchen. Emma was on the phone.

"Yes," I heard her say. "And we have to go now, before he gets home."

Who was she talking to?

"Okay, thanks. We'll be there in a few minutes."

She hung up and turned to me.

"Do you have everything you need?"

I nodded.

"Good girl," she said. "Give me five minutes to pack my stuff."

She disappeared into her bedroom, the one she shared with Daddy.

I sat down at the table and stared at the grocery list on the refrigerator. This house, this family, my school . . . all of them were gone now.

Emma reappeared with her duffel bag and backpack.

She laid a note on the kitchen table. It read:

> *Brannon,*
> *I just got a phone call from my sister, Clarissa. She ran away from her husband in Arizona. She's in Atlanta and I'm driving down there to get her. I'm taking Jenny with me. We'll be back tomorrow or the day after.*
> *I'm sorry I didn't get to tell you before we left. Don't worry about us. I'll call you later tonight.*
> *I love you,*
> *Emma*

"Come on," she said. "Let's go."

We carried our things to the car, got in, and Emma pulled out of the driveway.

"Where are we going?" I asked.

"First, to Shirley Rigby's."

I stared at her.

"Why are we going there?"

"Shirley left her husband once, and she went to a place not too far away, a convent where the nuns live. They let her stay and were very kind to her. She's calling them to ask if we can stay there, and I have to get the directions from her."

A convent? We were going to a convent to stay with nuns?

"It will be all right," she said, turning to look at me. "We'll be all right. Don't worry, Jenny, you're safe with me."

When we got to the Rigbys' house, Mrs. Rigby was waiting on the front porch. She ran across the lawn and hugged Emma tight when she got out of the car.

"I talked with Sister Frances, and they're expecting you," she said. "Here's the map; I've marked the route for you."

"Thank you, Shirley. You're a good friend."

"You call me when you get there and let me know you're okay."

"We will."

Emma turned to get back into the car and Mrs. Rigby caught her by the arm.

"Wait," she said, reaching into the pocket of her sweater. "Take this."

She shoved a handful of cash into Emma's hand.

"Oh, Shirley, I can't take that."

"You take it! You take it and go now, and be safe."

Emma hugged her again and got back into the car. She was crying now, and so was Mrs. Rigby.

"God bless you!" Mrs. Rigby called as we pulled away from the curb. "Be safe!"

42

Emma

I handed Jenny the map Shirley had marked for me.

"Can you read a map?" I asked.

"Yes," she said. "Daddy says I'm the world's best navigator."

I glanced over at her and put my hand on her knee. She was staring straight ahead. Tears ran down her cheeks.

"We'll be okay," I said. "We'll figure it out. Maybe there's an explanation for everything."

She said nothing.

"Okay, so where am I going?"

She looked down at the map.

"We go north on U.S. 68," she said.

I drove fast, trying hard to just concentrate on the road. My mind was like a twister roaring in all directions.

Brannon, my Brannon . . . how could I have been so wrong about him? How could I have been so wrong about everything? I'd never asked him about the other women in his life. And I had believed what he'd told me about Jackie. And about Hailey. My God, had he killed Jenny's mother?

"Emma, you're going too fast." Jenny gripped the armrest, her knuckles white.

"Sorry," I said, slowing to the speed limit.

"It shouldn't take us very long to get there," she said, staring at the map.

"Shirley said it's about half an hour."

"Do you think that's far enough away? Maybe we should go farther."

I shook my head. I wasn't sure I could drive even thirty minutes.

"Your dad has never even heard of this place," I said. "He won't know we're there."

"What if he talks to Mrs. Rigby?"

I shook my head again.

"He doesn't know Shirley and I are friends. She's the only person who knows where we're going. If he asks Resa or Angel, they can honestly say they don't know where we are."

The road was narrow and twisted through the hills. It would have been a beautiful drive on any other day. Just now, it was like a nightmare.

After what felt like days, I slowed the car to pull into the grounds of the convent.

"Wow," Jenny said softly. "It looks like an old castle."

"Shirley said it used to be a school where the nuns learned how to be nuns. Now it's mostly old women."

I parked the car in the small lot beside the building and we got out.

"Where do we go?" Jenny asked.

"Um . . . well, there's a door. Let's see if it's unlocked."

The heavy door creaked open and we climbed steep wooden stairs to a landing. We stepped into a large, comfortable-looking kitchen. It was empty, so we walked through another door that opened onto a long, wide hallway. Wooden floors gleamed in the sunlight that streamed through the window at the end of the hall. Several doors lined the hallway, all of them open.

"Hello?" I called. "Is anyone here?"

We heard footsteps behind us, and I swung about and stepped in front of Jenny, my arms tense, my hands in fists.

A tiny woman stood in the kitchen doorway. She wasn't even as tall as Jenny, and probably didn't weigh more than ninety pounds.

"Are you Emma?" she asked.

"Yes." I felt my arms relax.

"I'm Sister Frances," she said, smiling. "And you must be Jenny?"

I turned and Jenny was nodding cautiously, still standing behind me as though I could shield her from whatever came our way.

Sister Frances walked forward and extended her hand. I shook it.

"Welcome to Loretto," she said. "You'll be safe here. I've put you in a room on the third floor. There's a group staying there on retreat, so you'll need to be quiet when you're up there."

"Yes, ma'am," Jenny whispered.

"You don't need to call me ma'am," the nun said, laughing. "I'm just Frances."

She turned and walked toward the stairway.

"This floor is where the sisters live," she said. "This is our kitchen."

She waved her hand around the room.

"There's a kitchen upstairs, too. Come on, I'll show you where your room is."

We followed her up another long flight of steep steps. I was nearly winded by the time we reached the top, but the little nun seemed unaffected.

"This is the kitchen, and there are the bathrooms," she said, pointing. "There's coffee if you want to make some."

We followed her down another long hallway until she stopped in front of an open door.

"This is your room."

I stared at the room. It was beautiful, with high ceilings painted white and huge windows along one wall, framed in white shutters. Four twin beds lined the inside wall, each covered with a quilt. A padded rocking chair sat facing one of the windows.

"Wow," Jenny said. "It's so big."

"It's beautiful, Sister Frances," I said. "Thank you."

"You're most welcome," she said. "There's an elevator back here, in case you want to use it to bring your things up. It's not very big and it's not very fast, but it works."

I nodded, staring at where she pointed, not seeing anything except the pictures on the driver's licenses in Jenny's backpack.

"They are serving dinner in an hour, if you're hungry. And breakfast is at seven," Sister Frances said. "They'll ring a bell. Come downstairs to the second floor when it rings, and I'll take you to the dining room. It's kind of hard to find if you don't know where you're going."

"Thank you," I said again.

"Well, I'll let you get settled in. If you need anything, you'll find one of us on the second floor."

She turned and walked briskly down the hall toward the stairs. Jenny and I both just stood, watching her.

"She's a nun?" Jenny whispered when Sister Frances had gone. "She doesn't look like a nun. I thought they wore black robes and stuff."

"They used to," I said. "I guess they don't have to anymore."

We went back to our room and Jenny flopped down on one of the beds.

"It's really pretty," she said, staring around the room.

"We should get our stuff."

We walked down the stairs and outside to the car to collect our things. Then we hauled all of our stuff back up those long, steep stairs.

"Man," I said when we finally reached the top. "We'd be in great shape if we had to climb these every day."

Jenny said nothing. I looked back at her, but she didn't meet my eyes. She just stared at the floor as she trudged along behind me. When we got back to our room, I pulled the door closed and wrapped my arms around her.

"It's going to be okay," I said, kissing her head.

"How?" She pulled back and looked at me. "How can it ever be okay again?"

She threw herself onto a bed and began crying then, great, gulping sobs. I sat on the edge of the bed and rubbed her back.

"Shhh," I whispered. "You're okay, you're all right."

She cried for a long time while I sat there, rubbing her back and wondering what we would do next.

I glanced at a clock on the bedside table. It was past five. Brannon would be home in an hour. He'd be so sad to find us gone. Or maybe he'd just be angry. I shuddered at the thought of his anger. I'd always been stunned by how quickly he got mad, and how mad he got. But I never really thought he would hurt me or anyone else.

My phone rang in my purse, startling both of us. I looked down to see who was calling—Resa. I let the phone ring until it stopped, staring at it in my hand. After a minute, it chirped to tell me I had a voice message.

"Hey, honey. It's Resa, just calling to see how you're doing. You feeling okay? Do you want to have lunch tomorrow, someplace that's *not* Happy Days? We could get Chinese and then go to the thrift stores. Call me. 'Bye."

Tears filled my eyes. I would miss Resa. She was always so much fun to be with. Would I ever see her again, her and Harlan and the diner?

"You should turn your phone off." Jenny had rolled onto her back and was rubbing her eyes. "Turn it off in case Daddy calls."

"Smart girl," I said, turning off the phone.

Brannon would be frantic when he couldn't reach me. What would he have for dinner? Leftover chicken and potatoes? God, was it just last night that I'd made a special dinner for the two of us? Just this afternoon that I'd been so happy, buying baby clothes and making all kinds of plans? It felt like years ago, like a whole lifetime ago. It was hard to imagine it was still the same day, that Brannon didn't even know yet that we were gone.

"You told Mrs. Rigby you'd call her," Jenny said.

I nodded.

"You probably shouldn't use your phone, though."

I nodded again.

"I'll go downstairs and see if I can find a phone."

I rose and stretched, my hands cupping my lower back.

"Can I come with you?" Jenny stood, too. "I don't want to stay up here alone."

"Sure." I held out my hand to her, and she took it. "It's pretty quiet up here, isn't it?"

We walked downstairs to the second floor and stood in the hallway. The entire floor looked empty. Then we heard voices and laughter at the other end of the hall.

"Come on," I said, pulling Jenny by the hand.

We walked into the kitchen to find several women in chairs around the table, a pot of soup on the table before them. It smelled good.

"Excuse me," I said. "We were wondering if there's a phone we could use?"

"You can use mine." Sister Frances rose and handed me her cell phone.

"Thank you."

We walked back out into the hallway and I dialed Shirley's number. She answered on the first ring.

"Hi, Shirley, it's Emma."

"Thank goodness," she said. "Did you-all get there okay?"

"Yes, we're here and just settling in. Jenny can read a map like a pro."

"Can I do anything?" she asked.

"You've done enough," I said. "Seriously, thank you, Shirley. I don't know what we'd have done without you."

"Well, you just stay there and be safe. I'll come up tomorrow or the next day. Lucy can stay with Jasper. Is there anything you need? Anything I can bring?"

"I think we're good. But I'll be glad to see you."

"Okay, well, you take care and call me if you need anything."

"Thanks, Shirley. I'll see you soon."

"She's coming here?" Jenny asked when I hung up.

I nodded.

"But what if Daddy follows her?"

I tried to smile. "He won't, honey. He doesn't even know Shirley and I are friends."

"Does Jasper know we're here?" Her eyes widened. "Because he might tell someone if he does."

"I don't think Jasper would tell anyone," I said. "He knows what it's like to be afraid. Besides, I'm sure he doesn't know. Shirley wouldn't tell him."

We walked back into the kitchen and I handed the phone back to Sister Frances.

"Thank you," I said.

"You're welcome." She smiled at me. "Are you-all hungry? We've got some good soup tonight, ham and bean. And Genevieve made bread."

She pointed to a short, round woman with white hair and dark eyes, who nodded and smiled.

"Are you hungry?" I asked Jenny.

"Kind of." She was eyeing the soup.

"Well, sit down then." Sister Frances pulled another chair up to the table and Jenny sat. I dragged another chair over and sat beside her.

She ladled soup into bowls and set them before us. Another woman sliced bread and handed a piece to Jenny.

"There's butter," she said, pointing. "Or strawberry jam, if you want it."

"Thank you," Jenny said softly.

I smiled at the women around the table. "Thank you all so much."

Then I braced myself for a barrage of questions. Thankfully, no one asked us anything. They simply smiled at us, and then resumed the conversation they'd been having before we arrived.

"Anyway, I told Mary Margaret it was time to get the oil changed, and she said she would take care of it."

The nun across from me shook her head and frowned.

"But of course, she didn't. And now it's going to cost a fortune to get it fixed."

"Well, she's got a lot on her plate," another woman said, her voice soothing. "I'm sure she meant to get it done."

The first woman sighed heavily.

"She always means to get things done," she said. "But she never does."

I took a bite of bread and a spoonful of soup. It was delicious. I was surprised at how hungry I was.

Beside me Jenny ate in silence, her eyes fixed firmly on the bowl in front of her.

The nuns talked away about people and places we didn't know, and I was grateful for their presence and for the way they just accepted us at the table, no questions asked.

"Excuse me, Sister Frances?"

A woman stood in the doorway. She wore sweatpants and a T-shirt, and had short, spiky blond hair. She didn't look much older than me.

"Yes, dear?" Sister Frances smiled at her.

"I just saw Sister Agnes walking down the driveway toward the road. I thought someone should know?"

"Oh, dear." Sister Frances rose quickly. Two other women stood, too. They all ran toward the stairs.

"Thank you, Lorelei," the nun sitting next to me said.

"I was going to go after her myself, but she doesn't really know me," the blond woman said.

"That's all right," the nun said. "Frances and Anne will bring her back."

Jenny stared at them, obviously confused.

"Sister Agnes gets confused," the nun named Genevieve explained, smiling at Jenny. "Sometimes she wanders, and then she can't remember how to get back home."

"Hi," the blond woman said, extending her hand to me. "I'm Lorelei."

I shook her hand. "I'm Emma, and this is Jenny."

"Is this your first time here?"

I nodded.

"Are you staying on the third floor?"

I nodded again.

"Well, if you need help finding the dining room, just let me know. It's like a rat's maze trying to find it."

"Thank you."

"If you want a glass of wine later, come on down to the kitchen. We've got plenty to spare."

"Oh, no, thank you," I mumbled. "I can't drink alcohol. I'm pregnant."

"Well, come and have tea then," she said, grinning at me.

"Maybe," I said.

"Okay, see you later."

She turned and sprinted toward the stairs, taking them two at a time.

"Lorelei is here on retreat, too," the nun next to me said. "She's a very talented musician. You should have her sing for you. She has a marvelous voice."

The sisters began talking among themselves again. Jenny and I finished our soup and bread, and rose.

"Thank you all so much," I said. "It was delicious."

"You're very welcome," one of them said. They all smiled at us.

"Well, good night."

We walked back down the hallway and up the stairs to our room. It was just starting to get dark outside.

Jenny sat down on a bed and stared at the floor. She said nothing for a long time, then rose and pulled her laptop from her backpack. She turned it on and waited, finally looking up in frustration.

"We don't have Internet," she said.

"It's okay," I said. "You can go one night without the Internet."

She sighed. "I was going to show you the article about Briana. And maybe Google Ami and see if there's anything about her."

I put my hand on her shoulder.

"We'll find someplace with Internet access tomorrow. It can wait until then."

Jenny turned the computer off and shoved it back into her backpack.

"Wait," she said. "You didn't see this yet."

She pulled out a manila folder and held it out to me.

I took a deep breath before I opened the folder. I didn't think I could take much more.

I scanned the papers inside.

"Your dad had a sister?" I looked up at Jenny. "Did you know that?"

She shook her head.

"Well, apparently he loved her, because he named you after her."

She shrugged.

I put the papers back into the folder and began pacing the room.

"Okay, let's see. We know he had a sister, and we know her name. Maybe we should try to find her. Maybe she can tell us something about his childhood, something that might explain . . ." I paused and swallowed hard.

"How would we find her?"

"We've got the address for the adoption service. We could drive up to Indianapolis and just go there and ask questions."

"Emma?" Jenny was watching me, her eyes wide. "We have another address."

She pulled out the letter from Hailey's mother.

"Do you think she still lives in Indianapolis?"

"Maybe," I said. "There's only one way to find out."

"So we're going to Indianapolis?"

"I guess so."

"Are we going tomorrow?"

"I don't think so," I said. "I think the first thing we need to do is find someplace with Internet access and do some research. Besides"—I dropped onto a bed—"I'm exhausted. I think I need a day to just regroup."

"There's a lake out front." Jenny stood staring out the window at the gathering dusk. "We could take a walk in the morning."

"That sounds good."

"Emma?"

"Yeah?"

"I'm sorry."

"Oh, Jenny, you don't have anything to be sorry for."

"But if I hadn't gone up in the attic, then we wouldn't know about . . . everything. And we could still be at home and a family."

She dropped beside me on the little bed and I scooted to one side to make room for her.

"I know it's hard," I said, putting my arm around her. "But it's better to know."

"I guess so."

We lay there a long time. At last, Jenny fell into a fitful sleep, and I felt my eyes beginning to droop. So I rose carefully, covered her with a blanket, and climbed into another bed.

As I let myself drift to sleep, I prayed for the hundredth time that day: *Dear God, please take care of us. Please help us do what we need to do. And please protect us from . . . from anything bad.*

❦ 43 ❦

Jenny

I squeezed my eyes shut against the sunlight. I was so tired I just wanted to sleep a few more minutes. I must have forgotten to close the curtains the night before.

Then I heard it, someone else breathing in my room.

I opened my eyes and sat up, staring around me at the huge, unfamiliar room. Where was I?

The clock beside the bed said it was a quarter till seven.

I turned toward the breathing sound and saw Emma asleep in the bed next to mine. She was still wearing her clothes. I looked down. So was I.

Images of the day before came flooding back—sitting on the bed in Lashaundra's room, cutting open the boxes in the attic, showing Emma the lockets and the driver's licenses. I wasn't at home, in my own room. I was in a room on the third floor of a convent. Emma and I were hiding from Daddy.

I sat up and closed my eyes. When I opened them, I would be at home. The whole thing would just be a nightmare. *Please, God, let it be a nightmare.*

But of course, it wasn't just a nightmare. It was real. I had ruined everything.

I stared at Emma while she slept. I felt tears sting my eyes.

Emma was the closest thing to a mother I'd ever remembered having. She was pregnant with my little sister. I loved her. I had done what I had to do to protect her.

I had to pee.

I rose quietly and tiptoed to the door, pulling it open, praying it wouldn't squeak. Then I stepped into the hallway and padded barefoot toward the bathroom and relief.

I was washing my hands when the woman with the short blond hair walked in.

"Good morning!" she said, smiling.

"Hey," I mumbled.

"I hope you slept well?"

"Yeah, I slept okay."

"Did we keep you up last night?"

"Um, no. We went to bed early."

"Oh, good," she said, splashing water on her face. "We got a little tipsy and I was worried we were too loud."

"It's all good." I walked toward the door.

"Is your mom up?"

I stopped. My mom? She meant Emma, of course.

"She was still asleep when I got up."

"Well, breakfast is at seven," she said. "So if you guys want to eat, she should get up."

"Okay, thanks."

I walked back to our bedroom wondering if I should wake Emma or not. She was pregnant. She needed to eat. But she needed to sleep, too. And as long as she was asleep, she didn't have to remember why we were here.

"Good morning," she said when I opened the door.

"Hey," I said.

"Did you sleep okay?"

"Yeah. Did you?"

"Actually, yeah. I slept well. I'm kind of surprised I did. I was just so tired."

She was sitting up in bed, stretching.

"The lady we saw last night, the one with the blond hair who's not a nun, she said breakfast is ready at seven."

Emma looked at the clock. "Well, we're just in time then. Wait for me, okay? I have to go to the bathroom."

After she left, I made up the bed I'd slept in. Then I made the bed she'd slept in, too. When she got back, we both changed our clothes. Then we walked out into the hall, and there was the blond woman again.

"Good morning!" she chirped. "Are you-all going to breakfast?"

"I guess so," Emma said.

"Good. We can go together."

She led the way down the stairs, talking the whole time about Loretto, its history, the nuns. She talked fast and she walked fast. Emma and I had to hurry to keep up.

"I've been coming for almost twelve years," she said as we reached the first floor. "Honestly, I don't know what I'd do without this place. It's my spiritual home, and I'm not even Catholic. I mean, when my marriage ended, I was here more than I was home. And the sisters just let me be however I needed to be."

"When did your marriage end?" Emma asked. We were walking down yet another long hallway.

"Five years ago," the woman said. "I'm Lorelei, by the way. I don't remember if I told you that last night."

"I'm Emma, and this is Jenny."

"Are you-all from around here?"

Emma looked at me and I looked back at her.

"No," she said. "We're just passing through."

"So how did you hear about it?"

"Um . . . a friend of mine stayed here once. It was a long time ago."

Lorelei opened a door into a large, empty room. We followed her to another door on the other side. I was glad we weren't trying to find our way around on our own.

"So, when are you due?" she asked, glancing at Emma's stomach.

"September," Emma said.

"That's so exciting. I always wanted a baby but . . . well, maybe next time, right?"

She pushed open yet another door to another hallway. It really was like a maze.

"We were trying to get pregnant," she continued. "But it didn't happen. And then . . . well, then he decided to try with someone else."

"I'm sorry," Emma said softly.

"Oh, well." Lorelei just kept walking. "I'm glad I found out before I got pregnant, anyway."

I looked at Emma and wondered what she must be thinking.

"Here we are." Lorelei opened yet another door and we were standing in a huge dining room filled with women, mostly old women. Some of them even wore the hats I thought all nuns were supposed to wear.

"There's cereal and juice," she said, "and sometimes boiled eggs. The biggest meal is at lunch. Don't miss that. Then for dinner, it's usually soup and leftovers from lunch. It's not exactly gourmet cuisine, but hey, it's here and it's ready and you don't have to cook it."

We went through the line cafeteria-style. I got some Cheerios and a carton of milk and a roll. Emma filled a plate with fruit, a boiled egg, and a biscuit. Then we followed Lorelei to a table and sat down. She never stopped talking the entire time.

"This is Sarah," she said, nodding to another woman at the table. "She's from Louisville. And Pat's from Columbus." She nodded to another woman.

"This is Emma and Jenny," she said, pointing to us now.

"Hello," each of them said, smiling at us.

Lorelei chattered nonstop while we ate. When she paused to take a breath, Emma asked, "Is there any place close by where we can get Internet access?"

"Sure," Lorelei said. "There's a room just off of this one where you can get it. I'll show you after breakfast."

I ate my cereal and tried hard to block out the chatter around me. I wondered what Daddy was doing right now. Was he eating breakfast, too? Was he worrying about where we were? Had he discovered that things were missing from his boxes in the attic?

Finally, Emma stood up. "Where should we take our trays?" she asked.

"I'll show you." Lorelei rose and picked up her tray, then led us to the back of the room.

"Now, let me show you the Internet room."

She led us to a smaller room that looked like it had been a kitchen once.

"You can get on the Internet in here. They keep saying they're going to get it at the main house, but that hasn't happened yet. And you know what? I'm kind of glad. It's nice to be completely disconnected from the world, you know?"

She led us back to the building where our room was and sprinted up the stairs ahead of us.

Emma looked at me, winked, and smiled as we climbed the stairs.

"So, do you want me to take you back to the Internet room? Or do you think you can find it on your own?"

"I think we'll be fine," Emma said. "But thank you for showing us the way."

"No problem."

Lorelei stood a moment, just smiling at us.

"I know it's confusing at first, but you'll get the hang of it," she said. "This really is the best place in the world."

Then she turned and walked quickly down the hall to her room.

"She talks a lot," I said to Emma once we were inside our own room.

"Yes, she does."

We sat down on our beds for a minute, just relishing the quiet. Then Emma rose.

"So," she said. "Get your laptop and let's go see what we can see."

We got lost only once on our way back toward the dining room, ending up in a large chapel with wooden pews. But a nice older lady pointed us in the right direction, and we finally found the little room where Lorelei had said we could get on the Internet.

Two other women were already there, each in front of a laptop. Both of them smiled when we entered.

"Here," I said, sitting at an empty table.

I turned the computer on and waited, then connected it and us to the Internet.

"Can I check my e-mail first?"

Emma nodded.

There was only one message, and it was from Lashaundra.

Hey, where are you? it read. *Your dad was here last night asking if we knew where you and Emma were. He was really mad. And, I hope you won't be too mad at me, but after he left I told Mama and Daddy about the driver's licenses and what we found online. They kind of freaked out, and I know they are worried about you. So e-mail me and let me know you're okay.*

I showed the e-mail to Emma. Her brow furrowed as she read it.

"Damn," she said softly. "I didn't want to get them involved."

"It's okay," I said. "They won't tell Daddy anything. Not now that they know what . . . what we found."

She still looked worried.

"Can I e-mail her back?" I asked. I hated to think of Lashaundra worrying about me. And Mr. and Mrs. Johnson, too.

"I don't know," Emma said.

"It'll be okay," I said. "I'll just tell them that we're safe. That's all. Please, Emma?"

"Okay," she said, finally. "But don't say anything about where we are or where we're going."

I clicked reply and typed: *Hi Lashaundra. Don't worry. Emma and I are fine. We are safe. I miss you.*

"Is that okay?"

Emma read what I'd written and nodded. I pushed send and breathed deeply. At least they would know we were okay.

Then I pulled the stack of driver's licenses from my pocket, went to Google, typed in Cara's name and city, and scrolled through the missing people till we came to her spot. Emma read it, her face pale.

I typed in Briana's name and pulled up the newspaper article. Emma read that, too. She looked like she might throw up.

"Are you okay?" I whispered.

She nodded, but didn't say anything.

I found Ami's license and typed, *Ami Gordon, Fort Worth, Texas.*

Several items popped up, and I clicked on the first one.

LOCAL WOMAN'S DISAPPEARANCE
A MYSTERY FIVE YEARS LATER

FORT WORTH—When seventeen-year-old Ami Gordon left her parents' house in Haltom City on April 2, 2008, after an argument with her father, her mother thought she'd be home within the week.

"She only took her backpack," says Tammy Gordon. "Not enough clothes to stay away for long. She didn't have a credit card, and she couldn't have had more than twenty dollars with her. We figured she was staying with a friend and would cool off and come home."

But Ami Gordon never came home, leaving her parents and younger brother to wonder what had became of her. They are still wondering.

Emma was reading the story over my shoulder. I felt her hand shaking on my arm.

"Look," I said, pointing to the bottom of the screen. "There's a reward for any information."

"Look at her mother." Emma's voice was shaking, too.

I stared at a picture of an older woman sitting on a couch holding a photo of Ami. A man sat next to her on the couch, his arm around her.

"I can't even imagine what they are going through," Emma said. She had one arm wrapped across her stomach, like she was shielding the baby from the computer screen.

I said nothing, just clicked the back button and scanned through more entries on Ami's disappearance. She'd left home the spring before Daddy and I came to Texas. She'd lived with us a few months there and stayed with us when we moved to Tennessee. After she left, Cara had moved in with us.

"What about this one?" Emma held out a driver's license and I took it from her.

Laura Parker, Cincinnati, Ohio, I typed into the search engine. I clicked on the first entry that came on the screen, a newspaper article from the *Cincinnati Enquirer*.

"Missing Woman's Remains Found in Florida," the headline read.

I read quickly. The article was a lot like the one about Briana. Human remains in Florida had been identified as Laura Parker, missing for three years from Cincinnati. The article was dated 2007.

I stared at the picture on the screen, trying hard to remember the face. But no memory surfaced. I'd been so little then, and it was right after my mother died.

My mother . . .

I typed furiously in the Google search bar: *Hailey Bohner, Greenfield, Indiana.*

Nothing.

Hailey Bohner, Indianapolis, Indiana.

Still nothing.

Hailey Bohner, Cincinnati, Ohio.

I stared at nothing on the screen.

"What was her maiden name?" Emma whispered, her hands on my shoulders.

Hailey Wright, Indianapolis, Indiana.

Finally, a hit. I clicked on the link.

Local Woman Still Searching for Daughter

INDIANAPOLIS—Imogene Wright last heard from her daughter, Hailey, in January 2006. Hailey, then living in Cincinnati, wrote that she was afraid of her husband, Brannon Bohner. Wright wrote back, but never received a reply to her letter.

"I just know something went bad," Wright says. "We didn't always get along, but Hailey always let me know where she was and that she was okay. When I got the last letter, I wrote back to her and told her to come home and bring her baby."

Bohner gave birth to a daughter in 2003.

"I never got another letter," Wright says. "I drove down to Cincinnati a couple months later to the trailer park where her letter had been addressed from, but the man in the office said Hailey and Brannon and the baby had left a few weeks before. He didn't know where they'd gone."

Wright contacted Cincinnati police, but because Hailey Bohner had not been listed as missing by her husband, they had little to go on. Hailey and Brannon Bohner and their daughter, Jenny, were gone. Wright has not heard from her daughter since.

I was shaking so violently now I had to clench my hands together in my lap. I swallowed hard and stared at the picture of a woman standing under a sign for the Compton Hills Mobile Home Park. I squinted and stared again. That was my grandmother, the one I never even knew I had until I'd gotten into Daddy's boxes.

Another picture showed a smiling young woman with blond hair cut in a sleek bob—my mother. Hailey Wright . . . she had a last name now, and even a mother. And the last time anyone saw her she wasn't in Greenfield, Indiana, where Daddy told me she had died of the flu. No, it was at a trailer park in Cincinnati, Ohio.

I felt Emma's arms around me; her head rested on mine.

"Are you okay?" she asked, her voice very small.

I shook my head, but no words came.

Across the table, another woman sat in front of her open laptop, her eyes on us. She tilted her head slightly.

"Are you all right?" she asked, looking from Emma's face to mine.

"Oh," Emma said. I don't think she'd even been aware of the other people in the room. "Yes, we're fine. Just doing a little family history project."

I snapped the laptop shut, unplugged it from the wall, and carried it against my chest, walking quickly out of the kitchen-like room and into the maze of hallways.

"Jenny, wait."

Emma ran to catch up, wrapping her arm around me.

"He lied to me." I felt a catch in my throat. "He told me my mother died in Indiana, in Greenfield. But she was in Cincinnati before she died. And that last woman, Laura, is from Cincinnati. Maybe she moved in with us there, after my mom . . ."

I stopped to stare at Emma, and I knew my face was as pale as hers was.

"What happened to my mother? Do you think . . . did he kill her?"

Emma pulled me into a tight hug.

"I don't know," she whispered. "I don't know."

"Are you guys all right?"

Lorelei stood watching us, her eyes wide.

"We're okay," Emma said, trying to smile. "We've just gotten some . . . sad news."

"Anything I can do?"

"No, thank you." Emma took my hand and we walked back toward the main wing of the building that housed our room, then up the steep stairs. Her face was so white she looked sick.

"Are you okay?" I asked as we reached the landing of the second floor.

She nodded and stopped, holding onto the banister.

"I just need to catch my breath."

An instant later, before I could even put my hand out to her, she collapsed in a heap on the floor.

"Emma!"

I heard footsteps in the hallway, running toward us. More footsteps on the stairs below.

"Goodness!" Sister Frances knelt down beside Emma. "What happened?"

"She just . . ." I stopped, unsure how to go on. What had happened?

"Oh, my." I heard Lorelei's voice behind me. She stood on the stairs, gaping. "Is she okay?"

Sister Frances was patting Emma's cheek, calling softly. After a long minute, Emma's eyes fluttered open and she stared around her, as if trying to figure out where she was.

"You fainted, dear." Sister Frances patted her cheek more gently. "Can you stand?"

She took one of Emma's arms and Lorelei took the other and they helped Emma rise from the floor.

"I guess I'm not used to so many stairs," Emma said.

"Let's get you up to your room." Sister Frances took Emma by the elbow and began pulling her down the hallway. "We'll take the elevator."

Emma turned to look at me with wide eyes.

"Come on," Lorelei said, grabbing my hand. "We'll meet them at the top. The elevator's too small for all of us."

I ran up the stairs behind her toward the third floor, then down the hallway to the elevator. We'd reached the door before it opened. Emma stepped off, Sister Frances's hand still under her elbow.

I led the way back to our room, not looking back at Emma and the nun. I couldn't bear the look on Emma's face.

"Here you go, sit down." Sister Frances guided Emma to a bed. "Lorelei, will you get us a glass of cold water?"

Lorelei nodded and disappeared. I heard her feet pounding against the wooden floor as she ran to the kitchen. A minute later she was back, carrying a large glass with water and ice cubes.

"Now, just take a sip," Sister Frances said, holding the glass to Emma's mouth.

"I'm sorry," Emma said. "I don't know what happened."

"You passed out," Lorelei said, standing in the doorway. "You looked really pale and I was worrying, and then I heard you fall."

"Jenny?" Emma looked toward me and I tried to smile at her.

"I'm okay, are you?" I asked, willing her to be healthy and strong.

"I'm fine," she said.

She started to sit up, but the tiny nun's strong hands held her shoulders against the pillow.

"You're obviously not fine," she said firmly. "Lorelei, be a dear and call the infirmary. Ask one of the nurses to come, will you?"

The blond head bobbed and disappeared.

"Just sip some more water," Sister Frances said. "Try to relax. I'm sure it's nothing, but I'll feel better if a nurse checks you out."

Emma sighed and took a sip of water.

"I really am fine," she said.

The nun only looked at her, not moving from where she sat on the bed.

"Shirley Rigby said you needed a safe place to stay," she said. "Why don't you tell me what you're running from?"

Emma looked at me and I stared at her. Then she took a long, deep breath.

"My husband," she said, then paused. "I met Brannon last summer when he was working in Idaho. I followed him here to Kentucky and we got married in January."

Sister Frances said nothing, just took Emma's hand and held it in her own.

"Jenny is his daughter, my stepdaughter."

The nun smiled at me.

"Anyway, she was going through some boxes in the attic and found . . . well, she found some things that . . ." She looked up at me then, her eyes filling with tears.

"Daddy's had a whole bunch of women," I said, trying hard to keep my voice steady. "They come and stay, and then they go. Except, in the attic I found the jewelry Daddy gave them, and these." I handed her the stack of driver's licenses.

Sister Frances took the plastic cards and stared at them.

"These women all lived with your father?"

I nodded. "And they all left. Except, they wouldn't leave their licenses behind, would they? And then I started Googling them, and . . ."

"Two of them are listed as missing," Emma continued. "Two more are dead. One of them was found in Texas, her body, I mean. She was already dead. The other was found dead in Florida."

"We lived there," I said.

"In Florida?" The nun turned to look at me.

"And in Texas." I nodded. "We lived all over. And Trish lived with us, and so did Ami and Jackie and Cara and Briana."

A small noise made us all turn to the doorway, where Lorelei stood, staring with wide eyes.

"I'm sorry," she stammered. "I didn't mean to . . . I just came to tell you that Sister Paul is on her way."

"Thank you, dear." The nun nodded at her as if dismissing her.

Lorelei stood for a minute, then nodded back and disappeared.

Sister Frances turned back to Emma.

"Have you talked to the police?"

Emma shook her head. "I just found out yesterday, and all I could think of was to get out of there, away from him. Besides, we don't have any real proof that . . . that Brannon is involved in any of it."

"Well, for right now the thing to do is take care of yourself and your baby."

As if on cue, a woman appeared in the doorway, tall and thin and carrying a medical bag.

"Here's Sister Paul. She's a nurse and she'll take good care of you."

Sister Frances rose and Sister Paul approached the bed.

"I understand you fainted?"

Emma nodded.

"Well, let's check your blood pressure and temperature," the nurse said.

Sister Frances walked to the door, then turned back toward us and said, "Jenny, would you like a cup of cocoa? I have some in the kitchen downstairs."

I shook my head and she smiled and held out her hand.

"Come on, dear. Let's let the nurse check Emma out."

I looked to Emma. She nodded and smiled weakly. "I'll be fine," she said. "Go have some cocoa."

I followed the nun down to the second floor and into the kitchen.

"I'm afraid I don't have any marshmallows," she said, pulling a packet of instant cocoa from the cabinet. "Sister Agnes ate them all last week."

She smiled at the memory. "I came in here and found her sitting on the floor with the entire bag, just eating them and humming to herself."

"Is that the one you had to go get last night?" I asked.

"Yes, she gets confused." She shook her head. "It's such a mystery, the mind. Physically, Agnes is fine, healthy and strong. But her mind . . . well, it's like she's not really here anymore."

She poured hot water into a mug with the cocoa, stirred it, and put it on the table in front of me.

"How old are you, Jenny?"

"Eleven." I took a cautious sip of cocoa.

"And you've lived with your father always?"

I nodded. "My mom died when I was three. At least I think that's when she died. That's what Daddy told me. But now, I don't know if that's true or not. I don't know anything now."

I blinked back tears.

Sister Frances sat down beside me and put her hand on mine.

"I know it's very confusing," she said. "I know you're upset, and you have a right to be. He's your dad and you love him."

I nodded, but I couldn't speak because of the huge lump in my throat.

"Whatever turns out to be the truth," she said, her voice gentle, "you and Emma are safe here."

"Thank you," I mumbled.

She stood and began pacing around the kitchen, her hands clasped behind her back. I watched her while I drank my cocoa. I'd never met a nun before. She wasn't anything like I expected. She seemed just like any other old woman, just normal.

The nurse walked in then, smiled at me, and sat down.

"Your mother is going to be fine," she said. "She's a little bit dehydrated and the stairs were a bit much for her. But she and the baby both seem fine."

"Can I go see her?" I rose.

"Sure," she said. "Just keep things quiet and make sure she stays off her feet for a while."

"Thank you," I said. I turned to Sister Frances. "Thank you for the cocoa."

I ran from the kitchen, down the long hallway, and up the stairs—back to our room. Back to Emma.

44

Emma

Jenny's face was ashen, her eyes red, when she ran into the room. "Are you okay?" she panted.

"I'm fine."

She lay down on the narrow bed beside me and laid her head on my shoulder. I put my arms around her and kissed her head.

"The nurse said I'm a little dehydrated, that's all."

"What is she going to do?"

"Nothing," I said, patting her back. "I'm just supposed to take it easy and drink lots of water."

"Is the baby okay?"

"The baby is fine. We're okay, Jenny. We're going to be fine."

She sat up and stared at me, shaking her head.

"How?" she asked. "How are we ever going to be fine again?"

"I'm not sure," I admitted. "But I've been through hard times before, and I came out okay. We just have to be careful and think of what to do next."

"Should we call the police?" Jenny's voice shook. I knew she was worrying about Brannon.

"Not yet," I said. "Not until we know something, anything for sure."

"How will we know for sure?"

I tried to smile at her. She looked so scared and small, sitting there on the bed.

"Well, I think we should go to Indianapolis," I said, trying to keep my voice level. "Tomorrow, maybe, or the next day. Once we're sure I'm okay and the baby is okay. We'll drive up there and try to find Hailey's mother . . . your grandmother. Maybe she knows some things we don't. Meantime, we'll stay here. Brannon doesn't know about this place. He won't look for us here."

Jenny lay back down beside me then and sighed. For a long time we just rested there, wrapped in our own thoughts. Then she sat up again.

"I saw a bunch of books on a table downstairs," she said. "Do you want to read?"

"Sure," I said. "Go pick out a couple books."

She stopped at the door. "You sure you're okay?"

"I'm fine." I smiled at her. "Go get some books, so we don't die of boredom."

I heard her feet pounding down the stairs, felt tears slide down my cheeks. Jenny was so young, and everything she ever knew about herself and her father had been turned upside down. Maybe I should have left her with Brannon. He would never hurt Jenny, I felt sure of that. Maybe I shouldn't have brought her with me.

Then I shook my head. I couldn't have just left her there. I knew that. I loved Jenny. I couldn't leave her behind. Not knowing what I knew now.

Please, God, please help me to be strong. Please help me to protect Jenny and my baby. Please show us what to do.

I closed my eyes, trying to squeeze back the tears.

"Hey." A voice came from the doorway.

Lorelei stood, carrying a package of crackers.

"When my sister was pregnant, all she could hold down was crackers. I thought they might help." She set the package on the table by my bed and stood, looking uncertain.

"Thanks, Lorelei." I smiled at her.

She sat down on the bed next to mine.

"I didn't mean to eavesdrop," she said.

"It's okay."

"Do you think your husband is looking for you?"

I nodded and sighed.

"He won't look here," I said. "He doesn't even know about this place."

"What will you do next?" she asked.

I shook my head. "I don't know. I was thinking of going to Indianapolis. That's where Jenny's mother was from. We have a letter she got from her mother, so we have an address. It's a place to start, I guess."

"Can I see the address?"

I looked at her for a long time, trying to decide whether to trust her, this perky young woman with spiky blond hair. Her blue eyes met mine, not wavering. Finally, I handed her the envelope. She scanned the address and her eyes widened.

"My best friend left her husband," she said, handing the envelope back to me. "He beat the hell out of her, and eventually she couldn't take it anymore and left."

"What happened to her?" I asked.

"He killed her."

I stared at her, feeling my stomach clench.

"He went to the bank where she worked and he shot her." She shook her head and wiped a hand across her eyes.

"I made a promise to her at the funeral that I would never just sit by again. I knew he was hitting her. She denied it, but I knew. And I didn't do anything. And then it was too late."

"I'm so sorry," I whispered.

"So," she said, straightening her shoulders, "maybe that's why I came down this week. I wasn't scheduled to come. Carol and Lydia asked me, but I told them I couldn't. I didn't have enough vacation time. Then, the day before they left, I just decided, 'What the hell?' And I came."

She paused and looked at me, but I had no idea what to say.

"Maybe I'm supposed to be here now to help you."

I shook my head.

"It's nice you want to help," I said. "But I don't want to drag you or anyone else into our mess. If Brannon really did kill those women . . . he could be really dangerous, Lorelei. I don't want you to end up getting in the middle of it."

Jenny's feet pounded up the stairs toward us. Lorelei rose and stared down at me.

"Sometimes you have to accept a God-thing when it comes," she said firmly. "Pray on it, okay?"

"Okay," I said. "I'll pray on it."

Jenny came in carrying an armful of books. She stopped when she saw Lorelei, looking from her to me and back again.

"I'll be back," Lorelei said.

"What did she want?" Jenny asked after we heard Lorelei's steps echo down the hall.

"She wants to help."

"How can she help?" Jenny asked. "Is she a cop or something?"

"No," I said. "She's just a nice person."

"Did she hear you tell Sister Frances about Daddy?"

I nodded.

"What if she tells someone?" Jenny's eyes grew wide.

"She won't," I said. "She really is just a nice person."

She dumped the pile of books onto an empty bed.

"I wasn't sure what you'd want, so I just brought a bunch for you to choose from."

I scanned the books, settling on a novel with a picture of a haunted-looking little girl on the cover. Jenny chose another book and lay down on her bed.

"Emma?"

"Yes, Jenny."

"I love you."

"I love you, too."

We read until we heard the bell ring, announcing lunch.

Jenny stretched and set her book aside.

"Are you ready for lunch?" I asked, sitting up.

"You're supposed to stay in bed," she said firmly.

"I'll be fine," I said.

She shook her head and stared at me darkly. "You should stay in bed. I'll go down and get you something. You can eat it here."

I laughed and swung my feet over the side of the bed, searching for my shoes.

"She's right."

Lorelei stood in the doorway again.

"You stay here," she said. "Jenny and I will go get lunch and bring you up something."

"All right." I sighed, flopping back on the bed. "I'm outnumbered."

Jenny followed Lorelei out of the room. I lay on the bed, staring at the ceiling. My stomach growled. I hoped they'd be back soon.

"Are you feeling better?"

Sister Frances stood in the doorway, smiling.

"I'm fine."

"Can I bring you something for lunch?"

"Jenny and Lorelei went to get something," I said. "But thank you."

She nodded and turned to go.

"Sister?"

She turned back.

"Can I ask you something?"

"Of course." She walked into the room and sat down in the rocker by the window.

"Is Lorelei . . . can I trust her?"

Sister Frances laughed. "Oh, yes," she said. "Lorelei is a good person. I know she appears a bit . . . flighty at first. But she's got a good heart and a good soul."

"She said she wants to help me."

The nun nodded.

"She doesn't even know me," I said. "Why would she want to help?"

"Lorelei has some healing to do herself," Sister Frances said. "I think helping you and Jenny could be a part of that healing."

"She thinks she's here right now to help me. She called it a God-thing."

The nun laughed again. "Maybe she's right. Maybe God put her in your path for a reason."

"Do you believe that?"

She paused for a minute, then said, "I think God is here whenever we help one another. Do I believe God sent her here on purpose? Who knows? But she's here, and you're here, and she wants to help you. And that's God."

"That's not the kind of God I grew up with."

"Ah," she said. "You've had a bad church experience?"

I nodded. "I came out of it thinking the church is just a way for old men to control everyone."

"Do you want to know what I think?"

I nodded again.

"I think in the end, all churches are human creations. Some are just more human than others."

I stared at her.

"But if the church is a human creation, why did you become a nun?"

"I didn't say I didn't think God was real," she said. "I believe God is real. I know God is real. But the church . . . well, I think that's just our very human way of trying to understand God. And of course we can't ever really understand God. God is a mystery. But I think when we act toward one another with kindness, that's God showing up through us, letting us be his hands in the world."

"That's nice," I whispered.

"You get some rest," she said, rising. "And if you need anything, I'm right downstairs."

I lay there thinking about what Sister Frances had said. Was God real? If so, I definitely liked her vision of him better than the one I'd heard as a child.

After a while, Lorelei and Jenny returned, carrying trays from the cafeteria. We ate chicken and rice and broccoli that had been cooked to a mush, while Lorelei talked about her church in Indianapolis. She was the director of music there.

"Do you play the organ?" I asked.

She nodded. "I learned as a child. But I'm not the organist at church. I direct the choir. I choose the music. Sometimes I write the music."

"You can write music?" Jenny's eyes were round.

Lorelei nodded. "I majored in music at Butler University," she said. "It's the only thing I ever wanted to do. Maybe after lunch, you can come with me to the chapel and I'll show you how the organ works."

Jenny smiled at her, then looked to me for permission.

"It's fine," I said. "I've got plenty to keep me busy." I waved at the stack of books. "You go have fun."

After they'd left, I settled down to read again. But the sun streamed warm through the windows, and the bed was soft and comfortable. Before I'd read two pages, I had drifted off to sleep.

I woke sometime in the late afternoon. A bouquet of wildflowers filled a vase on the table by the bed, a note propped against it.

Lorelei is going to show me the ponds, Jenny had written. *We'll be back before dinner.*

I stretched and yawned, glad that Jenny had found a distraction.

"Are you awake?" The nurse stood in the doorway, smiling at me.

"Finally," I said. "I think I slept most of the afternoon away."

"That's good," she said. "You need the rest."

She took my blood pressure and my temperature.

"Everything looks fine," she said. "Tomorrow, you can get up and take a walk or go to the cafeteria. But you'll have to use the elevator." Her face was stern. "No more stairs for you."

Jenny ran into the room carrying still more flowers.

"Look what we found! There's snowdrops and daffodils and violas, and these are called coltsfoot, isn't that funny?"

"They're beautiful," I said, smiling at her flushed face. "I'm glad you've been having fun."

The nurse smiled at us. "Don't forget," she said as she walked from the room. "Rest today, limited walking tomorrow, and no stairs."

"Lorelei knows all about flowers," Jenny said. "And you should hear her play the organ. She's really good!"

"Where is she now?" I asked.

"She went to her room to wash up for dinner."

"Are you going to dinner with her?"

Jenny flopped down on her bed.

"Sister Frances said we should come downstairs and have dinner with her again. She said we can use the elevator."

So, with Jenny's hand under my elbow, we toddled down the hall, stepped into the tiny, ancient cage, and rode slowly down to the second floor.

"Here you are." Sister Frances waved us to seats at the table, where the same women who'd been there the night before had already gathered.

"I hope you're having a nice retreat," the old woman beside me said.

"It's lovely here," I told her.

"I saw you out in the meadow," the woman said, turning to Jenny. "Are you having fun?"

Jenny nodded.

Then the nuns began talking about repairs being made at the barn, and we were left again to ourselves to eat soup and cheese and bread.

After dinner, we rode the little elevator back to the third floor and walked slowly to our room.

"What are you reading?" I asked.

"It's a book about wildflowers," Jenny said. "Lorelei loaned it to me."

I smiled. Maybe Lorelei and Sister Frances were right. Maybe it was a God-thing.

❧ 45 ❧

Jenny

The next morning, Emma went to breakfast with me. We rode the elevator down and walked slowly to the dining hall. Lorelei waved to us from a table.

"I saved you some seats," she called.

We filled our trays and went to sit with her.

"I'm glad to see you up," she said, grinning at Emma.

"I'm glad to be up," Emma said. "I don't know if I could take another whole day of just laying around."

"Have you decided what you're going to do next?" Lorelei spread jam on a piece of toast.

"I think we'll drive up to Indianapolis and try to find Jenny's grandmother."

"That's where I'm from," Lorelei said. "The address on your envelope is actually very close to where I live."

"Really?" Emma stared at her.

"Like I said," Lorelei said, smiling, "it's a God-thing. You-all should follow me up and stay with me while you're there."

"Really?" I said. "Can we do that, Emma?"

"Oh, I don't know," Emma said, her cheeks reddening. "We can't put you out like that."

"You won't be putting me out," Lorelei said firmly. "You'd be helping me make good on a promise. Besides, I've got plenty of room. It's just me and the cats. You-all can have the guest room for as long as you need it."

Emma opened her mouth, but before she could speak her eyes widened. She was looking over my shoulder. I turned and saw Mrs. Rigby standing at the door, waving to us.

"Is she a friend?" Lorelei asked.

"Yes," Emma said, rising to hug Mrs. Rigby.

"God, Shirley, I'm so glad to see you."

"Me too, honey." Mrs. Rigby stepped back and surveyed Emma from head to toe. "Are you all right?"

"I'm fine," Emma said.

She turned back to the table. "Shirley, this is Lorelei. She's from Indianapolis, and she's been so kind to Jenny and me. Lorelei, this is Shirley. She's the one who told me about this place."

Mrs. Rigby sat down at the table opposite Lorelei.

"I came here years ago," she said. "My sister used to work in the kitchen."

Lorelei smiled and rose. "I'll let you talk," she said. "Meantime, think about my offer." She touched Emma lightly on the shoulder. "I'd be glad to have you stay with me."

Mrs. Rigby arched her eyebrows as Lorelei walked away.

"She wants you to stay with her?"

"She knows about . . . why we're here. She had a friend once whose husband was abusive. She just wants to help."

"Have you seen my dad?" I asked.

Mrs. Rigby nodded. "I was in the diner last night and he came storming in, yelling for Emma. Then he yelled at Resa that she'd better tell him where ya'll went. Harlan came out front and I thought they might come to blows. But Resa just kept saying she didn't know where you were, and finally Brannon left."

She turned to look at Emma. "I've never seen him look like that."

Emma nodded. I did, too. I'd seen Daddy mad before. Not often, but sometimes. And when he was mad, he didn't look like Daddy at all. I shivered slightly.

"Did he ask you where we are?" I asked.

"No, honey." She smiled at me. "He wouldn't ask me anything. I don't think he even saw me there."

"I'm sorry to put Resa and Harlan through that," Emma said.

"They're all right," Mrs. Rigby said. "They've seen worse, I guess. Harlan did tell Brannon he should call the police if he was really worried."

"Do you think he will?" Emma's face blanched.

"No," Mrs. Rigby said, shaking her head. "He won't call the police. He's in too deep, and he knows it. But he is looking for you."

She took Emma's hand and held it.

"I don't think you should stay here," she said. "Too many people in town know about Loretto. I'm afraid someone might tell Brannon about it."

Emma sat in silence, her face paler than ever.

"We should go with Lorelei," I said. "And we should leave today."

Emma looked at me, then down at the table.

"I just don't know what to do," she whispered.

"Honey," Mrs. Rigby said, "if this Lorelei has offered you a place to stay, maybe you should take it. Maybe it's God's way of telling you where to go."

Emma stared at her without speaking.

"Let's ask Sister Frances," Mrs. Rigby said. "She'll know what you should do."

We carried our trays to the kitchen, walked back to the main building, and took the elevator to the second floor.

"Sister?" Mrs. Rigby said, standing in the door to the kitchen.

"Oh, Shirley!" Sister Frances put down the dish she was drying and hugged Mrs. Rigby. "How are you? We've not seen you in such a long time."

"I'm fine," Mrs. Rigby said. "I suppose you heard about Damon?"

"We did." The nun nodded. "We said a novena for him."

"Thank you."

"And how are you now? How are you holding up?"

"I'm good." Mrs. Rigby smiled. "I have a job."

"Good for you!"

"Emma helped me get it." Mrs. Rigby turned toward us. "She's been such a good friend to me."

"And now you're being a good friend to her."

"We came to ask you a question." Shirley dropped down into a chair. Emma sat down, too.

"What is it?" The nun sat down opposite Emma.

"Lorelei has offered us a place to stay in Indianapolis," Emma said. "I don't want to burden her. But Indianapolis is where Jenny's mother is from. I'm hoping we can track down her mother, Jenny's grandmother."

"That sounds like a fine idea."

"But," Emma said, "I don't know if Brannon will come looking for us there. I don't want to get Lorelei into any trouble. Or . . . well, you know."

"Emma, if Lorelei has made the offer, she knows what's at stake. I think it will be good for her to have you stay. And good for you, too."

"I agree."

We turned to see Lorelei standing in the doorway.

"I told you, I have plenty of room and I'm happy to have you. Seriously, I want to do this. I need to do this."

I stared at her, wondering why she would need to do anything for us.

After a pause, Emma rose and took Lorelei's hands.

"Thank you," she said, her voice trembling. "I can't tell you how much . . ."

"Shirley thinks we should go soon," I said. "She said my dad is looking for us, and too many people in Campbellsville know about this place."

"All right, then," Lorelei said. "I'll go pack up, and you-all do the same. And then we'll hit the road. Okay?"

"Thank you," Emma said again.

Mrs. Rigby followed us to our room. Then she reached into her purse and took out a white envelope.

"Here," she said, shoving the envelope into Emma's hands. "I wish it was more, but it's all I could scrape together right now."

Emma opened the envelope, then tried to hand it back to Mrs. Rigby.

"Shirley, I can't take this. It's too much!"

"Nonsense," Mrs. Rigby said, backing away. "You were a friend to me when I really needed one. Now let me be a friend to you. You'll pay me back when you can."

Emma threw her arms around Mrs. Rigby and both of them cried. Finally, Mrs. Rigby pulled back, straightened her blouse, and gave us a teary smile.

"Call me when you get there," she said. "But don't use your phone. It might have a GPS on it, or something."

She turned and walked out of the room quickly. We heard her shoes clicking down the stairs.

"How much did she give you?" I asked, staring at the envelope.

Emma took a stack of bills from the envelope and began counting.

"Two thousand dollars," she said finally. "My God, I can't believe she did this."

"You-all about ready?" Lorelei's voice called down the hall.

"We'll be there in a minute," Emma called back.

We gathered our things, made the beds, and walked to the elevator.

"Where are you parked?" Lorelei asked.

"Right by the building," Emma said.

I said nothing, just clutched my bag and held my breath, waiting for the elevator door to open. I hated small spaces.

"I'll pull around and you can follow me," Lorelei said. "It's a white Honda."

We put our things in the trunk and got in the car, then pulled out and followed Lorelei down the drive, away from our safe haven at Loretto and toward an uncertain future in Indianapolis.

"I can't believe we're doing this," Emma said. Her voice shook a little. "I hope it's the right thing."

"I hope so, too."

PART 3

INDIANA

46

Emma

We drove west for a while and then turned north, covering the same roads we'd followed just a few months earlier on our way to Campbellsville. I thought about that drive, how excited I had been, how it all seemed like such a grand adventure. Now . . . well, now I was on the run from Brannon with Jenny, pregnant and scared to pieces.

What if Brannon did call the police? Could I be charged with kidnapping? What if there really was an explanation for the lockets and the driver's licenses? But how could there be? My head ached just thinking about it all.

We drove in silence for a long time. Jenny sat beside me, staring out her window. She held her stuffed bear in her lap. She looked much younger than her eleven years.

"Are you doing okay?" I asked.

She nodded, but said nothing. Her hands clutched the bear tightly.

"I'm sorry," I said over the lump in my throat. "I wish I could make everything all right."

She sighed heavily.

"I wish I could talk to Lashaundra."

"I know. I wish I could call Resa, too."

"Do you think we'll ever see them again?"

"I hope so."

"Do you think Daddy misses us?" Her voice was small.

"I'm sure he misses you, honey. And I'm sure you miss him."

"Will I ever see him again?"

"Oh, honey, I'm sure you will. We just need to . . . we have to figure some things out."

I glanced over at her and saw her lower lip tremble.

"Do you wish you never met Daddy?" she asked.

The question felt like a punch in the stomach; it nearly took my breath away.

Did I wish that? If I'd never met Brannon, I would still be at the campground in Idaho, living in the bunkhouse, eating at Zella Fay's, working with the horses. I'd be safe.

But if I'd stayed, I wouldn't have met Resa and Harlan, Angel and Shirley. I wouldn't know Jenny. I wouldn't have this baby growing inside me.

"No," I said at last. "I'm glad I met him, and you. If I hadn't, I wouldn't have this baby." I patted my belly.

"She's changing lanes," Jenny said, pointing to Lorelei's car. I pulled into the right-hand lane behind her.

Ahead, Lorelei's turn signal came on. I followed her off the highway and into a McDonald's parking lot.

"Okay," she said, walking to our car. "We're going to get onto the loop in a couple miles. We're going east. Traffic is heavy sometimes, so if we get separated, just keep on the loop until you see the exit for Washington Street. Then go straight ahead through the light and I'll be in the parking lot waiting for you."

"Washington Street. Got it."

"You doing okay, kiddo?" Lorelei smiled across me at Jenny.

"I guess so."

"We're almost there."

She got back in her car and we pulled onto the highway.

"Do you think my grandmother is still alive?" Jenny asked.

"I hope so," I said. "I really hope so."

"I wonder what she's like."

"I guess we'll find out."

"Maybe she can tell me about my mom."

"I'll bet she'd love to do that."

Jenny sat for a long time staring out the window.

"Will we have to tell her my mom's dead?" she asked suddenly. "Or do you think she already knows?"

Oh God, I hadn't even thought about that.

"I'm thinking she already knows," I said softly. "It's been eight years. She might still hope, but she probably knows your mom is gone."

Jenny sniffed and wiped her nose.

"I know it's awful," I said. "But I promise it will be better for her to know for sure, instead of just wondering. And . . . and she'll get to meet you. I know she will love to meet you. You're her granddaughter, you know."

"What if she doesn't like me?"

"Oh, Jenny, of course she'll like you. She'll love you. You're a wonderful, wonderful girl, and everyone loves you. Plus, it will be like a little bit of your mother coming back to her."

"Her letter said things were hard between them. What do you suppose that means?"

I thought a moment before answering, choosing my words carefully.

"Lots of mothers and daughters have trouble getting along," I said. "I loved my mother, but I didn't get along with her a lot of times. Sometimes, the people we love the most are the ones we hurt the most. But I'm sure your grandma loved your mom. And I'm sure she'll love you, too."

"Emma?" Jenny's voice was a mere whisper now.

"What?"

"What if she wants me to live with her?"

Another punch in the stomach.

"We won't worry about that now," I said. "For now, we have enough on our plates. Let's just get to Lorelei's first, and we'll figure out the rest later. Okay?"

"I don't want to live with someone I don't know," she said firmly. "Even if she is my grandma."

"Don't worry." I squeezed her knee. "I'm not letting you out of my life, Jenny. I promise you that."

I thought back to the day I'd left Micah's house, driving in the predawn, abandoning the car along the highway, making my way to Salt Lake City—all the while, worrying about my younger sisters, especially Clarissa.

I couldn't save Clarissa that day. But by God, I could save Jenny now.

"There's Washington Street." Jenny pointed to the exit sign. I pulled onto the ramp and followed Lorelei to the light. She waved and put on her right turn signal.

I followed her down the busy street into what looked like a small town surrounded by city. We turned right onto another busy street and then right again onto a drive lined with trees and tidy brick houses. Lorelei pulled into a driveway beside one of the houses, and I followed her.

"Here we are," she said, when we got out of the car. "Home, sweet home."

"It's pretty," Jenny said.

It was a charming little house, redbrick with green-shuttered windows. A flagstone walkway led from the sidewalk to the front porch, lined with tulips and daffodils. It looked like something from a movie, small-town America, any town.

We got our things from the car and followed Lorelei onto the porch. She unlocked the door and we stepped into a little foyer. A small bench sat just inside the door, with a mirror hanging above it. A huge orange cat appeared, yowling loud and rubbing itself against Lorelei's ankles.

"This is Simon," she said, stooping to pick up the cat. "He's my good kitty, yes he is."

The cat was purring now, almost as loudly as it had yowled before.

Lorelei showed us the guest room, painted pale yellow with matching quilts on the twin beds.

"You-all just relax and settle in," she said. "I'm going next door for a minute to let Mrs. Hanson know I'm back. I wasn't supposed to get home till Tuesday, and I don't want her to think someone has broken in!"

Jenny sat down on one of the beds, stroking the quilt softly.

"This is really pretty," she said.

I sat down beside her and gathered a corner of the quilt.

"The stitching is beautiful," I said. "I used to quilt, when I was younger. But I don't think I ever did anything as nice as this."

"Did your mother teach you?"

I nodded and smiled, remembering long afternoons in my father's house, sitting with my mother and sisters around a quilting frame, hands flying as fast as the gossip.

"Maybe someday you can teach me."

"Maybe I will," I said. "When all this is settled, maybe we'll get a quilting frame and I'll teach you."

Jenny sighed and lay on the bed, resting her head in my lap.

"I hope that comes soon," she whispered.

I stroked her hair, wishing with all my might that I could just erase the ugliness of the last few days and make it all better. If only Jenny hadn't gone into the attic. I shook my head. No, it was better to know. I had to know. I had to protect myself and my baby. If only none of it was true. If only Brannon hadn't . . . I couldn't even make myself finish the thought. Brannon had done awful things. As soon as Jenny showed me the licenses, I knew. I'd seen his anger, I'd felt it. And I'd told myself I could live with it. But now . . . now I knew. Now there was no going back.

I felt a bit of damp on my hand as I brushed Jenny's cheek. She was crying, not making a sound.

I began crooning the song my mother used to sing to me when I was a little girl and sad.

"Let me call you sweetheart, I'm in love with you . . ."

❦ 47 ❦

Jenny

"So, what's the plan?" Lorelei poured coffee into a mug and set it on the table for Emma.

"I'm not sure," Emma said. "Part of me wants to start looking for Jenny's grandmother right away, but I'm just so tired."

She looked tired. Her face was pale, her shoulders slumped, arms folded across her pregnant belly. She looked nothing like the Emma I'd met in Idaho.

"Well, then," Lorelei said, sitting down at the table, "how about we just have a quiet afternoon? You can always start looking tomorrow."

Emma smiled at her.

We ate turkey-and-cheese sandwiches with milk.

"Are you feeling any better?" Lorelei asked, watching Emma.

"Actually, yes," Emma said. "In fact, I'm thinking maybe we should find the house on Layman."

"My grandmother's house?"

She nodded. "You said it's not too far from here?" she asked Lorelei.

"Just a few minutes," Lorelei said. "Let's change clothes and I'll take you."

Soon we were in Lorelei's car, driving down windy, shaded streets.

"It looks like a Norman Rockwell painting," Emma said, gazing out the window.

"Irvington is a great neighborhood," Lorelei said. "I grew up here. It's been through some hard times, but it's making a comeback. I wouldn't live anywhere else."

After only a few minutes, she parked the car at the side of the street.

"That's it," she said, pointing to a small brick house with a screened front porch. An American flag flew from a pole beside the front door. A huge tree shaded the lawn. A black cat lounged on the walkway. I stared, blinking back tears. This was where my mother had lived, before she met my dad. This was where she'd walked home from school, maybe sat on the front porch reading books, playing in the sprinkler on the front lawn on hot summer days.

"It's pretty," Emma said. She turned to look at me. "Are you ready?"

I swallowed, took a deep breath, and nodded.

We got out of the car and stood a minute, just looking at the house. Was my grandmother inside? Would she be glad to see me? Or would she hate me because I was my father's daughter?

Emma took my hand, and we walked up the driveway to the porch, Lorelei behind us.

"Here we go," Emma said, raising her hand and knocking softly on the door.

A dog barked inside, and before I could say, "Maybe we should go," the door to the house opened and a young woman stepped onto the porch, a toddler on her hip.

"Can I help you?" she asked.

"We're looking for Mrs. Imogene Wright," Emma said, her voice shaking. "Does she live here?"

"Oh, Imogene." The woman smiled. "She used to live here. We bought the place from her four years ago."

My stomach dropped.

"Oh, well . . ." Emma stammered. "Thank you."

"Do you know where she lives now?" Lorelei asked, her hand on my shoulder.

"She moved into one of those town houses on Johnson," the woman said. "But you can probably find her at the store. She usually has it open on Sunday afternoons."

"What store is that?" Lorelei asked.

"Bookmamas," the lady said. "On Johnson, just around the corner from the Irving Theater."

"I know where it is," Lorelei said. "Thanks so much."

We walked back to the car. I was shaking so hard I thought my legs might just fold underneath me.

"Okay," Lorelei said firmly. "Bookmamas, let's go."

"Do you think we should just show up there?" Emma asked. "If she's at work, it might be kind of awkward."

Lorelei laughed. "I wouldn't worry about it. Bookmamas is pretty laid-back. You'll love it."

She drove toward the main street we'd driven down earlier, and I stared out the window at the little shops and restaurants. Then we turned onto a side street and Lorelei parked the car.

"There it is," she said, pointing to a little storefront in a big brick building. The bicycle rack out front was empty, but the sign read, OPEN.

We walked across the street and Lorelei pushed open the door to the shop. A bell tinkled, announcing our presence. We stood just inside the door, looking around at the shelves of books. The store appeared to be empty.

"Hello!" An older woman appeared from the back of the store, leaning heavily on a cane. "Welcome to Bookmamas. Can I help you find anything?"

"I, um . . . we're looking for Imogene Wright?" Emma smiled at the woman.

"Well, you found her." The woman limped forward and smiled back at her. "I'm Imogene. What can I do for you?"

I stood staring at her, this woman who was my grandmother, my mother's mom.

"My name is Emma, and this is Jenny." Emma pulled me forward slightly.

"It's nice to meet you, Jenny." The woman smiled at me now and held out her hand. "We've got some wonderful young adult books just back here." She turned and limped to a shelf. "Did you have something specific you were looking for?"

"Mrs. Wright," Emma said. Her voice faltered and she cleared her throat. "My last name is Bohner. My husband is Brannon Bohner."

The woman turned so fast, she nearly fell. "Brannon Bohner?" she whispered.

"Yes, ma'am." Emma nodded.

"Do you know Hailey?" she asked. "Where's Hailey?" She looked past Emma as if she might see her daughter standing there.

"No, ma'am, I'm sorry I don't know her. Do you want to sit down?"

The woman's face was white.

"Yes," she said, pointing to some chairs set in a circle at the back of the store. "Let me just lock up."

She limped to the front of the store, locked the door, and turned the OPEN sign to CLOSED.

"How can you not know . . ." She paused, removed her glasses, and wiped her eyes, sinking into a chair across from Emma.

"I met Brannon last summer," Emma said, her voice gentle. "He was working in Idaho at a campground, and I came with him to Kentucky last fall."

"But where is Hailey?" The woman stared at Emma, her voice shaking.

"Brannon told me that Hailey died several years ago," Emma said. "I'm very sorry."

"Oh." That was all the woman said, just, "Oh."

She sat for a minute staring straight ahead. I don't think she even saw us. Then she slumped forward and began crying, low, moaning sobs.

Emma rose and went to sit beside her, wrapping her arm around the woman's shoulders. They sat like that for several minutes, the old woman crying, Emma rubbing her back.

Finally, the woman raised her head to look Emma right in the face.

"But the baby . . ." she said. "What happened to Hailey's baby?"

"She's here," Emma said, pointing at me. "Jenny is Hailey's daughter."

The woman made a small, strangled sound as she stared at me.

"Her eyes," she whispered. "You have her eyes."

"Yes, ma'am," I whispered back. "That's what my daddy told me."

Everything seemed frozen for a minute. No one moved. No one spoke. I felt sweat begin to bead on my forehead. Would she tell us to leave? Would she hate me because of Daddy?

She rose then, leaning heavily on her cane, and held open her free arm.

Lorelei pushed me slightly, so that I rose, too. I walked to the woman, not sure what to say. But then I didn't have to say anything. She pulled me to her tightly and began crying again; her cheek rested on my head.

"Jenny," she whispered. "Jenny . . . I've wanted to see you for so long. Oh my God, Jenny. I can't believe it's really you."

I glanced over at Emma. She was smiling and wiping tears from her cheeks.

The woman, my grandmother, stepped back and stared into my face.

"You're so beautiful," she said, gazing at me. "How old are you now?"

"I'm eleven."

"And how old were you when Hailey . . . when your mama . . . died?"

"I think I was three," I said. "At least, that's what Daddy told me."

She looked over her shoulder then, eyes wide.

"Is he here, too?" she asked. "Is your father with you?"

I shook my head.

"We ran away from him," I said.

"Does he know you've come here?"

"No, ma'am." Emma rose and put her hand on the woman's arm. "We left while he was at work. He doesn't know where we are."

"You're afraid of him, too?"

"I wasn't," Emma said. "But Jenny found some boxes in the attic with a bunch of driver's licenses from women who'd lived with him before, and then we Googled them and some of them are missing and two of them are dead, so we left. We left right then. We drove to a place with nuns and that's where I met Lorelei." She nodded to where Lorelei sat, watching us all. "She brought us here and . . ." Her voice trailed off.

"I know I sound crazy," Emma said, sighing. "But yeah, I'm afraid of Brannon."

My grandmother put her arms around Emma then and patted her back.

"You did the right thing, running," she said. "I told Hailey she should run. I wrote to her and begged her to come home. I told her she could live with me, or with her aunt and uncle. But I never heard back."

"We found your letter," I said.

She turned to stare at me.

"She was writing back to you. We found her letter, too. It wasn't finished."

She groaned and sank back into her chair, covering her face with her hands.

"Brannon told Jenny that her mother died of the flu," Emma said. "But we're not sure if that's true. We think maybe he killed her, and the other women, too. I'm so sorry, Mrs. Wright."

The woman sat quiet for a minute, then raised her face. "No Mrs. Wright, dear," she said. "Everyone around here calls me MommaJean. That's what my grandkids called me, and it stuck."

"You have more grandchildren?" Emma asked.

MommaJean nodded. "Six," she said. "My son, Rudy, has four; my daughter, Lily, has two boys."

She rose and took my hand. "And now I have seven," she said, smiling at me.

"Come on," she said abruptly, walking toward the front door.

"Where are we going?" I asked.

"Home," she said. "We're going home."

48

Emma

Imogene lived just up the block from her store in a narrow, three-story brick row house set back from the street. We followed her to the end unit and she opened the door. It hadn't even been locked.

"Is anyone else at home?" I asked.

"No, it's just me."

"But your door wasn't locked."

She laughed. "I never lock it. Seems like every time I do, I end up losing the key. We're safe here; everyone watches out for everyone else."

I glanced next door before we went inside, and indeed, a face appeared at the window and an old man smiled and waved.

"That's George," Imogene said. "He watches out for me."

The small front room had high ceilings and hardwood floors—and it was cluttered. Books lay in stacks on tables and the couch and the floor.

"Excuse the mess," she said. "I'm not usually this bad, but with my hip, I can't do a lot of lifting. I'm going to get a hip replacement one of these days."

I sat down beside Jenny on the couch. Lorelei moved a stack of books from the wing chair and sat down. Imogene limped into the kitchen.

"Does anyone want a soda?" she asked.

"Let me help you." Lorelei rose and walked into the kitchen.

I put my arm around Jenny's shoulders and squeezed.

"So, how are you doing? You okay?"

She nodded. "It's just kind of weird, you know?"

"Yeah," I said. "But it will get better."

Lorelei carried a tray from the kitchen with four glasses. Imogene followed with a bag of cookies. She sat down in a rocking chair, put the bag of cookies on the coffee table, and stared hard at Jenny.

"I can see your mama in your face," she said. "Not the hair, of course. You must have gotten your father's hair. But your face and your eyes, my goodness, you look so much like my Hailey."

"I found a photo album in my dad's boxes," Jenny said. "It has lots of pictures of my mother."

Now it was my turn to stare. I'd heard nothing about a photo album.

"I didn't tell you," she said, turning toward me, not meeting my eyes. "I found it the first time I was in the attic, that snow day, remember? I was afraid you'd make me put it back."

"Do you still have it?" Imogene asked.

"It's in my suitcase at Lorelei's house," she said.

"I'd love to see those pictures. Meantime"—she rose and walked slowly to the steep wooden stairs—"I've got some pictures you might like to see, pictures of your mama when she was just your age."

She climbed the stairs slowly, her cane thumping on each step.

I took a sip of my drink and wrinkled my nose. Diet . . . ugh.

"She seems really nice," Jenny said quietly.

"Yes, she does." Lorelei had risen from her chair and was looking at a framed picture on the wall. "She has good taste, too. This is a Monet print."

I stared at her blankly. I knew nothing about art.

"He was an impressionist," she said. "He painted a whole series of these water lilies. Isn't it beautiful?"

We heard the cane thumping down the stairs.

"Can you take these, dear?" Imogene carried a stack of photo albums under one arm. Lorelei took them from her and set them on the coffee table next to the bag of cookies.

I picked up an album and opened it, as Imogene settled onto the couch on Jenny's other side.

"There," she said, pointing to a photo of a young blond girl holding up a blue ribbon and grinning. She was standing in front of the house we'd just seen on Layman. "That's Hailey when she was twelve. She'd won a ribbon at the county fair for one of her paintings. Did you know she painted?"

Jenny nodded. "Daddy has two of her paintings at home. One is of daisies and the other one is a tree in a big field."

Imogene's eyes opened wide. She struggled up from the couch and held her hand out to Jenny.

"Come here," she said. "I have something you'll want to see."

I followed them up the stairs, Lorelei behind me. Imogene was panting now. I wondered how she managed those steps every day.

"These stairs will be the death of me yet," she said. "Usually, I sleep on the couch. But you have to see this."

We walked into a bedroom and there, hanging above an unmade four-poster bed, was the same tree in the same field, only the leaves on the tree were orange and gold and red.

"That's just like mine," Jenny told her. "Except mine's in the spring."

Imogene sat down on the bed and wiped her eyes.

"That painting was the last thing I ever had from Hailey," she said. "After I wrote to her and never heard back, I got worried. I wrote another letter, telling her I was going to drive down there to Cincinnati and get her. Not a week later, I came home from work and found this on my porch, wrapped in brown paper. There was a little card taped to the paper that said, 'I love you, Mama. And I'm fine.'

"I thought maybe she'd come back then. I mean, she must have been in Indianapolis, right? She left the painting right on my porch. But she never did come home. And she never wrote or called again."

Jenny sat down beside her on the bed and took her hand.

"At least she said, 'I love you,' " she whispered.

I stood staring at the picture. Brannon had told us he'd sold the other paintings. How had this one ended up with Hailey's mother? Had Hailey brought it? Or had Brannon?

We walked back downstairs and sat on the couch again, looking at pictures of Hailey and her brother and sister. They looked like a normal, happy family, the kids playing in the yard, sitting at a picnic table in front of a huge watermelon, dressed in their Easter Sunday best and holding pastel baskets with brightly colored eggs.

"Where's her dad?" Jenny asked.

"Oh," Imogene said, sighing heavily. "Hailey's father died when she was six. Henry was his name. He was a good man, a good father. He had the cancer, you know, in his lungs. It nearly broke Hailey's heart when he died. She was his favorite, his special girl."

I stared at a picture of fourteen-year-old Hailey, dressed in very short shorts and a cropped top, her belly bare. She was tan and lean and pretty, grinning at the camera. No wonder Brannon had fallen for her.

"Mom?"

A young woman, maybe a few years older than me, stood in the doorway, her arms filled with grocery bags.

"Lily!" Imogene cried out as she stood. "Come here, dear. Come in. You'll never believe who this is." She pulled Jenny's hand until Jenny stood beside her.

Lily looked hard at Jenny, shook her head, and stared again.

"You look like . . ." Her voice trailed away.

"It's Jenny!" Imogene said. "It's Hailey's little girl, Jenny, eleven years old. Can you believe it?"

Lily stood staring.

"Well, don't just stand there," Imogene said, frowning slightly. "Come here and say hello to your niece."

Lily put her grocery bags on the floor and walked slowly toward Jenny.

"You sure do have her eyes," she said, wrapping her arms around Jenny.

"And this is Emma," Imogene said.

I rose and held out my hand.

Lily reached for it as Imogene continued, "She's Jenny's step-mama."

Lily's hand dropped. She glared at me. "Where's Hailey?" she asked. Her voice sounded like shards of glass.

"I'm so sorry," I stammered. "Hailey died when Jenny was three."

Lily looked from me to her mother and ran down the stairs, taking them two at a time.

"You'll have to forgive her," Imogene said, shaking her head. "Lily just idolized Hailey. Hailey was her big sister and . . . well, she took it real hard when Hailey left. Will you excuse me?"

She walked down the stairs yet again. I stared after her, wondering if we'd done the right thing coming here. Lorelei rose and gathered the grocery bags from the floor, then walked downstairs into the kitchen. We heard the refrigerator open and close, then a cabinet.

Jenny and I walked downstairs and sat back down on the couch together.

"I have an aunt?" she said. "And an uncle, too, I guess. My mother had a brother and a sister."

Lorelei walked back into the room and knelt in front of Jenny.

"You have family, honey—your mother's family. You don't know them yet, but you will. And they will love you."

I sat watching them, my stomach churning. Jenny had a family—a grandmother, an aunt, and apparently an uncle. And cousins. She belonged somewhere . . . somewhere without me.

Then Jenny leaned heavily against my shoulder and I draped my arm around her.

"I already have a family," she said firmly. "I mean, I want to know MommaJean and Lily and my cousins and . . . and all of them. But, Emma is my family. She's the one who loves me. She's the one that matters."

"Hey." The voice was soft, small. We looked toward the door where Lily stood, her eyes and cheeks red.

"I'm sorry I was rude," she said. "I just . . . it's been so long since we heard from Hailey. I guess I hoped . . . Anyway, I am glad to meet you, Jenny, so glad."

She put her arms around Jenny again and held her quietly for a long minute. Then she turned to me and extended her hand.

"I'm glad to meet you, too, Emma," she said.

I ignored her outstretched hand and opened my arms. She hesitated for just an instant, and walked into my arms.

"I'm so sorry to bring you such awful news," I said. "I wish I could undo what happened."

She squeezed me hard for a minute and let her arms drop.

"At least you brought Jenny back to us."

❧ 49 ❧

Jenny

It felt so weird, sitting in that small room with my grandmother and my aunt—my mother's mother and sister. They were kind, kept offering us more sodas, telling me how much I looked like my mother.

"Did you call Rudy?" Lily asked suddenly.

"Not yet," MommaJean said. "I just found out, it seems like. I haven't even thought . . ."

"I'm going to call him."

Lily walked into the kitchen, pulling a cell phone from her pocket.

"Who is Rudy?" Emma asked. She'd been sitting so quiet, just listening. But she'd never let go of my hand.

"That's my son," MommaJean said, smiling at her. "He's two years older than Hailey, her big brother. He always looked after her for me. He'll be so glad to meet Jenny."

Lorelei rose and stretched. "I need to make a call myself," she said. "I'll just be outside."

She walked out the front door, leaving Emma and me alone with my grandmother.

"She seems like a nice girl," MommaJean said, nodding at the door Lorelei had just closed. "Did you say you only met her after you left home?"

"Yes," Emma said, squeezing my hand, "we only met her yesterday. Or was it the day before?" She looked at me, but I didn't answer. I couldn't remember, either, it all felt so long ago and far away.

MommaJean looked confused.

"When Jenny showed me what she'd found—the licenses and . . . and everything—I didn't know what to do. I just knew we had to leave before Brannon came home."

She stopped then, lowered her eyes, and wrapped her free arm around her belly.

"So Mrs. Rigby . . ." I began.

"That's my friend, Shirley," Emma interrupted. "I called her, and she told me about a retreat center not far from where we were in Kentucky. We drove up there . . . it's a convent, actually, a place where the nuns retire."

"Nuns?" MommaJean sounded confused. "Are you Catholic?"

"No," Emma said. "But Shirley is, and she told me we could go up there to stay and be safe until we figured out what to do next."

"Shirley's husband died," I said. "He was real mean."

"He was abusive," Emma continued. "And one time Shirley ran away from him, and the convent . . . really, it's a retreat center . . . anyway, that's where she went. And so that's where we went, Jenny and me. I didn't know where else to go."

MommaJean said nothing, just waited.

"That's where we met Lorelei," Emma said. "She had a friend . . . oh God, it's such a long story. Anyway, I told her about Brannon and the letter we found from you, and she said she lived pretty close to you. And . . . and so we just came home with her."

"She works for a church," I added, thinking that might be helpful.

Lorelei walked back into the house then, snapping her phone closed.

"Thank you." MommaJean rose and limped toward Lorelei, her arms open. "Thank you for bringing them home to me."

"Rudy is on his way," Lily told us from the kitchen doorway. "He can't wait to meet you, Jenny."

"Well, we're going to need some dinner," MommaJean said. "Call Jockamo's, Lily, and order us some pizzas. Get a Slaughterhouse Five and maybe a Maui, and . . . what do you girls like on your pizza?"

She looked from me to Lorelei to Emma, still sitting on the sofa.

"We like anything," Emma said. She looked so tired and pale. I sat down beside her and took her hand in mine.

"Can we get something without meat?" Lorelei said. "Maybe the Cheese Louise?"

"Okay," MommaJean said firmly, "a Slaughterhouse Five, a Maui, and a Cheese Louise, all of them large. And get some bread sticks, too."

"What's a Slaughterhouse Five?" I asked. It sounded pretty gross.

"It's named after a Kurt Vonnegut novel," MommaJean said. "He was a famous writer from Indianapolis. Haven't you ever heard of him?"

I shook my head.

"Well, it's got five different kinds of meat—the pizza, that is," she said. "Pepperoni and sausage and bacon . . . and some others I can't think of right now. It's good; you'll like it."

Lily disappeared back into the kitchen with her phone.

"Are you all right, dear?" MommaJean was looking hard at Emma.

"I'm fine," Emma said, but she didn't sound fine. I held her hand tight in mine.

"It's all a bit much, isn't it?"

"It's a lot," Emma said. "I'm so happy for Jenny to find her extended family, and so grateful that you've been so welcoming. But it's a lot to take in."

MommaJean sat down by Emma and touched her cheek.

"Jenny is our family," she said firmly. "And so are you."

Emma's eyes filled with tears. She opened her mouth, but nothing came out.

"Honey," MommaJean continued, "you brought my granddaughter back to us, my little girl's little girl. And you're her step-mama, and that makes you family. You're stuck with us, whether you like it or not."

Emma smiled. "Thank you," she whispered.

"The pizzas will be ready in thirty minutes." Lily walked back into the room. "Rudy will pick them up on his way over. Oh, and I called Joe."

"Who's Joe?" I asked.

"That's my husband," Lily said. "He's going to bring my sons over to meet you."

"You'll love them," MommaJean said. "Jerry is nine and Danny is six. They're going to love you."

I held tight to Emma's hand. All my life, it had been just Daddy and me. Now I had a whole family of strangers. I wasn't sure how I would remember all their names.

"Can I use the bathroom?" I asked.

"Surely," MommaJean said. "Lily, show Jenny where the bathroom is."

I followed Lily upstairs and she pointed toward an open door.

I closed the door behind me and sat down on the edge of the bathtub. My head ached. I felt like I might throw up. Mostly, I just wanted to go home . . . but where was home now? Where was Daddy? I closed my eyes and remembered the day in Idaho when I knew Emma would be my new stepmom. Daddy and Emma dancing on the grass, Emma winking at me, the hot, still air in the trailer. If I could go back and undo it all, would I?

A light knock at the door startled me.

"Jenny?" Emma's voice was soft. "Are you all right?"

Was I all right? Had I ever really been all right? Would I ever be all right again?

I opened the door and wrapped my arms around her.

"I'm scared," I said.

"I know," she said. "I'm scared, too."

We stood like that for a minute, then she kissed the top of my head.

"I know it's kind of overwhelming, but it's pretty great that you have a whole family, that they want you in their lives. You can find out all about your mother, now. That's a good thing, right?"

I nodded.

"Okay, we'll eat some pizza and you'll meet a bunch of people and then we'll go back to Lorelei's and get some sleep. Does that sound all right?"

I nodded again, then took her hand and walked downstairs with her. The small front room was crowded now. A man stood with his arm around Lily. Two little boys shouted and ran from the living room to the kitchen and back again. Lorelei sat in her chair, just watching the chaos. MommaJean looked up from the couch and beckoned to me.

"Come here, Jenny," she said. "Come and meet your cousins."

The rest of the evening passed in a blur. My uncle Rudy arrived with the pizzas. Then Rudy's wife came, bringing two of their kids. The room was hot and crowded and incredibly noisy. I sat as close to Emma as I could get, trying to remember to smile.

I had a family. A huge, noisy family.

And I missed Daddy.

‒‒ 50 ‒‒

Emma

Lord, I was so glad to get back to Lorelei's. The house was cool and quiet and calm. I stretched out on my bed in the guest room and just breathed in the peace.

Jenny lay on her bed, clutching her stuffed bear.

"Do you miss Daddy?" she asked suddenly, her voice small.

I turned my head to look at her.

"Yes," I said. "I miss him a lot."

"Me too."

Neither of us spoke for a while. Then Jenny sat up, still holding the bear.

"Where's your phone?" she asked.

I sat up and reached for my purse, dug the phone out.

"Can we listen to the messages?" Her eyes were wide and wet. "Maybe he called. Maybe we can just listen to him talk, just for a minute."

"I don't know," I said. I was afraid to listen, afraid to hear what Brannon might say, and afraid to have Jenny hear what he might say.

"Please?"

I tried to turn the phone on, but the battery was dead. So I dug through my suitcase for the charger and plugged it into the wall outlet. I turned the phone on and looked at the screen—forty-six messages, almost all of them from Brannon.

"Did he call?" Jenny asked.

I nodded. "He called a bunch of times."

"Can I listen to the messages?"

I sighed. I was more tired than I'd ever been in my life. Honestly, I didn't think I had the strength to listen to any of Brannon's messages. But Jenny's face was so sad and so hopeful. I clicked on the first message and held the phone to my ear.

"Let me listen to them first," I said.

"Emma?" His voice filled my head. "Babe, where are you? I got your note. Are you in Atlanta? Why didn't you tell me you were going? Call me back, honey. Please call me soon."

Tears filled my eyes. I clicked on the next message.

"Emma, where the hell are you? It's almost eleven and I don't even know where you are. Call me back, damn it!"

The messages went on and on, alternately pleading and angry, promising and threatening. I clicked the last message from him.

"Listen, you stupid cunt! You think you can just leave me and take my kid? Stupid bitch! You bring Jenny back here and you do it now! She's my daughter, not yours. I will find you, bitch, and when I do you're a dead woman!"

"Are you okay?" Jenny stared at me, her eyes round and frightened.

"You don't want to hear them," I said. "He doesn't even sound like your dad anymore."

She lay back on the bed, her arm over her eyes, and began to cry.

I looked at the phone again. Three more messages, one from Angel, two from Resa. I clicked on Angel's message.

"Emma, I just want to make sure you're okay. We're worried about you and about Jenny. Brannon has been tearing around town like a wild thing. He showed up here last night, drunk and screaming. Michael finally told him he'd call the police if Brannon didn't leave. I know you're scared, but please let us know you're okay. Call me back, or have Jenny e-mail Lashaundra. Be safe."

Tears stung my eyes. Angel and Michael had been so good to me, after that disastrous start. I hated that they were so worried.

I clicked on the first of Resa's messages.

"Hey, darlin', it's me. I don't know where you are, but Angel told me what you found in the attic. You should go to the police, Emma. Do it before he finds you. And for God's sake, don't come back here. I believe he'd kill you if he could."

I wiped my eyes, and clicked on her second message.

"Emma, it's me again. I done told Wylie about what ya'll found. He said he's going to do some digging around, to see what he can find out about Brannon and all those women. Angel's little girl showed him the things she and Jenny found on the computer. You just lay low, you hear? Wylie will figure out what to do."

When I looked up from the phone, Jenny was staring hard at me.

"Angel and Resa called. They said your dad's in bad shape. He's been drinking, I guess, and he's pretty angry."

She nodded. "I've seen him like that," she said, her voice flat. "Once, when he thought I was asleep, I saw him hit Jackie. He hit her so hard she fell down. That was the night she left. I always thought it was because he hit her."

She came and sat beside me on my bed.

"He gets mad, I know. He's got a bad temper," she said. "I knew that even when I was little. But . . . but he's not all bad, is he? I mean, he was a good dad. . . ."

"No, he's not all bad," I said, hugging her. "I think he's got something inside that makes him lose it sometimes."

"Like a demon or something?"

"Not a real demon, like you see in movies," I said. "I think something is broken inside Brannon, and sometimes he can't control himself."

"Why?" she asked. "Why can't he control himself?"

"I'm not sure, Jenny. Maybe it's something from his childhood. Living in foster care all those years was probably really awful. Who knows what happened to him when he was a kid?"

"Maybe his sister knows," Jenny said. "Maybe she can tell us why he's like that."

"Maybe," I agreed. "I think tomorrow I will call that adoption agency and see if we can get any information about her. Or maybe I'll just go in person. It's harder to turn someone down when they're standing right in front of you."

"Can I go with you?"

I tilted her chin up, so I could look her in the eyes.

"Yes, you can go with me. We're in this together, Jenny. Whatever happens, we're in this together."

I didn't sleep much that night. I was so tired I felt halfway dead, but I still couldn't turn off the static in my head. Brannon's voice screamed at me. *I will find you, bitch, and when I do you're a dead woman.* How could I have fallen for a man like that? How could I have been so wrong? I swore when I left Arizona that I'd never be with an abusive man again. And now here I was, running from another disastrous marriage.

I heard Jenny's rhythmic breathing and wondered how she could sleep at all. I hoped she wouldn't have nightmares. God knows, we were already living one.

∾ 51 ∾

Jenny

The next morning, Lorelei let me use her computer to send an e-mail to Lashaundra.

> *Hi, Lashaundra. Emma got your mom's message last night. We are fine. I sure miss you. Love, Jenny.*

I didn't read all of the e-mails that filled my in box. There were just too many, almost all of them from Lashaundra.

We met MommaJean and Lily for breakfast at a place called the Steer Inn. Lily's boys were at school. Everyone else was at work. I was glad it was just the two of them.

"How are you this morning?" MommaJean wrapped me in a hug and kissed my cheek.

"I'm okay."

"How about you, Emma? You sleep well?"

"I'm fine," Emma said. She didn't look fine. Her eyes were red, her face was white, and her beautiful red hair was kind of a mess.

"You look like you could use a cup of good, strong coffee."

MommaJean waved at the waitress.

"We want three coffees and four orange juices," she said. "Do you want some cocoa, Jenny?"

"Yes, please."

The waitress handed us menus and went to get our drinks.

"Now this is on me," MommaJean said. "No, don't even argue about it. I have eleven years to make up for with my granddaughter, and I can surely buy her breakfast."

"You might as well let her," Lily said, smiling at Emma. "Momma doesn't ever take no for an answer."

"Thank you," Emma said quietly.

"Now, after breakfast I thought we could go to the old house, the one your mama was raised in. I thought you might want to see it."

"Actually," Emma said, "we have plans this morning."

"Oh." The old lady's face and shoulders sagged.

"It's just . . . we found some adoption papers in one of Brannon's boxes. Apparently, he had a little sister. We're going to the agency to see if we can find out anything about her."

"Well then, we'll go with you." MommaJean looked pleased with the idea. "Lily has the day off, and I don't need to open the store today."

"I really think it's better if we do this on our own," Emma said. "I don't want to overwhelm the people at the agency, or Jenny's aunt, if we can find her."

MommaJean opened her mouth, but before she could say anything, Lily touched her arm and shook her head.

"That's fine," Lily said. "You-all do what you need to do."

The waitress returned with juice, coffee, and cocoa.

"What can I get you today?"

"I'll have the biscuits and gravy," MommaJean said. "With a side of potatoes."

"Eggs Benedict," Lily said.

"Can I have pancakes?" I asked. "With chocolate chips on top?" Emma nodded.

"Veggie omelet, please," she said.

"This was one of your mama's favorite places to eat," Momma-Jean said, patting my arm. "When she was in high school, she and her friends came here almost every day after school to have a Cherry Coke."

"Is the high school close by?" Emma asked.

"Just down the road about a mile. We can go there sometime, if you want to see it."

"Okay."

I looked around, taking in the smells and sounds. My mother came here with her friends after school. Maybe she'd sat in this very booth.

"I'll tell you what," MommaJean was saying. "Maybe tomorrow I'll take you on a whole tour of Irvington. I'll show you where your mama went to grade school and where she got her hair cut and the old movie theater and the park. Would you like that?"

I nodded and smiled. She seemed so eager to please me.

The waitress returned and set a huge plate of pancakes in front of me, chocolate chips and whipped cream on top. They looked almost like the pancakes at Happy Days. A lump filled my throat.

"Go ahead, darlin'," MommaJean said, "taste them."

I took a small bite, hoping I could swallow it.

"It's good," I said.

"Your mama used to love pancakes," she said. "And French toast. Next time we come here, you'll have to get the French toast. That was her favorite."

After breakfast, we walked to the parking lot.

"Where is this agency?" MommaJean asked.

"It's on Churchman," Emma said, pulling a piece of paper from her purse. "Lorelei made me a map."

"That's not too far," Lily said.

"You call us when you're done there," MommaJean said. "We'll have lunch, maybe at Dufour's. How does that sound?"

"That sounds lovely," Emma said. "But I have to say, I'm so full I'm not sure I'll have any appetite."

"Oh, you will once you get there," MommaJean said. "They make their own bread. The smell alone will make you hungry."

She wrote her phone number on the map.

"Good luck," she said. "Call me when you're done."

"She's so nice," I said when we got in the car.

"She is," Emma said, nodding. "She really wants you to like her."

"It's weird that she's my grandma and I never even knew about her."

"Give it time. It will start to feel normal after a while."

We drove south for a bit and then turned west, eventually pulling into a parking lot beside a redbrick building. It felt like we were out in the country.

A receptionist smiled at us when we walked in.

"How can I help you?"

"My name is Emma Bohner," Emma said. "We're trying to find my husband's sister. Her name was Jennifer Adele Bohner before she was adopted."

"You'll need to see Karen," the receptionist said. "Have a seat and I'll call her."

We sat down in the waiting room. Pictures of happy families covered the walls.

A few minutes later, a middle-aged woman with short dark hair appeared.

"Mrs. Bohner?"

Emma rose and they shook hands.

"I'm Karen Mason. I understand you are looking for your husband's sister?"

"Yes, ma'am. She was adopted in 1992 through your agency."

"Come with me," the woman said.

We followed her to a big, cluttered office, where several more pictures of couples with babies smiled down at us.

"Now then," Ms. Mason said, "what was her name?"

"Jennifer Adele Bohner," Emma said.

She reached in her purse, pulled out the letters I'd found in Daddy's boxes, and handed them to Ms. Mason.

Ms. Mason put on her glasses and scanned the letters. Then she rose and walked to one of the big file cabinets that lined the walls.

"Bohner," she said, flipping through files. "Yes, here it is."

She pulled a file from the drawer and sat back down at her desk.

"Mr. Bohner wrote to us three years ago, looking for information on his sister. Unfortunately, it was a closed adoption and the best I could offer was to put a letter from him in his sister's file, in case she wanted to make contact. But we never received another letter from him."

She looked up from the folder and smiled.

"The good news is that Jennifer did contact us last year and indicated she would be willing to meet her brother. I have a letter from her here."

"Can I see it?" Emma asked, reaching for the envelope.

"I'm sorry," Ms. Mason said. "It's addressed to Brannon Bohner. I'm afraid he's the only one who can receive it."

"But she's my aunt," I said. "I'm even named after her."

I reached into my pocket and pulled out my school ID card.

"See, Jennifer Adele Bohner, just like her."

The woman smiled, but she still held onto the letter.

"Jennifer was very particular that only Brannon would receive the letter. She didn't want her birth mother to find her."

Her birth mother? How could her birth mother find her? She was dead.

"The thing is, Ms. Mason, my husband is very ill," Emma said.

I stared at her for an instant, then dropped my eyes, trying to look sad.

"He's in the hospital and all he wants is to meet his sister. He asked me to come."

Ms. Mason frowned slightly.

"I'm sorry he's sick," she said. "What hospital is he in?"

"It's Taylor Regional Hospital in Campbellsville, Kentucky," Emma said. "That's where we live."

Ms. Mason said nothing.

"Please, Ms. Mason, Brannon needs to see his sister again, or at least talk to her. He's afraid he'll die without ever finding her." Emma's eyes were wide as she stared at the woman.

Ms. Mason sighed then.

"Do you have proof that you are his wife?"

Emma reached into her purse again and pulled out another sheet of paper.

"Here is our marriage license," she said, laying the paper on the desk.

I tried hard not to look surprised.

Ms. Mason picked up the license and read it. Then she sighed again.

"Well, this is not the way we usually do things," she said. "But Ms. Bohner did indicate that she would like to meet her brother."

She rose then and held the envelope out to Emma.

"Thank you," Emma said. "Thank you so much. You have no idea how much this means."

"I think I do," Ms. Mason said, smiling.

Emma shook her hand, gathered the papers she'd brought, and put them into her purse, along with the letter from Daddy's sister.

"I can't believe you lied to her," I said as we pulled out of the parking lot.

"I had to," she said. "She wouldn't have given us the letter otherwise."

"Can we open it?"

Emma shook her head. "Let's wait till we get back to Lorelei's," she said. "I don't want to be reading and driving at the same time."

~∞ 52 ∞~

Emma

We sat on the bed and stared at the envelope. Finally, I tore it open and we read the letter. It was dated May 6, 2011.

> *Dear Brannon,*
> *I found out a few months ago that you were trying to find me. I got your address from your letters to St. Elizabeth's and wrote to you, but the letter came back. You'd moved and left no forwarding address. So, I'm putting this letter in my file, in hopes that sometime you will find it.*
> *My name is Jennifer Monroth now. That's my married name. My husband, Jack, and I have one child. His name is Henry and he's two years old.*
> *I was adopted by my parents, Mike and Monica Howard, when I was three. I've had a happy life with them.*
> *I don't remember much about before I was adopted. I was so young, and I think I blocked a lot of it out. But I remember you. I think I called you Bray, and you took care of me. I used to have terrible nightmares, and my parents took me to a counselor for several years. When*

*I was older, they told me what they knew about our
birth mother and what she did to us. I went through old
newspaper records and found out that she was put in
prison for child abuse. I don't know if she's still in jail.
I hope she is.*

*I would really like to meet you someday. I still live
in Indianapolis at the address above. My phone number
is 317-555-2484.*

Sincerely,
Jennifer Adele Monroth

I read the letter twice. Brannon's mother was alive. And in prison for child abuse. Why hadn't he told me the truth?

"Do you think that woman is still in jail?" Jenny's voice was small.

"I don't know, honey. But wherever she is, she can't hurt you."

"Daddy said she was dead."

"I guess to him, she was dead."

She leaned against me and I put my arm around her.

No wonder Brannon had so much anger. He'd been abused as a child. And it must have been very bad, if his mother had been put in prison.

"Poor Daddy," Jenny whispered.

I could only nod. The lump in my throat was too big to talk through.

"Why didn't he tell us the truth?" Jenny asked.

"I guess he just wanted to forget all about it," I said. "It was probably easier just to make up a story."

We sat a moment just staring at the letter.

"Are you going to call her?"

"I think we should," I said.

"When?"

I took a deep breath and stood up. "Now."

I went to the kitchen and dialed the number on the letter. After three rings, a woman's voice answered. "Hello."

"Hello," I said. "Is this Jennifer Monroth?"

"Yes." The voice was cautious. "Who is this?"

"My name is Emma Bohner," I said. "My husband is Brannon Bohner."

The line was silent for so long I was afraid she'd hung up.

"Oh my God!" she said finally. "Oh my God."

"I'm in Indianapolis," I said. "And I would really like to meet you."

"Is Brannon with you?"

"No," I said. "He's in Kentucky. That's where we live now. I just came up . . . to visit family and I told him I'd check in at St. Elizabeth's to see if we could find you."

"Oh my God," she said again. "Where in Indy are you?"

"On the east side," I said. "A neighborhood called Irvington."

"I know where that is," she said. "We took my son to the Halloween festival there last fall."

"So, do you think we could meet?"

I held my breath. Beside me, Jenny was shaking.

"I would love that," Jennifer said. "I can come up there this afternoon, if that works for you."

"That would be great. What time?"

"Is four okay? Henry, that's my little boy, he has a doctor's appointment at two. We could come after that."

"Perfect."

"There's a coffee shop in Irvington; it's on that little side street by the theater, right across from the bookstore."

"I know where that is."

"Great, I'll see you at four. And . . . I'm sorry, what is your name again?"

"It's Emma," I said.

"Okay, Emma. I'll see you at four."

I hung up the phone and wrapped my arms around Jenny.

"We're meeting her at four."

"Here you are!" MommaJean waved to us from a table in the little restaurant. "How was your morning?"

"It was . . . interesting."

We sat down and she hugged Jenny.

"What did you find out?"

"Actually, a lot," I said. "Brannon's sister had left a letter for him with the agency. I called her and we're meeting today at four at the coffee shop, the one across from your store."

"So you're going to have even more new family?"

Jenny nodded.

"Well, that's exciting. Aren't you excited?"

Jenny nodded again.

"You don't look very excited."

Jenny stared at her hands in her lap.

"It's just all so weird," she said. "I didn't even know Daddy had a sister until a few weeks ago. He never told me about her. But she has the same name as me."

MommaJean shook her head.

"Seems like there's a lot about your daddy he hasn't told you."

"We found out that Brannon and his sister were put in foster care because their birth mother was abusive," I said.

"She's in prison," Jenny said.

"Good Lord!" MommaJean's eyes opened wide. "That's awful."

"It's pretty bad," I agreed.

"So is this sister younger than Brannon or older?"

"Younger," I said. "She got adopted, but Brannon didn't."

"Well, that explains a lot, doesn't it?"

"What does it explain?" Jenny asked.

MommaJean shifted in her seat and cleared her throat.

"I don't want to talk bad about your daddy," she said. "But he had a dark side. When Hailey married him she was head over heels in love, happier than I'd seen her in a long time. But . . . well, that didn't last.

"She didn't want to tell me at first, how he'd get so mad sometimes he'd hit her. I tried to convince her to leave him, but then she got pregnant and she said he changed. He was real gentle with her then, she said, like when they first met."

"Did you ever meet Brannon?" I asked.

She shook her head.

"I didn't even know his name till after she married him. She called me sometimes just to let me know she was okay. But I never saw her again. Not once. After her last letter, I tried to get the police to look for her. But they didn't do much. They said she was an adult, and the only one who could report her missing was her husband, because that's who she lived with."

The waitress appeared with water and menus.

"Iced tea, please," I said. "And a glass of milk for you, Jenny."

"I'll have coffee," MommaJean said.

We sat a moment in silence. Then MommaJean cleared her throat.

"You don't know what hospital Hailey died in, do you?"

"No, ma'am. I'm sorry. The only things I know about Hailey are what Brannon told me. And he's lied so much, I don't know what's true and what's not."

"They were living in Cincinnati then," MommaJean said. "I suppose I could just start calling hospitals. Somebody has to have a record of her, don't they? I would dearly love to know where she's buried."

She dabbed at her eyes with her napkin.

"It's an awful thing to lose a child," she said. "But what's even worse is the not knowing."

I nodded.

"Emma lost a baby once," Jenny said.

"I'm sorry, dear." MommaJean patted my hand.

"Thank you."

"When are you due with this one?" she asked.

"September."

"Well, I hope it's a healthy, happy baby."

I tried to smile, but I felt like crying. I was bringing a baby into the world without a father. How would I support my daughter? And Jenny . . . how could I support a baby and Jenny?

"It's all right, dear." As if she could read my mind, MommaJean took my hand. "You're not alone. You're part of our family now. I told you, you're stuck with us whether you like it or not."

53

Jenny

We went to MommaJean's after lunch. She and I sat on the couch looking at pictures of my mother.

"That's when she was in high school. She was a pom-pom girl." She pointed to a picture of a young girl in a short dress and cowboy boots with tassels. "She did that for two years, but then her senior year she quit. I was sorry she quit. She was so good at it. But she met a boy the summer before she was a senior, and he hung out with a different crowd."

She shook her head. "I didn't like him from the start. But Hailey was just crazy about him, and the more I told her he wasn't good enough for her, the more she hung onto him."

She sighed heavily.

"She moved in with him in December and quit school."

"Was that my dad?" I asked.

"No, she didn't meet him until later, after she and Darren broke up. I wanted her to move back home, but she had a job out in Greenfield and was sharing an apartment with another girl. She didn't want to move back in with her mama. Then she met Brannon."

She sniffed and wiped her eyes with a tissue.

"I'm sorry," I said, leaning against her.

"Done's done," she said. "I couldn't stop her from making mistakes. I tried, but she was headstrong. Still, she made you, and you're a beautiful granddaughter."

She kissed my cheek.

"MommaJean," Emma said. "Do you have a computer?"

"There's one upstairs in the guest room," she said. "One of these days I'm going to move it down here so I can use the danged thing."

"Do you think it would be okay if I checked my e-mail?"

"Surely, darlin'. That would be fine."

Emma walked upstairs and MommaJean started talking about my mother's painting.

"She was just so good, so talented. I wanted her to go to art school. But she wouldn't even apply."

"How did she learn?" I asked.

"Lord only knows," she said. "She just had a gift. No one taught her; she just knew how to do it."

"I wish I had known her."

She hugged me close. "Me too, Jenny. I wish that, too."

Emma's footsteps pounded on the stairs.

"Is everything all right?" MommaJean rose.

"I have to make a phone call."

Emma dug her phone from her purse and turned it on. She walked into the kitchen, punching numbers.

"Resa? It's me."

I ran to the kitchen and stood, watching her as she paced in front of the sink.

"When?"

Pause.

"Yes, that's where we are."

Pause.

"Oh, hell!"

MommaJean stood behind me, her arms around me.

"Thanks, Resa. . . . No, really, thank you for letting me know. . . . We'll be okay. He doesn't know where in Indy we're staying. . . . All right. You too. 'Bye."

She turned the phone off.

"Brannon is coming to Indianapolis," she said. "He told one of the guys at work he knew we were here, that I'd gone through his personal papers and stolen some of them, and had probably come up here to try to dig up dirt on him. The guy told Michael about it."

"When?" I felt myself start to shiver.

"He left there a couple hours ago."

I stared at her.

"What if he finds us?"

"He's not going to find you," MommaJean said, squeezing me tight. "He doesn't know where I live."

"He knows your name," Emma said. "All he has to do is look in the phone book."

"Let him come!" The old woman raised her cane. "Just let him come. I'll kill him for what he did to my girl."

"MommaJean," Emma said. "We can't put you in that kind of danger. Brannon is . . . he's dangerous."

"Maybe we should go to Lorelei's," I said. "He won't know about her."

Emma nodded. "That's what we'll do. But first, we have to meet your aunt."

She looked at her watch. "In fact, we should go now."

"Maybe you should skip that, Emma." MommaJean's eyes looked worried. "I can go to the coffee shop and tell her what's happened."

"No," Emma said firmly. "I need to meet this woman. I need to find out what happened to Brannon. I need some answers."

"Well, if you're going, I'm going with you." She banged her cane against the floor. "I just got my grandbaby in my life, and I sure as hell am not going to lose her now."

We left our car parked behind MommaJean's house and walked the block to the coffee shop. Several people sat outside. It was a beautiful, warm day.

"We'll sit inside," Emma said, her eyes darting from place to place.

We walked in and blinked, letting our eyes adjust to the darkened room.

"Are you . . . Emma?"

A young woman rose from a couch, a woman with dark hair and

dark eyes. I stared at her. She looked so much like Daddy it almost hurt to look at her.

"Jennifer?" Emma extended her hand. "I'm Emma, and this is Jenny."

The woman stared at me, then dropped to her knees and wrapped her arms around me.

"You must be Brannon's daughter," she said. "You look just like me."

"Yes, ma'am," I whispered. "You look just like Daddy."

"Well, Jenny, this is your cousin Henry." She pulled a little boy forward. He had the same dark hair and eyes.

"Henry, say hello to your cousin Jenny."

"Hello," he said softly, staring at me.

"I didn't know Brannon had a daughter," Jennifer said. "And you're named Jenny, too."

"Jennifer Adele," I said.

"He named you after me," she said, her voice soft. She hugged me again.

"Jennifer, I'm so glad you could meet us," Emma said. "I have so many things I want to ask you."

"I'm thrilled to meet you," she said. "I have so many questions for you."

"Do you mind if we sit in the other room?" MommaJean pointed to a back room. "It will be quieter there."

"I'm sorry," Emma said. "This is Imogene Wright. She's Jenny's grandmother."

Jennifer shook MommaJean's hand. "It's nice to meet you."

"Yes." MommaJean sounded impatient. "Let's go to the back."

Jennifer cocked her head, confused, and then followed Emma to the back room.

We sat down around a low table.

"How is Brannon?" Jennifer asked. "The last time I saw him I was only three, but I have such a clear picture of him, standing in front of me, trying to keep some other kid from teasing me. He always took care of me."

Emma took a deep breath.

"Brannon doesn't know we're here," she began. "At least, I hope not. We left, Jenny and I left a couple days ago while he was at work."

Jennifer frowned.

"Henry," she said, "do you want to play with your Game Boy?"

The little boy nodded and smiled.

She pulled the console from her pocket, turned it on, and handed it to him.

"Use the earphones," she said.

She waited until Henry was happily engaged in a game, then turned to stare at Emma.

"He doesn't know you came to find me?"

Emma shook her head.

"Brannon is . . . we think he's dangerous. We think he might have killed some women."

Jennifer just stared.

"Before I met him, Brannon had a whole string of women. How many, Jenny?"

"Six, I think," I said. "Maybe seven. I might not remember them all."

"They lived with him and Jenny, and then just disappeared."

Jennifer shook her head. "Maybe they just left."

"That's what we thought," Emma said. "But then Jenny found a box in the attic with these."

She laid the driver's licenses out on the table, then set the lockets down next to them.

Jennifer reached immediately for the tangle of lockets.

"Oh my God," she breathed.

She pulled a chain from beneath her blouse. A silver heart dangled from it.

"Brannon gave me this when we were in foster care," she said. "I don't know how he got the money. He told me to always wear it, and that way he'd always be with me."

She looked up at Emma. "Did he give you one, too?"

Emma nodded, and pushed the licenses toward her.

"These are what really scared me."

Jennifer picked up one license after another.

"I Googled them," I said. "Two of them are dead and some others are missing."

Jennifer's face was pale.

"You think Brannon killed them?"

Emma nodded. "I've tried every way I can to think of an explanation. It's the only thing that makes sense."

"My dad told me once a few years ago, when I was thinking of looking for Brannon, that they had almost adopted both of us. But Brannon kept getting into fights in the foster home. One time he almost killed another kid. My parents thought he was too . . . damaged. They were afraid to take him."

Jennifer closed her eyes and sat for a minute.

"I guess I really hoped he'd come out okay," she said.

"He's a good daddy," I said, my voice shaking. "He's never hurt me. Not even once."

"He is a good dad," Emma said. "He loves Jenny beyond anything. It's one of the things I fell in love with."

"He got in those fights because of me," Jennifer said. "He was always trying to protect me."

"Well, Lord knows he didn't have to protect Jenny from her own mother!" MommaJean's voice was sharp. "My Hailey loved her baby. She would never have hurt her."

"Did he kill her, too?" Jennifer asked.

"He told us she died of the flu when Jenny was three," Emma said. "We just don't know."

"What we do know is that he's on his way to Indianapolis," MommaJean said. "One of Emma's friends called to tell her. And we're afraid he'll come to my house. He knows Emma came looking for me, and for you."

"Is your house close by?" Jennifer asked.

"Just up the block."

Jennifer rose abruptly. "I need to go," she said. "I can't have Henry here if Brannon shows up. I'm sorry. I want to help you, but I can't put my son in danger."

"I understand," Emma said. "Jenny and I are staying with a

friend. Brannon doesn't know her. He's never even heard of her. We could go to her house. He won't look for us there."

Jennifer stood a moment, looking from Emma to Henry. Then she shook her head.

"I'm sorry," she said again. "I can't."

She pulled the Game Boy from Henry's hands.

"Come on, honey," she said, picking him up. "It's time for us to go home."

"Jennifer, wait, please." Emma followed her through the coffee shop into the bright sunlight. I was right behind her.

"I'm sorry," Jennifer said again.

"Emma!"

Daddy stood across the street in front of the bookstore. In his hand was a gun.

❧ 54 ❧

Emma

I froze for an instant, then grabbed Jennifer's arm and pulled her back into the coffee shop, pushing Jenny ahead of us.

"Call the police!" I yelled.

The barista took one look at us and at the people scattering on the street in front of the shop, and bolted for the door, locking it.

"Get into the back room!" she shouted.

We ran to the back, and I heard Brannon banging on the door.

"Damn it, Emma! Get out here!"

"Oh my God," Jennifer whispered. "Oh my God!"

"Jenny, take Henry into the bathroom." MommaJean's voice was firm, steely even.

Jenny paused for a split second, then reached her hand out to the little boy.

Jennifer put her son down and pushed him toward the bathroom.

"Go with your cousin, honey. Okay? And stay put! You stay in the bathroom until Mama tells you to come out."

The little boy looked at her, confused, tears welling in his eyes. But he took Jenny's hand and followed her down the hall.

"Lock the door!" MommaJean yelled after them.

"Goddamn it!" Brannon bellowed from the sidewalk. "Emma,

let me in! Come on, babe. It's me; it's your husband. Just let me in so we can talk."

"This is Carrie Appleton—I'm at Lazy Daze Coffee House. Ten South Johnson in Irvington. There's a man out front with a gun trying to get in!"

The barista sat huddled against the back wall, her cell phone pressed to her ear.

"Damn it, Emma! Let me in!"

I crouched down on the floor, my arms over my belly.

An explosion of sound shook the building. Glass flew toward us from the shattered door. Brannon reached inside, unlocked the door, and stepped in. He was panting heavily and looked like he hadn't slept in days.

"Oh my God!" the barista shouted into the phone. "He shot out the door! He's in here!"

"Emma?" Brannon's voice was soft now, cajoling, pleading.

"Emma, honey, it's me. It's Brannon, your husband. Come out here and talk to me, babe."

MommaJean gripped my arm as he walked toward us.

"Bray?"

Jennifer stepped in front of me, blocking Brannon's path.

He stopped short, his mouth open, eyes wide. Slowly, he lowered the gun to his side.

"Jen?"

"It's me, Bray. It's Jen; it's your little sister." Her voice shook, but she stood where she was, planted between Brannon and me.

"Jen . . . my God! Jen, I tried and tried to find you."

"It's me," she repeated.

"Look at you, you're all grown up. Oh my God, Jen . . . I tried so hard to find you."

"I know." She spoke gently. "I'm sorry it took so long. I've been trying to find you, too."

She took a step toward him.

"I have a son now, Bray." She stood directly between Brannon and me. "His name is Henry. He's four years old. He's hiding from you right now. He's scared, Bray. He's scared of you. *I'm* scared of you, Bray. Please put your gun down."

"Jen, you don't have to be afraid of me."

Brannon smiled that crooked grin, the one that nearly broke my heart.

"I always took care of you, remember? When Mama came at you, I always got in her way. I took all of it for you, Jen. And when we were in that place—that awful place with those awful kids—I protected you. I always protected you. Don't you remember, Jen?"

"I remember some of it," she said. "I was so little."

"So little and so pretty and so perfect," he said. "And now . . . my God, you're all grown up, Jen. Look at you, all grown up. And a mother, too."

"Did you kill those women, Brannon?"

He froze, his eyes widening, and raised the gun again.

"I had to, Jen. I had to protect Jenny."

"You didn't need to protect her from her own mother, you bastard!"

MommaJean stepped up beside Jennifer, her eyes blazing.

"Hailey loved that baby with all her heart. She wouldn't ever hurt her!"

Brannon sneered at her for a long minute.

"She slapped Jenny's hand," he snapped. "I saw it. She hurt my baby girl. She deserved to die."

He looked down at me then.

"You *bitch!*" he shouted. "You took my daughter away from me. She's *my* daughter, not yours! She belongs with me."

"This is your daughter, too."

I rose to my feet and put my hand on my belly. "Are you going to kill her, too?"

Brannon took a step back, but he didn't lower the gun.

"I don't want to hurt you, Emma," he said.

And God help me, he sounded like Brannon again then, just like my own sweet husband, the one I'd fallen in love with.

"I don't want to hurt you," he repeated. "I just want my daughter back. Give Jenny back to me, and I'll go."

He cocked his head and smiled at me. He actually smiled. My stomach churned.

"She's scared of you, Brannon," I said as calmly as I could.

"Only because of you, you stupid bitch!"

He took a step toward me and aimed the gun at my head.

"If you'd just done what I said, if you hadn't gone snooping through my stuff, we'd be okay, all of us! We'd still be in the house, and Jenny would be in school. We'd be okay, damn it! But you had to go snooping through my things."

"Daddy?"

We all turned and my stomach dropped.

Jenny stood just behind me, touching my arm lightly. She'd closed the bathroom door behind her, Henry still inside.

"Jenny! Baby, come here. Just come with Daddy, and everything will be all right."

Brannon's voice came soft and sweet. He smiled at her.

"Did you kill Jackie?" Jenny's violet-blue eyes never left his face. "Did you kill Trish and Cara and Ami?

"Did you kill my mother?"

He paused for a long moment and then looked down at the barista, still huddled on the floor, her phone clutched in her hand.

"Get out!" he screamed at her. "Get out of here. This doesn't concern you."

She ran for the door.

"Baby," he said, turning back to Jenny, "I was only protecting you. That's what daddies do, they protect their children."

"Emma didn't go through your boxes," Jenny said. "I did. I found the lockets and the driver's licenses. I Googled Jackie and Ami and Trish and Cara and . . . and Briana. I Googled them all. Briana and Ami are dead, Daddy. They died where they lived with us. Cara is missing. I don't know about Jackie."

Her voice caught in a sob.

"Jackie was really nice," she said, staring straight at her father. "She was really nice to me. Did you kill her?"

"Baby, just come with me." Brannon's voice was pleading now. "Just come with me, and we'll go someplace new and everything will be all right. It will be just like it used to be, just you and me. Come on, baby." He reached his hand to her.

"I'll come," Jenny said, her voice shaking. "I'll come with you . . . but only after you let Emma and the rest of them go."

Brannon made a strangled sort of sound in his throat.

"Let them go, Daddy. And I'll come with you wherever you want."

He stood a long minute, his gun still pointed at me.

"Brannon, please," I whispered. "She's just a little girl. She deserves a real life."

"Get out." His voice was flat.

"Go on!" he shouted. "Get the hell out of here, all of you!"

"Henry," Jennifer called. "Come out now, honey. It's time to go."

I didn't blame her. She was protecting her son.

Henry walked out and stopped briefly, staring at Brannon and the gun.

"You're a bad man," he said.

Jennifer scooped him up and ran toward the front door.

"You too!" Brannon yelled, pointing the gun at MommaJean. "Get out of here, now!"

MommaJean stood still, her hand on my arm.

"You took my daughter," she said, staring straight into his eyes. "I will *not* let you take Hailey's baby, too, you son of a bitch!"

A single shot brought her to the ground.

"If you'd raised your daughter right," Brannon said, his voice flat, "maybe she wouldn't have been such a bad mother."

I dropped on my knees beside MommaJean and rolled her over. A dark red stain seeped across her stomach.

"No!" Jenny screamed, dropping to the ground beside me. "Nooo!"

"Drop your weapon!"

A policeman stood just inside the shattered door, his gun trained on Brannon.

"Get out!" Brannon screamed. "Get out of here! Just let me take my little girl!"

Jenny looked up at him and slowly rose to her feet. I grabbed her arm, trying to pull her back to me, back to safety.

"Don't!" I yelled. I don't even know who I was yelling at.

"I hate you."

Her voice was low, but it filled the shop, echoing from the corners.

"Jenny, baby, come on." Brannon reached his hand toward her. "Just come with Daddy now, and everything will be okay."

"I hate you!" She screamed it at him.

"Jenny . . ."

"I *hate* you!"

He stared at her for an instant, his mouth open.

"You *bitch!*" He turned and pointed the gun at me.

Please, God! Please protect my baby.

I waited for the noise that would end my life.

The police officer tackled him, knocking him to the ground. The gun he'd been pointing at me clattered to the floor.

"You bitch!" Brannon screamed again, raising his head to stare at me.

The officer put his knee firmly on Brannon's back, forcing him to lie flat.

"We need an ambulance!" I yelled, dropping back down beside MommaJean.

"It's okay," I crooned to her. "It's over now. It's all over. Please don't die, MommaJean. Please don't die!"

⋘ 55 ⋙

Jenny

We sat a long time in the hospital waiting room, tense and testy, avoiding one another's eyes, staring at the pastel blue walls. Lily got there first, with her boys; her husband came right after. Then Rudy arrived, all four of his kids with him. I couldn't remember all their names. One of them looked almost my age. Not long after, Rudy's wife, Anita, rushed in. Then Lorelei came. Had Emma called her? I didn't know.

Jennifer and Henry were there, too. And after a little while, Jennifer's husband arrived, rushing toward her, dropping down beside her, hugging her tight. He lifted Henry to his chest, clutched him, tears streaming down his face.

My family, I thought, looking from one to the other. This was my family, the one I never even knew I had, the one Daddy never told me about.

We were all waiting to hear if MommaJean was going to die. She might die because my father shot her. Right in front of me. Daddy shot her.

The whole time, Emma never let go of my hand. She held it in the coffee shop after the police handcuffed Daddy and dragged him away. She held it in the police car on the way to the hospital, sirens blaring. She held it still as we sat waiting in the hospital to hear about MommaJean. Emma never let go of me.

"Is Imogene Wright's family here?"

A doctor wearing blue scrubs walked into the room, carrying a clipboard.

All of us rose, walked toward him in a cluster.

"Is she going to be all right?" Lily asked, the only one of us who could form the words.

"She's going to be okay," he said, smiling at us. He looked tired. "She lost a lot of blood, and we had to give her a transfusion. But thankfully, the bullet didn't hit any major organs. She'll need to stay here a few days and we'll monitor her. But she's going to be all right. She'll live."

Lily started crying then, scooping her sons into her arms. Her husband leaned in and hugged them all, crying, too.

"Thank you, God!" Rudy hollered. "Thank you, Jesus, for your merciful grace!"

His kids gathered around him, and he held them tightly to him.

Jennifer, Daddy's sister, sat quietly. She held Henry in her lap. She didn't say anything, but her lips moved in a silent prayer. Her husband held her hand, stroked Henry's cheek, kissed them both.

I stood in the middle of all of them, Emma's hand still in mine.

I felt like I might throw up.

MommaJean was going to be okay.

I was so grateful. I was so glad she was going to be all right, this woman I didn't even know until yesterday—this woman who was my mother's mother. My grandmother, who had been so happy to see me, so welcoming, so brave as she stared down my father in the coffee shop.

My father shot her.

My father shot her.

My father shot her.

Daddy killed Jackie. He killed Trish. He killed Cara. He killed all of them . . . all of the women who'd lived with us, taken care of me, tried to love me. All of them.

Trish, who couldn't cook, but tried so hard, even when Daddy made fun of her. Cara, who did cook, who made fettuccine Alfredo better than anyone. Jackie, who always made me laugh and braided my hair so gently.

He killed them all.

He killed my mother. My mother . . . Hailey, who had birthed me and loved me and sang to me in a voice I could almost remember. He killed her, too.

He almost shot Emma . . . Emma, who was pregnant with my little sister, who convinced him to stay in Kentucky, who never let go of my hand.

And he said he did it to protect me.

I jerked my hand free of Emma's and ran to the bathroom. I threw up into the toilet. Then I threw up again. And again.

It was my fault. Daddy had said so. All of them were dead because of me.

"Jenny?"

Emma's voice—her dear, kind voice, the voice that almost was silenced today because of me—called to me from outside the stall. "Honey, are you okay?"

"No."

"MommaJean is going to be fine," she said. "Everything is going to be okay."

"Jackie won't be okay. Trish won't be okay. Cara and Ami won't be okay."

I heaved into the toilet again.

"My mother won't be okay."

I sat back on the floor.

"They're all dead because of me."

There, it was out.

"Jennifer Adele Bohner, open this door right now!"

I'd never heard Emma sound angry before. I unlocked the door to the stall, rising from the floor. She grabbed me hard, pulling me into her soft tummy.

"Don't you ever, *ever* let me hear you say that again! Do you understand? Never!"

"But it's true," I said. I started crying then. I cried so hard I almost threw up again.

"Jenny," Emma crooned, holding me tight. "It's not your fault. None of it is your fault. Your dad had a terrible, terrible childhood and it damaged him. That's not your fault. It's not your fault that he had an abusive mother. It's not your fault he got put in foster care and lost his sister. It's not your fault that he did what he did. Your daddy is sick, honey. There's something wrong in his head. But it's not your fault. None of it is your fault."

"Are you okay?" Jennifer stood in the doorway.

"We will be," Emma said firmly. "We'll be fine."

We walked back to the waiting room, and everyone there hugged me. My aunts and uncles hugged me. My cousins hugged me. Lorelei hugged me. They didn't blame me. They didn't say it was my fault. They just hugged me and let me cry.

We got to see MommaJean later that day. She was very pale and had tubes stuck in her arms, but she smiled when we walked into the room.

"There's my girl," she said. "Come give your grandma a kiss."

I sat on the side of the bed and held her hand.

"You were very brave today," MommaJean said.

I shook my head. "You were the brave one."

"Actually, I think all of us were brave today," Emma said. "We did what we had to do, and we're all going to be okay."

MommaJean smiled at her. "We're a strong family," she said. "A strong family with strong women."

That night at Lorelei's, I sat on my bed with the photo album I'd found in Daddy's box.

"Your mother was really pretty," Emma said, standing by the bed.

"I wished I'd known her. I wish . . . I wish everything had been different."

Emma sat down beside me and wrapped her arm around my shoulders.

"I know you wish that," she said. "But you can't undo what's done. You can only pick yourself up and go on. And you can do that, Jenny. I know you can. You are the bravest girl I've ever known, and I am so proud of you."

"I love you."

"I love you, too."

Then suddenly she sat up straight and smiled.

"Here," she said, taking my hand and putting it on her belly. "Do you feel that?"

A tiny bump moved under my hand.

"That's your little sister," Emma said. "She's moving."

I stared at the roundness of Emma's belly.

"Wow," I said. The baby moved again.

"Come September, I'm going to need a lot of help," Emma said. "Babies are a lot of work, and I'm counting on you to be my helper."

She leaned toward me and kissed my cheek.

"I've never been around babies before," I said. "You'll have to show me what to do."

"I think you're going to be a great big sister. This little baby is going to love you."

Epilogue

Emma

In the end, Brannon confessed to nine murders, including Damon Rigby's. He ran Damon off the road that night and left him to die in a ditch. And he confessed to killing Mrs. Figg, too. He'd pushed her down the stairs and then watched her die on the floor of her own house. He blamed her for my fall.

He confessed so that Jenny wouldn't have to testify at his trial. At least, that's what he said. But I think he probably confessed so he could avoid the death penalty. MommaJean and I went to his sentencing—life in prison with no possibility of parole.

He told the police where he'd buried the bodies of all those women who'd lived with him. And so, finally, Hailey came home. We had a graveside memorial service on a beautiful day in June, surrounded by family and friends. Jenny held MommaJean's hand throughout the service. Both of them cried.

The publicity was terrible at first. It seemed like everywhere we went, people stared at us and whispered. Reporters called Lorelei's and MommaJean's and the bookstore, trying to get interviews with me and Jenny. Our pictures appeared in newspapers and on the TV news. I tried hard to shield Jenny as best I could, and I watched proudly as she learned to cope with microphones and cameras and reporters yelling questions.

And then, two weeks after the first news story appeared, Momma-Jean got a phone call at the bookstore. My little sister, Clarissa, had seen my photo on the news all the way out in Los Angeles, where she had gone after leaving her own disastrous arranged marriage. A week later, she flew to Indianapolis. It felt almost surreal, seeing her again. All grown up with two young children of her own, she lived with her new husband in California. She had been trying to find me for years, she said. So I guess, in a way the publicity was both a blessing and a curse.

My worries about how to support Jenny and the baby were eased a bit when I got a call from a lawyer in Texas who represented Ami Gordon's family. There'd been a reward for information about her murder, a reward of fifty thousand dollars. I didn't want to take it at first, but MommaJean convinced me to accept it.

"You gave that family the same peace you gave me, honey," she said. "That's worth all the money in the world."

We used the money to buy a little row house just two doors down from MommaJean. I enrolled Jenny in school and took a job at the coffee shop, replacing the barista who'd called the police that awful day when Brannon arrived with the gun.

We've been down to Campbellsville twice, Jenny and I, to see Angel and Lashaundra, Resa and Harlan, Shirley and Jasper. I asked Jenny if she wanted to move back there, but she wanted to stay in Indianapolis, where her family is. We have a big family now, a big, beautiful, noisy family. Jenny has gotten to know her cousins, and on days when I work she often goes to Rudy's house after school to play with his daughters.

My belly is getting bigger every single day, it seems. We've been decorating the nursery with ducks and bunnies. Jenny loves to buy things for the baby. She is going to be such a good sister.

We haven't told MommaJean yet, but we've decided to name the baby Hailey.

THE SEVENTH MOTHER

Sherri Wood Emmons

ABOUT THIS GUIDE

The suggested questions are included to enhance
your group's reading of Sherri Wood Emmons's
The Seventh Mother.

DISCUSSION QUESTIONS

1. Zella Fay tells Emma that Brannon is carrying a lot of baggage. Are there any red flags in Brannon's behavior in Idaho that Emma misses? Is she foolish to leave Idaho with Brannon and Jenny? Have you ever taken a risk that big? Did that risk pay off, or not?

2. Emma grew up in the Fundamentalist Latter-day Saints community, which upholds the legitimacy of polygamy. Do you believe polygamous marriage can ever be okay, or is it fundamentally wrong?

3. Angel asks Emma if she thinks "white folks are the only ones who can hate," and says her father hated white people because of the way he had been treated in the South under Jim Crow. Does that hatred make Angel's father a racist? Or do you agree with filmmaker Spike Lee, who said in a 1991 interview with *Playboy* magazine, "Black people can't be racist. Racism is an institution."?

4. What role does Jasper Rigby play in the story? Is there hope for his becoming a better man than his father, or has his upbringing sealed his fate?

5. After Mrs. Figg's death, Lashaundra tells Jenny that people who don't believe in God probably go to hell. Do you believe in heaven and hell? Is belief in God a prerequisite to heaven?

6. Sister Frances tells Emma that all churches are human creations, but she still believes in God. Does that jibe with your experience of church? Why or why not?

7. Lorelei tells Emma that their meeting at Loretto is "a God-thing." Is that something you believe in, or is their meeting simply a lucky happenstance? Have you ever had an experience you would call a God-thing?

8. Jenny comes to believe that Emma is different from all of her previous "stepmothers." Yet it's Jenny's actions that precipitate their flight from Brannon. Is Emma really different from her predecessors, or has Jenny simply become old enough to start asking questions about her father's life?

9. Is Emma right to accept the reward money offered by Ami Gordon's family? Or does it seem like she is profiting from Brannon's crimes? Would you feel comfortable accepting such a reward? Why or why not?

10. Given Brannon's childhood experiences, is he simply a product of terrible circumstance? Does his background in any way mitigate his crimes? Is he in any way a sympathetic character?

11. Emma's first marriage was to an abusive man. After she left him, she tells Jenny, she followed a man from Salt Lake City to Rexburg, Idaho, because she thought he was "really nice." But he turned out to be not a good guy. Finally, she marries Brannon, who also has an abusive history. What in her background leads Emma into one abusive relationship after another? Is she doomed to keep repeating that pattern?

12. Jenny has seen her father's uncontrolled anger, and even episodes of violence. Is she in any way complicit in Brannon's crimes? Does she have a responsibility to warn Emma, or is she simply too young to be accountable?